M000033051

Strum

A NOVEL

NANCY YOUNG

PORTLAND • OREGON
INKWATERPRESS.COM

Copyright © 2013 by Nancy Young
Cover and interior design by Emily Dueker
Yellow Guitar © Thesovich. Dreamstime.com
Rural countryside landscape © Petr Jilek. Bigstockphoto.com
Blue Ridge Vista © Tim Mainiero. Dreamstime.com
La Bahaia Silhouette © Neonriver. Dreamstime.com
34590262 © Jupiter Images
Golden Blue Background © David Schrader. Bigstockphoto.com

Author photograph © Bo Struye

Publisher's Cataloging-in-Publication data

Young, Nancy, 1963-
    Strum : a novel / Nancy Young.
    p. cm.
    LCCN 2013908408
    ISBN 978-1-59299-937-8 (pbk.)
    ISBN 978-1-59299-938-5 (eBook)

    1. Woodworkers--Fiction. 2. Deaf--Fiction. 3. Music
    --Fiction. 4. Families--Fiction. 5. Love stories.
    6. Domestic fiction.   I. Title.

PS3625.O9678S77 2013   813'.6
                    QBI13-600085

This is a work of fiction. The events described here are imaginary. The settings and characters are fictitious or used in a fictitious manner and do not represent specific places or living or dead people. Any resemblance is entirely coincidental.

All rights reserved. Except where explicitly stated, no part of this book may be reproduced or transmitted in any form or by any means whatsoever, including photocopying, recording or by any information storage and retrieval system, without written permission from the publisher and/or author.

Publisher: Inkwater Press

Paperback
ISBN-13 978-1-59299-937-8 | ISBN-10 1-59299-937-9

Kindle
ISBN-13 978-1-59299-938-5 | ISBN-10 1-59299-938-7

Scan QR Code to learn
more about this title

All paper is acid free and meets all ANSI standards for archival quality paper.

1 3 5 7 9 10 8 6 4 2

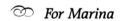 *For Marina*

Le cœur a ses raisons, que la raison ne connaît point.
On le sent en mille choses.
C'est le cœur qui sent Dieu, et non la raison.
Voilà ce que c'est que la foi parfaite, Dieu sensible au cœur.

— Blaise Pascal, *Pensées* (1669)

Contents

1

THE JOURNEY (ST.-GÉRARD), 1954

The melody had come to him in a dream. It was a haunting sound, refined and vaguely familiar, and it came through the absolute silence of an old-growth cedar forest not yet ravaged by the steel saws. Something in this music drew him out of his body and invited him to a sacred dance, the vision of the forest still vivid in his floating body. Although he was wandering in search of something he did not know, he felt a new sense of peace and purpose, not unlike a thirsty land quenched at last by a replenishing rain.

At the first light, with the dream more real than any event in his recent memory, Bernard closed the doors of his cabin and set out in the direction of the dawn. The music had come to the young man in his sleep, breaking the silence of his waking hours, which had been silent since he was five years old. But now, following the surge of the music in his inner ear, he walked purposefully beyond the lake and surrounding autumn landscape of his home like a scout embarking on his first tribal hunt. His feet paced out the rhythm of the music for eleven hours, yet he felt no tiredness, his sense of purpose still strong.

He reached La Pérègrine Creek taking the old loggers' road to where it met the Salmon River at the base of Mont-Mégantic, following its meandering and keeping just within sight of the undulating terrain of clear cutting. The area around Solpetrière was first settled by French fur-traders in the early seventeenth century near the junction of the creek and the river, and much later became a lumber town. By the time he found his way to this settlement, however, it had become a ghost town, abandoned for more than three decades. A scandal involving a priest, it was rumored, had sent the town into a downward spiral that decimated the once thriving timber camp. Whole families retreated from Solpetrière to other nearby towns, a few settled new camps downriver, and others packed up to move southward to New England, or back to Europe, until the sawmill eventually shut down for lack of willing workers.

Although he had set out at the first dim rays of dawn on foot, assisted by the occasional motor car, he did not reach this main bend of the river until nearly nightfall, much later than he had hoped. The low-grade light of the sun behind the tree-line now presented him with a dilemma. Finding it much too dark to proceed into the thicket, but too early to abandon his plan, he parted the low branches of the thick undergrowth on the periphery of the forest, brought himself up tall as a warrior, and searched the dense woodland floor with his eagle eyes for a trail, a path, or a clearing of some kind to suggest an entrance, a safe passage through the cauldron of this dark evergreen sea. Meanwhile, the sunset had begun to turn a deep dusky red, gold and navy against the black silhouette of the encircling trees.

Directly above, a white crescent moon made her half-sliver appearance, followed by the North Star, a frozen spark above the horizon's diminishing bonfire. He considered whether to enter the dense forest, which would inevitably obliterate the illumination of moonlight. With his sense of purpose still strong, he was keen to advance into the belly of the beast and discover the source of the pull which like a fish hook had lodged itself in a central space in his inner ear and was now working its magic to reel him in. He was a salmon swimming instinctively upriver, through a path of undeniable dangers, a night forest replete with predators. But he confronted his momentary fears with uncharacteristic disregard, for tonight logic and self-preservation were not his masters.

His initiation into the forest was a baptism of darkness. Almost immediately the dim moonlight disappeared, a lamp blown out by a phantom wind, and the darkness descended upon him, swallowing him in its jaws whole. Even the constant strains of music in his head ceased. He turned his whole body to see from where he had arrived though he was standing merely five steps from his entrance. He could not determine it, so complete was the blackness. For a moment he felt embalmed by it. Never before had such isolation permeated his being.

Without any internal sound or external sight Bernard was a tree in the darkness himself, suspended in time, space and all existence. And, disconnected as he was from his senses and even his earthly body, he soared, first like the night owl low through the trees and then higher and higher until he burst through the tree tops and at last found the moonlight that illuminated the view. From this vantage point he could see a single massive cedar standing tall in the very heart of the forest before a clearing that suggested the widest part of a creek bed or river. The tree stood regal and imposing, a beloved queen presiding over her subjects, a fearless but compassionate leader. Her benevolence and majesty, her very existence, was overwhelming.

Then suddenly and without warning, the tree swayed and toppled to the forest floor unceremoniously and seemingly in suspended motion. At that instant, as if the core of his being were transformed into a piece of lead or iron ore, Bernard felt himself sucked back down onto the forest floor just as the awful trembling began to subside. When his eyes opened he was supine on the ground but in a moment he was standing, now sensing the tremor through his feet and the shockwaves filtering through the branches and through his hair. Then, as if on cue, the music slowly began again, first imperceptibly then rising to a crescendo in his inner ear.

An undeniable force was now taking over. He was being pulled to the center of the uncharted forest as if a strong magnet resided there. He was guided on this journey by a vacillating equilibrium and disequilibrium dictated by that inner music. Approximating an internal compass, it instructed him, directing his progress and informing him when he was off the track. By the time he had walked and climbed a significant distance into the forest and finally reached the fallen tree, the late morning sun had created a cauldron of light in the clearing, a theatre stage set for a giantess — Ophelia lying in silent repose on her watery deathbed.

The tree was a mighty thing to behold and Bernard felt minuscule and insignificant in its proximity. At first he hesitated to approach it, as if it might abruptly spring to life, a wounded animal feigning death. From a distance he admired its great size — the girth at its widest part seemed as broad across as the width of the log cabin he had recently built. A tree of that size, he surmised, would surely be at least 700 years old, perhaps even 800 years. He had seen many trees nearly as grand as this one cut down by the loggers, often eight or ten of them at a time, each gripping one end of several saws needed to bring the giants down.

In his early years he had wept to see such beautiful creatures felled and turned into matchsticks and building timber. A thing of such beauty deserved reverence, he thought. To spare his soul the travesty, he had retired to the very last step of the milling process where the workers finished the planks and readied them for transport to the cities where the great building booms required the steady supply of construction timber. It was here that he was able to almost forget the tragedy of the majestic giants, and by a stroke of providence to discover the beauty of the fine grain hidden within.

But now at the river's edge he peered at the great cedar, as he stood close to its wretched tangled roots which reached to the sky, the torn limbs of a terrestrial monster tearing its way out from the savaged ground. The rest of the tree had fallen transversely across a wide part of the watery passage so most of its trunk was at least partially imbedded in the water. Swirling white-water rivulets formed around the half-submerged branches like long flowing sleeves draped across the arms of a water nymph suspended in a tragic moment of her dramatic dance. He could not even see the terminus of that colossal body from where he stood. It seemed to extend forever into the middle distance, its end view obscured by woody shrubbery, dust and debris still floating through the shafts of light through the tops of the standing trees.

Clearly the tree had passed of its own accord, perhaps of old age or some other natural cause. The rough bark was beautifully creviced and uniformly dark, rich and reddish brown. Several hollowed knots in its mid-section would have been home for many centuries to a host of small animals which he hoped by now would have found an alternative nesting place.

His first instincts were to calculate a way to bring the monolith back to the cabin with him. He hesitated, for the thought of utilizing large machinery to cart it away seemed disrespectful. On the other hand, leaving it to lie here unceremonious and soon sodden by autumn rain and the river's icy waters also seemed a sacrilege. He imagined the impossibly fine, golden grain hidden beneath the rough reptilian exterior, and the multitudinous rings that would reveal the tree's age, an ancient puzzle of sacred design. Each ring was a single phrase of exquisite music rising, rising in his middle ear. A soliloquy thundering like a white-water torrent edged with the deceptive calm of sonorous blue eddies. A simmering shiver traveled up his spine and set his hair on end.

As he followed the river farther down its wet and rocky edge, he realized that a large section of the tree's upper half had broken from the bottom when it made its terrible collapse to the earth. The separated section now lay like a sleeping fawn nestled against its hunted deer mother unaware of her demise. A dreadful sense of responsibility then overcame him, a grim and unexpected visitor intruding upon an intimate moment. He imagined the snow blanketing the fallen tree, then the river filling in the hollows of the creviced bark, eventually splitting it asunder with its winter expansion. He pictured the slow deterioration, the incessant growth of fungus, and the relentless burrowing of insects. He could feel the gnawing at his own body, as if he were the lonely corpse itself lying prone across the swelling riverbed.

Again, as if being pulled by a strong magnet, he moved toward the fallen tree. A woman's voice called to him in a strange language, speaking to him in an encouraging tone, beckoning him to come forward, to touch her. Another voice, this time a man's, seemed to add its encouragement to hers. The man spoke in yet another language, but like the woman sounded soothing and kind. They beckoned to him as if *he* were now the small animal separated from its mother.

Small rapids formed around his ankles and entered his submerged leather boots as he stepped into the cool of the river. Then they swirled around his knees. When he finally reached the half-submerged tree, the water had welled up to his torso and the freezing cold gripped his loins with a vengeance. With an almost delirious cry he leapt onto a branch and pulled himself clear of the icy water. He clung to the tree now as if it was a life raft. He rested his head upon the trunk and pressed his ear into the damp bark to see if he could make out the voices that had spoken to him earlier. No voices made themselves heard, but now he felt a presence in his heart and the slow return of the music. His heart raced to the quickening beat of a ceremonial drum. This was the feeling he had as a boy when his mother gathered him into her arms as he cried in muted rage about the ancient cedars as they were felled one by one. She had comforted him while his heart pumped with anger. But this time, his heartbeat quickened not with rage, but with excitement, as if he had discovered a long lost truth.

Bernard knew the answer to his dilemma. The tree sections would have to be separated completely and somehow floated down the river. He calculated that the job of extricating the smaller top section of the tree alone with only his sharpest handsaws would take him no more than three days. Then, it would be an excruciating wait through a minimum of five months of winter until the first thaw, before he could return to the bend in the river and recover this ancestor.

It is autumn now, he thought to himself. *In the spring this river will swell to a mighty roar with its icy white water spilling down from the glacier peaks. The river can carry this giant to another place, a safe place — to its home and mine.*

The swell of the music in his inner ear transformed into the mighty roar of rapids that he remembered from his early years when he could still hear as a very small boy in his father's large canoe. Carried down a river similar to this one, he felt the elation of the swift rolling action of the boat as it lifted, then crested on a wave, then dropped with a mighty wet splash. His small hands gripped each side of the narrow point of the canoe as his father expertly guided them past large boulders and the occasional drifting tree branch with his single wooden oar alternating side to side. After several hours of this wonderful ride, the gush of the river would quickly subside and swirl imperceptibly into the beckoning and expansive mouth of the glacier lake ahead of them. The boy would then know they had arrived at the special place where they would catch the most beautiful shimmering creatures he had ever seen.

It was an interminably long week before Bernard was able to make his way back to the forest. Into the back of his father's old hand-me-down pick-up truck he threw the camp gear and set of sharpened saws. As he made his way on the sealed road for the two and a half hours ahead of him, he thought only of that gravel road that would rattle the old truck mercilessly until the road stopped dead an hour and twenty minutes later. There the trail-head would lead him into La Pérègrine Creek Forest and to the tree that he knew would be there waiting for him.

Since the day the strange music led him to her resting place deep in the forest, the spirits of the ancient cedar featured nightly in his dreams. Each evening it was the same — floating over the treetops by moonlight, bringing him to the tall cedar whose nightly calamity befalls with a thunderous roar. Two spirits rise up to join him in this mystical flight, their presence stirring like the shifting musical fog filling the night air with its crescendos. Then suddenly they disappear, as swiftly as they appeared, back into the forest as the music explodes into a cacophony of sound.

Abruptly Bernard sat up in his bed and the melody ceased completely. The almost imperceptible whirring sensation in his head that accompanied him regularly during his waking moments returned to him in that instant. A mixture of shock, sadness, and relief overcame him as the music stopped and the solid reality of his grounded bed conspired with the crisp early morning air to fully awaken him. His first thought was that he could wait no longer; every day the nights grew longer and the days shorter. The first snow would not be far behind.

The trail into the forest was vastly different by daylight and he had to close his eyes and trust his instincts to arrive at his previous destination, like a hunted animal tracking its own scent to return to the den from which it had fled. Nearly overwhelmed by the difficulty of this task, he questioned his sanity on several occasions. Every turn seemed identical to the last, every excruciating incline leveled around the bend by a sheerer decline. Conjuring up the music again in his head served useless; nothing came to him except the strange confidence he felt in his gut that this was the right path.

Fourteen hours later disorientation and exhaustion became his companions. His rucksack was weighted heavily by the set of saws. The burden became unbearable; every step nearly decimated him. Not once had he stopped to rest or take food on his single-minded mission, and now, on the edge of utter exhaustion, he stumbled on a loose rock and spilled over the edge of the precipice as his hands groped helplessly at tangled roots and loose branches useless to break his fall.

The seconds that passed during his plummet down the cliff face expressed themselves like underwater minutes. Perhaps even an hour. When he came to an abrupt and miraculous stop a few tumultuous yards below, he found himself hanging in precarious suspension. His rucksack, which came off one shoulder, had wedged itself between tangled tree limbs, but the saws had come loose and separated from the pack during the tumble. They were now somewhere far below, at the bottom of the eight-hundred-foot ravine he guessed. *Better them than me,* he thought, comically relieved. A kind of delirium had settled in and he found himself shaking with desperate laughter. He had fallen feet first into a pocket of tangled tree roots that held him tightly onto the narrow ledge like a large swallow in a woody, pendulous nest.

When his laughter nearly exhausted the adrenaline that coursed through his every capillary and vein, he took stock of his situation and mentally searched his body for pain and signs of injury. Besides a burning sensation in both hands, he seemed to be unharmed, intact at the very least. An exposed tree root snaked above his head like a stream of smoke above a candle. This he grabbed with one raw hand and with the last vestige of adrenaline as his aide, extricated himself from the awkward hammock and hoisted himself carefully up along the crumbling dirt wall and back onto level ground. Scrambling quickly into a sitting position against the high side of the trail, he looked out into the expansive view that opened up before him. His heart leapt into this throat, throbbing and pounding in rapid beats. Scrambling quickly back to the edge, he peered down into the precipice. Here was a familiar view — in his dreams of flying this particular vista was always below him.

The jagged rows of conifers wound down, down, and down yet more; layer upon green-black layer, from where he kneeled on the ridgeline to the very bottom of the ravine. *And, sure as the day turns to night*, Bernard thought to himself, *there it is, that bend in the creek, and my beautiful giant lying waiting on her broken back.* It was several hundred feet down below, but the tree appeared to him as clear as day, almost as if clouds had parted and the vision was thrust upward to meet his retina in a perfect moment of electromagnetic transference. The vision was crystalline and inspired in him a notion of infallibility.

Through the burning sensation of hands scraped raw by thirty feet of rough-barked roots, Bernard's thoughts automatically returned to the dilemma of retrieving the saws. That morning he had loosely bound them together with a leather thong, wrapped them in a canvas bag which he cinched at the top, and tied them to the rucksack. As they dislodged during his stumble, the ties at the top may have come undone and the saws would have spilt themselves halfway down the side of the mountain and halfway across it. Would he risk his life to scramble down the steep side of the ravine to retrieve them, or proceed with his plan without them?

Either seemed like a pointless proposition — to carry out his plan of separating the two halves of the tree without a saw, or risk life and limb in the pursuit of a senseless task, for the prospect of finding one much less all three saws on the mountainside was as likely as finding the proverbial needle in the haystack. He cursed his luck and then cursed his own ineptitude. For a long while he sat frozen with derision, unable to carry on with either task. Then, it started again. The music floated out from within him; it began as a low vibrato that twinned his beating heart then rose out of the lower registers into a full crescendo of sounds. It lifted him from his dire mood and cleared away the self-scorn, but did not take him into the skies as it did the first time he entered this forest. Overhead the noisy cries of a pair of goshawks were beyond the realm of his hearing, but the unbelievably fast swooping of the raptors became part of the symphonic display.

These aerial guardians helped him to make a decisive move — he would carry on without the saws. In the rucksack he had packed a large Bowie knife in case he was required to hunt for his dinner or defend himself against a hungry predator. A knife like this has a blessing all its own; like the bald eagle it finds its quarry, quickly kills and carves only for the necessity of survival. This hand-knife he had owned for as long as he could remember, even as a small child. He remembered vaguely his first father putting it into his small hands without a word. Now he knew it would complete the job he came to do. There was no way he could guess how long cutting through jagged layers of ancient timber would take, but *if it took a month to accomplish the task,* he thought to himself, *then I will stay a month. I will stay as long as it takes.*

Bernard opened his pack to inspect the contents. In it he had provisions for three days, a pot, a water canteen, the hunting knife, a sleeping bag, rope, and a tarp. As long as he made it down the ravine without losing any more items, he was assured that he was well provided for and could survive any length of stay on the mountain. The light was fading fast and the young man was exhausted from his near brush with death, but he gathered up his pack and went in search of a suitable place to set up camp. That night, in his sleeping bag under the hundred million stars, he slept soundly. There was no music. No flying — just soundless, motionless, and formless sleep. In the morning he was the most rested he had felt in many, many months.

By the time he found his way down to the creek, this time without incident, he was well aware that a Bowie knife might be insufficient to complete his mission. But he was determined to do it, like a wild animal disposed to chew its own leg off to escape a trap. Once he came face to face with the giant tree, however, his resolve faltered. It was larger than he remembered and without his saws the task before him seemed insurmountable. He walked around and around it, examining the fracture from every angle. The diameter of the tree at its greatest width was more than twice his height, but at the fissure it was merely to his chest, and most of it was separated. What held the two pieces together was a thick untidy mass of outer bark and about twenty of the nearly eighty layered rings of decade growth.

Bernard took out his hunting knife and placed its edge along the line of an outer ring and drew it straight across. The circle was so large that his knife ran along its arch for quite a length before cutting into the rough layer of bark. The cut ran deep where the timber was soft, nearly pliable. Water from the running creek had soaked into the splintered edge of the tree and the inner wood was now swollen and spongy where it was exposed. A ripple of relief coursed through his body like the large wake of a boat sailing across a placid lake. He struck the blade back into an attached section of the tree and felt the soft timber yield to the knife point.

As if he had struck gold, he took to his task like a man possessed. The music was ever present now in his inner ear. The lilting turns and the melodious escapades inspired his rhythmic sawing and cutting motions and kept him apace for three days, only stopping briefly at intervals to sharpen his knife on a leather strop, drink from the creek, and eat a hurried meal of dried meat and bread. At the end of each long day he was chilled to the bone from standing thigh-deep in the creek, but under the stars each night he slept soundly, lulled into a dreamless slumber with the sensation of oblique excitement and sheer hopefulness.

On the fourth day he began to ration his food; on the fifth he did not eat. On the sixth day he neither ate nor slept, for the task was nearing completion and the temptation to work through the night to remove the last shreds of splintered bark was overwhelming, even in his famished and nearly depleted state. Working for the next three days like a crazed and maniacal soldier lost in the jungles of foreign enemy territory, he survived on the thin hopes of victory, working slowly but efficiently as the layers of timber came away in equal parts to the layers of skin on his hands, feet, wrists, thighs, knees, ankles, which worked in a disembodied, mangled frenzy alongside the sawing motion of his knife, and his chattering teeth.

Then the blade sliced through the final bit of unwanted wood and jimmied against a hairy sinew of bark. With all the might he had left in his embattled body, he leaned against the tree segment and rolled it back and forth in its place, working the fissure in the log until it seemed amenable, at least nominally acquiescent, to becoming free from its attachment. The stringy fibrous bark of the tree clung with every ounce of its reluctant hirsute sinew, until finally the two parts separated and the upper half rolled a few minor feet until it found its equilibrium again in a new resting place in the deeper waters.

He fell back on to the creek bank and collapsed with utter fatigue. His whole body burned as if it were a deserted ship tossed in a fiery and hellish sea, lashed against molten lava rocks, and broiled by biting winds driven by the devil himself. But beneath the excruciating pain he felt a dull euphoria lodged in a crevice of relief. Was it a feeling of accomplishment, or something more transient, like release? All he knew was that the job was done. He allowed himself to eat again and the sustenance was welcome, like the softness of the timber which was its saving grace, and for this he desperately thanked the flowing waters, aware that without the proximity of the river and its role, his task would have been impossible.

Bernard's slow return to his truck after his ordeal in the deep of the forest was as sluggish as the snow that evening. It dusted the ground without gusto, its fervor spent by the lofty wind that blew it all around and refused to let it fall. His careful and consistent pull-up and stabilize-before-moving-on pattern of climbing the side of the mountain was time-consuming and arduous, but the extreme patience and equanimity required of the young man was equal to his resolve. Exhausted and aching to a point of paralysis, the thought of returning to the sanctuary of his humble cabin on the lake was the essential vision formed and held firmly in his mind with a clarity only surpassed by purpose.

He had been in the forest at this point for nearly three weeks. In that period he had partaken of provisions for just three days, supplemented sparely by edible vegetation found along the forest floor: wild alpine strawberries and elderberries, brown field mushrooms, wild asparagus and leaves of geranium, clover, and cranesbill. They sustained him through the rigors of his exodus from the woods. Retrieving the timber in the spring thaw would be a terrifying challenge, both exhilarating and overwhelming. The alternative of returning with logging tractors and forklifts was tempting, but the thought of the ruthless machines, with their cumbersome, unwieldy, and dispiriting bulk, entering that sacred temple was beyond contemplation, even if they could reach that elusive uncharted ravine. He would stay with his plan to complete the second stage with the aid of Mother Nature — with the assistance of the weather and the elements, the alignment of the stars and seasons — and the purity of heart and spirit. What did not kill him would sustain him.

It was the longest winter the young man had ever experienced. Not since he had broken his arm in an ice-fishing incident four years earlier had he ever suspended his woodworking projects. Through that long frozen winter where his arm seemed unwilling to set and heal, he could not complete normal tasks other than stacking firewood with one hand. That was the most interminable winter, until now. His studio stood jarringly silent and empty, but no work could commence until he had retrieved the fallen timber and the familiar spirits embodied in it. Occasionally their permutations crept into his sleep with dreams of a disembodied metaphysical reality. The mundane world of his waking moments was reinvented into a formless and timeless landscape.

The comforting solace and protectiveness of the music was like a mother's hand on a sleepy child's head. The powerful twinned feelings of love and encouragement were cradled in the form of that symphony. As the blankets of snow came down layer upon layer over the wintry backdrop, the young man's internal landscape slowly became ever more vivid. By the time spring finally emerged through the long cold march of winter, the visions and auditory dreams reached a climax. The dreams came to him at once multifaceted and crystalline, their brilliance and emotional power overwhelming him to a point where joyful tears spilled over from his eyes unrestrained even before they were opened.

Then suddenly the scenery changed. One cold early spring morning a warm sensation embraced him on awakening. The faint scent of juniper and pine needles lingered like the fragrance of a woman's perfume in the air. The smell itself was the first tentative harbinger of spring and he knew at once that he could finally plow a path through the snow drifts from his cabin to the road. With chains already on his truck tires, the roads would make themselves available with some effort and caution. At first light, he set his father's canoe into the bed of the truck, along with provisions for a prolonged stay in a wild terrain and cold weather gear to protect against certain sub-zero temperatures. He made his way upriver slowly.

The minor roads were still sheathed in a thick blanket of snow and the truck struggled mightily at several points to make its way through the icy obstacles, wheels spinning and slipping hopelessly. His persistence paid off when he finally made his way to the junction of the main highway. A snow plow had been employed recently there and the truck, laden as it was with the heavy wooden canoe and his camp gear, was soon sailing along at a steady but controlled speed, bringing him closer and closer to his destiny.

Bernard was grateful for the progress however slow it had to be, and although it set him back several hours, he estimated that he would be able to reach Solpetrière, the deserted old loggers' camp, by nightfall. There was no chance of him entering the forest in the dark of night at this time of year, as he had done previously. He would have to make a bed somewhere that night in the old camp and take his chances in the morning. As the truck inched its way through the icy unplowed streets, he could make out in the near distance the steeple of an old church against the pale crimson and gray-blue sky.

When he pulled up to the entrance of the derelict old church, in the headlights he caught sight of a small animal, a muskrat scurrying for cover under the boards of the entrance. He smiled to himself, relieved to know that spring had definitely arrived if animals were out and about hungrily making up for the lean months of their winter hibernation. He turned off the ignition and dropped the lights down so as not to disturb the shy residents any further, leaving the low fog lights on as he stepped out of the truck to inspect the structure of the entry porch and check the door to see if there was any chance of taking refuge in the building for the night.

The boards of the landing were splintered and rotted away over the many years that the church, the whole town as a matter of fact, had stood empty. He trod very carefully where he could see the timber had maintained its integrity above the floor joists beneath. The small portico roof above his head had lost most of its tiles either to vandals or the weather he could not tell, but the gaps had caused water to come through and eat away at the floorboards. Inside the church would be no different. The ceramic roof tiles were a luxury in these parts and it was no surprise that some enterprising individual had stripped the building of its valuable parts for re-use or re-sale. The simple fact that it was a church did not seem to restrain the thief; he was thorough in his desecration of this tired old house of God. The entry lamp was gone and the doorknobs wrenched from the double doors.

Where the door handles once had been, Bernard put his fingers through the holes and pulled the doors open towards him. The truck's fog lights now threw an eerie yellow glow into the empty cavern of the church. Several broken wooden chairs were left upturned in the corners and what was formerly the pulpit was now a desultory heap of rubble, covered with a light layer of ice and snow that had come through the gaping hole in the roof overhead. Behind the dust heap was a large gothic arched window, the clear glass panels adorned with a random spiral of cracks which created a sinister spider's web backdrop to the ruined interior.

The temperature in this abandoned church was only a few degrees above the outside, but he determined it was better to be under shelter in case the weather changed. A set of stairs below the great arch of the window appeared to descend to a lower level at the back of the church. *Even better*, he thought, *more protection against the elements.* From his truck he retrieved his sleeping gear and a flashlight and now cut out the fog light. The immediacy of the pitch blackness engulfed him and for a moment he stood stock still, letting his eyes adjust to the dark and looking skyward to see if any stars had escaped the cover of the clouds. There were none.

His electric torch lit a way through the cavernous interior with its narrow tunnel of luminosity. The stairs were wholly intact and unlike the rest of the building in relatively good shape, as if they had been overlooked in the assault on the rest. The staircase made two left turns as it descended into the basement of the church. With the slight illumination afforded by the flashlight, he could see that there was a small room, perhaps a study, down below and at the bottom of the stairs stood a door that led out to the back of the lot, which sloped downward to a rear exit at a lower level. There seemed to be little else in this room, except a writing desk and a chair also in fairly good condition. *Perhaps they were brought here at a later date*, he wondered to himself, *after the building had been ransacked?*

Then the focused beam lit upon a tall, heavy but bare timber bookcase, its worn shelves sagging on several levels, the black paint on the backing board peeling and suspended with cobwebs in random corners. Several large rusted nails secured the bookcase to the thick stone wall behind it, and yet the whole structure stood at a tangent. He turned and dropped his sleeping gear onto the desk and settled into the chair. He contemplated laying out his sleeping bag in the small space between the chair and the bookcase, and then he noticed on the floor beside the bookcase evidence of scraping on the stone that showed the case had at least once been moved sideways. But the dust had settled over many years to obscure the mark, and it was only by virtue of the torchlight that he could see the phantom scrapes. He flew up suddenly and placed both hands at the top of the bookcase and with all his strength released the nails from their once-permanent places in the stone with one powerful pull that shattered the cobwebs and caused a copious amount of dust to rise unceremoniously into the darkness. The backboard splintered as he wrenched the case sideways and it fell in a heap beside the gap that was left by its absence.

Shining his light on it now, he saw that a low narrow doorway led into a small chamber, perhaps a closet or pantry. A cot was leaned against the far wall. On an adjacent wall was a small window barely wider in both dimensions than a man's hand, with its glass concealed by a wooden panel. Looking back to the cot, he noted the woolen blanket covering the mattress of the cot. Whoever used it last made sure it was carefully made, a small pillow positioned at its head and the blanket tucked neatly under the mattress. The wool was adorned with several large moth-holes and faded to a dusty grayish-blue but it still maintained a quaint and inviting quality to the grateful traveler. Bernard settled his sleeping bag over the cot and placed the torch on the floor so it cast a flood of light across the low ceiling and reflected down again. The exposed stone walls gave him the impression he was in a fortress or some medieval castle. He brought his hand up against it, felt the slight residual warmth, and understood why the room was so comfortable.

The timber panel across the window shut out the light and unwanted intrusions from the outside world. It was nailed to the frame of the window at several points but with his pocket knife, he was able to pry it off with minimal effort. In the darkness this small window provided no view of what lay beyond, but he guessed there would be a southern or southwestern aspect which allowed the stone wall to absorb the sun's warming rays. With the panel still on the floor below the window he returned to the bed, turning off the flashlight with one hand as he laid his body down. As his head landed resolutely upon the swell of the small pillow, he closed his eyes and waited the few minutes for them to adjust to the darkness before re-opening them. A luminescent ray of moonlight found its way through the small window and opened out a vista to him as he drifted toward sleep.

Snow covers the landscape like a coverlet of fine white lace. Silently he watches a solitary figure in the distance wend her way slowly through the forest toward him. She is wrapped head to toe in a thick cotton blanket and listening intently through the weave of the cloth for the sound of water. A small sleeping bundle is cradled in her arms beneath the blanket. When she comes upon the water she stops. Before her a colossal old cedar stands taller and straighter than all else in the wilderness. Its impressive trunk and ancient roots heave themselves above the earth. There she settles and begins to softly sing, rocking the baby in her arms. A teardrop falls upon the sleeping child; a loose wave of auburn hair escapes from her small black bonnet and spills down across her shoulders.

Her singing summons a young scout who appears amongst the snow drifts. He is draped in deerskins below the waist but above he is bare, his wide brown chest emblazoned with the black markings of a young Iroquois warrior. He slowly makes his way across the snowy ground, his moccasined feet making no sound at all. The young mother closes her eyes and releases herself to a deep sleep. Content with their sleep, the brave begins to climb the great tree, clearing the highest branches and disappearing into the tree top.

The woman awakes, peels away the blanket and stands up carefully, the child with her now much older. With a joyful laugh the boy runs off to chase a rabbit as it bounds its way across the spring forest. She calls out to him, but does not follow or appear alarmed. Her auburn hair now is crowned with gray and her pale translucent skin a soft freckled brown from the years of exposure and hard work. She pulls a black shawl around her shoulders and sinks back into the embrace of the tree. The roots seem to come alive and wrap their tentacles around her as she begins to sing a melancholy song, and the tree absorbs her into its bark as the last phrase trails off.

When the boy returns he is a young man of about seventeen, with long black hair tied behind his back. Hawk feathers adorn the thin braids that fall on each side of his face. He carries a guitar casually over his shoulder; it seems dwarfed by his tall frame but in his large graceful hands it becomes a thing of infinite beauty. Where his mother had previously sat, he leans now back against the tree and begins a slow lilting ballad, a haunting canto so full of sadness and passion it sounds like an emotion being forced from his body.

And then all at once the stone-walled room engulfed the dream, the dreamer, and the sounds and vibrations of the haunting ballad. Bernard abruptly awakened and looked about him and saw no one, but the notes of the song resonated as if they were bells chiming from the belfry of the church at a far distance. It was early dawn outside, he saw from his quick glance at the small windowpane. It was open fully, a square of pale light clearly framed by the dark gray stone wall. A nightingale landed on a low maple branch just above the window and began a plaintive song that complemented the guitar music. It trilled a laconic melody that permeated the small window and reverberated throughout the stone chamber.

He was fully awake now and looked to the small window for the bird outside, but there was nothing. He threw back the sleeping bag without a thought and was hit immediately with the frosty air, his breath making a cloud as he let it out sharply. He wrapped the still warm bag around him as he walked across the short distance to the window. Only then did he notice that he had slept with his boots on, a fortunate oversight considering the freezing temperature and the bare concrete floor.

He stood for a moment peering out across the churchyard. At a distance he made out a fence line that defined a cemetery, the vaguely luminescent tombstones dotting the small yard like haphazard teeth in an old beggar's mouth. *No one has swept out these stones for nearly a century,* he thought to himself. *I will pay a visit later.* But now he headed back to the bunk and reached down to retrieve the flashlight, which he believed had been kicked under the bed when he first alighted.

His hand felt nothing for a few minutes as he blindly patted the floor beneath the bed. Then, in the furthest reach of the cot against the wall, he felt something hard and significantly larger than the flashlight. Surprisingly it did not move easily with pressure. This discovery made his search for the flashlight urgent, and his random patting became more frantic. After a while he gave up and sat back on his haunches, only to nearly sit on the torch which was merely inches behind him. Flicking the switch, his momentary light blindness was discomforting but also brought with it a sense of relief.

When his eyes had adjusted he brought the light under the bed and found beneath the bedding, as far against the wall as it could possibly go, a large, oddly shaped and scuffed black case. Dragging it out carefully by its worn leather handle, he immediately recognized it as an instrument case of some kind. It was covered in a thin layer of dust and its single large clasp was barely attached, the original brass thoroughly tarnished and battered. The clasp came away in his hands. Carefully placing it to one side, he pried open the lid — there lay, nestled in the faded red satin of the lining, an ancient guitar, its five double strings strung loosely across an intricately cut rosette, but showing no signs of deterioration.

With two careful hands he lifted out the old instrument which he was certain would be over a hundred years old, perhaps two, and felt its solidity and smoothness like an old hymnbook he once sang from at Sunday mass. Something about the way its strings lay less than taut, but not limp, across the filigree sound-hole reminded him of sadness. Gingerly he laid the guitar on the bed and resisted the temptation to strum it or pluck the translucent strings, fearing the instrument would give way with the sudden force and disintegrate with the vibration after the unknown years — perhaps a century — it had lain untouched.

Beneath the space where the guitar had rested in the case, he found a thin notebook hand-printed on parchment. The archaic hand-lettering was replete with flourishes and the occasional inkblot; the words were also accompanied by exquisitely drawn pictures, detailed illustrations of musical instrument construction of the time. Leafing through quickly, he found the final illustration was similar to the instrument prone on the cot before him, but not identical. It had, however, very noticeably six strings. Lying beneath the notebook, a few thin and yellowed sheets of hand-inked music appeared as old as, if not older than, the notebook, perhaps of the same vintage as the old guitar. Across the top was written in a spidery hand, *"Per il mío caro Tomás."*

Altogether it was an unexpected find. Closing the manuscript and replacing the sheets of music, he carefully positioned the guitar back on top of the brittle and fragile pile of musical and personal memory. For how long it had lain there, he could only guess. The manual, he noticed, was remarkably detailed. What could have inspired someone to write down and draw such meticulous instructions on making these instruments, he thought? Was it the original maker? Or was it something extracted from an encyclopedia about musical instruments? And then he heard it again, a soft woman's voice humming a familiar lullaby in his ear. He could almost feel her breath.

It then struck him that this guitar was no stranger. The young man in his dream had played it against the large tree. *Could this be the same guitar?* There was no doubt in his mind; it had the same burnished reddish-ochre sunburst finish and a small filigree sound-hole encircled with an intricately braided red, brown, and yellow timber inlay. Finding it there under the bed where he had slept, however, was overwhelming and his mind was spinning with the largeness of the events that had unfolded in the last hour. All at once it came together in his mind. The melody was the same as those of his dreams in the last three months. Different arrangements, same tune. The music in his inner ear, the moonlight flight, the giant tree fallen in the river, the incessant dreams. And now, finding the guitar and the music — these were the newest pieces of the puzzle, but where were they leading him?

Subsequently he noticed that dawn had fully arrived and the room was no longer trapped in darkness. The soft rose light framed by the small window was comforting. Morning had brought a revelation, but also more questions. Bernard, however, was accustomed to life's mysteries and as per usual put the questions out of his mind. He did not like to dwell on uncertainties, choosing rather to proceed boldly and finding answers in time without ever having to ponder a question. Quickly he gathered up the guitar case and placed the broken clasp in the pocket of his flannel shirt. He wrapped the sleeping bag around the case and tied it with the short piece of rope he normally used to secure the sleeping bag. The large awkward bundle he carried under his right arm and in the other he carried the flashlight. He made a swift glance about the room, memorizing its dimensions and the details of its furnishings, then attempted to exit through the door beside the stairs.

At first the door would not open, even after he undid the various latches and locks. It refused to release its firm position in the frame. The years and the weather had warped the door so much it now stuck, not budging against the weight of his body. Bernard took out his pocket knife again and wedged it between the door and the frame just at the top corner above the doorknob. He felt something give slightly and with just a bit more downward pressure the timbers separated and the door scraped free.

He opened the door outward and before him was a welcome vision. The snow-covered churchyard was bathed in the morning's gentle glow and the row of maple trees created an intricate and gothic lattice of bare black branches. On closer inspection he could see the early preparation of greening buds bidding to rupture on every branch. He saw a lone warbler — or was it a cedar waxwing? — land on one of the lower branches and throw its head back to sing in earnest. But the effort was lost to him. He closed the door firmly behind him with some regret. He stepped off the concrete landing and his boots sank into the snow and did not yield until the crunch of ice was nearly up to his knees. He made deep tracks around the ruin of the church from the back door to the truck, which had burrowed and shoveled its way through the snow right up to the front vestibule the night before. It appeared from his perspective to be buried to the height of the flatbed. As he approached it from one side the canoe tied to the bed had the appearance of floating on the snow drift, and the picture brought a smile to the young man's face.

He would only have to reverse out of the position he left the truck in, he thought to himself. Luckily it had not snowed overnight; otherwise the new blanket of snow would have presented a fresh obstacle to his early departure. Carefully he placed the sleeping bag–wrapped guitar case upright onto the passenger seat and wedged it in place. It sat upright like a stately personage, and in a way Bernard felt he now had a traveling companion and a partner on his rescue mission.

When he reached the edge of the forest, he could see that the snow had begun to melt into a hard cover of ice on the forest floor. This was good news for he knew that the canoe would be easier to transport, gliding along with its central spine acting like a skate blade above the ice, than if the snow had still been powdery or the ice slushy. For a moment he pondered whether he should throw the case into the canoe to bring his companion along for the trip, or leave it in the truck to retrieve after his mission was completed. The thought of someone coming along and lifting the precious instrument from the truck while he was deep in the forest, however, left him with no alternative.

He removed the leather case from its seat, leaving it still wrapped in the sleeping bag, and hoisted it with care into the body of the canoe. He tied the loose end of the rope to the forward seating plank and secured it on the floor of the canoe alongside the rest of his provisions and camping gear. The possibility of the guitar becoming damaged by the wet or lost in the rapids did not escape him, but somehow he felt it was safer in his company than out of it. And, no matter how treacherous the journey might be, its presence provided grounding and a sense of direction that the music in his inner ear had previously provided.

It was with a new sense of purpose that Bernard placed ice cleats underneath the soles of his boots and proceeded through the rough terrain of the forest with the canoe tied to his waist and dragged behind him. The ice provided a frictionless surface for much of the journey, but at several unwieldy turns along the way he had to haul the heavy boat bodily and use all his strength to bring it back into a more viable position. At one juncture in the late afternoon he was tempted to heave the canoe over a ridge and let it free fall to the other side to conserve the small amount of energy he had left before he would collapse in exhaustion.

This ridiculous temptation lasted only a fleeting second, but it reminded him of his near fatal fall during the last trip to this ravine, and how it was the roots and brambles that had saved him from a certain death. He remembered feeling like a splintered old wooden boat after that accident, the bruises on his upper thighs and minor fractures on his ribs aching for weeks on his return and the blisters on his hands never entirely healing.

Learning from the previous incident he stopped in his tracks, secured the canoe on the flat, and lay down inside it. He felt the hard edge of the guitar case wedged into his ribs through the sleeping bag, and this reassured him. He closed his eyes momentarily and the darkness that fell felt like a soft blanket of infancy covering his head and eyes to protect them from the bright lights. Sinking further into slumber he felt a mother's hand on his head through the blanket and then heard a rhythmic murmuring sound that must surely be blood pulsing through veins and a beating heart, then total emptiness.

When he awoke, he felt refreshed in a way that only a short deep sleep can achieve. Looking down now below

the ridge where he had bivouacked, he realized that he
was again at the pass where he had previously fallen. The
bottom of the ravine was covered in ice and snow, which
obscured the river, but he was certain that the tree would be
lying in wait directly below. Buoyed by this discovery, he set
out once again with canoe in tow. When he began the steep
descent into the ravine, however, the boat became difficult
to restrain. Now it towed him, rather than he it, and he had
to use a series of calculated throws, tree and rope anchor-
ing, and rein-ins to strategically sling the canoe and himself
down the slope without losing person or boat.

It was a slow and treacherous descent but when he
reached his destination in two distinct and intact pieces,
the relief it brought was the sweetest reward. He was able
to tow the canoe behind him in the final hundred feet of
the trek that led him to the creek's edge, precisely to the
position where he had parted the two sections of the fallen
cedar. There it was before him, the snow and ice forming a
glass-like encasement over the tree.

The creek had already begun to thaw, and large rivulets
formed over boulders near the tree. He leaned into one of
the flows for a long wet drink, and the freezing cold bit
into his exhaustion with a fierceness that made his entire
body shudder. But the action cleared his head and the shot
of clarity and renewed purpose gave him the strength to
untie the canoe from his waist, settle the boat into a dry,
comfortable, half-upturned position under a large spreading
spruce, and prepare to make camp for the night. He lit a
spare fire, changed out of his damp clothes, and hung them
near the fire. When his clamminess finally dried away and
he was nearly paralyzed with cold, he layered on several dry
articles of clothing and socks before settling down before

the campfire to dine on a heated can of white beans and a half baguette. He savored the sweet taste of the bread and legumes, knowing they would provide his body with sufficient fuel for the long cold night ahead.

When the fire finally died down to a small glowing ember, he left it to crawl under the sheltering upturned canoe, wedging himself between the guitar case and the wooden paddles. The thick bed of pine needles beneath him gave off a pleasant scent that lulled him almost immediately into sleep. This night he did not dream. Even when the rain came down tapping lightly and steadily, then more urgently on the wooden canoe, he did not wake. By morning the rain had passed and he was surprised to find the sun already high in the sky above the tree line by the time he crawled out of the canoe tent. He had not slept this soundly for a long while, and with a wry smile that would not leave his face, he undertook his morning ritual before consuming a light breakfast of bread with butter and an apple.

The combination of pine canopy and canoe was a perfect foil for the dampness that permeated the site. The first rain was a sign that warmer weather was ahead and the creek would soon swell to a minor torrent. Already it was beginning to flow, thawing from the center line outward to the banks. Where the fallen tree was moored, the ice was visibly breaking away in large chunks. As the sun rose higher in the sky, he rushed to position the canoe with the precious cargo inside over the remaining ice ledge beside the smaller top section of the separated tree. The long rope emanating from the front of the canoe, whose other end was earlier attached to him at the waist, he now secured to the uppermost part of the tree. He strung the end of the rope around the trunk just below two top branches that fanned out like arms of a ballet dancer in pirouette. He secured the rope with a double bowline, and again around a branch.

Together the twinned logs would make their way down river as an odd pair — one hollowed and light and the other solid and unwieldy. The young man planned to ride the canoe through the slow icy rapids and carefully guide the log down the river before it became a swollen white-water rapid. From memory he knew there were no precipitous waterfalls but he could not be sure if there were rock ledges or other foreseeable obstacles to snare the linked pair. He placed his fate in the hands of the spirits that drew him to the forest in the first place, and believed with all his being that this journey was his destiny. If he made it through with his life and limbs intact, and his prized load not lost or destroyed, he was prepared to believe there was indeed an Almighty God who guided the lesser spirits of the trees, the animals ... and our human souls.

For a moment he had lost consciousness and when it returned, the ache over his right ear was excruciating. He looked out through half-opened eyes and saw only a brilliantly clear azure sky. He was rocking gently from side to side and realized then that he was still in the canoe and flat on the small of his back. He rose to a sitting position carefully and felt the throb in his head increase, and the buzzing in his ear amplified. He looked behind him and saw the small pool of blood on the floor of the canoe between the camp gear and the precious cargo where his head had just been cradled. With his right hand he felt the fleshy wound of the gash and the extensive swelling on the side of his head and knew that he had been hit by something large and very heavy.

He dipped his hand into the cold glacial water and washed off the blood, then took a drink from his cupped hand. It cleared his head a bit and brought the reality of the situation to the fore. He removed a bandana from around his neck and dipped it in the water to clean his wound, then tied the scarf tightly around his head to ensure the bleeding was stopped. He looked around him to get his bearings. To his amazement the canoe was still attached to the large log, which now swirled aimlessly in a wide slow-churning eddy formed by a shallow inlet carved into the open expanse of the river. The long tether that connected it to the canoe disappeared into the water for a few long seconds before it re-emerged again in a straight taut line and forced the canoe to mimic its movements like a caboose curving languor-ously far behind its long snaking drive-train. Bernard could not recall what had caused his black-out. The last thing he remembered was nearing what looked like a significant fall in the widening creek and paddling furiously to keep up with the rushing log to ensure the rope would not cause the canoe to be flung like a slingshot over the drop.

He had dipped the paddle into the white-water on his left-hand side in order to steer the boat wide of an upcoming boulder when next thing he knew, his forward passage was suddenly stopped short. Although he was unaware of it, he was knocked sideways and then rolled face down, wedged tightly under the seating planks and scattered haphazardly in amongst the damp gear on the floor of the boat. The canoe continued its precipitous journey, cruising unpiloted over the falls. The front end of the boat rose like a timber tidal wave as the back of it spun around in the jostling currents of the slipping water. The boat splashed down miraculously in a cataclysmic but upright position, its seismic contortions causing his unconscious forehead to come into jarring contact with the side of the seating plank and bringing him conversely into a slow consciousness just as the widened river abruptly ceased its angry gyrations.

Bernard came to in the calm of the swirling eddy and wondered for a moment whether he was in heaven. But the sky was a natural blue and tufted with the familiar clouds of an earth-bound atmosphere. He remembered his vow to believe in an Almighty Spirit and took a moment to close his eyes and thank whoever or whatever it was that guided him to safety. It might have been a low-lying branch swiping his head as he looked in the opposite direction, but he remembered that the river's edge had been some distance away so it would have had to be a tree growing in the middle of the river, which was unlikely, or a rock fatefully dropped by an eagle or osprey onto his head as if it was target practice. A large rock from a raptor's beak was even more unlikely and basically unheard of. The other possibility was divine intervention. He would never know, but for what it was worth he was still alive, albeit with absolutely no recollection of how he managed the waterfall without losing the cargo, or how the boat and log were able to ford the rapids unmanned and find safe passage into the wide calm inlet.

He was uncertain how much farther or for how long he needed to continue downriver before he could find an outlet reasonably accessible to the road. Once launched, the precipitating log pulled him in the canoe at a frighteningly rapid speed. He figured he had traveled at that speed for nearly three hours before the accident occurred. He had no idea after that of how long he had floated unconscious downriver. By the position of the sun it was afternoon and he could be anywhere between the headwaters of Peregrine Creek and the junction of the Salmon River.

He scanned the horizon for landmarks. There were no mountain tops to give geographic proximity, just a sea of green — luxuriant waves of emerald, jade, viridian, khaki, olive, lime — washed across the landscape in infinitely watering-down layers one behind the other on both banks of the river and beyond them. The unstoppable lateral movement of water downstream shunted him into an illusory sense of progression in the opposing direction although his canoe was at a virtual standstill in the slow churning of the eddy. Then he saw it in the corner of his eye — a silvery flash, a flicker in the water that could only mean one thing. Finally it heaved itself fully out of the water for a fleeting second, long enough for him to see that the fish was real. His best guess was that the rapids had brought him into the Salmon River and he was now only a short distance north of the old camp town.

In the half dark, he swung the canoe around to a forty-five-degree angle to the embankment of the river, struck his oar into the pebbled sand, and heaved aching legs and a drenched body over the side of the boat. Landing uncertainly, he pulled the heavy craft onto the shore, and with the very last vestiges of strength beached the battered canoe and secured it with several large rocks he hauled one by one into the canoe. It made a substantial pile that acted as an anchor for the boat, which was tethered to the floating log intermittently straining against the fraying rope.

The darkening sky gave little light to his efforts and when the ominous clouds issued their first distant roll of thunder, he felt it come up through his feet. The lightning flash in the corner of his eye sent a chill through his body. He had never felt so fatigued in his twenty-three years, and his bones felt as splintered as the oar he had earlier struck into the ground. Instinctively he ran to the boat and removed the layers of tarp, clothing, and camp gear to uncover the guitar case that was still tightly wrapped in the sleeping bag. It was relatively dry considering the sodden condition of the canoe floor. He was relieved to find the case had managed to repel the river's waters, even as the canoe itself had not.

He rolled all the contents he could carry into the large tarp and dragged it several yards up the sandy embankment to higher ground. The line of trees thickened as he advanced into the forest edge and there he found bone-dry pine needles under the enormous spreading boughs of an old spruce. When the rain finally descended, it was filtered to a fine mist through fifty feet of interlaced and cascading branches. The danger of bears advancing on him in the dark of night now presented him with a gruesome challenge; rather than ponder it, he immediately began searching with his torch for well-placed tree branches well above head height that he could throw tarp ropes over to create a large hammock for his provisions. For himself he planned to climb the large tree and settle into it for the night. It would not be the most comfortable bed, but after such an extended battle with the river it would be a tragedy to succumb now to the grip of a hungry, aggravated, and post-hibernation black bear.

In the morning, Bernard was thankful to find he had not fallen out of his elevated perch nor had the provisions and gear been raided. Everything was in its place, including the black case which was wedged beside him in the intricate web of structural branches that made up his crib. The scent of freshly crushed pine needles filled his nostrils and made his stomach rumble with hunger, but he was content to lie back in his high-set loft and review in his mind the events and outcome of the previous day. He drifted back into sleep again and awoke two hours later to the screech of a goshawk in the near distance.

Eventually forcing himself to climb down the tree, he inspected the log and the boat, and was much relieved to find the anchored boat still moored on the riverbank and the tethered log lapping now on the water's edge. On its precipitous ride downriver the log had been stripped of most of the longer low-lying branches. The relatively green upper twigs and branches however still clung tenaciously to the body of the sectioned timber and it was these that reached out of the water like the frail flailing arms of a drowning swimmer. This image made the young man suddenly sympathetic to his cumbersome and exhaustingly weighty burden.

Over a quick spare breakfast of oranges and sodden arrowroot biscuits, he calculated the time and distance required to retrieve his truck and return to the site. Having traveled yesterday for approximately three hours at a relatively moderate speed downstream from the junction of Peregrine Creek along the Salmon River, he calculated that he must be within striking distance of Solpetrière. Heading west through the forest with only the guitar case, sleeping bag, and his torch, he reckoned he would eventually run into the road that ran parallel to the river and with luck might be able to flag down a truck driver who would give him a lift to his own. When he had the log rolled and winched onto the pebbled beach out of the reach of the water, he set about planning a system of physical landmarks to guide a vehicle to the site.

He followed a circuitous path determined by the distance between trees which he believed a truck could pass through. With his pocket knife he cut low twigs and branches and laid them in an obvious cross directly on the path. Three hours later the forest opened into an expansive clearing and emptied the traveler onto the man-made route.

The first vehicle on the deserted loggers' road was a tractor that ambled along more than an hour and a half later. At his wave, the driver stopped to enquire if he needed a lift. The chatty old farmer was more than happy for a bit of company, and Bernard was able to understand him even if he did not respond in kind, and so he delivered the young man directly to the door of his waiting truck. It was only after jumping in and turning the key in the ignition that the younger man discovered the battery had worn itself out waiting for his return. The farmer reversed his tractor and pulled alongside Bernard's truck.

"Guess you'll need a bit more of a ride. Or maybe we can recharge your batteries with this old tractor?" the man asked. "No cables?" he continued when the young man shook his head sadly and gestured the lack of cables.

"Never mind. Hop in. I'll take you wherever you need to go. I was headed out to Scotstown for parts. This old thing has never broken down and she can take the distances better than my pick-up truck."

The farmer initially thought he misunderstood when the young man indicated that he needed to return to the forest to retrieve a large heavy boat. But with the help of a pen and paper, he soon understood Bernard's dilemma and to his own surprise agreed to help the stranded hitchhiker.

During the slow and steadfast reverse trip, Bernard learned that Sean Gascoigne's family had owned a dairy farm in the area since the 1840s. His mother was a Scotswoman and his father French, but they were raised Presbyterian and "free from the debilitating guilt" of the Catholic Church. His father was one of the few Frenchmen in Québec Province who encouraged his children to pray to Jesus instead of the Madonna, and had a distinct disdain for priests.

"My father's family, you know, settled in Solpetrière only a few years before the scandal. They had given very generously toward the building of that church. Do you know about the church?" The younger man nodded his head and gestured that he had slept there.

"You slept there?" the farmer asked incredulously, facing his passenger. "But no one's lived there since about 1890 or so. It's become an absolute ghost town. I've heard it's been reclaimed by the forest. But I've never been there, so it's only what I have heard. The canton is about to demolish it and resell the land to hoteliers."

The young man's eyes widened at the thought of a hotel on the site of the church. He was glad that he had retrieved the guitar when he did.

"I suppose you've heard about what happened to the priest?" the farmer continued. With this bit of information the young man shook his head. "No? Well, it's an old rumor now so I suppose it might be just one of those tall tales designed to scare little children and keep them away from ruins. They say the priest who built that church had a young Iroquois murdered when he found out his niece was carrying his child. The Indian died of gunshot wounds to the stomach. This devastated the niece so much she stabbed her uncle in the heart, right inside the church. No one knows what happened to the niece, or the child."

His eyes now widened with disbelief. Could his dream have been wrong? There was much love and tenderness, he recalled, and the music was only sad, not sinister. "I don't believe it," Bernard said suddenly, surprised to feel the vibration of his own expressed voice in his head. The farmer turned in surprise to look at his previously silent travel companion.

"That's all right, *mon ami*," he replied. "I don't believe it either."

They continued in silence for a fair while until they reached the spot where Bernard knew he had exited at a natural opening in the forest. The tractor made a sharp right turn and treaded a circuitous path into the woodland following the young man's lead, jogging on foot several yards in front of the machine and fossicking for crossed landmarks like cairns on a snowy trail, while the older man maneuvered the tractor like the expert farmhand he was. The tractor made light work of retrieving the log and canoe and both were loaded onto the machine with an ease he could not have imagined earlier. The young man continued to Scotstown with his rescuer to retrieve the tractor parts and battery jumper cables, and dropped into the local mill to have the log cut into manageable lengths. The two men bid farewell, and Bernard was on his way back to St.-Gérard arriving just at nightfall at his cabin by the lake in the full glare of the wolf's moon and under the luminescent cloak of the Milky Way. In the clear night sky the stars appeared like a million points of enlightenment and he was certain that old Sean Gascoigne was an angel sent to him by his guardian spirits. Divine intervention had again placed the right tool at his disposal at just the right time.

2

ISABELLE (FORCALQUIER), 1880–1881

At Le Havre, the captain waited impatiently at the dock for the loading of the émigré passengers, cargo, and mail packets. He was setting sail for Liverpool shortly, where the majority of these passengers would embark on the great transatlantic Allan Line Steamer ship to the port of Québec. From there some would carry on further to Montréal, Ontario, New Hampshire or Maine; some would remain in the old fort town. Ten-year-old Isabelle and her uncle were traveling by coach to his small parish in Solpetrière, slightly more than a camp at the base of Mont-Mégantic. But she would not know that yet, not until the two weeks of her sailing trip would bring her to the start of a very bumpy ride. The girl picked up the heavy leather trunk with all of her thin body straining at its great weight. Inside were her life's meager treasures and the items of necessity for a girl of ten on a journey to the New World. Although she could barely manage, she kept the trunk close, fearful that it would be lost from her on the long journey. A plain brown pinafore fell to below her stockinged knees, ending well short of the scuffed brown leather boots strapped meticulously in worn but polished metal buckles.

Above her, the tall lean figure of her uncle in a cassock and cloak of heavy black wool stood on the ship's loading area calmly issuing muffled instructions to the milling wharf-hands, rough ageless yet worn-out men with dirty beards and thick fingers who hefted the large trunks over their shoulders as if they were sacks of goose down or sawdust. The young girl looked upward toward the imposing priest whom she had met only a fortnight earlier and observed him closely. Regardless of time or place he was immaculately dressed in black from head to toe, the white clerical collar the only exception. Everyone's attention led directly back to this impressive man of the cloth, and those around him ultimately found obedience and cooperation where otherwise there may have been idleness or neglect.

In an ad hoc but coordinated fashion, the coterie of rough men carried the trunks up the latticed loading ramp and piled them neatly to one side in the ship's vast cargo hold. Without a word, the last case was hoisted into its place with the others in the pile and the last wharf-hand rambled down the plank nonchalantly toward the young girl. On reaching her he gently leaned forward and took the girl's trunk from her effortlessly with one calloused and leathery hand.

"I'd like to keep this with me if at all possible, sir," she cried with urgency, her small hand not letting go of the heavy case even as it nearly dragged her along as the man pulled it to him.

"Whatever you say, Miss," he replied, releasing the case and with the same hand reaching out to steady the girl as she nearly tumbled over with the weight of the valise back in her possession. With a small bow of his damp head he enquired, "Where would you like it placed?"

"That's all right. I'll carry it myself," she retorted, turning her back on the man and straining to drag the case behind her.

"Careful you don't hurt yourself there, Mademoiselle!" he called out, one eyebrow raised in amusement. He watched her move away awkwardly with the worn brown valise, forcing slow progress down the side of the sailing ship to the passengers' entry. The girl's small body, a slanting starfish as the free arm swung up to balance the other one, strained to the breaking point. The weight of the books she had carefully packed in the case the night before nearly caused Isabelle to wish she had left them behind. With all the resolve she could muster, she urged the bag toward the entrance, but in the end acceded to the unperturbed wharfie's assistance when the access ramp up to the ship's opening proved too much.

Sitting alone now in her small cabin aboard the ship, she pondered the two long weeks of the ship's journey to her new home, still considered the "New World" by residents of modern Europe. And, although a revolution of progressive industry and new scientific methods was taking hold in Europe, people's lives were not abruptly improved as they had been promised. In the cities, and even in provincial France where she had lived, Canada held a promise of freedom and a fresh start. Tales of fur-trappers and timber merchants making fortunes in the wilderness of that wild frontier became modern legend. The French government encouraged their patriots to continue to emigrate to British-controlled Québec in order to redress the balance of French-British presence there since the turning of the tides in 1763, after the Seven Years' War.

The night before she had tightly wrapped her favorite books in a large handkerchief and tucked them carefully into the small space between a pair of black shoes, two pairs of wool stockings, a dressing gown, undergarments, two dresses, and a spare wool coat. The half dozen books were the only ones that she allowed herself to take on her highly anticipated journey to the new territory. The others were returned to Father Pascal's library. Her wardrobe was spare and she made the decision to leave most of it with the needier children of her village as they were now too small and not befitting a future school teacher, as she hoped to become one day at her uncle's church in Canada. The new dresses were donations to the church where she and her mother had lived and worked for as long as the girl could remember.

On the bed beside the large valise was the final, most valuable item for her journey — a beautifully worn hand-crafted guitar bequeathed from her dead mother. It was nearly one hundred years old, and as it lay now open in its case on her bed, it reminded her painfully of her beloved Maman. Lifting it gingerly and running her thin fingers delicately along its edge, she remembered her mother and the fevered wish she bestowed upon her before she died. It was late last year and the fever had already taken hold in the village and many of the frail and elderly had succumbed. The shock was palpable in their small parish when her mother succumbed as well. The memory of her luminous face and the fine bones of her long fingers lingered like a bittersweet aftertaste in her young mind. Her dreams were filled with her mother's presence — teaching music to the children, a weekly Saturday occurrence that brought young ones happily to the church; making rounds to tend to the sick; providing meals for the children of the poorest villagers. Father Pascal missed her presence as well, but finding a replacement for the church's caretaker became a priority. Mother and daughter had lived at the church for as long as Isabelle could remember. Her mother was cook and housekeeper for the now octogenarian priest, Father Pascal, and as the caretaker of the small church, she was seen as the mother of the congregation with its three hundred souls, and Isabelle felt she had a large family about her.

While young Isabelle was still in her cloth nappies, music was her mother's special gift to her. Even before she could speak her first cogent words she was taught to make beautiful sounds with strings and bows. She had her own child-sized guitar, which she gave away to a small boy from the next village when she outgrew it. Like her mother she wanted to encourage the love of music and nurtured talent when she saw it. Her mother's regular Saturday musical sessions were a high point in all the children's week. When her mother's fever prevented her from holding the weekly gathering, children and their parents came to her bedroom window to play little songs for her. As the fever wracked her mother's thin body beneath the crumpled damp sheets, Isabelle continued to play ever so softly. Starting with the very first song her mother taught her, and following with every piece she learned since then, Isabelle meditated slowly and deliberately on bringing forth the comfort of music to her sick mother, never believing that she would eventually succumb.

Her final serenade played on its own accord as the mother's fevered moans turned into a groan and ended just as the last breath was squeezed out. Mother, daughter, and guitar lay in silence on the bed for nearly two hours before the priest returned from the church to find the sad group. He sought to comfort the now motherless child by reading long passages of the Bible, but each night for two long months Isabelle cried herself to sleep in her small lonely bed.

"Isabelle, my child," Father Pascal reminded her, not unkindly, "you are a big girl now, and if your Maman was still with us, God rest her soul, she would not wish for such tears to be shed. Go to sleep now and remember all the goodness she provided to the people she cared for."

"But Father Pascal," the distraught girl answered through her tears, "Maman comes to my dreams each night as if she was really still with us, and all I can feel when I awake is that she is no longer with us. She will never play her music to me again. I wish I could go to sleep and never awake again too." Her sobs continued, the cries of a lonely dove.

"Sleep now, my child. Your mother will play her music to you again. She may be gone, but surely she will play with the angels in their choir, and her music will be with us for an eternity."

Isabelle tried with each passing day to release her mother's memory into a reliquary of the past which did not cause so much pain. She dedicated herself to taking over where her mother had left off until a new caretaker could be found. Father Pascal considered her too young at ten years of age to shoulder the immense responsibility of his congregation, but he did not rush as urgently as he might have had she not proven to be rather equal to the task. She cooked meals for the old priest just as her mother had, dusted and cleaned the church hall and his library to a spotless shine, ordered the poultry and meat from the butcher and shopped at the markets each week, just as her mother had done. Several of the village ladies volunteered their assistance in preparation for the Friday and Sunday mass, and even organized a christening. She tended the *potager* herself and learned through trial and error how to stake certain climbing vegetables, when to apply dressings of ash to others, and how to harvest pumpkins.

Nearly six months passed and the harvest moon brought one evening a tall stranger to Isabelle's attention. He was introduced to Isabelle as her uncle, Father Jacob, her only living relative, and he had arrived from his own parish in a remote part of eastern Canada — New France they still called it, although the British had wrestled control over the place just over a century ago — to take her back with him. They would set sail in less than a fortnight. He was dressed in black, resembling a much younger Father Pascal, but over his robes he wore a long traveler's cape lined in red. At first Isabelle worried that Father Pascal would be left with no one to care for his and the church's daily needs, but the old priest assured her, in front of her uncle, that he could easily find another caretaker. It seemed that quite a few petitions had already been made to him, but he had let her continue with the role for half a year knowing it would be curative for her young soul, so recently devastated by the loss of her mother.

"Your services are required over the seas, my dear," Father Pascal began, "to work with your uncle in ministering to the needs of the loggers' souls in New France. You have learned the tasks of providing for a congregation well while your blessed mother was alive, and over these past months you have acquitted yourself well."

"Thank you, Father," she replied humbly, not daring to look at her newly discovered relative. Father Jacob sat silently and deferentially at the more senior priest's table and listened tangentially, with his thin face expressionless but not unkind.

"I am confident your uncle will be pleased that his new charge is so well equipped for the ministrations of a church, and skilled domestically at so much. In two weeks' time, you shall gather all your belongings and make your way to your new home."

"Yes, Father."

"Go, my child. Go and be a dutiful daughter of Our Good Lord and light the way for others so that His Word will ring as loudly in the frontier as it does here in our small village. You are a daughter of the world. Be a blessing to your uncle, as you have been to me. May the Lord bless you, my child." For the first time in many months Isabelle felt a faint stirring of hope. The possibility of honoring her mother by becoming her likeness in a faraway place appealed to the bright and earnest young girl.

"It will be good to be needed, Father Pascal. I would like to do that. And ... " she looked hopefully to her uncle, "I would also like to teach the loggers' children how to read and write. And play music as Maman did." Her uncle did not volunteer a reply, for he was proving to be a man of very few words, but his overall appearance seemed amenable and her hopes rose further.

Fourteen days later exactly, on the eve of her departure, Isabelle replaced the delicate antique music instrument into its black leather case, which lay beside the larger trunk on her small bed. Wedging the instrument case lengthwise along the widest part of the trunk, with a silent prayer for the safe journey of her belongings, she closed the heavy lid of the leather trunk for the last time in her old bedroom and secured the lock. Her own self she laid down on bedding spread upon the floor beside her bed and blew out the diminishing stub of candle.

As her eyes slipped closed and the half-light of the moon through her curtained windows retreated to slivers, she heard the strains of music from her mother's favorite piece, a nameless tune she played with such passion and sadness that Isabelle often wondered from where the source of emotion could have come.

"Good night, Maman," Isabelle whispered as the soaring music reached its summit and loosed its final crescendo of falling notes. Angels and ordinary men wept from the sheer beauty of its sound.

Once they reached Liverpool and boarded the amazingly large steamer ship, Isabelle felt a new mixture of dread and excitement well up inside her. The future she saw before her was simultaneously laden with great possibility and terrifying unknowns, grand new vistas and frightening unseen savagery. If she believed the stories and idle rumors of those around her before she set sail, she would have been overcome with dread. But Isabelle was gifted with the ability to withhold judgment until she could prove to herself whether, behind cavalier words and well-meaning but unwarranted advice, there lay veracity or untruths. Quite precociously she had noticed that, when one was as young as she, others were wont to give unsolicited advice. Wisdom, she assured herself, came from those who had traveled far and wide, like her uncle Father Jacob, who would not see fit to take his niece to the New World if he believed it was full of danger and angry savages.

Her desire for knowledge had begun at a very young age when she first entered the clergyman's library with her mother and discovered that books were the source of the greatest knowledge and could transform a person who sought to be elevated by them. As she tidied the books on Father Pascal's shelves and carefully ran the feather duster over them, her small hands caressed the numerous leather-bound volumes as if they were precious stones with mystical qualities. Following her mother around the large library, Isabelle marveled at the books he had collected from all over the world. Her fingers lightly brushed over the imposing tomes as they revealed themselves to her: *La Commedia;* Goethe's *Faustus;* an eighteenth-century translation of the *Tao Te Ching;* a collection of Greek tragedies; a directory of New World medicinal plants.

When her mother was busy in another room, she would creep back to the library and pull out a volume, admiring the cryptically printed letters and staring with wide-eyed amazement at the exquisitely executed ink drawings and the rare gilded figure of an angel swooning in ecstasy on a book sleeve. At eighty-two, the priest was well-traveled and revered, having witnessed new worlds discovered and old dynasties collapse. He considered himself a scholar of the New World Order and a messenger for God, placing his belief in the new scientific methods and the forward march of industry just a step behind his faith in the Holy Trinity.

The heady embrace of the catechism and old books was Isabelle's nursery; however antiquated they were, these tomes were the building blocks of her child's playground. And, as her world contracted into the tiny constricted space of her small ship's bunk, it was her steadfast belief in God and Knowledge, and her ability to recall in her mind the great uplifting magic of her mother's music, that sustained her on the two-week journey across the vast open seas. To her dismay, her relationship with her uncle, whom she continued to call "Father Jacob," as he was introduced to her, did not deepen during the long voyage.

Speaking always quietly in dulcet tones, his calmness was fortress-like in its reserve. His gaze was set permanently upon the horizon and because of his great height he appeared to look perpetually above the heads of his fellow travelers. He almost seemed not of this world. But, did he simply choose to look beyond the mortal world to divine answers from the heavens and the greater universe, the girl questioned herself, or was his distance and lofty arrogance a sort of protective shield against wounds he feared to sustain in this very material world? She was filled to the brim of her small body with questions unasked and more unanswered, but feared her towering uncle in his pious and immaculate robes would be impervious to her questions.

"Father Jacob," she enquired timidly one morning, as they gathered in the dining cabin for a breakfast of bread, butter, and a dollop of bee's honey, "how much longer will it be before we shall see land?"

The priest looked beyond her to the flickering gas lamp hung from a peg above one of the cabin's four portholes and at length replied, "Not long, child. One more week and we shall round the coast of Newfoundland, God and weather permitting." Isabelle looked behind her briefly to see the porthole where her uncle's eyes were fixated. A muted and barely perceptible arc of horizon floated between the lifeless sea and the colorless sky. No swoop of albatross or clot of cloud interrupted the grayness. The morning light was weak and uninspired but the unrevealing clouds belied the dawn of potential.

Before the breakfast china could be cleared away and her opportunity lost yet again, Isabelle cleared her throat and addressed her uncle with a question that had niggled at her for weeks but she had little courage or incentive to pose.

"Father Jacob," she began timidly again. "I have a question that I hope you may be able to answer." She waited for a reply, which did not come until much later, after she had actually forgotten she ever spoke. His words nearly startled her out of her chair.

"Not now, child," the man of cloth replied with only a hint of annoyance in his dry brittle-leafed voice.

"It was about my mother," she interjected quietly.

"I must attend to my books this morning. Your question can wait until a more suitable time." The towering cleric rose hurriedly from his seat and exited the cabin, leaving Isabelle to wonder if there was not a sliver of avoidance in his retreat. She felt suddenly ashamed and abandoned, as if she had proposed a war and her uncle chose not to be enlisted.

Returning to her small cabin, she had no recourse but to seek exclusive comfort in her own company. For the first time during the slow journey west, a tiny imperceptible tug on her sleeve as from a small child emanated from somewhere underneath her tidy bunk. With barely room enough to move the large valise, Isabelle maneuvered herself nimbly and retrieved the instrument case from its dark cramped confines. Lifting the guitar from out of its case immediately transformed the small room; the sterile greeny-white eggshell walls turned a faint yellow-orange reflected with the half-light of the small porthole above. Even the scratchy gray wool of the cot blanket mellowed with softness.

The instrument against her body felt alive and her drab mood fell away, warming to the soft dawn-lit patina. The first plucked sounds of the strings surprised her. Its pitch was preserved. The instrument had not lost any of its tonal perfection on the journey and now gave its music effortlessly, a meadowlark at the first flush of spring. Its familiar smoothness and comforting shape were welcome like a well-worn pair of shoes. Her mother's arms seemed to close in about her. As she moved her fingers tentatively at first and then relaxed instinctively into the assuredness of the ancient strings, her tempo gradually coordinated itself with the steady rhythmic rise and fall of the boat on the sea, a troupe of Spanish dancers gliding across the wooden planks of a ballroom floor in a guileless glissando.

Her mother's compositions were haunting melodies, exacting in their mastery of form and by their beautifully balanced structure, first a major then a minor key with interwoven harmonies that caused a well-spring of emotion which seemed to rise from the very inner being of the soul in anyone who heard her play. Isabelle knew that it was as much the player as the compositions themselves that elicited that kind of emotion, and her mother was the most silently evocative person she knew. The guitar spoke for her, its words all bittersweet melancholy in homage to some place or someone now long gone. In the large rollicking boat en route to a strange new land, the daughter played the melodies as if in conversation: a vibrato was a question strung out to await an answer, a rubato a slowing to receive it.

For the next several days, there was little reason to leave her small cabin. She responded once daily to the bells that announced the afternoon meal, the uncle meeting her at the

German cook's cabin, satisfied that his charge was safe, and not questioning her activities of the forward-marching morning and night. Isabelle counted the days and weeks, and the day on which almost a fortnight had passed since her last breakfast with her uncle, she turned eleven. She would address him again with her important question. This time, she resolved to herself, she would phrase the question differently and with hope elicit a less elusive and more favorable response from her relative.

"Uncle Jacob," she began confidently. "Today is my birthday; I am now eleven." She paused, feeling her assurance slowly fade as Father Jacob, having been addressed directly by the girl, gathered himself up taller than ever at the table. She continued despite her waning conviction. "I miss my mother very much. Did you know her well when you were children?"

"Yes, child," the uncle replied.

"What was she like?" she countered immediately.

"As God was her witness," he said slowly with a long drawn-out breath, "she was not afraid of hard work."

Father Jacob closed his eyes and reluctantly brought forth memories of a past that he had not evoked in over two decades. His twin sister was a devilishly strong-willed person; that he remembered. The farming life was only ever a duty to him, as the only son. She was his father's right hand, and his sister embraced her responsibilities like a girl possessed by a demon. She worked on the land side by side with both male relatives, her small frame only half his father's height and her fine fingers nearly bleeding, but they toiled until sundown each day, and at the end of the week there was no one who could bring customers and money to their market stall like she could.

While he resolved to leave the land and become a priest as soon as his father would allow him, his sister's attachment to the land and her enduring enthusiasm for the abundance of the harvest and increasing income from their labors never faltered. The proud radiance on her small face as she handed the weekly earnings to their Papa was invincible. And then he remembered their father's betrayal — suddenly Father Jacob's broad angular shoulders relaxed of their own accord and Isabelle sensed that the drawbridge over the fortress moat was being lowered momentarily for her to enter.

"Did she play music too when she was young?" the girl asked boldly now.

"No, child. She did not. There were fields to plow and harvests to gather, constant repairs and winter stores to attend to."

"Then where did she learn to play music like an angel?"

"Like an angel indeed."

The priest hesitated, his eyes beginning to search the walls of the cabin to avoid the niece's gaze. The bridge was starting to rise once again and quickly she followed up her line of questioning with a query that required a simple aye or nay. Her heart began to race and she felt a simultaneous panic and exhilaration in her breath like a fast rising tide.

"Did she learn to play at a convent in Notre-Dame?" the girl continued, her eyes wide and beseeching the older man.

"I would imagine so," he said nodding his head, his eyes still trained upon the gray-white wall.

"And was she at the convent for a very long time?"

"Yes," he murmured almost imperceptibly.

"How long, Father?" the girl continued, her hope rising. "And how did I come to be born?"

Her uncle now looked at her with little compassion, although in his formless but steady gaze she could see nothing of the anguish which began to rise in him as he looked upon his niece. For a moment he looked into the girl's face and saw for the first time a painful likeness to his sister — the pointed chin and the broad forehead fringed with auburn rather than black, but the same pale translucent skin that evinced a finely formed porcelain mask over the young face; the eyes and lips so like his sister's yet also so different. Where his sister's eyes were amber like his own and her lips full, this girl's eyes were the color of the forest. There he stopped short. The emerald green eyes of someone he once knew. He did not notice that her lips were small like a budding rose.

The life her mother led before she was born remained a mystery. When Isabella discovered books in her mother's meager belongings that bore the imprint of the convent's seal, the only explanation she received was that her mother had once devoted her life to God. But she was a woman of few words. Her twelve-year vow of silence had made a lasting impression; even when she found herself eventually outside the strictures and confinement of the convent walls, her silence remained like an invisible cloister about her. She was impermeable to the rest of the world. Isabelle often felt she was on the outside of this wall looking in, for she knew very little, practically nothing, of her mother's inner life.

The camp was smaller than Isabelle had envisioned. As the coach approached in the failing light that early spring evening, the girl felt weary to the bone, having traveled for three consecutive days on rough roads that jarred and jumped under the wheels of the horse-drawn carriage. Her bones seemed rearranged by the journey and she clutched her seat as if her life depended on it. On the long jaunting trip her uncle's formidable attention was focused on a large, heavy, leather-bound bible in his lap, which he used as a sort of ballast to keep from pitching forward and sideways as the coach careened its way southeast into the interior of the wild Canadian landscape.

The horses and coach drivers were changed every day on the journey and the last driver kept up a continuous monologue aimed at his passengers regardless of whether they could hear his words or not. Isabelle was not glad for this distraction, but caught a large enough fraction of his interpretation of the landscape to understand that they were nearing their final destination — the furthest eastern endpoint of the invisible line she had drawn from their original staging point at the port of Québec. They kept to the only road in the area, originally a horse trail regularly used by the natives, then recently cleared and widened by the loggers who had set up the new camp not seventeen years earlier.

Of the original six passengers that disembarked from the ship and gathered to charter the coach three days earlier, only the girl and her uncle remained. By the time the road-weary carriage horses strode into the camp with their heavy hooves, the last rays of the sun were bleeding out and less than two dozen gas lamps formed a sparse constellation across the campsite. An early salute from a barn owl broke the settling silence.

Isabelle could barely fight through her fatigue to alight from the coach and remain standing, as the driver handed down their baggage. A dark rounded figure carrying a kerosene lamp above her short frame rushed out of the cabin and with head slightly bowed, welcomed the priest and his charge to the camp.

"I hope you had a tolerable journey, Father Jacob," she said with motherly concern. "I hope your back did not bother you too much." Then she looked at Isabelle quickly up and down and said, "And you must be Isabelle?"

"Yes, Madame," the girl replied with an awkward and regrettable dip of the knees.

"You're not as little as I imagined you to be. Sorry to hear about your mother."

"Yes, Madame."

"Welcome to Solpetrière, Isabelle. I am Madame Lowell. I am your uncle's housekeeper. Why don't you both take yourselves into the house and I shall be there shortly."

"Yes, Madame," was all the girl could manage.

"I will just help the driver here with the bags."

Father Jacob strode up beside Madame Lowell at that moment and stooped above them with his hand on the older woman's shoulder for support.

"Thank you, Madame Lowell," the priest said quietly. Then he corrected himself self-consciously, "Amalie." These were nearly the first words that Isabelle had heard from her uncle's lips since they commenced their coach journey that morning. The tall man turned on his heels and moved toward the cabin slowly. Isabelle followed a few paces behind him unsure of her legs but keen to discover what a log cabin looked like from the inside. Isabelle did not stop to take up her bag although for a moment she dreaded to think how her precious cargo had survived its three-day journey through purgatory.

She caught up to her uncle, who had already stepped through the threshold of the house, not waiting for her to find her way up the dark steps. Her new home was small with warm cedar log walls and simple rough-hewn timber furniture. To one side was a large iron pot-bellied stove upon which was nestled a black iron kettle steaming upon a glowing bed of coals, and a fat copper soup pot beside it, the lid only perfunctorily holding back the succulent warm smells of supper, a reward for their timely arrival.

The priest motioned his niece to seat herself on the small lounge as he disappeared into his private room. Isabelle was glad of the seat, but decided to remain standing and moved slowly across the room to look more closely at the books and photographs lined up along a small rough bookcase against the opposite wall. Two daguerreotypes leaned against the back of the shelf just above her eye level. The girl immediately thought it must have been Madame Lowell who put them there, as certainly her uncle would have placed them higher, at his eye level. She could just see in the dimly lit cabin the figures that faced her, standing with an eternal moroseness. The photographs fascinated her as she had never seen one before. Although the solemn pairs of eyes that stared back at her were unfamiliar, in one she made out the possible image of Uncle Jacob dressed in a black robe and standing beside another man in different robes, and yet another man in a soldier's uniform.

At that moment the baggage arrived with the house-keeper and the coach driver and together they arranged the cargo in a small pile in the corner of the cabin. Father Jacob appeared out of his room wearing a clean frock with a freshly scrubbed look about his countenance. The driver enviously eyed the soup pot, but bid his farewell and exited to tend to his horses for the night. Father Jacob picked up two leather valises and carried them into his room as Madame Lowell hurried behind him with two more, quietly urging him to be careful of his back.

Madame Lowell was much older and plumper than her mother, Isabelle observed. She was stout and sturdy as a tree stump and twice the width of her reed-like Maman. Above her flushed and rounded face was a mop of silvery gray hair pulled loosely back in an untidy bun at the back of her creased neck. Her small mouth was shaped like a beak and overall her appearance was of a clucky old silver hen. Madame Lowell, Isabelle would eventually discover, was a Swiss-French widow who had been married to an Anglican minister, with whom Father Jacob had been acquainted in his earlier travels through Canada.

Standing alone in the corner was Isabelle's now somewhat bedraggled valise and she wondered if she should move it. But not knowing where to place it, she simply went to stand beside it and waited for the housekeeper to return to give instruction. Subsequently, Madame Lowell re-entered and without due consideration picked it up as if it was a mere feather duster. The plump rolls on her arms wobbled slightly but she did not seem to struggle at all with the weight.

"Come along, child," she motioned to Isabelle, "Your room is yet to be finished so you shall stay with me in the back house. Is this all you have?"

"Yes, Madame," said the girl with her eyes cast downward to avoid revealing the anxiety she felt at Madame Lowell's careless waving of the bag about her as she spoke. The priceless contents were unknown to her; only Isabelle was privy to their preciousness, and she nearly reached out for the bag but realized that Madame Lowell was only being kind to assist her as she did, and might be offended by her protectiveness.

"You'll want to wash up a bit before supper too," Madame Lowell now said, looking concerned at the girl's dusty, crumpled, and bedraggled clothes and hair. Her shoes in particular were the worse for wear even though Isabelle had taken great pains to polish them with a bit of rag before she disembarked from the ship.

Isabelle stood still.

"Come with me," Madame Lowell continued. "We'll get you out of your dusty clothes and scrub you down. I suppose two weeks in a sailing ship and three days on the road without a decent bath would make anyone look like a street urchin!"

Like a tired baby chick trying to keep up after its mother, Isabelle giddily followed the matron. They picked up the kerosene lamp from its peg on the porch and carried it down the steps and around the house to another small bungalow behind the main house connected by a covered walkway. With the cold seeping in through her thin frock, Isabelle picked up her step and kept close to the dark figure below the bobbing lamplight. Then the door of the cabin was prised open and immediately a waft of lemon polish and lavender found their way into Isabelle's nose. She cried out with a half-anguished, half-delighted gasp as the rich warm smell all at once took her numb memories back to Father Pascal's house, which her mother had always kept beautifully polished with lemon oil and freshly scented with the lavender flowers that bordered her lush *potager*.

Madame Lowell turned around to study the girl's face and saw quivering lips and tears welling up in the two emerald eyes behind the dusty mask. Without a word, she placed the valise carefully on the floor and, with a knowing sigh, put both her matronly arms around the girl in a soft maternal embrace. The tears rushed down her grimy cheeks carrying the salty grit and emotional detritus of the past months into her trembling lips. These she pressed exhaustedly into the plush and welcoming bosom of Father Jacob's housekeeper.

"Now, now, now," Madame Lowell cooed, "You go ahead and cry. You must be very, very tired. We'll wash your face and get you undressed and into the cot for a good sleep. You can have your bath in the morning."

She led the weeping girl into a bare closet-sized room with a tiny window set quite high, and a small cot which had a thin cotton gown folded neatly upon it. Isabelle let herself be helped out of her dusty shoes, barely able to remain standing on the cold timber floor, as Madame Lowell helped her undress, scrubbed her quickly with a washcloth, and pulled the nightshift over her. Pulling back the woolen covers, Isabelle slipped into the bed with a small whimper and was asleep before Madame Lowell bid her good night and closed the door behind her.

The evening passed without dreaming for the exhausted girl. While her uncle dined in his room in the main house, she floated in the euphoria of a deep sound sleep, not even waking when the large russet bantam roused itself before the first light of dawn to announce the start of his day. At one point she drifted out of her slumber briefly to be met with the essence of lemon oil, but on this occasion it brought comfort rather than tears, and softly lulled her along on the placid ocean of sleep.

When she finally awoke several hours later to the sounds of a dozen chickens clucking and rousing each other in the poultry joisting ground below the small window, she sat up in her cot to look around the room for the first time. It was small and likely a storage closet at one time as several deep shelves lined the wall opposite her. They held a veritable supply store's variety of cleaning implements and old rags, including a bottle of oil that surely was the source of the lemon polish essence that had sent the homesick girl into a frisson of tears the night before.

Across the room a small high window was left slightly ajar, rendering the sounds of the poultry below particularly distinct. The window beckoned her, and with the help of a small step-stool and standing on her toes, she was just able to take in the view afforded by the windowpane. Outside, the expansive view took her breath away. In the foreground, from the house to the animal shed a few yards away, the scene was familiar — under a large bare-limbed maple tree a dozen or so chickens scratching at a hard-packed dark brown surface bordered by an expanse of fresh lime-green grass glazed in parts with gleaming patches of melting ice. Beyond the roofline of the barn, the contours of evergreen treetops fanned out from every direction, extending higher and further than her eyes could comprehend. In varying shades of green from a deep emerald to a greeny-gray goose egg color that disappeared into the white of the clouds above the peaks, the vertical sea of conifers was as vast as the ocean she just crossed. Above the floating cloud line, the sky graduated to a brilliant azure blue that she had only imagined in her dreams.

A firm knock on the door caught her gazing at this splendid view and woke her from the reverie of the scenery. Stepping down carelessly from her perch upon the stool, she suddenly found herself in a crumpled heap on the floor and gave a small cry. The door opened smartly and Madame Lowell came whirling in with her long skirt flying, nearly dropping the small tray in her hands, and her mouth opened in a small *"Caw?"*

"Isabelle," she clucked, "What are you doing there on the ground? Have you hurt yourself?" She placed the tray of breakfast on the cot and bent over awkwardly to assist the collapsed girl. Her ankles were weakened from standing on her toes for so long peering out the window, and when she alighted on the ground from the height of the stool they had given out from under her.

"I'm all right, Madame Lowell," she replied quickly. "I just tripped over the stool. I am all right now." Scrambling to her feet with the woman's help, Isabelle hobbled over to the cot, sitting down abruptly and nearly disrupting the omelet and piece of toast on the small tray. "Oh, thank you so much for the breakfast, Madame Lowell. You needn't have gone through so much bother for me. I was on my way out to help you with the housework. My mother was the housekeeper for Father Pascal in my hometown, you know. I always woke up early to help Maman with the chickens ... "

"You never mind the housework today, my dear. I will expect some help soon enough, but today we shall get you cleaned up and fed, and then we will see what Father Jacob needs done." Madame Lowell picked up the tray and motioned with her silver-gray head for Isabelle to follow. "Come on now; let's sit you at the table to eat your omelet properly — parsley and onion to give a tired girl some energy. I will go and warm the well water for your bath, so don't delay with the breakfast."

Isabelle sat for a moment longer and pondered her new life thus far. She remembered Madame Lowell's motherly embrace the night before and realized that this woman was kinder to her than anyone she'd ever known. Her own mother remained distant in her silence, as did her uncle. Madame Lowell however kept up a constant dialogue and seemed genuinely concerned for her safety and comfort.

I shall not let her down, Isabelle thought to herself. She gathered herself off the cot and limped in her bare feet out to the small hand-hewn kitchen table where Madame Lowell had left her breakfast.

After she completed her ablutions in the warm copper hip-bath, Isabelle was grateful for the opportunity to pull on fresh undergarments, a clean dress and stockings retrieved from her case stowed underneath the cot. The temptation to pull out her guitar case and examine the instrument inside for any damage was on her mind, but instead she crept back into the kitchen in her stocking feet and found her shoes near the back door. They had been dusted and polished to a dull sheen. She lifted them to her nose and smelled the slightly rancid odor of animal fat on them, but was grateful that the job had been done for her. Putting them on, she felt like a newborn person.

How strange and wonderful it feels, she thought to herself. *The ground no longer rocks, or rattles my bones!*

The elation was short-lived, however, for when she returned to her traveling suitcase to examine her precious instrument, she was devastated to discover that the guitar case was missing. It was only then that she realized that she had failed to replace the precious cargo into the larger case at the end of the ship's long voyage. It must have remained under the bunk of her cabin as she herself was being bundled off the ship and into the jostling carriage. The thought of this crushed her into the small of her own soul.

Isabelle wept hopelessly as she realized that she might never see her mother's beloved instrument again, and this brought more tears and an angry fist on her thigh for her carelessness. She felt disheartened beyond redemption, but in time realized that regret would not remedy the situation. No more tears, she promised herself resolutely. The loss of her mother's guitar meant she must leave her childhood behind and embrace her new life here as an adult. And like her mother, she too would not be afraid of hard work.

The months quickly passed and Isabelle found that life at her uncle's home was not unlike her previous life. Like her Maman, Father Jacob was a person of few words, yet he managed to supervise the construction of a new house of worship in the camp, just as her mother had been able to inspire a whole generation of young musicians in her small village back home. The priest's distance, however, meant that he did not feature largely in her daily routine for nearly a year. The new church was to be constructed of saw-milled timber and roofed in fired-clay shingles. It would be the first European style structure in Solpetrière, and it was a momentous occasion when Father Jacob stepped up to the open-air pulpit to preside over the ground-breaking and blessed the site, sanctifying the land with a sprinkle of Holy water and a kiss from his own dry lips.

When he had arrived seven and a half years ago, the camp contained merely a handful of log cabins. Many of the workers still lived in stretched animal-skin lean-to tents and cooked on a campfire. There was no milling shed and the logs were transported by a team of six draft horses to the closest mill nearly a day's journey eastward. Father Jacob's work was mainly to provide a weekly sermon to a dozen fellows, fortnightly confessions and absolution to the same men, and the occasional last rites to a dying logger felled either by consumptive conditions or a fatal accident.

The last year and a half brought a sharp increase in the population when it was decided that Solpetrière was a productive area and the quality of its timber out of the ordinary. The ancient cedars found just north of the camp were fine-grained, barely knotted, and remarkably easy to cut. The priest found that his congregation had more than doubled in that time, including the arrival of a few reluctant young — and not so young — ladies, and their requirements expanded rapidly to include an occasional wedding, weekly confessions, and eventually a few baptisms. The donations to the church construction grew fast. Over a six-month period, just before he departed for France to pick up his orphaned niece, the funds reached a sufficient level to warrant his dispatch to the Holy See, along with the Archbishop of St.-Boniface of Manitoba, to seek approval from the Bishop, and perhaps the Pope himself, and pay the required liege to the almighty Catholic Church.

By the time the Church's superiors had appropriated their handsome shares, quickly blessed what was left of the monies, and sent him back to Canada forthwith, the priest felt fleeced like a senseless sheep, dismayed and fretful. The recriminations his congregation would lay upon him for the paucity of remaining funds allocated to their much-anticipated church played in his mind. It weighed heavily upon the prudent priest throughout the entirety of the return journey, and right up to the moment a week later that the first sod was turned on the building site as the loggers cheered. Father Jacob kept up a beneficent appearance but underneath the fine black robes his nerves were on edge and lurched with anxiety while his sermons were not equal to the grand occasion.

The issue of the unforeseen reduction of funds initially outraged the congregation, but quickly indignation turned to resignation, and soon the most able of the members stepped forward to volunteer their labor and skills in the name of the Church. Among them were the original settlers of the camp, those men who had no wives or children but secretly hoped the building of the church would help attract more feminine prospects. Construction took place every evening after the mill stopped operation and before the sun dropped below the edge of forest, completely obscuring the workable light.

So it was that the church came to be built over the course of a year, while its interior remained unpainted with bare rafters and hand-finished timber benches instead of polished Italian pews imported via Montréal. Father Jacob himself was required to act as the construction foreman, as the wages for a hired one were no longer available. Working with plans sent to him by the Church from other similar construction sites in New France, the priest was quickly overwhelmed by the complexity of the task, and prayed frantically each night in a delirious dialogue with The Lord begging him in bring the project to a satisfactory end.

Slowly the construction lurched toward completion — first a foundation, then a sheltered structure, then timber cladding. More than once, roof trusses and floor joists required re-cutting to an appropriate length, and a window frame or two moved to line up with its opposite. The bell tower, which was to be structured out of bricks, fell a few feet short due to an underestimation of the quantity of required bricks, but in all, the project moved forward at a respectable pace, and by the end of autumn, just as the muskrats were completing their own frantic efforts for the long winter, the congregation enjoyed its first Sunday mass under the roof of their own spare and rough-hewn cathedral.

The only thing amiss was the large stained glass window, which was promised by the Archbishop but never delivered. In its place the men fixed ordinary panes of glass shaped to fit the gothic arched frame, but as clear and uncolored as a cloud-covered sea. Through it, an expanse of evergreen was majestically framed, creating a magnificent backdrop to the parishioners' eventual realizations that the ever-present cedar was as much a suitable depiction of their Almighty Savior as any other.

As the church construction progressed throughout the spring and summer, Isabelle found little time to lament the loss of her music. Madame Lowell was a kind and compassionate woman who never hesitated to give her new charge a motherly embrace when she looked like she needed one, but she was also an immaculate housekeeper and expected the girl to follow suit. Each morning, Isabelle was awakened at the first light to collect the eggs, tend to the boisterous chickens, and milk three moody cows. By noon she would have dusted and polished every piece of furniture and shelving in her uncle's house, as well as mopped the floors and scrubbed the pots from the previous night. Madame Lowell was pleased by the girl's dedication and handiwork and praised her heartily to Father Jacob, who only smiled wanly, then returned to his nightly inspection of the building plans with a distracted stare.

The late afternoon hours were free while Madame Lowell had her daily nap. Isabelle would have liked to spend that time playing the guitar or composing a new piece of music, but that was not to be, and soon she discovered that the fragrant woods and meandering creeks and rivers beyond the camp offered a whole new fascinating world of unfamiliar sights and sounds, animals, plants, and an occasional breath-taking vista. As summer approached and the daylight hours stretched to their maximum, the church construction efforts picked up and Father Jacob did not often return to the house for his evening meal until almost dark — nearly eight and sometimes nine o'clock. Preparations of the meals became later and later, and Madame Lowell's naps grew longer and longer, ironically stretching nearly to bedtime before she was required to rise. But Isabelle delivered her chores regardless of the season and used the additional hours of the summer to distract herself with new activities. At her usual time in the early afternoon, she peeled the potatoes and prepared the soup stock, or plucked and trussed the occasional chicken.

At the first opportunity, the girl headed out to explore the wilderness, first on foot then eventually on a horse that was given to her uncle — the priest had stepped up on behalf of one of the parishioner's sons who fell afoul of the law, and helped defuse a potential tragedy. The old gray mare was a gift he could not refuse. Quite to her surprise the horse became Isabelle's new charge and she accepted with reluctance. The haughty beast was skittish initially but with the assistance of the young man, who owed his freedom to her uncle, she learned quickly how to feed, groom and ride it and before long the girl came to appreciate the proud animal. By the following summer she was confident with saddling and riding the horse, and her daily errands on horseback became a pleasure with purpose. She renamed the horse Béatrice.

One mid-summer afternoon, Isabelle saddled the mare and wandered into the forest. On a previous visit she had seen that there were large patches of forest that had been cleared of their particularly large trees some years before, and the open area around the stumps was often covered with grasses and herbaceous plants not found elsewhere on the pine forest floor. She arrived this day with eager plans to gather herbs she knew were edible, and bring them back to the house to identify using Father Pascal's *Directory of New World Medicinal Plants*, a hand-illustrated volume that looked as enticing as the plants themselves. She also brought a small notebook and drawing pencil which Madame Lowell had given her as a belated birthday present, not long after their arrival at the camp.

It took less than two hours to arrive at her favorite clearing in the forest, following the meandering creek which gave the camp its name. It was very shallow in parts and just barely flowing as it had not rained for nearly two months. And, although this lack of precipitation aided the church's construction considerably, it also worried many of the residents as dry hot summers sometimes spelt disaster in the form of ravaging fires caused by sparks from the logger's saws at the cutting sites. As Isabelle approached along the winding creek, she noticed it was particularly well-lit from above. It was her first mid-summer day in her new world and the high afternoon sun seemed brighter and more intense than any sun she had seen before. As she brought the mare into the clearing, however, the horse saw something that spooked her and abruptly reared and bolted, with the girl hanging on desperately, screaming at the top of her lungs. But the frightened horse shot through the forest as if she had seen a ghost and galloped for a mile or more before she managed to lose her rider. Girl and basket spilled unceremoniously from the saddle at a sharp bend in the creek where the horse turned suddenly right and the girl fell left. The spooked horse kept running and all Isabelle hoped was that the mare would somehow make its way home without her.

Isabelle was amazed that she managed to remain in her saddle for the wild ride as long as she did. It had taken her deeper into the forest than she'd ever been, crossing several shallow waterways that may have been tributaries to her familiar creek — or not. She felt hopelessly lost and her heart was still pounding long after the sound of the horse's hooves had disappeared into the forest. In the relatively open and benign clearing alongside the water, she picked herself up and checked for scratches or bruises. Surprisingly there were none. The soft pine floor had been her salvation; it was nature's own cushion for life's painful spills and falls. The notebook and basket fell not far from her and she gathered them up, surprised and amazed that the pencil had managed to stay wedged between two pages of the book and was unbroken. She sat down again, now more calm, and leaned against a cedar whose branches nearly swept the ground with its low pine cones. Her eyes closed for a long moment.

When she re-opened them they scanned the ground and re-focused on the multitudinous shades of green and yellow in the grasses that sprung up between the low-lying shrubs. Not far from where she sat, a long wavering line of red army ants marched resolutely through the dry blades like soldiers to a battle. She watched patiently as the ants delivered randomly cut pieces of leaf from a low-lying bush, holding the ragged green sheets vertically in their strong jaws while their nimble feet traced the exact steps of the warrior ant before them. Watching them disappear one by one under a fallen branch directly in front of her, she surmised that they would eventually re-emerge on the other side to continue their journey to an unknown anthill perhaps a great distance from where she witnessed their initial foray.

Her gaze was interrupted by a rustle and a movement in the bushes to her left, caught in the periphery of her vision. For a moment her heartbeat quickened again and she thought with trepidation of all the large creatures Madame Lowell had cautioned her about: the deer-like creatures called "moose," and the frightening black bears of which she was particularly fearful. They sometimes came into the camps and disturbed chickens and the occasional unfortunate human, but then she rationalized that many small harmless animals also inhabited the forest. *My fears are unnecessary*, she thought to herself, for this rustle in the trees sounded decidedly smaller. She relaxed for a moment and sat absolutely still waiting for another rustle in the bushes to confirm her thoughts.

No sound came after a long while so she resumed her position against the large tree and relaxed her shoulders. There was no reason to panic, she convinced herself. Whatever was there was now gone. She had come to draw, enjoy the afternoon, and gather herbs; a fall from her horse was no reason to abandon her plans.

"Just a few minutes more and then I shall find my way back," she declared loudly to herself. "Béatrice will likely return to the stables and with luck Madame Lowell will send a rider back to get me." Reaching for the notebook and pencil, she looked about slowly to find a suitable view to render. The curve of the creek rounding another large tree caught her eye where the sparkling water formed a small waterfall over some large rocks caught up in its roots. Never having had drawing instructions, only good hand-to-eye coordination and the willingness to discipline it, she tentatively began a sketch.

Painstakingly she labored at the drawing, taking her time and not rushing the lines onto the page. Then, just as her first drawing began to take shape, the small movement in the bushes suggested itself again, in the same spot out of the corner of her eye. With her pencil held in mid-stroke she looked to the left and caught sight of a dark eye peering at her between the tall blades of grass and shrubbery. She stared back at it, determined not to appear frightened as she was instructed to do if ever faced with a dangerous animal. For what seemed an eternity, the two individuals stared at each other, both determined not to show fear or aggression. It was Isabelle finally who put down her pencil and notebook and stood up with open hands to show she was not armed or dangerous.

The boy who saw her through the tall grass looked with curiosity at her pale skin, strange curving dark hair that gleamed coppery-red like a hawk's back feathers under the sunlight, and even stranger eyes that seemed the color of the forest. The skin and hair were no surprise, but he had never really come this close to the White Man before, and this girl with her bottled glass–like eyes was fascinating. He was not much older than she, and when she stood up he realized that she was quite small.

Walk-Tall had been coming to this particular area of the forest since he was old enough to hold a bow and arrow and allowed to wander out of his family's campsite alone. He had walked nearly two hours this morning to arrive just as the sun reached its highest point in its summer arc and had been taking a nap in the shade of the tall grass when he was awakened by the sound of a horse approaching in the distance. He had sat up calmly to discover the nature of the intruder, and it was with all his willpower that he did not stand up straight away to help the rider whom he saw thrown from the horse just a few feet in front of him. It was his nature to help others, but he had been given strict instructions to avoid contact, if possible, with any of the members of the White Man's people. When he saw that she was not hurt, however, he felt much relieved.

But now, with the pale girl standing facing him boldly with her hands strangely turned out toward him, he felt he must do the same and show a similar boldness, and also respect her turned-out hands. The lines on her pale pinkish palms were very clearly marked, he observed, and wondered if that was the reason she held them out to him. He stood up slowly, parting the tall grass so he could step through it and move closer to inspect the girl's palms. She stood completely still with her hands held awkwardly out as he stepped closer and closer. When he was near enough to reach out and touch her he stopped, amazed that she suddenly closed her eyes, as if to say, *I trust you, but you may kill me if you desire.*

His desire at that moment was only to look into her eyes and see the forest reflected in them. "Please open your eyes," he said slowly in his own dialect of the Iroquois nation. He did not expect her to understand and was startled to see her eyes abruptly open. A smile quickly followed the look of surprise on his face, and as the girl opened her eyes to discover the friendly face looking at her, she felt a huge relief that must have been apparent to her observer because he then began to laugh, shyly at first then more heartily, shaking mirthfully in his moccasins.

Isabelle could not believe her eyes. Here a "Savage" was standing before her and she felt completely unencumbered with fear. It was helpful that he was not much older than she, but it was the timbre of the boy's laugh that relaxed her, and she recognized the boyish mischief in that laughter, knowing that it was in his heart as well. His plain buckskin vest was trimmed with a simple pattern of small wooden beads which revealed to the observant girl that a mother had lovingly sewn these intricate beads into her beloved son's clothing. Observing that he was taller than she was by a head and wore his long hair in braids tied up with animal hide and a few brightly colored bird feathers on his adorned plaits, she also saw that he was a strong and good-looking young man; all at once she felt shy and embarrassed.

He now held out his hands so she could see the lines on his palms. Surprised to see that they were nearly as pale as the back of her arms, although his face and body were a sun-burnt reddish brown, she peered eagerly into his hands and then dropped hers to her sides. Looking up at him again, she was abashedly aware that he was now looking intently at her, searching out her eyes as if they were newly discovered gems imbedded in a rock. To satisfy his obvious curiosity, she opened them wide and moved them sideways and back like a barn owl would. Again he laughed and she decided that his was one of the best laughs she'd encountered anywhere; it was so natural, but also so full of an animal's cunning and innocence at the same time. He lifted one arm toward the sky and she followed it with her eyes and thought she saw his jaw drop as he caught the glint of the sun in the brilliant emerald starbursts of her squinting eyes.

For a moment his heart lurched and his head seemed to spin; he was afraid he would drop to the ground, felled by such an astonishing pair of eyes. Looking away and focusing momentarily on the close bark of the cedar where she had been seated helped him find his equilibrium. He had seen fish scales this color and a bird feather that mimicked the forest and gleamed brilliantly in the sunlight, but to see it in this human creature was almost overwhelming. *Why were these people to be avoided,* he wondered? *Eyes this brilliant must mean something good or close to the hidden parts of nature that we could benefit or learn from.* In nature, bright colors and shiny reflective features were assets, or at the very least a protective measure, like the poisonous red berries, or the snake whose lethal venom often matched the brilliance of its patterning.

These thoughts raced through his mind and there seemed no rational explanation for putting a distance between them. A smile was certainly mutual to all good humans and he showed his readily as he took one of her hands in his and led her back to the tree where she was previously seated. To show his intentions, he sat down first into a cross-legged position and motioned for her to sit as well. Gathering her skirts around her she returned to her sitting position against the tree, but this time copying the crossed-legged posture and watching him carefully to see if there was something else he expected of her.

The position felt decidedly good she thought; strangely it had never occurred to her to sit in this way before. It wasn't natural, but it was certainly a way to feel steadier on the ground and it gave her a sense of communicating friendship, of giving herself freely as less a stranger and more a friend. Sitting this way also had a calming effect; although she was not panicked in any way, there was a certain tension she felt which had never entered her before.

It was exciting and abashing at the same time, as if her body felt wholly alive but her mind was trying to shut down this joy with a yoke of confusion.

If he felt the same mix of joy and unease, he did not express it. There was no awkwardness now as he sat before her. Earlier he experienced the strange weakness of the knees and a palpitation of the heart that threatened to floor him, but now he only felt a strange joy. Reaching across to the notebook she had abandoned on the ground, he lifted it with a question in his eyes and a broad smile across his sharply chiseled face.

This face becomes more handsome with each new smile, she thought to herself.

He held up the thin layer of paper which held her pencil rendering and placed his other hand over his chest and said in his own tongue, "I love your drawing."

Although they understood not a word of each other's language, there was enough perception in their earnest gestures to suggest they had a kindred spirit. Isabelle felt she had found her first new friend in this new country. The procession of pictures she drew for him was generally admired, bar one of a sailing ship, which he understood but seemed to dislike. In return he drew a few awkward pictures for her as well, including a long patchwork tepee and a jumping horse. Time seemed to stand still for them until the sun abruptly dropped below the line of trees and Isabelle gasped with the realization that she had a two-hour return walk ahead. If she did not make it back before the darkness set in, she would be doomed.

The boy looked at her with concern and put both hands on his chest to say, "I will not hurt you."

Isabelle understood his gesture and smiled at him, making a quick walking motion with two creeping fingers in the air and pointing at the sun, then moving her finger down and down past the horizon and into the ground. This he understood well and quickly stood up. He looked about for a moment as she gathered her notebook and the basket and then he bent forward to help her to her feet. The delicate feel of her arm through her thin cotton sleeve caused a new flutter in his stomach and he wished he was still sitting cross-legged on the ground.

In her mind, the strength of his helping hand on her arm was exhilarating. Intuitively she knew to follow him when he turned and headed through the trees on a path that he saw clearly like a track in fresh snow, but to her was just a brown and green pine needle–strewn forest floor where every step seemed identical to the next.

Moving in the opposite direction from where he had come, he led her along the river toward the camp as if he already knew her destination. Isabelle instinctively trusted him and followed closely behind. At one point at a bend in the creek, he continued straight ahead instead of following the curve of the waterway. Isabelle gestured the other direction, finally recognizing the few landmarks in the forest that she knew, but Walk-Tall simply nodded and walked resolutely through another clearing in the trees, following the footpath that only he knew.

When they neared the final clearing, Isabelle caught up to the scout to see the camp lanterns beginning to light. The gratitude in her heart felt like a warm drink on a frigid day; she could feel the relief wash down into her stomach as she walked toward the lanterns, the last rays of sunset burnishing the echoes of hammers that sounded steadily near the edge of the forest. As if on a visual cue they all came to a halt. At that precise moment the sound of crickets seemed to come into the cauldron of air and shadows of the camp, and Isabelle turned to say goodbye to her guide. But once he had seen the lights he had turned back and was long gone before she knew it.

3

BERNARD (ST.-GÉRARD), 1932–1959

"We don't bite the hand that feeds. Do you understand what that means, young man?"

Every month of every year, as the loggers cut deeper into the virgin forests, the young boy watched with horror from a distance as the familiar chain-line of cedar trees disappeared one link at a time.

"Bernie's heart is too big," Ellen Tenderfield would interject quietly, defending the boy's inconsolable tears at every tree-felling season. "He's a sensitive lad. Remember what he has already experienced..." Her voice trailed off as she remembered the horrid carnage of the mill accident not five years ago.

"This boy is going to learn a tough lesson. Nobody cries for trees..." replied her husband Col, examining the boy's stricken face from a distance through furrowed brows and shaking head. "He's got a hell of a lot of pain coming his way."

In that bitter cold winter of 1932 when Bernard was born, St.-Gérard held no special place amongst the hundreds of mill towns across the Eastern Townships of Canada — old villages whose primary purpose was to supply trapped fur to ready buyers in Europe, and timber to the burgeoning ship-building industry in Nova Scotia, New Brunswick, and Québec. Over a short century these towns had become home to thousands of enterprising French, English, and Scottish fur-trappers, traders, and loggers. They carved an increasingly lucrative existence by their desecration of nature: the brutal felling of trees and the clearing of old growth forests daily for the limitless requirements of industry. All in the name of a new religion called Progress.

Bernard grew up with a brooding sense of indignity at the relentless rapacity around him across ever-enlarging stretches of virgin forests where 800-year-old trees were brought to their knees with a screech of un-abiding metal. Thundering vortexes of swirling air shifted and displaced life itself. Doubting the virtue of the timber industry was like questioning the existence of God. For the sensitive boy, however, the certainty that God *was* the tree, or at the very least resided in the most ancient of trees, was apparent. Over time, however, he learned to keep the knowledge to himself, hidden from the laughter of other boys, away from the unbending beliefs of those who would not understand, and away from the parents who adopted him and loved him, but *could* not understand.

Col Tenderfield was the superintendent of the saw mill where Bernard's natural father had worked since he himself was a boy. His father's fatal accident orphaned him at age five, as his mother had died shortly after his birth. She was a poor, nearly deaf French girl whose family disowned her for running away with an Indian. Her unexpected passing left the boy's father bereft, but determined more than ever to make a decent life for himself and his son. He refused to find a family to adopt the newborn and so brought the unfortunate young soul to the mill every day and entrusted him to Providence, and the Good Grace of God. After the accident, the Tenderfields took the boy in as one of their own among their four older boys.

Bernard's world began with the shrill roar of circular saws and planing machinery, but at five it become muted. His fate was truly in the hands of a merciful God who took away the sordid sound of the trees being cut piecemeal in their prime, and reduced it to a low resonating vibration and the whisper of displaced air, a ghost passing unperceived. It was not hard to imagine that the trauma and horrendous carnage of his father's accident, which the boy had witnessed, had an implicit and undeniable impact on his disability.

Through the refuge of a large close-knit family, young Bernard grew up in his own teeming world to become strong of character but gentle in demeanor. He stood tall and straight and eventually even imposing among the cedars that bordered his family's modest log home. As he grew to become a man, his square jaw and chiseled eagle's profile revealed his Native constitution, but the heavy dark eyebrows framed intensely green eyes, which were deep-set and fringed with thick dark eyelashes. The copper red facial hair which appeared at puberty created a further mystery of his origin. Although his voice was not lost, his desire to use it diminished with each passing year. To his young mind, he was simply the son of God-fearing mill-worker parents, and brother to four older brothers. There were few questions worthy of asking.

Ellen took it upon herself to home-school her adopted son, teaching him spelling, reading, and arithmetic, a basic sign-language of simple gestures, and lip-reading. At times both mother and son would reach a mutual impasse in this arduous learning process, and would draw a truce. As adolescence approached, Bernard's hearing rapidly declined and by thirteen he became completely deaf. The roar was silenced, replaced with a monotonous hum. That same year he began an apprenticeship at the saw mill while his brothers joined the war effort. The brothers — John, Jordan, Aidan, and Callum Tenderfield — were all trained to pilot the locally built Hurricane fighter bomber planes, and prepared to fly them in Europe. It was an unhappy time for the envious young boy, but out of a sense of duty he learned to wield the saws and stack the boards without complaint.

The tears of the cutting season had stopped several years earlier but no one knew the agony he continued to bear inside his heart as the timber succumbed seasonally to the saws. As diligently as any one of the young men keeping the wheels of the industry turning, Bernard worked the timber. The constant noise of the saws made wordless communication the norm amongst the workers, mostly older men now, even several who came out of retirement to fill in the places of the younger men who were sent off to pilot training or to the European Front. Through this period, a silence seemed to fall over the infrequent social gatherings as if everyone was in silent prayer.

The outside world had impinged very lightly on this tiny community over the years, even during the first war, but the second war came to claim heroes even from the smallest hamlets across Canada. Very few words escaped the lips of those who were left behind. The women deferred to the silence of the older men, only speaking when instructing the children and keeping social interaction to a minimum. Everyone was in a waiting mode. And then one day, the war came abruptly to an end. John, Aidan, and Cal returned to St.-Gérard decorated as heroes. Jordan, the second brother, did not return; his Hurricane Mk1 had heroically taken down two Luftwaffe bombers before it was shot down over London. His Atlantic Star arrived at the Tenderfields' door one evening the following winter. The young RCAF officer bearing the medal had trained with Jordan at the RCAF camp in Montréal and it was his honor to hand-deliver it to the mother's trembling hands.

With the long war over, life began to resettle into its normal pace. The mill, which had nearly shut down during the war, now became a bustling factory — building resources hit the highest level of demand ever in the history of Canada — and expanded exponentially over the next five years. Now seventeen, but his services to the mill no longer as essential as they had been during the war years, Bernard discovered the underlying beauty in the grains of the sawn timber that revealed themselves gradually with the assistance of planing machines, careful hand sanding, oiling, and polishing.

In the slope of the evenings after the mill-workers called it a day, working half by lamplight and half by the feel of the grain, he coaxed arresting pieces of furniture and exquisite and sometimes curious objects from the off-cuts of timber. Eventually it overtook his time and efforts during the normal hours and propelled him into a different echelon of timber craftwork than could be expected of an untrained craftsman.

The noise of the saws around him made no impact on his tranquility as his steady hands moved the jig-saw across the wooden slabs, with the precision and deftness of a surgeon saving a life. In a single continuous cut he revealed the forms that transformed the damaged timber into things of beauty. If it was not for the families of the camps who were willing to give a fair portion of their hard-earned savings to purchase these items, he would have forfeited his artistry within a short time to assist with the supply of construction timber whose demand increased manifold after the end of the war.

Bernard became regarded by the residents of his home-town of St.-Gérard as an artist of major talent. After years of dedication to his craft, the income he derived from his gift allowed him to purchase a small plot of land not far from his family's home fronting Lake Aylmer. There he built his own modest timber-framed cabin from logs he lovingly cut and milled from the surrounding cedar forest. In his constant and soundless world, he worked the timber alone, using the full power of his strong lean body to lift and rotate larger and larger slabs of wood. Well before the cabin was complete, he set about creating an adjacent woodworking studio.

The pieces he wrought from the bare wood rang out with a remarkable truth, simplicity, and purity. In a time and place where rough manners and the monotonous drone of machinery dominated lives, the sublime beauty of the fine furniture and decorative art objects were a kind of salve for the mothers who secretly promised themselves someday more glamorous, or at least more respectable lives beyond the timber-yards. These very women created a competitive clientele base for Bernard's output, swarming his studio like honey bees, or protective hens, keeping others at bay without actively appearing to. They came to watch him carve and tame the timber with his large graceful hands and admire the placid almost beatific expression on his finely chiseled face. Over time he realized that their feminine aura helped his creative efforts, but he never wittingly encouraged their presence even as his fan club grew exponentially.

Lorraine was the exception. Being seventeen and the only child of overly protective parents who sent her away to an exclusive Catholic girls' boarding school, she had never heard of the wood artist. And when she arrived that fateful summer evening, he considered her to be the second most beautiful creature he had ever seen. Her father, the tool-making Scotsman and engineer Glen Stewart, owned the small specialist hardware store which supplied Bernard with his growing arsenal of precision wood-working tools. Her mother Sylvie-Marie Bédos Stewart, a Breton woman who also had some very distant Native ancestry, made sure her only daughter was raised with the love of Our Lady in her heart. Lorraine had just returned after graduating from the exalted Catholic girls' school Sacré-Coeur des Trois-Rivières, when her father suddenly fell ill one Friday afternoon. She arrived at the studio late in the afternoon to deliver a custom-made awl Bernard had ordered some weeks earlier.

In the door of the workshop she leaned her petite frame, straight thin legs turned in like the pegs of a stork and a white cotton dress nearly opaque in the late afternoon sun. Her soft brown hair fell in waves over her shoulders to the middle of her bare arms, which were crossed now over the heart-shaped neckline of her summer dress. A gold chain around her neck suspended a small gold cross that shared its space below her collarbone with a small mole. Her face was luminous as only a blossoming teenage girl's complexion could be. She was the picture of a Titian Madonna with high pale and peach cheekbones, finely appointed eyebrows arched above light golden brown eyes, and pink rosebud lips thin, small, and sensuous.

The girl knew the young man by description from her father, but when she saw him in his studio working, never lifting his head once during the thirty-five minutes she stood diffidently at the entrance, she knew that he was a true artist, as she had never seen that kind of focus in someone her age before. When finally the head rose up and a pair of green eyes met hers, their emerald brilliance locked on her gaze and they both knew something was about to change.

It took all her concentration to make her hands steady as she gathered her dress about her and swept gracefully into the studio. Surveying the workroom, she quickly found a low round stool a few feet in front of his work table and perched herself upon it, spreading out her skirt like a parasol. He nodded and returned to carving the large ornate jewelry box. But his heart was beating too fast and he could almost feel the small bead of sweat begin to form on his smooth brown forehead. Little butterflies began their flight in his stomach and he felt uncharacteristically self-conscious. Eventually he downed his tools and looked up, just barely finding the nerve to look back at his maddeningly beautiful audience of one. Her smile seemed to light up the darkening studio and when she stood up and brought the soft curves of her face, neck, and shoulders closer to him, it caused his whole body to riot, and the normal buzz in his eardrum to change into a stirring march.

The romance lasted for three volatile months before Lorraine began to feel she could no longer bear the young

man's silence. Together they had made a pair of polar oppo-
sites. While she had a ready and knowing smile but suffered
no fools, he had a silent brooding quality that belied a gentle
unassuming manner. She announced her departure by packing up her night-market trinkets while Bernard was away
on an errand. Her collection of ornamental keepsakes was a
catalogue of her soul — a Fabergé egg, exquisite cloisonné
ring-boxes, brass camels, finger bells and toe rings acquired
at the St.-Gérard markets brought to Bernard's workshop
to inspire him on her frequent but short-lived visits. She
harbored a gypsy heart that could not stay in one place for
long. She left him a page-long letter expressing her sadness,
but resolute in her decision that it would never work.

Bernard mourned the loss of the girl fiercely but secretly,
for even as he felt the emotion burn hot in the inner lining
of his heart and soul, he knew he could never have kept
such an exquisite creature in the cage of his secluded life.
She was meant for the larger world. With time he began to
feel only gratitude for having shared intimate moments with
a person as exceptionally beautiful as she. After the girl,
there was a procession of older women, some married and
some widowed by the war, who could afford to accept his
silence and even appreciate it.

For days after he returned from his journey into the forest
of spirits, he stared at the large timber sections lying prone
on his workroom floor. On his workbench lay a single slab
which he had sanded and lightly oiled to discover its true
color under a clean finish. The reddish gold hue and rich

textured grain were mesmerizing. The lateral cut revealed a radiant core more perfectly symmetrical than he had ever seen. Its complete radiating arcs were like the rings of an onion, no irregularities marring their precise and translucent circularity.

After the fourth day the music returned and in his nightly dreams he found himself in a workshop; all around him were unfamiliar tools, grips, and vises, and his own hands appeared to be the hands of a woman. Rather than formless and timeless images as before, they were now clearly defined and absolute, and bathed in a soft warm light, the particular kind of sunlight one imagines illuminates lush mountaintops in a more temperate climate. The dreams were so real he had the sensation of working the wood with these delicate hands of his, knowing the precise pressure to use on every tool. The familiar melody now emanated from him through his own lips in a low melancholy hum. When he awoke he moved into his studio and stared for hours at the old guitar expecting it to vibrate *molto appassionato* of its own accord and initiate the tune that once again dominated his dreams. Only then did he realize what he had to do next.

The extraordinary timber was all and everything Bernard hoped it would be. Its tight straight grain on planing and sanding displayed a remarkable warm tone akin to the color of mead and honey. It was also miraculously free from knots and burrs and aesthetically it was like nothing he had seen before. He knew this timber was destined for objects finer than furniture or even sculpture. He imagined that the whole tree would have made an exquisite grand piano like the ones he had seen in his mother's coffee-table books, and his only sadness now was in knowing that this could never be. But Bernard did have a guitar in his studio and it beckoned to him with its achingly familiar sunburst. After the arduous journey through the forest they travelled together, he was infinitely relieved to find it had sustained merely the slightest scratch and minimal damage from the dampness. The sheet music and manuscript however did not fare so well. Some of the hand-inked writing was lost, some of the words transferred onto the back of the page before it, and others smudged into an unintelligible blur.

Even if he could understand the writing or read the music, Bernard did not suspect they were meant for him. Nonetheless he carefully blotted everything dry and took care not to overheat the room so as not to dry the paper, parchment, leather, or guitar too quickly. The antique musical instrument stood drying separately from its case on an upright stand, and the unbound pages were laid out carefully in their original order on a long bench cut from a single piece of maple. The log had been cut into five discrete sections, two the length of his own height, two half the length of the other two, and one the thickness of a table. The diameter of each was more than equal to the width of his workbench.

Strung above his workbench between several exposed beams were the individual pages of the manuscript hung from wooden pegs like a line of laundry, or sun-bleached prayer flags in a Himalayan village. On his workbench, Bernard brought the two pairs of book-ended quarter-sawn pieces of wood together and examined their beautifully colored, mirror-imaged and perfectly straight grains, instinctively knowing that this fine-grained solid wood would make the perfect soundboard top, allowing the instruments to vibrate harmonically at perfectly true frequencies and producing a tonal quality that would be strong, dynamic, and ultimately equal to none. Without ever having played a guitar except in his increasingly vivid dreams, he knew intuitively that it would resonate with a rich, sweet, mellow sound reflective of the lively emotions he felt in his heart as he created the instruments.

He worked obsessively and intuitively, but also unhurriedly, taking each step of the construction process as if it was part of a slow sacred ritual. After a brief kiln dry, he shaped the instrument bodies as closely as possible to the images drawn in the manuscript, somewhat foreshortened from the antique guitar, which now rested in its private corner providing quiet inspiration. Near the door of the studio the old guitar stood guard, a radiant sentry with the provocative aura of a lioness, its color changing with the light that came in through the window opposite, as Bernard delicately set the decorative braided timber inlays that circled the sound hole which he had meticulously carved out of cherry and spruce and inlaid with the help of small tweezers. This elaborate design took nearly two weeks to complete but when the last minuscule piece was inserted, he felt as if he had just performed life-saving surgery on two of his closest friends.

Creating the proper hour-glass shape of the instruments presented a less exacting, but more complex challenge. He created his own methods based on the drawings from the manual and created his own freely interpreted translations of the foreign language text into his own, enabling him to construct a functional framework that turned out to be truly inspired and nearly perfect in its simple symmetry. He steamed and braced the sides as instructed and mixed and stretched the animal gut glues and strings described in the manuscript while he waited for the forms to sustain their required shapes. For the neck and headstock he shaped long pieces of silver leaf maple which he normally reserved for chair legs and arms, as their dense structure provided the required lateral and longitudinal stability and tensile strength. He sanded each neck to the exact specifications of the manuscript while feeling instinctively for the correct smoothness and a width that felt comfortable in his hands. Two carved and hand-sanded bridges and saddles were created along with twelve individual tuning keys. Satisfied with the outcome of these, he then assembled and glued all the various parts, clamping and joining them one at a time with a whole arsenal of grips, vises, and weights. To this he applied four coats of a traditional polish to each sound-board, neck, back, and side, and hand-sanded and buffed the instruments meticulously between each coat, waiting a day to allow the lacquer to dry completely to a glassy sheen.

It had been nine months since he commenced the creation of these two masterpieces, and it was autumn again. He noticed the dried leaves fallen on his doorstep and across the expanse of his small lawn, which needed a good sweeping. Along the edge of the lake, the brightly colored leaves of the maple trees clung to the ever-denuding branches and were a welcome sight for his sore eyes. Each long day spent in the dimming light of the studio blurred his vision further. The early April sun had streamed in like a flood of spring itself when he had started the project. Keeping his studio door closed but the shades before his large windows open to the public meant that visitors arrived in a steady stream. But eventually the faces appeared less and less frequently as the project wore on and the leaves began to blow across his doorstep like brittle brown announcements of a return to cold weather and early evenings. It was a little startling for Bernard therefore to glance up one late afternoon a few weeks later to find a pleasingly familiar face pressed wanly against his window.

Lorraine had waited patiently for Bernard to complete his finishing ritual, standing back from the window as he brushed the final coat of French polish lavishly on one of the guitar bodies with a flourish of his brush, oblivious to her presence. He held the beautifully glossy instrument up for a moment to inspect the finish in the muted light, and in doing so finally noticed her and calmly focused his gaze upon her. At last moving to the door, he opened it leisurely and greeted her as if they had never parted, kissing her tenderly on both cheeks. To Bernard's surprise she had changed little in the three years since they saw one another, albeit she seemed more beautiful than ever. He, on the other hand, had changed tremendously and was no longer the boy she once held in an innocent kiss. He had grown into a man since that time, and the maturity in his face and body brought a strange warm sensation as she gazed at him. She longed to hold him in a long intimate embrace and smell his skin or taste his lips. Those feelings surprised her for she had not come expecting to have such a strong attraction; she had only returned from a break in her university studies in Québec to visit her parents, and had planned a cordial visit to see his new studio.

Bernard sensed a difference in the way she looked at him. Her brown eyes peered up at him through her eyelashes coyly, and her lips, with their frozen smile, looked as if they were pursed for a kiss. He decided he would take the chance and leaned into her without hesitation and swept her up in his arms, carrying her into his cabin before she could utter a word of protest. With eyes resolutely closed, Lorraine let herself be carried away like a damsel into the dragon's lair. When he laid her out on his single bed, she could only murmur a small unheard protest before he laid his body over hers and kissed her with an urgency she could understand and appreciate. At seventeen and twenty-three they had stroked intimate parts of each other's young bodies, but respected the small-town laws of chastity before marriage. But now, after three cosmopolitan years away in the big city, the young woman was ready to embrace his manhood, and he on his part, felt a need to give her what she seemed to want.

Not long after their initial frantic love-making, they repeated the coupling once again at half the speed, taking the time to stroke each other like old lovers and tasting the strange but familiar lips. Afterward, it was Lorraine who felt the need to explain her long absence from his life. She chattered on, only partly aware that, particularly in his half-drowsy state, he would have caught but a small fraction of her words as her face turned momentarily toward the moonlight now cast through the bedroom window. The words lost on her lover didn't seem to matter for she simply needed to exorcise the demons that haunted her after her abrupt departure years before. She had not meant to hurt him but felt the letter she left had been rather curt. It was simply easier, she had rationalized, to read her goodbye on paper rather than see it on her agitated face. They were, after all, just children back then.

The soundless banter and the vibration of her voice on his bare shoulder left Bernard feeling relaxed and joyful. He knew instinctively what she was expounding upon and just nodded earnestly whenever she sought out his face with a questioning look in her eyes. If his nod was accompanied with a smile, the result was a smile in return or huge sigh of relief. She was exorcising some sort of guilty demon or purging feelings of remorse or regret, this he knew. The confessionary look on her wide heart-shaped face in the moonlight made him think of the religious paintings he had seen on Christmas cards sent to his family. This image brought on a virtuous smile that spread joyfully across his face until it was stopped in its tracks by a barrage of kisses.

The young woman reappeared in Bernard's life at precisely the moment the two guitars were completed. For a few days she disappeared back to her parents' home to complete her visit, but she returned again to his rustic cabin and made it her home for nearly three weeks. All the while she harbored no expectations of him and required no reply to her complex musings on the current politics of the territory of Québec, or an answer to her many rhetorical questions about the nature of relationships and family dynamics. The mysterious age of the antique guitar was a baffling question, and she offered to research it for him on her return to the university — classical guitars were a passion of hers stemming from her days at the Catholic girls' college at Trois-Rivières. The school had given her the opportunity to study the violin as part of her matriculation, but she was passionately obsessed with classical guitar, which was not part of the curriculum. She sought out private tutors in the myriad of older European men more than willing to share their talent and skills with her. Bernard watched her carefully inspect the delicate body of the instrument with her eyes and hands, and examine the withering sheet music and manuscript with the careful eye of a scientist.

Then, without comment or warning, she rose from her seat and dragged her chair noisily to the place where the animal gut strings were strung to dry from laundry lines across the rafters of the studio. Climbing the chair, she brought them down in one hand, smoothed them out, and quickly strung them onto the two guitars, tuning them expertly by ear and strumming them affectionately before readjusting their tuning again. She ran an eight-note arpeggio up and down each neck, amazed by the rich sound they produced even as virgin instruments. Bernard brought the sheet music to her and placed it upright on the table in front of her. She glanced nonchalantly across the score, hearing the melody in her mind, then placing one foot on a low stool in front of her chair. She held the guitar up nearly vertically as she would if dancing a tango with it, and moved her fingers over the strings to make a soulful sound like an autumn breeze tumbling leaves across a golden expanse.

Her fingers flew up and down the fret board marking out a *recuerdo* both passionate and lamenting, and with her other hand she plucked a rhythmic discourse with fingers moving almost inverse to the other. Her gypsy soul found a platform in the soundboard of the instrument and with it the dying embers of her passionate spirit were rekindled and stoked into a blaze. Each rising arpeggio was an ascent into the upper reaches of a Vesuvius summit and the descents a plunge into infinite sobriety. The near madness of the moving fingers felt familiar to Bernard as he watched fascinated while her hands moved autonomously seeing waves and patterns of movement within. Without thought he picked up the second guitar and instinctively strummed chord patterns in unison with her picking. Like the verses that had flowed from him in his dreams, a harmonizing strum flowed from his instrument in a rhythmic pattern not unlike the somnambulant chant of Benedictine monks. He closed his eyes, letting the waves move through his fingers, and felt the blended vibrations move into a stratosphere of vibration that broke into a metaphysical symphony of sound in his inner ear.

Lorraine had stopped her own playing to observe with absolute awe her deaf lover play the guitar like an impassioned and seasoned musician. She had never witnessed a miracle such as this. But she was not a very devout or superstitious person, resistant to the number of miraculous "rapture" stories instilled in her by the fanatical nuns of her Sacred Heart convent school; her logical mind revolted against what she witnessed and suddenly she was overcome with dread. And then like the creature from the lake, she disappeared again, presumably back to the university to complete her studies.

He received a letter from her nearly a month later explaining that she had just been accepted into the university's law school. She apologized for leaving so abruptly but she hated goodbyes and didn't know how to explain to him that she was only meant to be away from her studies for a week, not the *three weeks* she had spent in his arms. Perhaps for the holidays she might manage to see him, but it might be a long while before she would have the chance to return to their small town. At the bottom of the page she had written: *Je t'embrase, Lorraine.*

He stared at her letter for quite some time admiring the steady hand in which she wrote, and memorizing every flourish of the long consonants. The writing was beautiful as he expected, and written on a sheet of pale blue linen paper enfolded in an envelope of matching texture and hue. The edges of the elegant stationery were delicately ragged, mimicking the antiquated edges of old parchment and reminiscent of the pages of sheet music he had found with the guitar. For the first time in months he thought about those papers and went to the drawer in his studio desk and pulled them out.

"Per il mío caro Tomás" was written in a shaky but florid hand across the top of the first page. The affectionate address was nearly obliterated by the yellowing and recent dampness, but contained a lifetime of sentiment within its five small words, written by an unstable but loving hand. *Who wrote this piece of music and why was it dedicated to this man, Tomás? Was he a beloved husband or brother? A son perhaps?* Bernard looked to the antique guitar standing guard in the corner of his studio. *He must have owned this instrument. Was he the man playing in my dream?*

Bernard replied to Lorraine's letter several days later and informed her that he would visit her in Québec if that fit in with her schedule. The days and nights that intervened between the writing of the letter and the careful preparation for his wintry traverse of the Haut Saint-François to the City were painfully slow. He imagined the train gathering passengers from New York en route to Montréal, making a minor collection of travelers there from Sherbrooke, and then on to Québec. He was prepared a week before departure, the late December air crisp and frosted with ice and snow shaken from the tops of the bare maples as he stumbled from his porch to the path leading to the frozen lake.

Christmas with his family at the Tenderfield home was filled with the prattle of young nieces and nephews, cousins and aunts, and the detached observation of the growing brood by grandparents now in their retirement years, and showing the wear and tear of nearly forty years of minding the mill. In the corner of the living room stood a six-foot Douglas fir decorated with the fine shreds of silver tinsel and red glass baubles collected over nearly four decades of Christmases by three generations. An assortment of presents nestled under the tree like a well-tended garden of delights. The crackling roar of the inferno blazing in the stone-lined fireplace stoked the excited chatter of children, and its visual fireworks created a focal point to which all eyes were drawn as they gathered for the opening of presents.

Spared the relentless and increasingly boisterous prattle of the young ones, Bernard sat unperturbed like a Buddha on the hearthside rug. His contentment glowed like a well-oiled lantern when the wide-eyed squeals of delight from the children peaked with his every gift-wrapped offering. Without delay they were scattered about the living room, a menagerie of finely carved fantastical animals, wooden spinning tops inlaid with intricate designs, and an astoundingly clever toddler's push-cart.

One of the hand-crafted guitars was propped against a wall beside him, unwrapped but fitted with a small card and gleaming warmly in the glow of the fire. It had gone unnoticed in the maelstrom of gifts and baubles until now. In its physical microcosm of air, light, and cellulose, it held tight the many trials and tribulations of Bernard's recent past. No one in the room could possibly guess what he had undergone to retrieve the source of its timber manifestation or the mystical notations that drove him to discover it. They were secrets that he kept under the surface of his ever-beatific smile and silent gaze. Or how, with a tyrannical largess, the towering pines had opened their branching staircases out to him like a hymn or a mantra to his evanescing search for lightness and meaning. Not easily giving up the secrets of their formidable cult, the roiling rapids had also, with their constant troubling toil, dealt him an unduly harsh hand, but he played well, plunging his embattled oars into the waters with little or no fear, and winning the unfair match with absolute fierceness.

Ellen did not guess for a minute that the present before her was a trophy. As she looked upon it, the glossy beautifully varnished instrument seemed to have a life all its own. It breathed faintly and emitted a low sonorous sigh as if its rounded curves shouldered sadness within it. Through her increasingly far-sighted eyes she made out the words which flowed before her in a swirling unfamiliar hand, and read them out loud.

> *Music and silence within this timber contain*
> *Treasured for a lifetime in moments declared*
> *The solace of tenderness in tempered refrain*
> *Love, much happiness, of sadness repaired.*
> *With a pure heart planted this fruit of my labor*
> *Indebted to you, your care, kindness forever;*
> *Beholden to life so fierce benighted*
> *Once alone now with kinship requited.*

"This is lovely," she said facing her son. "But who wrote this poem?" Bernard understood the wonderment in his mother's face. He had penned the words earlier that morning as he gathered the gifts. The poem seemed to come through the pen from a source within him that he had no control of. And now as it was read in the jostling backdrop of grandchildren and a roaring fire, the message was like a great ship sailing silently through rough and tumble waves. He gestured to his mother with his hand to his chest, *I did*.

"Oh!" she exclaimed with surprise, and then was stunned into a silence as the enormity of it struck upon her. It seemed her adopted son had suddenly transformed into a sixteenth-century poet. A cool stream of air breezed past her left arm and as if in counterpoint to her surprised cry, which still hung in the air, the guitar sounded in a low harmonizing bass. Ellen and Bernard turned to look at the instrument and then each other. In innocent collusion their eyes met and they both turned simultaneously toward Col, who was standing with the black iron poker in the enormous fire and his back turned. Apparently no sound had disturbed his concentrated efforts at stoking the already raging fire.

"Bernie," Ellen finally said, signing the words as best she could as she spoke them, "this is extraordinary. This guitar is exquisite. I didn't know you were making instruments now. How did you learn to do it?"

It came to me in a dream, was all he said, signing the words to his mother in the abbreviated language they shared. His placid facial expression flashed momentarily with a nearly imperceptible flicker of anguish and pain, but gave away none of the ordeal of nearly a year ago when the dreams tormented and tantalized him in equal measure. Nor did they suggest the physical hardship he endured at his own conquest of nature to salvage the colossal timber. His obsession of the past nine months however was metaphysical and inexplicable. The old manuscript revealed itself in surges of elucidation during waking dreams for which the whir of his saws and planers seemed to provide a perpetual vibrational frequency that powered the visions.

"You know what is even more extraordinary — that you somehow knew that I played the guitar? You couldn't have known, but before I married your father, I grew up in quite a musical family in Boston, filled with Christmas carols by the fireside — with me on the guitar, my mother on the piano, and my sister Rose on the violin. Rose became a rather successful violinist with the Boston Symphony Orchestra."

It is the work of my love and I hope you will cherish it, he replied.

"I will. In fact, there's something I've been meaning to tell you, Bernie," she began in a conspiratorial whisper. Whether it was because he had lost his hearing quite young, or whether he was just the baby of her clan, Ellen felt the closest to her adopted son. They were kindred spirits of sorts and she felt then, as now, that he understood her even without words. Before her this gentle giant of a young man stood, with eyes that melted hearts and a smile that turned heads against their will. Where did the source of the verse come from?

As a small boy he was fascinated by books and volumes of poems by the English poets — John Donne, Milton, Eliot, Keats, and Browning — but she never guessed that her words were anything more than a monotonous vibrational hum in his inner ear. She looked into his face, his knowing head tilted to one side and his lips slightly parted as if in mid-sentence, waiting patiently and attentively for her secret. The yellowish glow of the fireplace danced a light and shadow play on his chiseled jaw, casting a roguish gleam on his otherwise boyish face. She could have sat silently for hours just staring into his fine and familiar face.

"Your father and I are considering taking up a missionary post in Thailand next year," she finally said. "Now that you and your brothers are all settled down, and all the grandchildren are growing so well, we thought it might be time to do something important in our lives. Your father is growing very restless in his retirement."

A look of surprise and relief overtook his calmly patient visage as he whispered, "When will you decide for certain? Have you told the others?"

"Only John and Judith," she replied. "It was her suggestion in the first place, and through her close work with the Ministry and Father Lesley, we were selected amongst quite a few applicants across Canada. We will announce it to everyone when we decide for certain; probably early in the New Year. I wanted to make sure you were all right with it."

"Of course it is all right. You and Papa have always done important things in your lives," he signed. *"I am happy for you. You must take the guitar with you."*

Ellen rose out of her chair and put her arms around her youngest son. There they stood embraced for a long while, as if it was already a parting. Feeling that it might be the last time her boy needed her for comfort, she drew back and lifted the guitar and held it in her arms like the small sleeping child he no longer was. She moved with it over to the fire to hold it more clearly in the light, and to tell her husband of over forty-five years her revelation.

"You might think you know someone, and then one day they surprise you with the most astonishing gift you didn't know was possible."

The older man looked at her questioningly. "Ehh?" he muttered, still preoccupied with turning over a flaming log to create a more even burn across it. "Is that your new Christmas present from Bernie?"

"Yes. It's for both of us really," she answered.

"It will make a fine decoration. Warm this room up a bit." Absently Col hoisted another log onto the fire with the iron tongs and poked prodigiously until it settled neatly into an infernal niche between the glowing embers. "He's got real talent, that boy," he continued. The new addition refused to absorb the inevitable flames, its timber striped black and unyielding against the ephemeral orange radiance of the well-contained blaze.

And then, whether it was in his ear or just in his mind, he thought he heard the guitar make an incredibly subtle and spine-tingling melody as his wife cradled it upright, facing outward in her arms like a small papoose strapped to the chest of a native Indian woman working in a field. Her clasped hands had not moved from their position supporting the lower curves of the body, but the blur of strings was undeniable. His eyes moved suspiciously from the strings to her hands, then to her expression. They met an incredulous smile and a wide-eyed look reflecting his own on the woman's face.

Bernard found himself jostled along by a crowd of harried travelers herding baggage and uncooperative children along to their proper carriages at the train platform in Sherbrooke, which swarmed with holiday traffic. It was the afternoon of the last day of the year and there was little decorum left once the train's powerful engines and the whistle had fired, letting passengers know it was time to say the last farewell, grab the children, and board the vehicle. Vehement white steam fissuring from the steam-chute above the engine gave final warning of the impending departure, causing agitated travelers to become even more so. The young man was grateful for the lightness of his load; he had almost no luggage except for the efficient leather guitar case he had strapped across his shoulder.

En route to the elevated old fort city, he watched impassively as the landscape rushed past in the large square of his carriage window. In the glass-enclosed cabin he shared with a boisterous Glaswegian family visiting relatives in Canada, and an elderly nun in a light gray habit who sat directly across from him reading a bible opened on her lap, Bernard dozed off on a few occasions between being awakened again by a loud cry from one of the small tartan-bedecked children. Every few minutes the nun glanced furtively in his direction with a mutter under her breath. She found him alternately asleep or looking dolefully through the small circle of clarity in the window made by his ungloved hand. She seemed to be recounting an event or perhaps a prayer in her mind and his presence was a reminder.

The train progressed slowly as it made its way through the icy winter landscape. A frozen backdrop of snowy white drifts, patches of blue-gray ice, and prickly bare tree branches met his gaze everywhere he turned. In its monotony the countryside was most beautiful, stretching into infinity as anonymously and indiscriminately as an eternity. All that frozen whiteness made him feel at home, and yet he nearly quaked in awe at its sheer vastness. Looming up ahead, a stone church presented itself: a boldly upright steeple, its sides too vertical for the snow's blanketing grip but its beige serenity at one with the softly molded surrounds of blended whites.

The children in the carriage had no qualms with the colorlessness of the scenery; they squealed and squawked with delight at each spotted landmark as if discovering a treasure at every turn. Ice skaters making circling figure-eights on a frozen lake in the distance were colorful marching ants, while a lone barn sheathed in white — bar the small patch of blood red beneath the shallow eaves of its slanting roof — was a witch's hideout. To them the wintry playground was as richly hued as a summer landscape with castles and lochs among its heath.

Bernard closed his eyes and imagined the same magical landscape in the summer colors of emerald and pine green, the red barn a beacon in the sea of green and sky blue. He pictured his cabin sheathed in a thick blanket of snow and with the brushstroke of his imagination brought it to life in living color: warm timber logs, a black pitched roof, red-breasted robins bobbing along the painted blue rail on his veranda, an explosion of pink and white blossoms on the apple and peach trees in the small orchard behind the house. He imagined Lorraine standing on that verandah in her thin nightgown, a ceramic mug of coffee in her cupped hands and a radiant look of love on her beautiful face.

In the darkness behind his curtained eyes, and beneath his seat the rhythmic vibration of the train was soothing and persistent, but inevitably led to thoughts of another rhythmic motion. Immediately his body reacted to the memory with the gesticulating heat of a forward-thrusting steam train. He placed his open hand and cheek upon the cold misty windowpane and the icy shock pinched and drew out the heat in the other part of his body almost instantaneously. He imagined her completely covered in the thick layers of winter from head to toe like an Eskimo maiden, her light brown eyes peering out at him with an impish glint.

He wondered how she would look when he presented the guitar to her. Would she be incredulous like his mother had been? The vibrations of the strings when he plucked them felt good, not dissimilar to the sensation of the antique guitar, but whether its music was adequate to the job was lost on him. He would read her face and measure her reaction. If it proved to be unsatisfactory, he had another gift to present to her, a circular wooden box he had fashioned out of cherry-wood and maple, its round lid carved with an elegant design of intertwining vines. Inside was a poem that again had soared out of his pen like an eagle in full flight. Together, the guitar, box and poem were nestled inside the case on the open luggage rack, hanging over his head like unfinished business, and he grew annoyed with the slow progress of the train, wishing it would not stop and linger at each insignificant station as it did. It was not often that the laconic young man was impatient, but on this night he was anxious to see whether her face would be marked by delight or indifference.

He was confident the intricate gifts would be appreciated; he was less sure if she would be ready for his appearance at her apartment door. She had not replied to his letter informing of his decision to visit on New Year's Eve, but he attributed that to the fact that he had written her just over a week before Christmas. The holiday post was unpredictable and there was no other way he could contact her before his arrival. He was prepared to find a taxi cab to deliver him to her address if she was not at the station, and fate would decide whether she would be at home on his arrival.

The train entered the grand old Du Palais Station in Québec a mere twenty minutes after it was scheduled to arrive. It was the final day of the year and despite the snow and freezing temperatures, the train slipped into the station platform like a metallic silver limousine arriving at a red carpet event, bells and lights flashing as the evening bustle of the busy station greeted the arriving travelers. He alighted on the platform with his case in hand and scanned the crowd for a familiar face. Lovers and friends re-uniting for the year's last festivity greeted his searching glances and several wished him a happy new year. He nodded his head at the well-wishers, and to himself observed with a furtive smile that hardly a soul standing sober now would be doing so in four or five hours' time.

Slowly advancing along the platform to the stairs that led down into the bowels of the station, Bernard kept up his search for the woman he ached to see, hoping that fate would be on his side this night, particularly in this unfamiliar site. A last glance behind him brought him face to face with her. Her open arms were a welcome sight and they embraced with urgency so familiar. Finally disengaged from the embrace he guessed that her rosy cheeks were flushed from having raced through the crowded station in search of him, dark brown locks falling around her face loosened from the beige wool cap adorned with delicate white snowflakes pulled down over her arched eyebrows.

Exiting the station, she hailed the taxi which brought them home to her apartment in the old city beneath the towering shadow of Le Château, high on the fortified hill overlooking the grand St.-Laurent. The old silver Citroën raced around icy corners and up the precipitous streets of old Québec before edging into a narrow alleyway of two windowless brick walls facing off in the half-cast darkness of the gas street lamps. The snow in the alley was thick and hard-packed; several other cars sat boxed in neatly by it. Inside her small apartment on the third floor of the solid old brownstone building, the glow of the gas lamps through the expansive bay windows combined with the warmth of the large rumbling radiator provided a romantic ambiance as the two bundled themselves into the welcoming living room.

As Lorraine disappeared into the bedroom just inside the front door, Bernard placed his case on the lightly stained pine flooring of the foyer, and then settled himself upon a somewhat frayed chaise longue embroidered with a lavender-flowered chinoiserie pattern. Beside the divan on a lamp table a mélange of trinkets he well-remembered was displayed: a macramé bracelet festooned with brass finger cymbals, a sterling silver box with several small toe rings, a collection of brass camels, and a miniature hookah. A photograph of her parents standing in front of the old tool shop was propped up against the lamp behind the bric-a-brac collection.

"You know, Berne," she called out from the other room, "I only received your letter announcing your plans to visit this very morning. It arrived as I was preparing to..." then she remembered that he would not have heard a word of it. She returned to the lounge room and found him stretched out on the chaise. "Would you like to freshen up...?" she trailed off as she noticed that his eyes were closed, the look on his face as if he had finally arrived home after an arduous journey. She walked quietly across the room to the chaise and sat down on the edge of it at his feet. He opened his eyes and their emerald moonshine made her feel suddenly overcome with light-headedness. The snowflake cap was now removed and her hair fell in luxuriant waves to her shoulders. Without the wool overcoat he saw that she was dressed in a ribbed carmine sweater dress whose shawl collar revealed a lovely white neck and the familiar gold cross at the end of its delicate chain. He breathed in quickly and smiled, yearning to kiss the soft smooth skin on that neck.

"Berne," she said slowly with a slightly remorseful look on her face. "I have something I must tell you." He looked at her questioningly, his smile momentarily faltering.

No … wait, he replied, gesturing simultaneously with the palm of his hand. *I have something I want to give you,* he whispered. He rose out of the chaise to retrieve the case and returned to unbuckle the two leather straps encircling it. Lorraine sat still, following his movement with her eyes and head but not moving her body. She feared that he would have gifts that she could not reciprocate as his arrival was a surprise of only the past few hours.

He opened the case with the lid facing her so she could not see the contents. He hesitated for a moment, his hand poised above the case; then he drew out a small paper-wrapped box and closed the case. As she took it in her hand and carefully removed the wrapping, her face was appreciative but he could sense a fleeting reticence, as if the gift might represent something too much to accept. Her smile immediately brightened as the wooden lid with the intertwining vines presented itself.

"It's beautiful," she exclaimed. "Thank you, Berne. Your gifts are always so precious."

Open it, he said, gesturing for her to take off the lid. She admired the detailing and its confident bold design, fingering it delicately and not hurrying to open the box. She followed one of the vines with her index finger and traced its path around the lid, underneath another vine and back to its origin. Carefully she prised the lid off the box and pulled out the small piece of writing inside it.

Awake my love do not forsake
Songs my muse she cannot make
These dreams of you I mistake
For bitter winter trials partake
Days emerge from battle right
O divine fire once so bright
Lead me to her with your light
Beauteous visions of the night

"Did you write this?" she asked after reading it twice, more surprised by the language than by the message it held. She raised her eyes to look at him and found him nodding his head slowly. Then, without letting her say another word, he opened the case once again and withdrew the guitar. He held it to her and she took it reluctantly but could not conceal the delight in her eyes at seeing the exquisitely crafted instrument again.

"You have been learning to play it, haven't you?" she asked with genuine curiosity. She saw him shaking his head and smiling as if he was offering her his greatest possession, which he was. It dawned on her slowly that he was giving her the fine hand-constructed guitar and her heart leapt into her throat; a desperate sob came to her lips.

"But no, Berne, you must not give this to me," she cried out loud. "I don't deserve it. No. No. I can't take it. It's too ... too precious."

She stood up abruptly and handed the instrument back to him, his face a question mark and his flashing eyes beginning to shimmer with emotion. *But you are more precious,* they said. Barely able to face his questioning face, her eyes fixed themselves to a dark knot on the pine plank of the floor as she drew up her courage to speak the words she had meant to tell him weeks before.

"I can't, Berne...I...I...just can't," she began, stammering. "I have to tell you something important, but I know it is going to hurt you," she continued, sighing heavily. "I'm getting married, Berne. Tomorrow, actually...I am flying to Paris tomorrow. We will be married in four weeks." At first he thought he misread her lips.

"Married?" He spoke to her slow sorrowful nod.

"Getting married," she repeated. The words punctured like an awl, his resistance a slab of timber solid and true, but eventually it pierced through, leaving a clean round hole where his heart still throbbed. The fierceness of emotion left him bereft of logic. It stunned him — her ability to keep up intimate relations with him while she was already engaged to another man. Was it anger at this betrayal? Or was it remorse for having waited too long, too long to renew his love? In his cabin she had promised him nothing. Their naked bodies intertwined like the vines imbued in his rosette box, feeling as if they had been born that way. But the question was never asked whether her heart was also entwined with his. Or whether another in the city held it hostage, while she retreated to the countryside for some sort of refuge?

"Paris? Who is this lucky man?" he whispered, speaking as if he didn't believe his own words. *Paris?* Placing the guitar on the divan where the warmth of her body still radiated, his hands rose mortified over his face so she could not see the anguish. She stood before him limp with regret,

vacillating between the urge to take him in her arms and a need to flee, to run away and hide her guilty heart. In her bedroom the cases with her wedding trousseau lay ready. His unexpected letter announced his 6:30 PM train arrival. For much of the afternoon she had wandered in a daze, packing the last items into her traveling case without conviction. *Is it a sign? Why has he come just today, on the eve of my departure?* Her marriage was in less than a month's time and all at once the doubts drifted to the surface like fish unwell. Could she see him for a last time and not feel the contradiction of her situation, or damage his trust with her infidelity?

At his cabin on Lac Aylmer, the ruggedness of that wild country set her free. His love was like the clear glacial lake that surrounded them; in his impassioned embrace every nerve and follicle on her body was alive. But in the calm of his presence she was relaxed and feminine, a drifting yacht completing a tranquil summer scene, or a feline luxuriating on the lap of a man who was not her master. She had no need to craft words carefully or make intelligent statements about politics or the recent new world order. They were no defense against his unforced charms anyway.

But now he sat in her divan with his hands covering his anguish, annihilated by her betrayal. More accustomed to his placid affection and peaceful admiration, this new emotionalism left her alarmed and ashamed; it was beyond her understanding, but still she castigated herself for her unfair assumption that his tranquil bearing was equal to an unflappable emotional resilience. Perhaps it was a reflection of her own lack of moral rectitude, or was it her need to fly beyond the bounds of her impending marriage? A cultured and cosmopolitan life in Paris was all she ever aspired to; from meager beginnings as a shop-keeper's daughter in a small timber town in the wilds of the Eastern Townships, she was willing — no, looking gladly forward — to delay her further studies and career in order to become a diplomat's wife. She had already acquired, since her small-town years in St.-Gérard, a refined taste for red wine and dinner parties, and traded her rustic winter parkas for the cashmere and wool of a city dweller. Gone were the days of listening to monotonous tales of salmon fishing and moosehunts, and of minding her father's dismal little tool shop on Friday afternoons and holidays.

"His name is Joël de Vogel-Larochette. He was a LL.M. student," she began, continuing after a small pause. "His father is the cultural attaché to Canada … from Paris." Despite her misgivings for having played too freely with his heart, there was no question in her mind that she would proceed with her plans regardless of the sad state of their affairs in her small apartment. Retreating to the kitchen, she returned a moment later with two glasses ready with her mild offerings of red wine to rally against his disappointment. Placing them on the table, she folded her arms and body around her distraught lover in a firm embrace that made him recoil at first, and then submit with a resignation that told her he was a good man. Apologies were whispered passionately into his ear, which he may or may not have heard, but St.-Gérard would never replace Paris, Copenhagen, or St. Petersburg — all the places that she would grace in her future as a part of a diplomatic pair.

"Paris … St. Petersburg." He felt and understood the words from her lips; they were the signposts of her broader humanity, her destiny in a world far beyond his humble and meager life. She had always soared high above the mountainous cedars and colossal firs of their hometown like a graceful peregrine in full flight, brown and white feathers spreading like a Spanish fantail in the sky's invisible thermal, as precious and stately as the jewels on a mullah's crown. Her gypsy heart would soon fade into the past and in its place would grow a diamond-hard aristocratic core.

Bernard was lost. He felt a strange coldness in his feet and at his center, while his hands and face seemed to burn. Without thought he reached to the table and brought the wine glass to his lips, tipping its entire contents down his throat in a single toss. The warm dry liquid scorched and soothed his esophagus simultaneously; then the heat spread through his body. It calmed him but did not take away the sting in his heart.

"Please take it with you," he voiced, indicating the guitar with his outstretched arm. The contrite young woman was also at a loss for what to do. She gulped her wine and then joined the guitar on the divan, placing it on her lap as she sat down beside him. She held it close to her body and he watched her stroke it, wishing, not for the first time, that the guitar body was his own body, and that the sounds it now made were the clear true tones of his own voice.

Bernard sat lost in his own agony. Oh, to be gifted at this moment with the ability to speak out strongly against her mistaken notion that his lack of wealth or future was an obstacle to their happiness, to supplicate a change of mind, to turn her own decision to leave against her. He was more certain than ever before that she was born to be with him, to bear his children, to grow like the reeds on the lake around his home into beautiful lily-flowers in their ripe old age. But the words were stuck like honeycombs inside the hive, his thoughts buzzing frenetically, maddeningly around in his crowded head, their fulminated heaviness like nails in his coffin.

A slow sad tune of a medieval lament found life from the picking of her thin fingers, accompanying the softly uttered words memorized from the handwritten poem encased in the wooden box on a small piece of paper. His tears of frustration were too much for her to bear. She stopped playing and held him again, his strong body leaning into her as his quivering lips sought hers. With his broken heart in her hands, she led him to the bedroom, the array of bags creating a complex obstacle course for their empassioned tango to the bed. Giving himself up entirely to his ache at first, the heat of his anger and defeat eventually crept into his heart and consumed him. He let the dying embers of his love flare, and if he could enter her heart through his forceful thrusts he would try. Their moans were like the ravenous resuscitation of a once choked fire and when it reached its climactic conclusion they both were swelled with tears of ecstasy and emotional depletion.

When he awoke long after the dawn, she was already gone. Staggering like an injured beast into the living room he saw that she had taken the guitar with her. The wooden rosette box, however, was on the lamp table beside the divan. He opened the box and found inside her note along with a key. She wrote,

Although my body belongs not to you
Know that my heart will always be true.
Je t'aime, mon amour,
Je t'aime beaucoup...
L.

From the great height of the bay windows in the small apartment, he leaned frigid against the glass and wretchedly observed, now in the cold bright light of day, the imposing edifice of Le Château Frontenac as it loomed in the far distance. Below it the gritty ancient masonry walls of the old fortress tumbled. The excruciating wounds of his unrequited love burned. They fissured his heart more than the unforgiving drudge of his ascent into the breathlessly steep and thorn-brambled mountains during his delivery of the tree. Neither the relentless unforgiving forest nor the wild furrowing rapids were a match for Venus's spiteful whip. *She's gone. Lorraine, she is gone. Forever — out of my life.* He longed to touch her skin again and the ache for her clutched at his chest and burned like an ampoule of fire flung at him from a lowly place, the place where he had lost his soul and all of his bearings. All directions now led to a desolate end, without her. He smelled the faintest trace of her lilac scent in the small piece of paper he held to his face. It made his heart drop like a crumpled carcass into the base of his stomach.

The old Citadel stationed resolutely beyond the fortified walls beckoned for him, the prisoner, to conjure up with his shattered spirit invisible yet familiar armor around his heart. The achingly beautiful scenery enveloped by the blue-gray serenity of the wide and mighty St.-Laurent began to reach him. It made him understand why she needed to conquer the vast exterior world. From this vantage point she must have felt at once sequestered in the tantalizing lap of ultimate luxury and barricaded on the fringe of an old crumbling garrison. To remain in the grip of a tepid or crippling past was no way to live.

A seagull made an arc across the clouded sky, circling the turret-like wings of the Citadel in search of a landing point, or perhaps its mate? None presented itself. The bird not content to search in vain, opened is beak wide and made a heart-wrenching screech and continued on, disappearing beyond the battlements, perhaps toward the cannons of Artillery Park inside the St.-Jean Gate of the old city, searching for a more formidable foe. He could not deny her a cosmopolitan life, so what was it he thought he could offer her? He could not even hear the cry of the gull in its wretched search.

With Lorraine's words locked inside the timber box, Bernard deposited the relic of his love into the inner pocket of his winter parka and faced the bleak city streets where his aloneness felt heavier than the leaden letter upon his chest. He spun down into the brutal place that was the darkness of his soul and from there descended the slick, foot-worn stone steps of the oldest man-made stairs on that continent and paced the cobblestones hour upon hour, as if his life depended on it. Only for a moment did he contemplate the fall from a great height that a misstep would offer, the thought blurring even as it came to him. He scrambled like a hunted animal for an eternity, beating his heart into submission. Beyond the fortifications he reached the boardwalk along the cliff below the walls of the Citadel, his pace quickening, and then it broke him into a sprint. The paving and his rough boots ruined his feet and ankles but that was small torture. His was a dark, closed dungeon of a world where only physical, bodily pain was an emollient to his aching heart.

ADRIENNE (REILLANNE), 1859–1869

The austere and imposing gates of the Chartreuse Notre-Dame swung open momentarily to allow a young woman followed by her hesitant father to surreptitiously enter one morning in the spring of 1859. The eremitic convent on the outskirts of Reillanne in the Alpes-de-Haute-Provence was reticent by all accounts, and obscured on all fronts. In a thicket of trees, a meadowlark warbled out of turn in the quietude of the encircling pines, which otherwise blanketed the convent in perpetual silence. The farmstead on the outskirts of Forcalquier where the girl of thirteen managed to grow up in the company of only a father and a twin brother lay not more than a five-hour carriage ride from the alpine base of the Lubéron.

For three years the headstrong girl persevered in her demands of her father to allow her to join the Carthusian Order of the Sisters of Notre-Dame. Adrienne Sébastiani desired to become a novitiate like other young girls wished to find a husband. Her father's resistance did nothing to break her resolve. Constant prayer, she assured him, *lectio divina* — the daily reading of the Scriptures — and the absolution of solitude and simplicity in a cloistered existence were her true calling. When her mind was made up no entreaties, not even a herd of the wild horses, could change her course. Nor did the pleas of her twin brother, Jacob, for whom she was always the protector. Even though they were identical in age, they were opposite in demeanor. While Jacob was given to flights of fancy and his head was perpetually in the clouds and mist, Adrienne seemed as grounded as a flightless bird.

But no one truly knew what storms raged underneath her placid heart. She began her vow of silence well before her father finally granted her wish. To be admitted into the gates of Chartreuse Notre-Dame was not an easy thing; she had secretly written beseeching letters to the Sisters a full two years before this occasion and began her ritual silence nearly a fortnight before this. Those gates were shut tightly on the arrival of the father and daughter, but the large bell perched atop the iron palings rang out boisterously at Adrienne's insistence, and summoned Sister Teresa forthwith from her morning prayers. Father and daughter were greeted by a young nun not much older than the girl herself, and motioned silently to follow her along the long path which meandered through a perfected garden which led to the convent itself. Sister Teresa was a "converse sister" and her responsibility was to greet visitors at the gates when the infrequent non-convent resident called. Without a word Sister Teresa led them to a small chamber within the convent where visitors were met, then turned and left them to return to her prayers.

The Prioress greeted them at the door and motioned them to enter. She put her hands together and silently prayed with the visitors for a few moments before she bestowed a beneficent smile upon them. Arnaud Sébastiani was visibly startled when she spoke her first words. "I am Sister Wilhelmina. I am the Prioress here at Chartreuse Notre-Dame," she said. "Thank you for bringing young Adrienne up here today, Monsieur Sébastiani. Did you have any trouble finding it? We are quite reclusive here."

"Not at all, Blessed Sister," he replied, bowing his head respectfully. "My daughter Adrienne has asked me to bring her here for three years, and only now have I been able to make the arrangements to do so." He waited for the nun to reply, but no words came from her lips. "Thank you for replying to my letter. You know it is my daughter's choice to come, not mine." The nun nodded her head. "I am very sorry to leave her here ... no, I mean ... I am not sorry that she has given her soul to God, but I am sorry that I may never see her again. She is my only daughter." The nun nodded her head again. "She has made up her mind so I will just have to carry on as if I never had a daughter."

A moment later a light tap on the door announced the arrival of the converse nun. Sister Teresa entered, her head nodding almost imperceptibly to Sister Wilhelmina, and gently led Adrienne away to the small room of the postulancy that she would make her own for the first ten days of her convent life. Arnaud thanked Sister Wilhelmina and handed her a small sum of money, not knowing that his daughter had already sent her sizeable contribution in advance. He never saw his daughter again.

Adrienne found the silence of the nunnery soothing to her tremulous soul. For a young woman who had never had a mother and who had been no stranger to back-breaking work, which she shared equally with her brother and father on their small farm, the presence of so many Sisters and the fine handiwork to which they seemed to be confined made it an alien world. Most of her short life had been spent up to her small knees in rich black soil planting beans and cabbages and handling the heavy tools familiar to farm work. Each Sunday from the age of five, it was her special responsibility to sell the produce at the village markets. It wasn't long before she began to wonder why the other families that sold at market had a mother amongst them, but hers did not.

One late autumn afternoon when Adrienne was ten, she returned from the market to find an unfamiliar woman in the kitchen surveying the few items in the larder. Even with her rod-straight back turned to the girl, she could sense the woman's rising disdain for the sparseness of the farmhouse provisions. The girl quickly looked about her and saw the frayed and untidy furnishings of her home as if for the first time. An awful feeling deep in the pit of her stomach hit her like the striking of a sharp hoe into dry soil. Her heart constricted with the sudden sense of dread. As her mind raced and heart pounded, she found she could not express what the feeling was. She had no words to describe the betrayal. But even then she knew it was not her place to question her father, and her misgivings would be the source of strife.

Adrienne did not dare or choose to speak of it — not when the woman turned to face her with an uneasy smile, not when her father returned to the house later that evening to introduce his children to his new mistress, soon to be his wife, nor the next day when she found herself cleaning the kitchen from end to end while the woman monitored her progress. When winter finally arrived with the first silent snowfall, she built up the resolve to pose a question to her father.

"Papa," she quietly said as he sat in his armchair before the fire with his pipe. "Who was our Maman? What happened to her? Why have we never known her?"

Looking squarely into the eyes of his only daughter, Arnaud Sébastiani knew she was a strong young woman and he never once felt that she struggled under the yoke of hard labor or resented their life of toil. The blisters and calluses that this life gave her seemed only to toughen her stubborn nature and make her impermeable to the rumors and gossip of the other young girls of her village. When he peered into her eyes — there was an amber fire ablaze that belied the calm in her voice — he knew it was time she was told the truth. "She died giving birth to you. And Jacob," he added. Then continued: "Your brother was still mostly inside her when she suddenly..." he hesitated again, "...when she died. I had to pull him out with my own hands. I thought it was too late — he was the color of a frozen lake and limp. But his color changed all at once and he came to life. It was a miracle that he lived. That you both lived."

Adrienne let the words sink in slowly, a weighty stone dropped into quicksand. At first the thought resisted absorption, and then it was sucked in all at once. It was not just a hoe striking her heart, but a knife twisting itself at the very core of her being. She was frozen; no words surfaced to her quivering lips. The crackle of the fire thundered in her ear and it was with difficulty that she finally turned and retreated to her bedroom. There she resolved in her roiling mind to never speak of it again for as long as she lived.

The stand-off that ensued between daughter and the new wife made Arnaud's life unbearable. As a last resort, he gathered up his divided family and delivered them to church. Every Sunday after that he prayed to the Lord for an answer that would bring peace back into his household. The answer he received after nine months was not as he expected. The spring morning his new wife declared that she was with child, Adrienne, unexpectedly animated, made it known that she was going to become a nun. She had sought details through the Church on the requirements to join the silent order of Chartreuse Notre-Dame, and she started her vow that very day.

After many entreaties and even a strike across the face in a desperate and frustrated rage, the father could not break his daughter's silence. Two years and several months passed before Arnaud finally gave in to his daughter's request and by that time she had saved enough extra income from the farmer's markets to make the requisite donation in order to enter the gates of the convent. Almost as soon as Adrienne stopped selling the produce through the usual vendors' method of loud and competing entreaties and waving vegetables at passing customers, her income increased threefold from customers drawn inexplicably to her beautiful but silent fruit and vegetable stall. Her polished and finely displayed vegetables attracted the discerning buyer seeking quality over price, yet they lingered about, enquiring about her father which was met with more silence. That silence spurred them to expand further on inquiries, asking her silent opinion of their most pressing worries and eventually unloading terrible burdens. It seemed they felt much better for the telling, and in time she learned that they sought not just fruit and vegetables but the ultimate freedom of her silent pardon, bestowed upon them with her beatific smile.

Before long they came to give confession almost as a trial before they presented themselves to the parish priest. If she granted a cleansing smile upon them, they knew they would be given absolution by the priest. If she did not, they hesitated and found other smaller sins to seek forgiveness. They could rely on young Adrienne and fear not that their troubles and sins would be relayed on to others. Generous donations weekly found their way into the plain ceramic dish on the edge of her confessional table, which always contained her rosary and a few starter coins. By the end of two years, she prepared to enter the convent without her father's monetary contribution or his blessing.

At Chartreuse Notre-Dame, the weeks and months passed slowly and silently between the convent walls. The young novitiate grew each day more patient and skilled at filling her free moments between prayer, Scripture study, and convent duties with some other purpose, mental if not physical. Initially, as a converse nun — although she never exercised this freedom of speech — she was assigned the daily duty of maintaining the convent's library, secretly reading the elaborately printed texts, hand-written manuals, and collected manuscripts as she delivered borrowed texts to the cells of the cloistered nuns who left written notices at the library requesting them. She found the required items in the library's storeroom and slid them through the nuns' *guichet,* or food-hatch, carefully recording the delivery and return details in the meticulously kept record book, which as far as she could glean dated back to 1265.

One evening between vespers and her supper, Adrienne discovered a book that had been in the library for some time, which had not seen the light of day for at least a century. The delicately bound handwritten manuscript was inadvertently obscured behind a much larger volume which had been returned to the shelf in haste well before her time. On inspection she found that the pages of the manuscript contained exquisitely detailed and numbered illustrations on the fine art of musical instrument making, particularly featuring the "new" six-string guitar.

Enlarged detailed drawings depicted the various angles of the instrument to be constructed, but between the drawings was hand-written text she could not read. On the back cover was written: *Fabbricatorello, Napoles, anno 1792.* Adrienne stared at the text, eyes scanning slowly over the curvaceous lettering. They resembled the Latin she learnt in the study of the Scriptures, but she struggled to make meaning out of them. It was clear that cutting and assemblage required understanding of precise dimensions, but she could not calculate them without comprehension of the detailed descriptions. She resolved to devote herself to mastering the new language in order to decipher the manuscript with full appreciation.

Motivated by a new-found purpose, Adrienne solicited her friend Teresa, whose mother she knew hailed from Siena, to seek assistance in the Italian language while on their weekly *spatia mentum*, a walk beyond the cloisters lasting about three hours during the course of which each nun was able to talk in turn with the others. Sister Teresa gladly spent many intensely dedicated hours with Adrienne during their walks translating long passages of Italian because it gave her spiritual connection to her family, whom she missed quite passionately. Adrienne in the secret quiet of her cell copied a page at a time onto long strips of paper or cloth and wound them around her wrist beneath the long wide sleeves of her habit. Once they were out of the view of the others, she unraveled the transcriptions and Sister Teresa would give her the interpretations quietly and solemnly as if they were the Scriptures. Once completed, Adrienne returned to her cell to transcribe the passages in French into a notebook. Within a year the entire text had been translated, and the complete set of illustrations lovingly reproduced in the notebook. While the other nuns stitched and embroidered their tapestries, wove their fine linen and muslin and made hand-bound cloth books in the solitude of their cells, Adrienne discovered her talent for working with wood.

With the aid of a small handful of ancient woodworking implements she stumbled upon in an old maintenance shed once used by the convent's early builders, she made her very first simple, but carefully handcrafted lute. While on one of her cloister walks with Sister Teresa, she discovered several large blocks of soft spruce salvaged from the convent's wood-pile by the shed. Its large rosette was carved into a grille of three intertwining vines to represent her father, herself, and her brother. There was room for no more. Initially, Adrienne kept her prolific creations to herself, but eventually Sister Wilhelmina discovered them. Adrienne had never played music or known of orchestras, but over the course of five years she created in the solitary confines of her cloistered workshop a dozen perfectly formed instruments, including lutes, mandolins, baroque five-course and six-string guitars, and a *viola-a-mano*, each with a unique shape and more importantly, a faultless sound. Although the playing of musical instruments was not normally considered an occupation within the statutes of the Carthusian Order, the Prioress recognized a God-given talent and an opportunity to raise funds for the much needed repairs to the convent.

As word spread through the Alpes-de-Haut-Provence that the solitary nuns of the Chartreuse Notre-Dame convent were manufacturing exquisite hand-made instruments, there was no shortage of buyers for the special instruments thought to embody the liturgical prayers of the Sisters. At times it took many months and several attempts to cut and plane the soft woods, carve the exquisitely executed rosettes, or wind the metal around the sheep's gut strings to Adrienne's own exacting standards and satisfaction. Once completed, however, the instruments made the most beautiful sounds — haunting melodies and soaring lullabies as if they had a spirit and a voice of their very own. More than one customer returned within a year to commission a second and even third instrument to add to their collection and perhaps to atone for a recent trespass. They were never allowed to visit the nun however much they supplicated or offered donations. It was said that her pieces surpassed those made by ordinary luthiers; notwithstanding the fact each strum of the instrument was equal to a "Hail Mary" directly to the Holy Mother. They were exquisite and seemed to emit music even when no hands were laid upon them. And inside the convent no eyes had ever witnessed Adrienne at work in her solitary workshop.

On a particular warm autumn afternoon in 1868, exactly one day before Adrienne was to renew her vows for the next stage of her consecration as a virgin of Christ by making a profession of stability, obedience, and conversion, Tomàs found himself at the gates of the convent, almost vexed with anticipation as if he were meeting his destiny. Nearly a half day's travel brought the monk to the convent bearing a variety of finely formed goat's cheese and braids of rye bread. A curiously shaped leather case was strapped securely to his back while he balanced the gustatory offerings in round woven baskets over his shoulders and arms. He had walked the entire distance on foot with absolute anticipation for he had heard of the extraordinary nuns who made music instruments in silent prayer on top of the great hill and was convinced that his offerings of brotherly love in the form of fresh bread and exquisite cheeses would win the favor of even the purest of ascetics.

Sister Teresa met him at the gate just as he began to gingerly rebalance his burden to free a hand in order to sound the bell atop the gate. "Thank you, Sister," the friar declared. "You have saved me from dropping these baskets before I even have the good grace to offer them to you." The sister smiled.

"Good afternoon," he continued with a deep bow, hands clasped in prayer, surprised that the nun had smiled. "I am Fra Tomàs. I've brought you my freshly baked bread and our specialty — *Chèvre et Banon, nos fromages saints des Alpes-de-Haut-Provence*. May I come in?"

The friar revealed the contents of the frayed willow basket, pulling back the hessian cloth to reveal seven small rounds of goat's cheese, including the *Banon* wrapped ceremoniously in brown chestnut leaves and raffia, as cheerful and inviting as the faces of little children peering through a candy shop window. She motioned for him to follow her through the garden and into the convent. When he entered the convent and passed through the refectory doors, he was struck by the lightness and calm that surrounded him. Unlike the Barcelonette monastery, which was heavy with dark beams and masonry, the interior entry hall of Chartreuse Notre-Dame was bathed in light. He was abashed by the austere but decidedly feminine aura of the place and felt rather ashamed for his rough appearance and filthy sandals.

As if he had spoken the words out loud, Sister Teresa motioned for him to drop his baskets on a waiting table, and led him to a private washroom at the far end of the building. Years of silence had gifted the nuns with efficiency in reading the most subtle of facial expressions and unspoken impressions, answering requests well before they were made.

In the washroom, Tomàs removed his guitar, heavy robe, and leather sandals, and washed himself and his sandals thoroughly, giving thanks to the Lord for this small mercy. When he arrived back to the table where he left his baskets, he found a note written on hand-made paper where the baskets had been. It read,

Fra Tomàs ~
Thank you for your offering. May we, the Sisters of Char-treuse Notre-Dame, invite you to stay for supper, which will be served after the vespers in the mezzanine?
Please wait in the hall until someone comes for you shortly. I trust you will be comfortable waiting here.
Faithfully yours,
~ Sister Teresa

He folded the note carefully and placed it in a hidden pocket of his robe. He surveyed the hall to find a seat where he could rest his feet for a while. His sandals were damp and made a squelch as he turned to go. He decided that it would be best to walk about outside to allow his sandals to dry on the warm pavement before he was required upstairs. Taking his guitar in hand, he found his way through a side door, which led to a small courtyard lined on opposite sides with espaliered apple and pear trees and adorned with a diamante herb maze in the central space. The slanting sun cast an ochre glow on the few remaining apples on one tree. Tomàs found a comfortable seat on a low brick wall facing the trees and positioned his guitar against his body. Its smooth wooden curves and familiar weight made him immediately feel at ease.

Slowly he tuned the instrument and began to pluck a dainty *repicco* from the baroque instrument. He played it several times slowly in different keys and then began a more impassioned *punteado*, unaware of a figure watching and listening from an adjacent window on the far side of the courtyard. His fingers danced over the strings, first slowly then faster, and then with an urgency that transformed the *passacaglia* into a heartfelt plea.

Adrienne read the entreaty with her eyes and ears through the glass of the small vestibule window. She had been informed by the Prioress that a young friar had arrived at the entry gate with a musical instrument and several baskets of food. As she put away an obscure volume brought to the convent early that morning by an itinerant bookseller, she wondered with some agitation why a guitar would be brought to her by a monk. Would he ask her to play it for him? Or worse, ask her to repair it?

But now, as she watched him play rapturously and with abandonment she had never witnessed before, a small shudder quivered at the nape of her neck at the thought of making speech with him. It was the first time in nearly twelve years that she had a desire to speak. Watching him lost in his music was an entirely new and unsettling experience. She herself had often been lost in a melody as she brought a new instrument to life, but never before had she watched

133

someone else do the same and with the entirety of his body. As she continued to watch captivated by the performance, she strained to keep herself from blurting out, knowing that as soon as he realized she was watching he would stop playing, and this she wanted to avoid. Like a child watching a fearsome lion in a mesmerizing circus, her enthralled and beating heart prayed that the show would never end.

The young friar now felt eyes watching him closely. His early years as a street musician prior to entering the monastery gave him a sense of an audience's mood, and he could instantly identify an individual in the crowd who connected to his passion or felt his pain. They did not have to speak or express their appreciation. It made his music resonate more fully, as if another instrument had joined in. And right then, he could not see her, but he felt an undeniable connection to a presence somewhere in the proximity of the courtyard. He could almost feel the beating of her heart in time with his own, and the timbre of the song taking on a wider and more complex vibration than he had ever experienced.

But he could feel restraint as well, as if tears were being held back, or an invisible hand held over a mouth to keep in a cry of intense joy. Somehow he knew that this was no ordinary bond. Without that restraint, he thought to himself, the linkage between them would surely be overwhelming. He pressed himself to continue playing on, desperately tempted though he was to look up and around to see who held him in thrall. And then, as quickly as it was formed, the connection was lost. He stopped his playing and ran to a dark window, but no one was there. He ran to another window and still no one. Whoever had been watching him was now gone. Desperation gripped him. Slowly he laid aside his guitar and dropped to his knees in prayer.

"Dear Heavenly Father," he prayed in silence, "in the name of the Father, Son and Holy Ghost do not forsake your lost lamb, for I know I have strayed many a time in my lowly existence. My human mind and body are weak, but my spirit is pure. Please help me find the right path. If my destiny awaits me here, please assist me to find the way that the Lord has designed for me. Let me not stray from that path. Amen."

He crossed himself, kissed the rosary beads around his lean waist and rose slowly to find Sister Teresa waiting for him in the doorway from which he had come, her plump hands crossed on her chest with her crucifix nestled between them. He followed her through the door and across the long hallway to the staircase leading up to the dining hall. When they arrived, the nuns were all seated at their tables, some of them silently praying to themselves and others silently communicating with the nun opposite them. One seat opposite Sister Wilhelmina remained empty.

The friar seated himself carefully there as he was motioned to do by Sister Wilhelmina, who bowed her head and waited for him to bend his head before she began her prayer out loud. Tomàs started, his green eyes flashing as he glanced quickly around the table looking for the one he knew he would recognize without hesitation. But she was not there. He bowed his head deeply with silent disappointment as the sisters began to recite the Lord's Prayer without a sound. As Sister Wilhelmina's prayer reverberated throughout the dining hall, each heard in their own inner spirits the collective voices of the room. Then a bell sounded and an almost audible unified "Amen" reverberated across the rafters of the hall. After dinner was finished and as the plates were cleared from the table, Tomàs plucked up the courage to ask Sister Wilhelmina whether he could be introduced to the nun who fashioned the musical instruments by hand.

"Unfortunately," Sister Wilhelmina replied, "Sister Adrienne took ill just before supper and has retired to her room. I'm afraid she wouldn't be well enough to show you her instruments." The nun gestured for the friar to pick up his supper plates. This he did and followed her to the kitchen. When they returned the nun continued, "Sister Teresa tells me you play the guitar incredibly well. 'Like a true performer' were her exact words. Where did you learn to play?"

"Oh, she exalts me," he replied modestly. "I am but the Lord's humble servant. My father was a self-taught musician and poet from Seville who traveled Europe far and wide as a performer. His playing was compared once to his compatriot Fernando Sor, but he was not a conformist by any measure, and his flame did not shine as brightly as that celebrated composer. My father was more like a street performer — a troubadour. He composed the most beautiful ballads and that won him the favor of many a fair maiden from Seville to Paris to Amsterdam. Until the day he met my mother, a rising young opera singer in Vienna. She convinced him to leave his traveling days behind. But my mother's family was most unhappy with the liaison and so they ran away to be married, leaving behind her promising career to live happily, but with a meager existence, in the San Salvatore mountains near Lugano. They raised goats and produced the finest *chèvre* in the region. My mother sang to them marvelously to achieve the exquisite goat's milk. Unfortunately, the Lord decided to take both of my parents from me when I was eight — the influenza I believe." Both nun and friar crossed themselves reverently.

"So, what brought you to France, and Reillanne in particular?" The nun enquired.

"I was taken in and raised by the Jesuits in Lugano, you see. I spent fourteen years there before I took the vows of monkhood myself. My father had taught me to play the guitar and mandolin, and I basically mastered any instrument I could lay my hands on. But it was during my years training for the priesthood that I grew to understand the divine power of music and spirit of our ancestors which can live on in a beloved instrument. This guitar is the one thing my parents left me when they passed on. In its case my father had left me a few sheets of his hand-written lyrics and music, and that was all. Those are my only worldly possessions."

The nun smiled beatifically and urged the friar to continue. "When I was twenty-three, I left the monastery and traveled to Paris, then Prague, then further north as far as Oslo, Bergen and Stockholm. I performed like my father all over Europe, as a troubadour *and* a man of God. Most often I made my concerts outside of churches and cathedrals. The donations fed me and kept brothers at my table. The town folks at the Viking *kyrka* in Bergen were receptive and particularly generous. Without my guitar, I would be just another monk in sandals. With it, I am who I am. *Fra Tomàs, Il Musicista de San Francesco d'Assisi.*"

Sister Wilhelmina smiled. "It has served you and Father Francis well."

"Yes. I believe it was my destiny to bring music to the world, whether I was a brother or not. The legacy of the troubadours continues with me. I shall never let it die ... until of course, I do."

"So, you came to Chartreuse Notre-Dame to perform for us silent Sisters?"

"No, I came to discover the secret of your instrument-making. I have heard about the exquisite instruments made by one of your own, which I hear are kept locked behind glass cases in the homes of the wealthiest men in this countryside. Such a shame it is that such fine instruments will never be played for the pleasure of an adoring crowd. I have also heard that each instrument seems to have a voice of its own, even when no one is playing them. Is this true?"

"That surely could not be true, Frère." Sister Wilhelmina replied. "Do you believe such a thing could be possible?"

"Anything is possible when instruments are created — or played, for a matter of fact — with the essence of our spirits in them. I have known an instrument to play along, when another nearby is being played. The specific combination of forces and resonance of one imbues the other with a singular vibrational kinship, manifest in sound, like a ghost ship seen only on certain nights and in certain weather conditions. It is eerie and a phenomenon to behold!"

"Like the spirit of the Holy Madonna when she makes herself appear in a stone, on a hillside, or even on a milk-bottle. It is truly a phenomenon to behold."

"Yes, exactly," Tomàs replied. Both friar and nun stopped to reflect on the comparison of holy phenomena.

"Praise be the glory of God," declared the Prioress.

"Praise be the glory of God," replied Tomàs. "Amen."

"Amen," she echoed. "Frère, I can offer you lodging for the night in the hermitage that houses our converse Carthusian brothers. I must let you know, however, that the

Carthusian way may be quite regimented to those not initiated. Our day begins at one AM with a prayer to Our Lady, then at one-fifteen, we hasten to the church for our night vigils. Through them we express our watchful expectation for the Savior and for a dawn of resurrection to rise over the darkness of the world."

"Amen."

"Amen. I do not expect you to be there for the night vigils, but at eight-fifteen the Brothers join us for the Celebration of the Eucharist. Together we chant the convent's liturgy — our own rendition of Gregorian chant — the sisters join in silent prayer of course."

"Thank you, yes, Holy Sister. You are providing a 'room at the inn' for this humble servant of God, and I thank you."

"You are welcome, Frère. When it is time to gather to sing the Terce, Sext, and None in the chapel, the bells will ring accordingly to announce each office. Please feel free to join us during any or all of our solemnities. Let us now walk to the monastery."

The Prioress rose and Tomàs followed. She was an imposing woman of substantial height and moral rectitude, which was reflected on her exceptionally high-bridged nose and regal, thinly arched eyebrows. Below them her stern but compassionate gray-blue eyes emitted a clearly pious and virtuous probity. When she walked her gait was floatingly smooth and did not undulate, as if beneath her gray habit she was supported by an army of angels lifting her up a few inches from the earth. Her gray habit was correspondingly smooth and without a crease, except where the folds of her gown were meant to lie starched into a perfect pleat. Her crucifix, suspended from a delicate gold chain about her neck, provided the only accoutrement to such faultless tailoring. When they stepped out into the open night air, Tomàs took a deep silent breath and followed his pious and immaculate hostess, keeping two small paces behind her as she glided effortlessly through the spare but manicured garden.

"Hopefully in the morning, after Sister Adrienne renews her vows ... " the nun announced as she led him to the front terrace of the hermitage.

"She is renewing her vows?" he asked, somehow surprised.

"Yes. And for that, I am sure she will be improved enough in the morning, and will join us. Tomorrow we hold our colloquium where we engage in deep discussions and exchanges on how we can incorporate the Scriptures into our daily lives. This may be a perfect time for you and Sister Adrienne to exchange views on how your God-given gifts protect and nourish in your hearts the fire of Divine Love — the Love that unites us all as the members of the same body."

"Amen. That would be a most enlightening discussion, Sister," he replied, as they entered the monastery. The monk observed that this stone hermitage like the convent had the appearance of a more open and welcoming structure than he was accustomed to at the Franciscan monastery. "You are certainly far from a silent order."

"No, we are not. We are the *voice and heart of the Church,* which through us presents to the Father in Jesus our humble request for pardon, as well as our praise, supplication, and adoration. The Sisters have the freedom to choose among the diverse forms of liturgical prayer — silent or not. Choosing a life of solitude does not mean deserting the human family. Union with God, if authentic, does not shut us on ourselves;

rather it opens our spirit and expands our heart to embrace the entire world and the mystery of Christ's redemption — it is written in the Carthusian Statutes." Tomàs had let his mind wander while she expostulated on the Carthusian way of life and the human family. It found its way back once again like a wayward foot-soldier to the garrison of the elusive Adrienne and her small troop of sacred musical instruments.

"You know," the nun began, reading his thoughts, "I too have often felt it was a pity not to share Sister Adrienne's beautiful instruments with the public. Unbeknownst to her, I offered several of them a year ago for funds to make repairs to our convent, and quickly a competition formed to acquire them. As soon as Sister Adrienne heard of this, however, she asked me to lock them away in the storeroom and refused to make another. You have my permission to convince her to offer them to the world. Perhaps she will begin with you?"

"Perhaps ... " he replied, now lost in thought. He remembered the deep connection he felt earlier this day in the apple courtyard. He was certain now that it was she. Adrienne, whom he had not yet met, but whom he knew better than anyone he had ever known. He knew precisely how she would appear and the exact intensity of her gaze. He knew how she would hold a lute, run a bow against viola strings, and pluck a melody from a guitar. He now understood her reticence, understood her need to raise and maintain her guard, lest, like the ghost guitar, she make a sound against her will.

Adrienne stood at the upright gates of the convent for the last time. She looked up to the matching pair of brass archangels in bas relief on the heralded banners arching over each hinged wrought iron gate wing. Their simple flowing gowns and woven hair were frozen in breezy heaviness while their lips pursed eternally in silent remonstrance. A small bundle was tucked under the young woman's arm and the guitar that had been the cause of her unholy trespass was clutched in one hand.

As she swung open the heavy gate and stepped through, the dull ache in her heart intensified. The cold dampness of the early morning gripped her like frozen snow applied to a fresh wound, the ensuing numbness brought slim relief but the deep underlying pain continued to throb. She hesitated momentarily under the watchful eyes of the archangels and remembered his face close to hers, his half-opened eyes deeply patterned with an emerald brilliance the color of the forest.

"Speak to me," he said softly. He held her gaze for a long tender moment, and then his lips found hers in a kiss that she felt was full of sadness. "Please tell me something that will free me from the remorse of what I have just done."

But she could not speak. No words formed in her mind and nothing but a small mute cry came to her lips. She could only turn away and free herself desolately from his arms, the weight of her broken vow of chastity now a heavy yoke on a lumbering beast of burden. They sat in a frozen silence for an eternity, the stillness of the stone tower as austere and foreboding as the cavern of an ancient Roman cathedral and less forgiving. A thousand thoughts but no absolution came to her. "Come away with me," he ached to tell her, but those words he knew would place her in a unmitigated quandary, and him in the worst possible light for forcing her to choose between his selfishness and God.

When she had fatefully met him in the exterior convent gardens softly strumming his guitar just before midnight, it was without design that she had taken his hand and waited with him silently there until all the sisters had retreated to the chapel for the night vigil. Then, as they wound their way in darkness up the winding stone stairs to the apex of the tower with only a slim stub of candle in a wrought-iron holder balanced in her free hand, she knew that he would delight in the treasures they would find there. The instruments were lined up meticulously against the rounded tower walls on individual wooden plinths in chronological order of their construction. *This is no storeroom,* Tomàs thought to himself. *This is a sacred temple.*

He stood before a yellow-ochre pear-shaped lute with curved cedar top and ran his finger along the intricately carved rose of braided intertwining vines. Beside it a *colascione* rested against the stone, its diminutive reddish-orange cherry-wood face beaming like a child's. Its tiny abalone shell tuning keys reflected their subtle iridescence in the dim candlelight. Tomàs hesitated to remove an instrument from its pedestal, but Adrienne placed the candle down on a table not far from the entrance of the room and selected a small guitar which she held out to him. He looked at the golden sunburst radiating from the circular rosette soundhole in its finely crafted body and saw that it was nearly a replica of the guitar his father had bequeathed to him but somehow more refined, and he was nearly overcome with excitement at the prospect of making music with this excruciatingly exquisite instrument.

He took it from her, his hand curving over hers as he grasped the neck of the baroque guitar and drew both of them to him. Adrienne dropped her eyes to the stone floor in a moment of reticence, removing her hand from beneath his pleasingly warm and easy grip. She turned and walked as solemnly as she could to the opposite window where the moonlight seeped seductively through in a shadowy silver stream, illuminating a dark red mahogany mandolin shaped in a circular wave, its double strings gleaming. Stopping before it she carefully released the instrument from the small linked chain that held it securely against the wall.

In a single motion her body spun around to face him, brought the crest of the mandolin up against her stomach beneath her breasts and plucked a *tremolo* chord from its taut strings with her right hand before opening into an *andante* with a series of *legato* scale passages and more sustained *tremolos*. The first chord and every note following was in perfect tune, for she had that morning, as she did every morning, begun her day after her morning prayer with a slow methodical round, circling that tower tuning every instrument and playing an equal measure of music on each to season them, a nurturing mother lavishing her love upon her many children.

Tomàs listened intently to Adrienne's *tremolo*, admiring the purity of the sound and her controlled passion. He could tell that she had never taken a lesson and very likely was not a reader of music, but her own compositions were exalted and if angels could herald music with the flutter of their golden wings, the glide of her harmonic scale and hypnotic chords progressions would certainly be of the angels. He longed to stroke the alabaster arm that held the mandolin to her body and the serpentine fingers that shifted grace-fully up and down the length of the elegant neck. He longed to release the full power of that silent and reticent passion with a kiss. But with solemn restraint he returned his attention to the familiar guitar in his hands. His first rolled chord resonated through his body like an emotional response. It rose from him and joined her rising *arpeggio*, his next falling with it in perfect sumptuous harmony.

For an eternity they exchanged and interchanged melodies in faultless union, their harmonies intertwining with ease as if they had played together since childhood. They changed instruments and sampled the entire collection, varying and experimenting with the tempo, harmonics and chord progressions to adapt to the new instruments and combinations they invented. When the candle finally flickered and drew its last breath, he put down the *colascione* and drew her to him in an impassioned kiss. She yielded completely to him, her lute keeping them only for a moment chastely divided in its position between their aching loins.

The memory of their impassioned and unbridled coupling now embattled her. With her instruments as silent witnesses, they had fallen to the floor in an embrace that made the rock-solid tower and world around them melt away, as her perpetual veil was removed by tender hands followed by urgent lips. Intertwined as they were, the strange yet familiar exultation they experienced together was a new kind of enlightenment not unlike a trance achieved through prolonged prayer and meditation, combined with the arousing highs of a perfect rapturous harmony.

But, as the light of a cold moon shut down the last quiver of passion and gave rise to the guilty agony of abandoned vows, they rose in sudden shame nearly stumbling as they moved away from one another to opposite sides of the round tower. Adrienne slowly turned her back to Tomàs and began a ritual straightening of the instruments, returning them solemnly to their rightful positions without a word. At the last, tears sprang to her eyes and streamed hot down cheeks; shoulders collapsed shaking beneath her tousled hair.

Tomàs watched her achingly, the stone in his heart hammering an unholy void in his soul.

"Please tell me something that will free me from the remorse of what we have just done ... what I have done."

But still, no words could break free through her wretched silence. The pair stood silent in remorse for what seemed an eternity equally to each.

"If you cannot speak," he finally moaned in a half whisper, "then I must leave." His heart hung heavier still with the guilt of his trespass. Only moments had transpired since they were entwined in an ecstasy he had never before experienced, but he knew that this act would be his soul's torture of the rest of his days. His body ached to hold her in his arms again and feel the softness of her reluctant yet yielding lips. His mind continued to whirl with thoughts on how he could make it right for her, right for them, and right for God. But it was no use. He could see in her silent and angled repose that she found no sanctuary in his words. "You shall never see me again," he sighed, barely able to move or turn away.

The young man walked for two days in a clouded state before he even realized that he had abandoned his guitar at the convent. Knowing that he would never be allowed to enter those reclusive gates again, he spent that night in anguished remorse and in the morning, in the cold cradle of an alpine river, he found his passage back to God's Holy Kingdom, a helpless and repentant soul adrift in the bulrushes reclaimed and at last forgiven by the Holy Spirit.

But Adrienne would never know of this, and now poised at the precipice of a new beginning, the young woman cast aside the last vestiges of her cloistered and other-worldly existence. Her heart wrenched silently with the memory of her mortal sin — her sordid moment of digression played over and over again in her mind like a spinning wheel weaving a yarn so rich and lavish she dared not look. The instinctive actions of two young creatures coming together in the fumbling heat of animal passion had transported them both to an extraordinary place filled with sensations and sounds tantalizingly close to the real substance of salvation.

Yet those unsanctioned actions were aberrant to her cloistered world of rosaries, prayer and virtue. In the morning she was expected to renew her vows of silence and chastity in a profession of obedience. *But how could I do this now? My hypocrisy is writ large on the wretched scorecard of my soul.*

A long abject silence had ensued after their passions had been played out in coitus and Tomàs stumbled out into the darkness before she could turn around to face him — perhaps even forgive him. He had slipped out, leaving behind his only possession as if he were ready for the next world. Had she murmured a word his heart would have lightened, but her silence gripped him with the severity of its seeming reproof.

As Adrienne passed through the gates with her erstwhile lover's abandoned guitar and her sparse belongings, the profound remorse in her heart battered against her like gale-force winds against the tattered sails of a lost ship at sea. But miraculously, as soon as she stepped into the open arms of the broad reaching pines that edged the convent and swept through the hills and countryside around her, the winds abated. All of a sudden her lungs no longer felt they were squeezed in a vise, rather they felt as if the trees were breathing life into her as they surrounded her with an unconditional and unqualified acceptance akin to absolution.

5

LORRAINE (PARIS); ELLEN (ST.-GÉRARD AND BANGKOK), 1959

Passengers on the diplomatic flight between Québec and Paris were uncharacteristically sparse due to it being New Year's Day, and Lorraine felt conspicuous as the only passenger not suited in gray Pierre Cardin or sporting a cravat. The small cohort of traveling bureaucrats from the French and Québécoise diplomatic corps fell silent for a fleeting second as she entered the cabin. In front and behind her, the men rose briefly from their seats as she moved down the aisle. Once she was seated, they returned to their lively comments about the recent election of Général Charles de Gaulle, the new President of the Fifth Republic of France.

She was painfully aware that she was the only female in the sparsely populated plane, but the empty row of seats beside her was a relief. She did not desire conversation at this moment, and was grateful for the opportunity to be alone with her thoughts, which immediately dropped down to the plane's cargo hold, to the guitar sequestered there in the cold cabin below. She wondered at the rationality of her last-minute decision to take it with her to Europe. With her bags already delivered into the waiting car, she had unexpectedly asked the driver to wait in the limousine as she re-entered her apartment and retrieved the instrument. Bernard was still asleep — or pretending to be — and she gently closed the door so as not to wake him, and carried the case like a sleeping child in her arms out to the waiting car.

As she had descended onto the pavement in front of her apartment, a distinct rustle of skirts and the name *Isabelle* suddenly sounded in her ear, forcing her to glance briefly behind her to see if someone, perhaps Bernard, had crept up behind her and whispered the name in her ear. But no one was there and the driver looked on curiously as she swiveled her head around again surreptitiously, as if she might catch someone deliberately hiding from her.

"*Mademoiselle*," the chauffeur said curiously, "have you forgotten something again?"

"No, no. I just thought I heard someone say something. Did you hear it?"

"*Non, Mademoiselle*, I heard nothing. Would you like to go to the airport now?"

"Yes, thank you. *À l'aéroport, s'il vous plaît.*" But soon her mind returned to the voice, the name. *Isabelle.* She considered the two women she knew by that name. There was one in her French military history class last year with whom she shared a few study hours before the exam, but she was not a lasting friend. The other was an ancient friend of her mother, but she had met the old lady only once and nearly ten years ago. There was no one in her neighborhood or her family by that name, so why had it sprung up so abruptly and urgently just now? And so clearly? It was a mystery — like that guitar. She thought back to Bernard's efforts that first time she saw him with it. She had strung the instrument at his cabin before Christmas. She could not be sure if it was this guitar, or the other that he played, but it was miraculous that someone without any music experience could play as if he had been immersed in music since childhood. She had to admit it was only some basic chords he had strummed, but the other factor was his deafness.

Could he have heard the song she was playing? Could he have felt a resonance that echoed his own strumming? And what about the fingering of the chords? How could he have known? Could he have mastered them in the intervening years between when she first knew him and now?

She momentarily put aside the mysterious and unfathomable thoughts and focused her attention on the passing landscape as the limousine glided swiftly over the precipitous lanes of the City, absorbing the undulation of the cobbled streets without effort. The battlements were now above the level of her eyes and the morass of French colonial and English Tudor–style houses and commercial establishments sprang up at various angles from the oblique streets like a spread of toy building blocks strewn about the foot of a childish monolith. A taxi jostled with the limousine for space on the narrow streets and several young men on bicycles riding in convoy across the lane ahead of them made the trip painstakingly slow.

Lorraine wished for the car to speed away as quickly as possible so she could not dwell on the possibility of turning around and going back to her apartment. *He* was back there, but her *life* was ahead of her, on that diplomatic plane, in a one-carat diamond ring in her bags in the trunk of the car, in an elegant hotel on the Left Bank in Paris.

"Notre hotel-appartement est situé sur la Rive Gauche," he had written to her. *"Dans une rue calme du cœur historique de Paris. A courte distance à pied du Panthéon, du Jardin des Plantes et des Arènes de Lutèce...Tu peux ainsi découvrir ma Paris et ses nombreuses curiosités."*

As she read that letter, she became excited about the possibility of discovering not only Paris's numerous sights, but conquering his milieu and the whole of Parisian society. In her arms, however, was *his* gift. And it had spoken to her. As the car approached the wide open and spare gray avenues of the airport terminus, her thoughts wandered aimlessly through the nearly unspoken conversations and high emotions of last night — her last night in Québec, filled as it was with the silent but impassioned entreaties of her heartbroken lover. Her guilt over choosing a life of abundance with a man born into means — Joël, the *avocat* son of the French cultural attaché — over an unknown future with her achingly beautiful and soulful first love.

For a moment she pondered the possibility that she was marrying the wrong man, that *he* was her soul mate. But Lorraine did not believe in soul mates, miracles, magic, superstition, or the supernatural. *No*, she told herself, *surely all those things have no place in the reality of this world.* No nun or Sunday school priest could ever convince her that the miracle of the Creation story — Adam, Eve, the Garden of Eden, the apple, and most of all, the pestilent snake — was more than a metaphorical morality tale. No trance-inducing incantations of thirty-five Hail Mary's or Glory-be's with the assistance of an artillery of rosaries could bend her pragmatic, almost scientifically rigid mind from her logical truths.

Fortunately, she had learned very early on in her girlhood that she was better off to keep these truths to herself. She was accustomed to remaining silent against the contradictory possibility of dialogue with more devout and fanatical members of her own convent school's nuns and cohorts, notwithstanding her own devout parents. She sometimes felt she was a fraud, but in her mind her dedication to her studies and to her music was as true a devotion to God as any other.

In the hold of the plane beneath the high-speed chattering of the passengers, below the deliberate wandering of the flight crew up and down the wide single aisle of the plane with a silver tray of liquid, savory, and sweet refreshments, under the unsettled heart of a young woman about to marry a privileged son of a diplomat she hardly knew, the guitar that held Isabelle's passions sighed a bass-heavy vibrato of solemnity and passing sadness. No one was there to hear the groan, but it raised an echoed companion complaint in a guitar many far-away miles in St.-Gérard, leaning all alone against the cold hearth of the Tenderfield home.

Col Tenderfield stood transfixed before the barren fireplace in his spacious living room. It was the first morning of the New Year and he thought he heard a sad lowing sound emitted by Bernard's gift as it stood leaning against the cold granite. Could he have been mistaken? *No, there it was again ... in the clear light of day, no doubt about it this*

time. The low-register humming had now graduated to a slow rising aria of an angelic choir. The disbelieving man braced himself against the mantelpiece and shook his head as the musical tones completed their summit and fell again. *No, it can't be … Oh, the madness of it!*

The remains of last night's fire lay inert like the blackened stumps of a landmine victim. As his eyes fell on them, the shock of the horrendous vision left the elderly man utterly agitated and nearly breathless. He had lived through two World Wars — been at the front in the First and seen firsthand the travesty of war, and then lost a son to the Second. The corrosive edging-ahead of time left Col Tenderfield morbidly aware of his own mortality. His observation of the unnerving foreshortening of time during these latter years of his life was also disturbing. *And now, to suddenly hear things that are not there? What hope is there for me now — nowhere to go but down, and then further down again that slippery slide toward senility?*

Grasping the guitar tightly with his hand, Col Tenderfield brought the unbelievably light instrument closer to his face to examine the phenomenon. Its lightness was surreal; he had expected more weight from the guitar, human-scale heaviness at least. As soon as his hands closed on the neck and strings the sound began to diminish and by the time it reached his temple the music had ceased completely. Only a small vibration remained encased in the instrument, but as for sound there was nothing to assure him that any music had ever come from it. *But from where else could that melody have come?* Then from behind him a small wave of cool air brushed past the back of his neck and disappeared. He felt all the hairs on the back of his neck bristle and stand on end as he slowly turned around. *Surely that was a draft from the window*, he thought, *but there's no movement in the curtains and the windows are tightly closed.*

There was no indication of a breeze from within or without. Outside of the window it was still and white, as he would have expected. But then, in the corner of his eye, he saw a person walking just outside the window between the bare trunks of the silver-leaf maples. Moving quickly over to the window, he could just make out a tall black-haired man, perhaps an Indian, disappearing into the grove of trees. From behind it looked like it could have been Bernard, but he was almost certain the man was wearing buckskin and moccasins, and nothing else. *In this weather? He must be crazy. Or am I?*

While her husband was lamenting the tribulations of aging and its afflictions, Ellen Tenderfield was making the short drive with five grandchildren to Bernard's cabin. She had recently learned to drive and found an opportunity to practice that skill — taking the young ones ice skating on the frozen lake. His fireplace would be ablaze and he would obligingly escort the children down to the lake, where the frozen pale blue and gray cover of ice would be perfect. She expected he would be at home working in his studio; like every other year before this, New Year's Day would be like any other twenty-four hours on his calendar, if he had had a calendar. Her youngest son seemed to have a timepiece built into his head; he knew instinctively the exact moment of dawn, dusk, mid-day, midnight, and the day of the week, regardless of the fact he wore neither a watch nor owned a calendar. She was so certain that he would be home that she quietly panicked when she found his cabin door unlocked and no one inside.

The eldest of the grandchildren, Aidan's fourteen-year-old daughter Jocelyn, found a note on the kitchen table beneath a ceramic cup and read it out loud.

I am only gone a few days, a week at the most, so no one will probably notice. But if you are looking for me, I must be on my way back from Québec right now.
B. Dec 31.

Ellen felt a wave of relief wash over her. She guessed that his visit to Québec was to see Lorraine, who she knew had been visiting recently. She wondered why he had not thought to inform her he would be absent for their annual New Year's Day ice skating? It was not like him to go away for more than a day without letting her know. But then, she realized that those were the days before he built his house here on the lake. She could no longer know his comings and goings as before. It was only after this revelation that she realized he had grown into a fully independent adult. She felt abruptly redundant.

The children's clamor woke her out of her momentary depression. Their uncle's absence disappointed but did not dampen their enthusiasm; they rushed out of the house excitedly, goading each other to get there first and stopping only just before the edge of the lake to step into skates and pull on woolen mittens. Ellen no longer skated with the children, but was glad to see Jocelyn and the older children look after the littler ones in their uncle's absence. She sat on the veranda and watched from that distance as the small blades carried their joyful giggling passengers in variously delightful and wobbly circles, figure-eights, and angel spins. Beyond the small gliding and circling collection of miniature skaters, the natural amphitheatre of pines, maples, and sycamores encircled them like a colorful clutch of onlookers at a street performance.

When Ellen returned to her home late that afternoon after dropping off the grandchildren, she found her husband sitting in the living room staring into a full blaze inside the fireplace. She pulled her own armchair over to the fire and warmed her hands in its pulsating heat. The fire had a life of its own, spitting sparks and crackling loudly as small molecules of water in the logs met the energetic heat of its flames. Something had disturbed her husband and by the simultaneously weary and exalted look on his craggy and once very handsome face, she knew something extraordinary had happened. He was not usually this quiet and still.

"Are you thinking of New Year's resolutions?" she asked light-heartedly.

"No ... well yes, in a way; I've been thinking," he replied. "I think we should go to Thailand. Take up the post."

Her eyebrows lifted in small surprise. Over the past twelve months she had been staging a gentle revolution in their house, campaigning lightly for a change of scenery and cajoling him with offers and suggestions to undertake charity work abroad. Ever since Bernard had removed his belongings from their house, she felt the need to forge a new direction in her life. She felt snow-bound and landlocked. "Well, it's decided then? Shall we go visit with Father Lesley tomorrow and make the arrangements?"

"Yes. The sooner we leave the better." He turned to the fire again and immersed his full focus into its flames, as if he would find the answer to life's uncertainties in its flickering ephemeral energy.

"Fine," she replied, then a moment later added, "And what finally made the decision for you, may I ask?" She turned away from her husband as if he were a patient on her therapist's couch instead of on his favorite armchair in front of a fire.

"A strange thing happened today. While you were gone with the kids," he began. "I don't know if I'm starting to go senile, Ellen. I don't think so, but I swear I heard an angel in that guitar today!" He pointed at the instrument now lying innocently on a divan before the large window of the living room.

"So, you heard it too?" she replied. Their eyes met; for a moment there was surprise in Col Tenderfield's eyes, then a silent pact was made between them. The sound was real, that was determined. And, they both heard it. Col contemplated telling his wife about the tall Indian, but decided that may truly have been a figment of his imagination, spawned by the unlikely events that had taken place earlier in front of his fireplace. Perhaps they were related; perhaps not. Whatever the case, a change of scenery seemed advisable under the circumstances. Early senility could be stemmed by a change in environment, he was sure of it.

Col's father had lived to ninety-eight and his mind was sharp as a tack until the day he died. His mother had gone quite early, however, before he, the eldest was fifteen. The old man was a master ship-builder, moving his entire family — all five boys — out to Canada from Glasgow after his wife died. They had come to Halifax during the middle of the previous century when ship-building was at its peak; their lives were steady and hard work their motto.

When Col was twenty-six he met Ellen May, a headstrong Irish Catholic girl from Boston who had come up to Nova Scotia to teach literature at his youngest brother's school. They were soon married and decided to try their luck further into the hinterland and settled in St.-Gérard where the timber mills were starting to boom and the need for skilled labor was at a premium. As the hardworking young man advanced through the ranks and eventually became the main superintendent of the mill, his family grew and became the bedrock of the town. The day the horrific accident happened at the mill planted a sorrow in Col's heart that never truly left him. Bernard's father had been a worker at the mill for nearly eleven years. He was one of the few Native Indian workers at the mill and how he came to be an employee was Col's doing.

Joseph Berber was an Iroquois from St.-Régis, and when the mill manager met him, he was a young man of seventeen. The older man was seeking a new apprentice and was keen to extend the opportunity to a deserving boy from the reservations. Col posted a notice and the word was put out through the Indian grapevine. Joseph was the only real contender. The Council of Elders had already decided that he would be the one. His father, Adrien Walk-Tall Berber, was from this area but had a somewhat vague and mysterious background; he had left as a young man to become an ironworker for a brief time in New Brunswick before returning, settling into the St.-Régis reservation, and marrying Joseph's mother, a local Caughnawaga girl.

It was well known that Joseph's father left their family when he was just a boy. One day — soon after their second child, a girl, died at birth — he suddenly heard his higher calling and retreated to a Cistercian Trappist monastery in Oka, which had recently been established, and was never heard from again. His mother never married again. The elders believed that because Joseph was bereft of a father, he should be given the opportunity to learn a skill in order to support his mother. Joseph had a quality about him which Col Tenderfield liked straight away and proved in the end to be strong and direct, yet gentle in his demeanor, and a dedicated man who worked hard and well with others.

Three years into the job, the Elders sent Joseph a Caughnawaga girl as a blind date to ensure that he remembered his Iroquois roots while living and working amongst the White Men. Her name was Marianne and she was a plump young woman of twenty-one who was working as a waitress in St.-Régis. Her uncle was an Elder, as well as friend of his mother. Joseph was very shy and awkward with what seemed to him to be an outdated, old-fashioned tribal offering, and sent Marianne politely back to the reservation. It wasn't known to the Elders that Joseph had already found a young woman, Jeanne — a partially deaf French girl and sister of one of the temporary mill-workers who visited regularly from Montréal. After the "incident" of Marianne, Jeanne decided she needed to visit St.-Gérard more frequently and was pregnant within months.

But tragedy struck and she died of a bowel obstruction four months after the birth. Joseph could not bear to send his son to the reservation and could not leave the mill which had been so good to him, so he resolved to raise the little boy himself with limited help from the local wives. It was more than Christian charity when Joseph's accident four years later left little Bernard an orphan and the Tenderfields took him in as one of their own. Joseph's mother died less than a week after the funeral, presumably from heartache. Col Tenderfield felt the burden of responsibility for all the tragedy squarely on his shoulders. Over twenty years later, he felt perhaps he had finally heard his divine calling, and it came from a hand-made guitar.

Lorraine crossed the ocean in style and landed at Orly as gracefully as a diva. Feeling somewhat compressed after the tedious fourteen-hour flight, which included a stop in Montréal to pick up three passengers, she rose from her seat to stretch her slim and nubile frame, and no fewer than three gentlemen simultaneously offered to retrieve her hand-bags from the overhead compartments; two proposed to carry them for her. The new Parisian was surrounded by a veritable flock of well-mannered, immaculately dressed, and excellently manicured middle-aged men from both sides of the Atlantic, and each one was enchanted with the newest arrival to the French diplomatic landscape.

In the arrival lounge, another well-dressed man with refined manners stood waiting for her. As if to make up for the lack of an official departure party in Québec, Joël met his fiancée at the Orly Aéroport with an entourage of close friends, family, and personal assistants. The small crowd of strangers engulfed the young woman in embraces and multiple *baises* as they introduced themselves. Unexpectedly she knew what it meant to be someone, to have the world eating out of your hand. She felt like a movie star, a celebrity — Marlene Dietrich. Amelia Earhart. Perhaps a heroine returned from a remarkable around-the-world solo journey, or from long bloody war?

When the crowd finally worked its way through introductions and kisses, they let Joël into the inner circle. He held out a large bouquet of pink roses to Lorraine, and welcomed his fiancée cheerfully into his arms and kissed her lightly. Suddenly she felt shy and embarrassed in front of the adulating crowd; was she not a fraud, a faithless fiancée? Had she not just left another man in her bed? *No, stop yourself, you fool,* she silently reprimanded herself. *You are no more a fraud than every other woman who marries correctly, who finds the path of least resistance, who needs to firmly feel solid foundations beneath her.* She gently pushed him away, in seemingly shy deference to the waiting relatives and friends.

They whisked her away in a fleet of limousines that awaited them, as if they were already a wedding entourage rather than an airport welcoming party. Lorraine considered it a practice run for the ceremony in a month's time, to take place at the family's château in Aubigny-Sur-Nère in the Loire for 200 guests. It was all taken care of by her mother-in-law and her various secretaries and assistants. The dress, which she was yet to see, had been made for Joël's great-great-grandmother, the Comtesse de Vogel, in 1795, and now Lorraine would be wearing it. She wondered if Joël had actively sought out a fiancée who would fit the dress, like Cinderella's glass slipper. As the second son of a family with no daughters, the honors were bestowed first on his brother's wife, and now it was her turn.

She had no misgivings about donning a wedding dress well-worn by royalty. She only hoped to do it justice and to live up to everything the dress represented: *antiquity, family, responsibility, duty, royalty … loyalty … and … fidelity.* All at once the dress seemed much too heavy for just one girl. Quickly she swept aside the overbearing thoughts and focused on the passing landscape. A light snow covered the sparse woodlands of the Valle du Marne which fanned out in all directions, divided only by the spare streets of the town of L'Hay-Les Roses, with its painstakingly planned garden paean to the ubiquitous English rose. The Rosaria was a favorite of Joël. He had been part of a plenary committee, as a stand-in for his father, and had a small section dedicated to white blooms named after the family. The sprinkling of snow over the woodland park reminded her of Québec in the fall, as the sycamores and chestnuts begin to lose their definition and stature amongst the blue backdrop of cedars and plane trees. The one tree missing was her favorite, the sugar maple. She was no longer in Canada.

Minutes later the breath-taking spire of the Tour Eiffel struck the girl's vision and formed, there and then, a permanent snapshot of that monument's significance in her long-term memory. Its waffled grid-iron scaffolding of steel rose up before her, higher and higher as they approached the City of Light with its wide avenues and circular mayhem. A rolling tour of Paris commenced for her pleasure: Tour Eiffel, Arc de Triômphe, Louvre, Champs Elysées, L'Opéra, Tuileries, Notre Dame, on and on. Before her eyes, the cavalcade of sights passed in an orgy of gothic and Roman architectural wonder, like picture postcards on a carousel spinning at a rousing speed. As she admired these enduring landmarks of the Third Republic, the limousine convoy realigned themselves to ensure that the honored guest was first to alight upon the welcome doormat of the hotel-apartment's front door.

On arrival, the welcome party dispersed as they entered the grand lobby, each with a separate purpose as if they had arrived at an ornate film set and everyone had rehearsed and staked out their positions. Their names were vague in her mind and the connections even more so. Lorraine felt she was the only one who did not have a script; she had not a single inkling of what she was meant to do. It seemed that large white lilies sprouting from Grecian marble vases graced every table top in every corner of the ostentatiously spacious lobby, and exuberant candles and incandescent lights were trained strategically on gilded mirrors on each and every wall. The combination of soft whiteness and the fairy-glen-like glow had the effect of a magical winter wonderland brought into the vast interior.

Her baggage was being loaded into an ornate gilded elevator and she suffered a panicky moment. Where were her possessions going without her — upstairs to Joël's apartment, of course — the guitar too, presumably? Seeing the look of consternation on her face, Joël took her hand and led her to the grand staircase that divided the vast lobby evenly down the center. It led to a mezzanine level that looked down on all the splendorous gilding and crystal sumptuousness. From that lofty position, Lorraine could see the young female assistants shed their winter coats and underneath they were dressed in dark evening dresses.

"I will take you upstairs to freshen up, and then I have a surprise for you." Her weak smile was acknowledged and they retreated to a small private elevator which opened up seven stories above and directly into his apartment. Lorraine was relieved that the apartment was spared the overwrought gilding and tastefully adorned with a combination of traditional and contemporary furniture. The overall effect was decidedly Louis XIV with a bold, masculine brush of Bauhaus. She chose a chaise longue and reclined wearily onto it.

"Do not get too comfortable," he said ever so sardonically. "This is my apartment; I will take you to yours in a minute. Would you like a little tour?" She was taken aback by the news that they would be living in separate apartments.

"I...I didn't realize," she stammered. "Are we to live separately on a permanent basis?" She sat upright.

"Oh, *non, ma petite, non* — just until the wedding of course! I wouldn't think of it!" His mood seemed to change mysteriously, and he laughed heartily at her mistake. She was quite relieved and offended at the same time. She stood up and walked stridently to the door.

"Don't ridicule me, Joël. That is very cruel of you. How was I to know?"

"Forgive me. It is my mistake. I should have told you before. I assumed you would want your own toilette, etc., until we are man and wife." Then he added, "It was going to be a surprise, but I couldn't wait. I thought you would be pleased."

"I...am pleased. Yes. I just didn't...I misunderstood you."

"I see. Well, I am glad you are pleased. Shall we have a tour now, or would you prefer later?"

"Later, please. I would like to lie down for a moment. The flight was dreadfully long, you know. No opportunity to recline...most inconvenient."

When Lorraine arrived at her apartment exactly one floor below, she saw that it was as sumptuously decorated as Joël's, but more Louis XIV and less Bauhaus. Hothouse orchids and white lilies graced every tabletop. The gilded wall mirrors gleamed, multiplying the incandescent light of the crystal chandeliers in their reflected brilliance. Through the large balcony doors, the rise and fall of the black tile rooftops across the Fifth Arrondissement and the Rive Gauche formed an indelible matrix in her visual memory, which years from now would, like the minute red, blue, and white ferries plying the icy gray waters of the Seine in the distance, creep through her veins like a pulse.

In the bedroom, her luggage was laid out carefully on various sofas, chairs, and dressers, wherever the porter could find a horizontal surface that was not the floor or the bed. The leather case was propped on top of a Louis XIV armoire. She pulled a chair up to it and brought the case down, laying it carefully on the luxuriously quilted queen-size bed. When she opened the case, the instrument made a slight cooing sound as insignificant as a sigh escaping from the tiny beak of a captive dove. Despite everything happening around her, Lorraine began to feel that the guitar was like a friend — an actual living person whose happiness and freedom depended on her — this mysterious Isabelle perhaps? Even as she sat immobile during most of the long trans-Atlantic flight, she could not keep her mind off of the guitar, the lush music it made, and the rustling of skirts that seem to accompany it.

Stripped of her heavy wool traveling clothes, she lay down on the broad expanse of bedding in her underwear and brought the guitar to her body, lightly strumming the open strings, listening to the rich low vibrato of the gut strings and feeling the tingling sensation of the soundboard transferring wave upon wave of sounds down to the soft flesh and viscera beneath her bare stomach. The head stock lay flat against her forehead and the feel of the timber on her skin was cool and consoling, its smoothness like a well-spent afternoon in the sun after a cold winter, and its resonation like the comfort of a contented feline by her side. The weight of it was another thing. It had a modest heaviness which eased upon her like the weight of a careful lover. With an exhausted sigh she drifted into a perambulatory sleep.

She is wending her way through a familiar pine forest carrying a young child, and the accompanying sound of running water tripping over slippery rocks is like a lucent lullaby pulling her in and holding her captive in the cradle of the dream. The warbling of tiny birds invisible in the thicket of trees tells her it is spring. A wide path winds around the monolithic trees and follows the cut and curve of the creek-bed, at one point ascending into a steep glacial ridge of cedars blue with mist and replete with the cries and caws of a mating pair of goshawks, and then it descends, falling fast into a glade of ambling deer. Six pairs of doe's eyes stare at her with laconic indifference, as if she were one of their ilk.

At the end of this forested walk a magnificent château looms — or is it a convent? In a white dress and bare feet she enters the stone gateway onto a huge expanse of lawn. She carries not a child now, but a guitar in her arms. The stippling sound of water has become a soaking rain, besieging the stone with its pillaging wetness. She runs for cover in her quickly ruined dress and tries unsuccessfully to shield the instrument from the elements. Which direction? Ahead of her in the farthest reaches of the expansive court-yard, a small chapel offers refuge. A heavy door yields to her pressure and she peers into the darkness ...

Lorraine was awakened by a melodious disturbance. It was the doorbell for the second time, followed by a polite knock on the door. Startled, she alit off the bed, realizing she had been lying for several hours unclothed, with the guitar as an inadequate blanket. She was chilled to the bone and caught in the dizzying interlude between half sleep and wakefulness. She found a thick cotton robe hanging from a rack beside the armoire and stumbled blearily to the door.

"Who is it?" she called out wearily.

"*Excusez-moi, Mademoiselle.* Hotel management. I have your evening's itinerary here for you. Shall I slip it under the door?"

"Yes please. *Merci.*" A small white envelope was extended under the door. It was addressed on the cover with her name in a flowing hand.

"I will also leave this package, Mademoiselle, outside your door. *Merci, bon soir.*" With this information delivered, the attendant quietly left her to discover the large white box at her door. She retrieved it quickly, and then unceremoniously opened the invitation. Her presence was requested for dinner at seven PM at a concert in the Imperial Suite of the Hôtel Ritz. The white box contained a creamy peach ball gown festooned with a swath of white roses designed to span demurely across an otherwise revealing décolletage. On the back of the dress, a long train with matching roses trailed to the ground. Also in the box was a pair of matching evening sandals and a rose and orchid wrist corsage. Wearily she laid the evening ensemble on her bed beside the guitar and prepared herself for a bath. She had less than two hours to make herself the belle of the ball. Could she do it?

Never had the young woman felt so weary. The rigors of trans-Atlantic flying and maintaining decorum with a crowd of well-meaning strangers left her with little resources to revitalize her flagging energies. *I will have to get better at this,* she reprimanded herself for the second time this day. It was beginning to seem like her time was not her own; the rigors of belonging to a not-so-distant royal family were nearly too much for the shop-keeper's daughter and it was only her first day. Her previous visits to the family had been formal and quite brief. She imagined her fiancé fighting with the family to accept his choice of wife. She was a commoner, albeit an extraordinarily beautiful one. But from the colonies no less! If there was a whiff of rebellion in his swift engagement to Lorraine after only three months at the end of his one-year LLM studies in Québec, it had escaped her until now. Was there any hope of a reprieve in the proceedings? Would she be given the opportunity to shed the time delay that plagued her?

The steep learning curve was the price she would have to pay for purchasing a fairy tale destined for someone born prepossessed of the silver spoon, or with more ambition and avarice. The five-course dinner was interminable, and Lorraine found herself nodding sleepily in her seat next to Joël and his family, as the large string ensemble expertly wended its way through the four seasons of Vivaldi and then closed with a defining G-major quartet by Mozart. Only at the closing announcement of the concert did she realize that the performance was dedicated to her. Her embarrassment was complete as she realized that as she lightly dozed in her elegant chair, all eyes would have been on her before Joël's hand on hers awoke her during the last strains of the quartet. When she returned to her bedroom late that evening, she cried with exhaustion into the sound hole of her only familiar friend.

Col and Ellen Tenderfield stepped out into the hustle-bustle of a steamy afternoon on the outskirts of Bangkok and were greeted with the sounds of a people and a culture in constant movement — it seemed a hundred clackity *tuk-tuks*, the single bicycle-drawn carriages that carried elegantly dressed ladies and busy gentlemen through the throngs of traffic, jostled for attention. A pair of identically cleanly shaven, burgundy and yellow–robed monks in deep conversation crossed the street in front of them oblivious to the dozens of bicycles and cars swerving around them with deferential flair. The couple was headed northward, strolling solemnly in the direction of a large white-walled *wat*, a retreat of Buddhist calm just a few blocks from the Tenderfields' temporary accommodation at the Bang-kok YWCA, whose building squatted not far from one of the floating markets — on the Chao Praya River with its colorfully chaotic tangle of produce-laden rowboats. At the Y, the travelers found a veritable community of long- and short-term expatriate American, Canadian, Australian, New Zealand, British, and other European nationals.

The expulsion of the Church in China, and the eventual termination of missionary delegations there a decade earlier, had not been the case here in Thailand. It was a revela-tion — hundreds of years of Buddhism and a royal family passionately loved by its own people — the honey-coated haven of a country seemed positioned on a higher moral and communal plane than its neighbors, even while the politi-cal and social fate of Southeast Asia and the monolith that was China was poised to rend itself into shreds. Nascent threats of insurgency and turmoil, however, had sprung up of late in the hill-country area around Chiang Rai where their missionary placement was centered. This sent chills quietly up the spines of both Tenderfields, although neither one spoke of their inner panic.

The first week was the hardest. A shock to the system even for some seasoned travelers — the heat, the unrelentingly crowded streets and the low sea-level altitudes — all cause for the kind of oppression experienced by first-time divers. The pressure was claustrophobic and the panic debilitating, causing an emotional revolt edging on hysteria. If Ellen felt it, she kept it well hidden beneath the starched layers of her well-bred Bostonian reserve and erudite decorum, but Col almost succumbed to the tropical malaise of quiet terror. The three-week delay for the church administration to organize their posting in the countryside left them at loose ends and without their worldly goods.

International postal services on both sides failed God's laborers and ruined their maiden sojourn with uncharted inefficiency and disorder. While their purpose was to proffer services in the name of God, the job ahead seemed daunting when stripped away from the familiar and when life's irreconcilable mysteries were thrust in one's face. Separated from their belongings, the Tenderfields felt painfully unsettled. The only items they had carried with them on the plane were Ellen's handbag, Col's camera, and Bernard's guitar, safely secured in a curvaceous black leather case acquired for the trip.

The Church-organized accommodation was at capacity with budget-conscious antipodal travelers from Australia and New Zealand, and a small group of free-spirited Americans from San Francisco, en route to an ashram on the

Ganges. Between them all, the Tenderfields were suited up and supplied with personal toiletries sufficient to tide them over for a few days. In their borrowed cotton tunics, and traveling with only the guitar case in hand, the Tenderfields were mistaken for touring musicians and treated like entertainers and show-people. They learned to smile wanly and wave like minor celebrities until they finally paid a visit to the Canadian Embassy, where the staff happily opened up a special supply room in the back of the agency which could have posed as a flagship of Taylor's department store.

At the mention of Chiang Rai, however, a look of astonishment came over their fellow travelers. Known as one of the tri-corners of the notorious Golden Triangle, Chiang Rai was not for the faint-hearted, and unseasoned travelers were warned to avoid that particular den of iniquity. The Tenderfields' hero-status soared at this point when they shared their mission and itinerary.

"If God's will be done, you will both be sainted before the year's end! And please put in a good word to His Lordship on my behalf, would you?" exclaimed a jocular Australian.

Ellen was entirely disbelieving of the spurious claims of her fellow travelers. According to her own research, Chiang Rai was home to numerous indigenous hill-tribe populations with quite remarkable but harmless cultural practices, such as the elongating of necks to increase a girl's marriageability, accompanied by pictures of smiling children and elegantly toothless grannies.

They would never find out the truth of those claims for within a few days of arrival, the Church organizers received word that their belongings had mistakenly been transported to Kathmandu instead of Chiang Rai, and there were no personnel in the Nepali mission capable of transferring them on to the Thai village. Ellen had not researched such a drastic change in their itinerary, and the fear of an unknown country began to give away signs of her panic. This occurred, fortunately, just as Col was beginning to overcome his own malaise. He found himself laundering their limp and sweat-soiled clothes in the Y's small bathroom sink, while Ellen sat plumbing the precipitous depths of her resolve for the imminent travel.

The pair flew from Bangkok to Kathmandu, the second highest-altitude capital city in the world from one of the lowest — on a rather shabby plane which looked to be a retired vehicle from a previous decade. Perhaps it was purchased from the Chinese military, for most of the signage was in undecipherable characters, forcing Ellen to spend the majority of the time in mid-air trying in vain to make sense of them in case of a mid-air emergency. Meanwhile her husband slept soundly in the plane's cool environment, the first they had enjoyed in a week. Looking out the small fogged window of the plane, she was astounded to find them ascending into a mountainous country not unlike her own in terrain, if not temperature. Far below her the stretch of peaks and valleys lay like the humps of a moose's back and the thought brought tears to her sleepless eyes.

The tumultuous landing of the plane was like a stampede over a cattle grid before a river-crossing, but then it came to a halt. Ellen silently thanked the Lord for their safe arrival, while Col shook himself violently in its wake. Taking the guitar case securely in hand, Ellen marshaled her husband to the front of the plane to quickly disembark. But when they entered the terminal building, they were surprised to find themselves face to face with an imposing row of a half

dozen armed military guards, their Indian Civil Service–
issue shotguns and rifles pointing menacingly at them.

Col recognized these legendary Gorkha soldiers, fierce
and dedicated Nepali soldiers who fought bravely with the
Indian Army in their fight for independence from the British not long before. Their trademark crinkle-bladed *kukri*
swords were sheathed menacingly at their sides, a badge
of extraordinary courage and duty. Col instinctively raised
his arms in surrender and hastened his wife to follow suit.
But Ellen had the guitar case in her hands and did not know
what to do. One jungle-camouflaged soldier wrenched the
case from her hands and pointed his gun at her head, causing the weary woman to completely collapse in an unconscious heap at his feet. Pandemonium broke out and Col did
not know whether he would be shot if he tried to attend to
his wife, but his worries were allayed when the guard's superior, a stern, older-looking soldier, relayed a curt apology to
Col before he ordered two younger men to carry the woman.

Col was ushered again at gunpoint into a special detain-
ment area where Ellen was laid out gingerly on a rather
soiled rug by the two soldiers. Col was then asked to open
the case, which he did gladly at this point. All eyes were on
the case as the lid was pulled open and the gleaming guitar
revealed. An audible, almost shameful, "Aaaawwhhhh"
spread across the room as each soldier, Col amongst them,
smiled in relief and embarrassment at the harmless and
beautiful, almost heavenly glow of the glossy instrument.
The captain of the troop reached across and inspected the
guitar as he would a regulation issue rifle. Suddenly, launch-
ing a surprise guerrilla attack, the leader of the Gorkha band
ran the back of his nails across the strings of the soundboard and the room burst into the warm astonishing sounds

of the open strings, quickly tranquilizing the agitated men and engulfing the metallic sterility of the terminal with its calming sounds. He then removed the guitar to inspect its interior and to peer beneath it. Satisfied that it was not an implement of military insurgency, the captain handed the guitar to Col and indicated for him to entertain the crowd.

Behind the gathered men, Ellen had gained consciousness and witnessed the effect of the guitar on the group. She gathered herself up off the floor, brushed herself off, and tapped Col on the shoulder. With a surge of absolute relief, he handed the guitar to his wife. All eyes were on her as she drew up a chair and proceeded to play for the first time in nearly forty years.

Her fingers were hesitant with the fret board at first, but it seemed that, with her earlier descent into temporary unconsciousness, something unrecognizable rose to the surface of her brain and now directed the ascendance of the first rousing round of sounds she made on the guitar — an entire winged sailing fleet of *tremolos* and *arpeggios* accompanied by a concordance of hypnotic chords, which unexpectedly turned on their heels and danced a flamenco waltz of *lento* then *allegro vibrato* scales until they descended into the penultimate *arpeggios* of the unrelenting harmonic finale. Carulli's "Andantino" was a miracle of classical artistry and the men nearly cried with newly stirred passions, but she followed the emotive serenade with a fiery "Tarantela" that sent the men into a frenzy of whooping and applauding that did not cease, in Ellen's feverish mind, for an eternity.

In another place, on the far side of the rotating earth, a lonely heart soared momentarily as the serenade roused a tandem ghost in her bedchamber and granted her a much-needed reprieve from the frenzy of wedding preparations and the cold clutch of a medieval castle deep in a fertile valley not far from Carulli's own City of Light. Even against the crush and commotion of wedding preparations next door, Lorraine distinctively heard the melodious tune play itself quietly in the tranquility of her chamber, an intimate concert for her personal pleasure.

Sleeping pills and tranquilizers had done their work almost as soon as her head touched the pillows of her canopied bed the night before. With morning firmly ensconced in the château window reflected in her mirror, however, the fog returned to its defiant post inside her head, draped though it was in a luxuriant bridal veil. The team of hired professionals who had washed her hair, swept it up in a perfect chignon, moisturized her entire body, manicured and dressed her, then completed her cosmetic transformation, were finished and now performing their rituals on the bridesmaids next door.

Lorraine sat in mild amazement at the detailed finery of her toilette upon her dressing table, and pondered the blur of her vision and the overly adamant coloring of the rouge on her pale cheeks. Then, a solemn string of *legato* notes came to her like the lament of a funeral march. Glancing at the guitar perched at her bedside like a guardsman flanking a prison door, she sensed a motion in its strings; its sonorous tune mixed flawlessly with the trills and twittering of four bridesmaids rushing about the dressing room adjacent to her bridal chamber, which was cavernous by her own estimation. On the far side of the room, just beyond her ornate door, the frantic bustle of the servants and caterers flummoxed by the arrival of the wedding guests did not disturb her equanimity.

The bride looked somberly at the guitar, contented that it had accompanied her here and everywhere without complaint. It had provided companionship to the otherwise friendless young woman from the Haut-Saint-François. It was now her rabbit's foot, the charm without which she could not step outside the hotel-apartment, to the great consternation of her fiancé, who kept his distance under the guise of preserving their intimacy for the wedding day. He seemed more like a stranger to her each day, and as she prepared herself reluctantly for the upcoming nuptials, her nerves were as brittle as a denuded willow branch blighted by the bitter cold of winter, and her mind just as tortured, if not more so. She was sorely tempted to lift the guitar onto the lap of the heirloom wedding dress and strum a riotous gypsy rondo, but instead she stayed her hand and sat resolutely before the large mirror of her grand Louis XIV dressing table and made a comical face at her own reflection. Satisfied with the ridiculousness of her image, she next put on her steeliest, most regal, and most devastatingly beautiful countenance and stood to face the ceremony like the warrior-saint, Jeanne d'Arc, off to the wheaten battlefields.

A mysterious fog surrounded the medieval château as the haunting sound of the French horns signaled the start of the wedding ceremony. A solemn procession of nearly two hundred attendees led by the royal members of the wedding party made its way regally across the vast courtyard and then hesitated ceremoniously before the chapel, awaiting the completion of the first traditional hunting song by the cornets. When the last notes were drawn, the procession entered the chapel, dividing neatly between left and right, and filling the pre-arranged seats systematically with relatives and close friends of the bridegroom's family.

As the last blasted notes of the somber hunting tune faded into the past, Lorraine, as solemnly as a widow, methodically and regally paced down the aisle in her royal gown with all the decorum that the weighty dress required of her. Accompanying the bride was her father, the frail and closed-mouth tool-shop owner from St.-Gérard who had flown in on the overnight flight with his wife, to Aubigny-Sur-Nère via Montréal and Paris the night before. All heads and eyes turned to the main attraction beside the man, a vision in white luminescence like the first blanketing of snow on a virgin landscape, whose demurely downcast eyes led all eyes below to the voluptuous, precipitously draped bustline where a thin line of moss green velvet ribbon delineated the fashionably cinched Empire waist while majestically lifting two ripe winter melon–like breasts, forcing them skyward.

Below this unbridled display of the bride's feminine assets, the formidably understated gown obliterated any curves she might have had behind the formless two-century-old gossamer and lace train, which trailed behind her like a peacock's burden, while two capped sleeves floated like confections upon the ends of her sloping shoulders. A sheer white veil wafted around her head and bare shoulders more like miasma than lace, and crowning the entire vision was a large diamond and emerald-encrusted tiara, perched upon her head like a defining moment.

With cheeks flushed from the piercing cold of the diaphanous fog, Lorraine bit her lips to keep her teeth from chattering. Her knees felt weak and her flat satin ballet slippers offered little insulation of her bare feet from the cold cobblestone of the medieval courtyard. She clutched in her arms between frozen fingers and forearms two dozen white roses encircled with a stanchion of greenish-white lilies and tufted pussy-willow branches, all tied together into a large stately bouquet with silk and flax. She minced her way up to the pulpit before the majestically robed priest, and nodding her head as her husband-to-be nonchalantly joined her. It seemed to her, in her frozen and compromised state, that he was dressed in some sort of military uniform or a riding outfit complete with boots butting up to his knees, jodhpurs, and riding breeches. Perhaps the customary wedding tuxedo was too bourgeois for royalty. She was in no position now to question it.

The rest of the ceremony presented itself to her as a blur; on her aching knees for what seemed like an eternity with nothing but a delicate, elaborately embroidered satin cushion separating her from the cold stone floor. She meditated on the cadence of the priest's chants and instinctively repeated the appropriate "Amens" in a demure yet decorous whisper. They sealed their vows with the blood of Christ sequestered in a medieval gem-encrusted silver goblet, the bride's gleaming wedding band clinking decorously against the cup as it was passed to her quivering lips.

Later, en route to the grand salon, the fog had lifted neither from the château grounds nor from the bride's mind and spirit. Long sabers were drawn by the groom and his strutting royal brothers of the hunt — their vintage red riding coats masculine yet pristine in their black-lined squire sensibility. The swords were unceremoniously pressed into service to uncork an arsenal of champagne bottles, releasing a cheerful fountain of foam which found its way miraculously into the enameled goblets of the hearty revelers. A banquet table of food spilled over with many varieties of baguettes and French breads, platters of Valençay goat cheese, large ramekins of wild-boar pâté, and piles of Mediterranean fruits provided for the celebration. As more horns announced the imminent commencement of the official fox hunt, champagne flutes were raised by the four groomsmen as a single squad, and the celebrated union was dutifully toasted by one and all.

Then, as if prepared for battle, the squad of groomsmen led the battalion of equestrians, both male and female — excluding the bride, who kept on her royal gown and noble decorum while staying out of the hunt — through the salon doors and to the royal stables where they all found their assigned horses and saddled up for the hunt. The horn bearers wore their large circular brass instruments over one shoulder, with the horn at their waist, facing behind them. The groom's grand-uncle, Comte Georges de Vogel, as Master Huntsman, began the chase by releasing a frantic white hare onto the trailhead of the fog-gutted forest behind the château and then let loose a pack of frenetic hounds.

The large hunting party rode off in pursuit of the terrified rabbit, just as the bride and the wedding parties' less sporting women retired to the comfort of a row of chaise longues arched around the salon's grand fireplace. With the occasional blasts of the hunting horns in the far distance, the ladies made short order of the champagne and listened jauntily through a light-headed fog to a quintet play a touching but sonorous and drawn-out round of Bach fugues and then two movements from Saint-Saëns' *Le Carnaval des Animaux*, the hypnotic "Cygnet" nearly finishing off the giddiest of the ladies.

The musicians seemed to have materialized out of the stonework, and the weary bride wondered if they indeed were waiting in the wings while the ceremony, like the champagne, spilled languorously over into the afternoon. On a stroll alongside the stables the night before, she had seen the white hare huddled, too dull to be frightened, in one corner of the small dreary cage, and now she pictured the animal making its frenzied escape as a pack of blood-thirsty hounds and drunken royal hunters made hot pursuit after it into the forest. She wearily imagined herself as a witch flying invisibly through the dark of the woods and plucking the poor rabbit out to safety from its hopeless escapade.

The hare was she, and she the hare, living on borrowed time and a half-future. She called herself a wife. If only she could grab the ghost guitar fully in her hand and make magic of her false life and soar with it. She was no more than a barefoot Esmeralda. And Berne was her sad, silent and beautiful monster Quasimodo, awaiting her return to their lakeside sanctuary. A return he will likely never see.

A raucous applause broke out from the teetering audience and Lorraine was shaken out of her trance with a start. A strange trick of light cast by the fantastically large chandelier suspended from the ornate ceiling made an oboe, two violins, a viola, and a rotund cello appear to dance before her as if come alive from a murky incoherent dream. The musicians waved their bows in appreciation as they dipped again and again from their black waist-coats, presenting their respective instruments as if they were the true stars of the ensemble, and then bowing deeply at the bride's direction. From Lorraine's position front and center, the black suits of the musicians blended into the heavy dark tapestry that hung on the wall behind them. Festooned with a dozen prancing goats, ladies, and unicorns around a precisely executed knotted medicinal herb garden, the tapestry covered the wall completely, from the architrave along the vaulted ceiling to the granite flooring and from the edge of the cavernous limestone fireplace to the large picture window near the rear egress of the hall. Lorraine's eyes moved involuntarily to the uncurtained window and she was startled to discover an identical herb knot repeated in the courtyard beyond.

The surreal and bizarre revelation brought her feeling of delusion to an implausible peak. She gathered up her flowing skirts, excusing herself curtly to the revelers around her, and retreated quickly from the room to her chamber, moving like a startled chameleon in deferred flight. Ascending the stairs with heavy legs and the beginnings of a champagne-fueled headache, Lorraine wished vehemently for the end of the evening, to lie on her quilted bed and obliterate the light with the goose-down covers. *Would anyone notice? The quarry has been caught.*

Momentarily she heard in the distance the sonorous cry of a victorious hunting horn declaring conclusion of the chase. One of her ladies-in-waiting arrived at her door to dress her for dinner, which was to commence on the return of the hunting party. It seemed that one or two stragglers had been left behind, but all in all the revelers were buoyed by the vigor of the hunt. The rabbit was trussed like a Christmas goose and presented at table to the stunned bride. At the wretched sight Lorraine nearly gagged with revulsion. She quickly averted her eyes to hide her horror, and excused herself to squelch the queasiness in her stomach, discreetly emptying its contents in the stone confines of the small amenities closet beyond the scullery.

On Lorraine's return, toasts were made before a fine selection of de Vogel wines from the family vineyard in Chambolle: their legendary Musigny, Amoureuses, and several Bonnes-Mares.

"Aaahh, the wines show a tight, spicy herby nose which is medicinal and full," declared the Vicomte François de Vogel, one of Joël's several royal uncles. "Firm and savory — the palate is dense and full with immense structure; quite evolved. There's an earthiness underpinning this palate. A very savory wine with some future, yes!"

"But, ahhh," he continued, transferring his impressive attentions on the Musigny. *"Le Musigny à l'odeur d'un jardin sous la rosée...de la rose et de la violette à aurora."* The Vicomte likened the bride to the violette, although Lorraine knew it was the rose with which her new husband was enamored. The uncle also compared the various de Vogel wines to his family members.

"The Amoureuses represent our women," he expounded. "Musigny are our fathers, and Bonnes-Mares — they are the unmarried uncles! Explosive... masculine in style... powerful, long-lived... but acquiring a sweet, velvety richness with age... just like me!" Raucous applause broke out from the family cohorts and guests and it was not long before empty bottles piled high behind the wine counter left little room for the bar attendant to continue his job.

Toasts were made all around to both the bride and groom, and scornfully to the hare. This final remark was interrupted by the announcement of dinner. The five-course meal began with beluga caviar en croute and a selection of pomegranate, truffle, and vermouth-embroidered foie gras, and then followed by the main course of — luckily for Lorraine — not hare, but pheasant. The sumptuous dinner was finalized by a beautifully architectural *pièce montée*, the traditional wedding cake, dripping with dark chocolate and honey like the Hanging Gardens of Babylon. Throughout the meal and during the presentation of the cake, Joël continued his reserve and kept an uncommunicative distance. The hunt was his unique contribution to plans for the wedding ceremony, and although his mother initially disapproved, she capitulated when her grown son put on a familiar pout, both petulant and persistent, which he apparently never outgrew.

The mother also was well aware that the bride neither rode nor approved of hunting, but it seemed like such a grand idea, full of pomp and ceremony provided by a dozen French horns on the grounds of one of the family's estates. Very patriotic it was — particularly for the newly formed Fifth Republic. Le Général Charles de Gaulle himself was invited, but unfortunately the requirements of his renewed office kept him away. This may have been the cause of the groom's displeasure, but certainly the bride was not to blame for this slight? The priorities of the French Republic certainly trumped the importance of their nuptials, but the visibly annoyed groom was not to be consoled. Neither the vigorous hunt nor the sumptuous meal seemed to mitigate his irritation. He simply saw it as a vital missed opportunity to make a personal campaign to the new President for a diplomatic post and he was most unhappy. That night Lorraine collapsed on her bed with a murderous migraine headache and did not notice until the late rays of dawn that it was the guitar, rather than her husband, that lay comfortably and loyal, but motionless, on the bed beside her.

6

ELLEN (JIRI); LORRAINE (PARIS AND ST.-GÉRARD), 1959–1960

The soldiers wound up Ellen's performance with their own rousing rendition of a musical. The young one, who had previously taken the initiative to scare Ellen completely out of her wits, put his rifle down for a moment, licked both hands, and ran them through his glossy black hair to make it stand up high off his dark brown forehead like a slick wave off a balmy surf beach. Tucking his thumbs into his brown leather belt where several clips of ammunition hung down one leg of the camouflage trousers and his sheathed kukri — the famed Gorkha hatchet-knife — down the other, he wiggled his eight skinny brown fingers, parted his legs wide with knees crooked, and began moving his hips in a sporadic and jerky motion.

The others took their cue and joined in by clacking their sheathed kukris loudly against tables and chairs, or guns if they had no knives, in a unified syncopated beat. They gathered in an uncoordinated line behind a row of chairs and continued their tribal rhythm, *"Won, juu-juu... Won, juu-juu... "* while the young one cocked his slicked-up head to one side, curled his lip into a seductive snarl, and turned his dark eyes toward the stunned foreigners.

"Da warrden threw a partee at the county jail... " he began to sing, *"... the prison band was there, they began to wail. The band was jumpin' and da jawnt began to swing... "* Both arms and legs abruptly turned out wide on his two tipped toes and the boy strutted about like a baggy khaki-clad starfish writhing to the beat of the knives and gun-butts. *"You shoulda heard dem jailbirds sing... "* A chair was thrust in front of him as he grasped it in both hands and shook his thin shoulders in a writhing shimmy. *"... less rock! Ebreebawdee, less rock!"* Suddenly he was spinning on the floor in a circle around one bony hip. *"Ebreebawdee in da whole cell block... "* Standing now with legs apart, rocking sideways from one foot to the other, as one knee began a dance of its own jerking left to right. *"... was dancin' to da jailhouse rock!"*

Their captive audience of two stood speechless as a free-for-all took over the rest of the song. Five of the younger uniformed men began gyrating across the room like The King himself singing the verses in ragtag unison, while the rest of the band pranced about the room beating their sheathed kukris and the butts of their guns against tables and chairs in the syncopated rhythm that might have actually ingratiated the viewers had it not been performed with real, and presumably fully loaded, guns. Even the captain of the group reluctantly joined the troupe near the finale in the role of jail warden, wielding his gun cautiously, but nonetheless lightly bashing one of the Elvis-pretenders over the head with its butt.

When the singing finally ended, they surrounded their stunned captives like a pack of wolves or outlaws in a western movie. The boys repeatedly asked, "You know Elbis Presley? You know Elbis?" punctuating the question with excited assertions in Nepali interspersed with a healthy dose of swearing in their native Gorkha. *From the mouths of babes*, Ellen thought to herself. *And so dangerous*, with imposingly large guns in their scrawny arms and a maniacal air about them that made every hair on her arms and the back of her neck stand on end, even as they guffawed and merrily performed the impressive production number again, as if they spent most of the hours of their soldierly days rehearsing the piece. One of the boys picked up the guitar and made a fairly decent attempt at strumming along to the song as the others continued their prancing, singing, and wailing.

Eventually the prison party came to an end after the third rendition, when the mission's representative, a large-boned, red-haired Australian fellow finally broke through the military and administrative morass and released the Tenderfields from their grip. They were bundled into a large shell of a truck out on the tarmac along with the Australian and a few of the Gorkha soldiers, to be delivered presumably to the site of their lost luggage. But first the guide took it upon himself to give them a cursory tour of downtown Kathmandu, where small children skidded from out of the shadows of black and yellow latticed timber doorframes in every direction of the dusty dirt-floored square, forming a short parade behind the truck as it approached the ancient central square of Kathmandu. Dramatically sloped rooflines and picturesque temple structures stood timelessly throughout the village and the travelers admired the ancient architecture with awe, feeling as if they were being shuttled through an open-air museum.

To Col the dark tar-stained roof trusses appeared thousands of years old, mitered and carved with a level of detail that astounded him. Having worked with timber for a lifetime, to see such spectacularly dramatic and ornate craftsmanship was a revelation. The simple plain lines of their own glorified log cabin back home in Canada seemed a dull facsimile of these ancient architectural displays of human creativity and ingenuity. Prince Siddhartha himself could stroll regally through the square at this moment — with his bright yellow ochre robes draped across a square brown shoulder and trailing in the fine dust of the square behind him, his majestic head plaited in a tight glossy black swirl, and piercing dark kohl-rimmed eyes trained on the enlightened path before him — and he would not be out of place.

Aside from themselves, and the occasional weathered and ancient-looking Tibetan woman chanting a perpetual hymn, *"Om mani padme hum,"* on an ornate rug beside an open shop door, a face like a beautifully dried apple and the mesmerizing spin of her miniature prayer wheel like a watermill on a floss, the faces around them were red-cheeked and cherubic, set against a background of beautiful, taut, smooth skin the color of red tanned cowhide.

All around the periphery of the square, rows and rows of red and black lanterns and lines of multi-colored prayer flag–adorned shops selling rugs, silver jewelry, fabulously colored silk and cotton fabrics, brightly striped black Tibetan yak-wool wrapskirts, more prayer flags, and lanterns spilled out onto the plaza as if the plenitude of their wares uncontrollably outgrew the constricted dimensions of the shops over a protracted period. From somewhere inside the bowels of a shop, the mumbled, yet lightning-paced and frenetically urgent monologue emanated from a tinny quartz radio.

"What are they saying?" Col asked the Australian, who stopped to listen to the rapid-fire Hindi for a moment.

"Radio India is proclaiming the successful outcome of the first ever parliamentary election here in Nepal, which is enjoying support from Calcutta. The Nepali Congress is now moving towards implementation of land and agrarian reforms," he continued, " ... improving prison conditions, building up a police force to maintain law and order, eradicating corruption, and setting up economic programs ... " A muffled whooping and cheering, punctuated by happy cries in Nepali, could be heard from inside the small shop.

"The promise of a bright democratic future doesn't seem to have any impact on that old woman sitting outside this shop," Col remarked drily. They all turned to look at the toothless, leather-faced old woman who continued her chanting, and in her trance-like ecstasy of wheel spinning, ignored their merry-making. Not far from her, a small group of round-faced Tibetan children, half naked in the warm afternoon sun, stared boldly up at the strangers smiling. *Their cherubic red, sun-burnt faces need a good scrubbing,* thought Ellen to herself.

The Australian suddenly answered the rhetorical question seriously. "Perhaps her long tenure under the oppressive all-powerful Rana Regime has forced her into this meditative religious state?"

"What?" Col replied.

"While other independent countries in the world have gone through a scientific and industrial revolution," he continued, "Nepali society is frozen in feudalistic isolation, becoming one of the poorest countries in the world."

Looking around her, Ellen took in the profusion of colors, collections of gold, brass, and silver jewelry and trinkets strewn across blankets and rugs, ubiquitous ragged and endlessly flapping prayer flags strung across every doorframe, and got the impression that this well-preserved ancient square would have appeared exactly as it did had she arrived a century or two earlier by horse-cart or on foot bearing goods and chattel from Europe via India to trade with these enterprising people. All around there was private commerce; whether they had been trapped in a feudal society or not, these people certainly took it with a smile.

The trip to the mission at Jiri required a five-hour drive in the old military jalopy, and their small village, the Australian informed them, was better known as the trailhead for trekkers and mountain-climbers making an assault on the South Col of Mount Everest.

"For a privileged few, flights can be secured from the Kathmandu airport to a tiny airstrip in Lukla," he explained. "Beyond the treacherous Khumbu Ice-flows and on the cusp of the final ascent on Mount Everest — or *Sagarmatha* to the Nepalis, meaning, "Goddess of the Sky." Or *Chomolungma* to the Tibetans and Sherpas, meaning, "Mother Goddess of the Universe."

"That's very interesting," Col remarked. "You really know your Nepali stuff, don't you?"

"Yes. Well I've been here for a fair few years and picked up a little Nepali and Hindi. I met Sir Edmund Hillary once when I was a younger man on one of my first attempts. Did you know that the much less expressive 'Mount Everest' moniker known to the western world was established in

1865 in honor of Sir George Everest, the British surveyor-general of India who in 1841 mapped the location of the world's highest peak?" He continued, "Its height was measured by others, but the peak officially became Mount Everest in the English lexicon. Prior to this it was known for a time simply as Peak B, and then Peak XV. Hillary told me that himself."

The guide's monologue continued for most of the journey, punctuated sporadically by Col's interjections, but after the third or fourth hour Col's attention flagged and he found himself dozing to the sonorous sounds of the Aussie's drone. When he awoke, it was to see the truck pull into a clearing where a ramshackle old wooden building stood forlorn and uninviting.

"So, is this where our luggage ended up? It's a long way from Kathmandu. The message said they were somewhere inside the capital." The village, it would appear, had no other distinction besides the two important nominations of being Sagarmatha's trailhead and the site of the hospital and school. These two, however, were enough to warrant a dozen or two hangers-on to climb aboard the convoy of trucks and bus and literally hang off the side of the vehicles as they made their way wafting and backfiring across the precipitously steep, death-defyingly narrow and winding cliff-side roads from the outskirts of Kathmandu to these small dusty and sand-soaked hamlets. About half an hour before the final destination, all but one of the hangers-on alighted from their precarious perches on the trucks and tossed a few coins into the hands of the driver.

Not long after that brief stop, the trees and foliage re-appeared; a distinct drop in temperature and a clearing of dust occurred like a miraculous parting of the sea.

Ellen allowed herself to doze a bit while the gravelly road wound higher and higher into the tree cover, and then was awakened with a start when the convoy came to a sudden stop at a place where the light green canopy of trees and light speckled ground cover seemed to consume what little road was left in its arid green jaws. There was no room for the bus to turn, but somehow it did and the driver shut the engine with the bus facing the opposite direction. The silence was nerve-shattering.

Thanking their armed escorts profusely with smiles and waves, although their knees were jittery and achy and their jaws not yet unclenched, Col and Ellen began to disembark from the truck, holding nothing more in their sweaty palms than the guitar in its case and Ellen's handbag. One of the young Gorkhas at the front of the bus jacked up his rifle across Col's chest to suggest they were not quite ready to release their captives into the wild. The driver held up a handful of rupees in his fist and waved them slowly under his eyes. Col put up his hands as if in surrender, looked at the Australian, sitting silently now in his seat, then reached into his trouser pocket and removed a folded U.S. ten-dollar bill. With smiles, the driver snatched up the note.

"Again?" he said, as more a demand than a question. Col dug deep again and this time surrendered two Canadian twenty-dollar bills. He and Ellen were allowed to disembark. As they exited the camouflage-painted truck, they saw two soldiers carrying several boxes from the bus onto the veranda of the hospital.

"What's going on there?" Col asked the Australian.

"I presume those are your things," he replied sheepishly.

"What things?" Ellen inquired, her eye now catching a familiar leather trunk being lugged up the stairs by a scrawny boy soldier. "Oh! Those are OUR things!" she declared, abruptly panicking. "You've brought them here along with us! Did you know they were with us all along? Why didn't you tell us?" Her eyes rolled involuntarily as she thought about the last seven or eight hours of bumpy careening road dust. "We were meant to pick those up and take them back to Thailand with us!"

"No, Ma'am, I didn't know they were in the truck. I'm in the dark as much as you. I'm so sorry. I was told to accompany you lovely people here to make sure you arrived safely. I'll just be heading back now with this burly lot. Here is my number in Sydney, if you get in a bind." He handed them a crumpled calling card which read:

> *Darren Grimes*
> *31 Elizabeth Street*
> *Surry Hills NSW 2010*
> *Australia*
> *+61 2 9215 9190.*

The driver interjected, "Instructions to take you and your tings here to Jiri. For hospital-school. We are very much here now. *Namaste!*"

With this announcement he fired up the loud shotgun engine and sped away, spraying copious amounts of dust and gravel at the travelers before they could say another word, their jaws slack in spite of dry dust settling unceremoniously on disbelieving lips.

The hospital was a plain raw timber building, a school-house in a former guise. While they were careening on the cliff-bending road into Jiri, Darren had explained to them that it was built by a doctor from New Zealand about ten years ago after he arrived as a "tourist-slash-mountaineer" and discovered the good natured half-naked Sherpa children running about in the spring snow with "…nary a stitch of warm clothing or a pencil to write with." Illiteracy was never considered a handicap in this part of the world, but the altruistic young doctor raised the funds back in his native New Zealand and returned a year later with medicines — penicillin, antibacterial ointments, and aspirin — plus a substantial stash of funds to build a two-story, seven-roomed house that doubled as a school and a temporary surgery for his annual five-week holidays in Nepal, during which he undertook to perform the most pressing medical or surgical procedures required during the first week, before packing up his rucksack again and trekking up to Sagarmatha.

Initially the Sherpa villagers flocked to the doctor to have themselves prodded and poked and a stethoscope held to their children's tender chests. But over time the prodding and poking were deemed unnecessary, and eventually the doctor found his schoolhouse abandoned and announcement of his annual visits eliciting a major exodus of residents to the higher reaches of the mountain ranges during the summer months he was due to be in residence. Recent efforts, however, to recruit teachers from New Zealand and Australia, as well as the occasional medical locum, were met with some enthusiasm, and there was hope that the school at least would be resurrected in the next year or so.

It seemed that Ellen's qualifications as a teacher were the reason she was redirected to Nepal, without her prior knowledge of this, rather than Thailand, where, as it turns out, somebody else was assigned to administer a hospital run by Catholic missionary doctors and nuns on the outskirts of Chiang Rai. After several unsuccessful attempts to attract the attention of the caretaker of this particular hospital-school by rapping vigorously on the door and every window they could reach, the Tenderfields sat down among their boxes and luggage to consider what to do.

After a time, they found an unlocked window and Col crept into the building with less alacrity than he would have liked, and let his wife in through the proper threshold. Not surprisingly, no one was in residence or attendance, and from what they could see, no schooling or medical activities had occurred in there for quite some time. A light layer of dust covered the floors and remaining few bedraggled school desk-chairs. Half a dozen child-sized chairs with attached desk tablets were shoved in one corner of the large room; the expansive black chalkboard was covered with some sort of Nepali graffiti, scratched out across the slate with a small stick of white chalk which lay now in pieces on the floor below the board. Where the teacher's desk should have stood, Ellen pulled up a small desk-chair and laid down the guitar case, which she had never let go.

"This is not what I planned for us, Col," she sighed. "We are supposed to be in Chiang Rai right now, tending to the needs of those poor tribal children, not sitting here in an empty schoolhouse with *no* children to teach or tend to. What shall we do?" To her surprise, her husband was smiling wanly as he looked around him at the empty room.

"I think this is a rather good alternative, my dear," he replied cheerfully as she shot back a perplexed and annoyed expression. "I didn't want to tell you this, but I had heard from one of the sources at the Y in Bangkok that the mission in Chiang Rai was actually a leper colony! Imagine us there?"

"A leper colony?" Her annoyed expression transformed into a look of horror. "Really? You should have told me!"

"Yes, I know, dearest. I was going to tell you as soon as we collected our items and were heading back. I didn't expect this... this diversion. Of course, that source could have been wrong, you know. But, I tell you, I think this could be a very good diversion indeed!"

"Do you really think so?" Ellen was now curious at her husband's rather gleeful look.

"Yes, I do. Come now, we'll gather up the children from the various villages, and eventually we will figure out a way to bring some new books and pencils up here to these wretched mountains, and teach them ourselves."

"We will?"

"Yes. I'm rather keen to try my hand at teaching math."

"You are?"

"Yes! It will be refreshing. And you can teach them to play the guitar, on top of everything else you will teach them. Now, if I recall correctly, Darren — before he turned into a rather dodgy character — said there had been a recent recruitment drive for teachers and a doctor in New Zealand and Australia; soon enough there will be a swarm of others here to help."

"And if they don't come?"

"And if they don't come? Well, then we will have to build it up ourselves. Simple."

"Yes, I see what you're saying," she concurred finally as the possibility of resurrecting the school became a rather interesting challenge. She imagined all those cherubic cherry-cheeked children filling the seats before her. Children in clean uniforms seated in rows of desk-chairs, eyes gleaming, tidy heads neatly plaited and bobbing with excitement as the roster is called. One by one they call out sweetly, "Present, Missus Tenderfeeld!"

All at once her husband changed the subject. "Now, let's hear you play that guitar again!" he bellowed.

"What?" she stammered still lost in thought.

"The guitar!" he protested with a wry smile. "The guitar; let's hear you play it again! Not only is it a ghost instrument, but it's a receptacle of secrets. What next from this extraordinary creature? Will it dance a jig at the next full moon?"

"What?" she replied indignantly. "What are you going on about, Col? Honestly, one would think you have completely lost your mind. First you want to do the impossible and resurrect a school no one here wants — in fact you absolutely abhor anything that is impractical! And then next you want me to teach them something as unproductive as playing guitar?"

"How can you say that? I like music — just never knew your ability to play it so well. You never taught the children…" Col opened the guitar case, lifting out the instrument in question and handing it ceremoniously to his wife of forty-five years, "… and while we are on the subject of music, how could you have kept that a secret from me all these years?"

"Probably the same way you kept the secret of the lepers of Chiang Rai a secret from me!" she retorted, taking hold of the finely crafted instrument.

"Hardly the same thing!" Col replied. It was then that they both heard the haunting melody again. It was slow, rhythmic, and ceremonial like a tribal dance and it lifted their spirits as the weakening light from the pale dusky sun darkened beyond the dusty window.

The approaching spring season proffered a potential to Lorraine which required much physical and mental preparation. She drifted aimlessly and mostly alone for the two weeks of the honeymoon, which was spent at the manor following the arduously drawn-out wedding celebration. It was near the end of that time that she came to suspect that something was different in her body. Much of the time she felt tired and irritable. Unfamiliar guests appeared on the château grounds out of nowhere and addressed her intimately like family, making her nerves rattle, her heart race, and a cold sweat break out on her brow. Her secret conspired against her. Only her mother, who stayed with her only daughter beyond the wedding, knew something was not right with her. But Lorraine insisted it was only a touch of the flu or something harmless that made her feel unwell. After a week at the château, Sylvie-Marie reluctantly left her daughter, an alien now in the ancestral castle.

The one person who seemed not particularly interested in speaking to her was her husband, Joël. Perhaps he already recognized the flushed look on her face, or the queasy stomach she nervously clutched behind her new rabbit fur. If he suspected anything, he did not let it show. He was cordial and took a genuine interest in her well-being and comfort within the confines of his family's expansive estate, but — as far was bedtime rituals were concerned — he continued to leave her mystified by his dispassionate distance. As soon as dinner was finished he retired to the smoking salon with his many cousins and childhood friends. Amongst the merry band of gentlemen Lorraine tried to identify a special one that might become her ally, but the close coterie of school chums seemed determined to close ranks against her and keep cheerfully to themselves in cigar smoke–filled rooms. By the final week, however, she began to worry that their lack of consummation would bring suspicion, particularly if she began to show prematurely.

At dinner on the penultimate evening of their Loire Valley stay, Lorraine placed a warm hand on her husband's thigh as they drank yet another champagne toast at the start of the first course. She felt his leg contract suddenly and he nearly spilled his champagne as he turned to stare at her with indignant eyes.

"*Que c'est-?*" he stopped himself abruptly and she watched as his outrage was immediately checked, and his expression turned theatrically into embarrassment. "I'm sorry, my darling," he corrected himself. "What was that you were saying?" Lorraine smiled wanly at this sudden change of deportment.

"I was just saying … uh … um … " she stammered, whispering now. "Uh, that this champagne is quite nice. Makes me quite giddy, you know." Her eyelashes flew up and down as she stared expressionless at his champagne flute. Both hands, now above the table, moved to the tall glass, which she grasped in one hand and began to stroke with the other ever so slightly. A light-headedness overtook her and the sudden pallor of her face alarmed him.

"Are you … are you all right?" he queried, taking hold of her hands strangely cold, almost clammy.

"I'm so sorry," she replied, closing her eyes and shaking her head. "I think it's already gone to my head. I must have played too much tennis this afternoon. Will you take me to our bed, *right now*?"

The request was made rather loudly, causing the older guests to shift in their seats and clear wobbly throats, while the younger ladies, particularly the unmarried lot, chirped and blushed, attaching lips to champagne glass to quiet giggles and avert stares.

"All right, my sweet," Joël replied in a sugar-coated voice. "Right away; let us go." He stood up, asked his mother across the table if they could be excused, then helped his new bride from the table. Holding her upright, they retired from the room. Lorraine continued the charade all the way up to the bridal chamber, where, once inside, she locked the door with the large brass key and threw it out the window. As he looked on in surprise, she cornered him beside the bed.

"We are alone now, Joël. I'm not sure what game you are playing, but I know you can do this."

"Okay. Okay, Lorraine. Of course, *naturellement.*" He removed his dinner jacket and unclasped his gold and onyx cuff-links. "I was planning to come very soon. Tonight in fact." A cuff-link fell to the ground and rolled toward the guitar. He bent his body over to retrieve it. "I see you brought your beloved guitar? Very well."

"Yes, Joël. It has been a better husband than you. At least I know where it is when the sun goes down. Tell, me Joël, who is she? Is she here? Do I know her?"

"No, no. Lorraine, please. Don't ask me. Please, be reasonable."

"Reasonable? How can I be reasonable, when my husband is making love to another woman? Or...perhaps it is another man? Joël, if it is a man...just tell me. I think I can..."

"No, no. It's not that," he cut in. "I am not a homosexual, if that is what you think."

"Then it *is* another woman. Why, Joël? In Québec you said you loved me. I did think it was strange that you proposed to me with a letter, *after* you had returned to Paris. But, why? Why me? Why did you ask me to marry you if you love some other woman? Why?" A suppressed sob finally escaped her. Even if she was not devastated by the possibility of his infidelity, she was still deeply hurt by the betrayal and the shame of it.

"I did love you, Lorraine. You are very beautiful, and young, and perhaps the most brilliant girl I have met in a very long time ... "

"You *did* love me? But you do not now?" She covered her face with her hands and sobbed loudly now, her humiliation dawning upon her.

"No ... I mean yes. I loved you and still do. But, I am promised to someone else ... someone who ... whom I cannot marry." The confession was wrenched out of him, but after the words were out of his mouth, he felt a monumental burden lift. Lorraine simply looked at him impassively with her streaked and stricken face, and drew away when he tried to wipe her tears with his neatly folded handkerchief.

"So, you wish you were married to this someone else?" she asked with feigned emotion, wiping her face with the back of her slender hand.

"Yes. I guess you could say that." He hung his head, but still his relief was apparent. The relief was also now in her own heart. "I am very, very sorry, Lorraine," he continued. "I should not have done this to you. But, my mother has hoped and hoped for years that I would forget this other woman and marry a nice French ... *Catholic* ... girl. You were my best friend when I was in Québec. I missed my ... my ... umm ... my beloved very much. But you were such a beautiful girl ... bright as a bird. When we made love that once, you were like the silver lining on my dark stormy rain cloud." *Yes, and we are in the same crazy, sad, and pathetic boat,* she thought to herself.

"That is very sad, Joël. That makes me so sad." And again the tears flooded as she held out her consoling arms to her husband. They embraced like brother and sister for a moment, then, with a woeful sigh, she sought out his lips and kissed him deeply. "I forgive you, Joël, but you must do the right thing now, and consummate *this* marriage. That is all I ask."

The contrite groom obliged. Afterward, as they lay silently in the dark, she smiled wanly and heard again the sad, lamenting tune of the guitar by her bedside, as the scale ascended in a *legato vibrato.* When the *tremolo* scale finally descended and then subsided into an open-stringed chord, the curtains rustled dimly like the brush of long skirts. "Good night," she whispered. *"Et merci."*

Lorraine's newly apparent condition brought with it myriad delicate personal duties, which were a welcome reprieve from her formerly demanding spousal responsibilities. With significant assistance from his father with regard to lobbying Le Général, Joël secured himself an assistant attaché position in Vietnam where his father had once been Chief Diplomat and Attaché Cultural until a year before independence was declared at the end of the Indochina War in 1954. Joël had attended primary and secondary school during these early years, while his mother taught conversational French to other diplomatic wives in Saigon, along with her other domestic and diplomatic spousal duties. Times had changed significantly and the unstoppable Ho Chi Minh now was the man in charge of that former French colony.

Joël's position, like France's position itself in Vietnam, was very tenuous. But he was happy just to be returning to his boyhood home. Lorraine guessed without any doubt that her husband's "beloved" resided there. Never before had she seen him so amiable. They achieved an easy truce. Although they returned to Paris and to their separate apartments, for his mother they presented a united marital front, and to his government colleagues they were the perfect diplomatic couple. When the new civil servant was apprised of his new appointment in Hanoi to commence the following year, he wrote impassioned letters to his mistress, who was revealed, when pressed by Lorraine, to be, rather unromantically, a teacher of western medical science at the new National University in Hanoi. When pressed further he revealed that the woman had been his childhood sweetheart, a brilliant girl whose parents, a doctor of traditional Chinese medicine and an herbalist, scraped together enough funds to send their exceptionally bright daughter to the exclusive French International School in Saigon.

After a politically fraught graduation from their school, they eloped. Joël and the girl both turned eighteen within a month of each other, and decided they would abscond to her family home in the countryside south of Saigon as his own parents were determined to leave the colony and return to France before the embassy could be closed down with violence during the political crisis of those final years. Their elopement was short-lived; they were quickly found by the diplomatic services department and Joël was brought back forcibly to Saigon without the girl. Although he tried desperately for days to convince his parents to allow them to marry so they could sponsor her immigration to France, his mother refused point blank, and his father capitulated to her wishes.

Madame Marie de Vogel-Larochette was solidly built, stridently feminine, and formerly a blonde, but her carefully coiffed bouffant hairdo now gleamed silver like an ornate shield ensconced above a pair of forged steel eyebrows and an ice-blue stare. Although it was her husband, Émil, who was the grandson of the Marquis Georges de Vogel and traced his family back to the Hapsburgs, it was her regal bearing that identified them as royalty. Next to her rather effete husband, she was a formidable queen.

"I liked the girl enough when you were just naïve little children playing after school," Madame de Vogel-Larochette proclaimed to her distraught and unhappy son. "But her family is probably Buddhist. And they are poor country mice, are they not?" She waved her hand in the air vaguely.

"What of it, Maman? What if they are Buddhist, or from the countryside? The young man challenged, looking to his father, who stood silently beside his wife as if awaiting the verdict.

"They are probably one of those revolutionaries. What are they calling themselves these days?" she asked rhetorically, disdainfully spitting out the word. *"Communistes?* These are reasons enough for the girl not to be a suitable match for you," she retorted with certainty. "Or, for that matter, to be trusted!"

"I assure you, Maman," he countered, now just barely containing his fury beneath a furrowed brow, " ... that Mae Anh is *not* a *Communiste* and can be trusted absolutely. And furthermore, I know for a fact she would readily be baptized into the Roman Catholic Church, if I asked her to. She has already suggested this!"

The young man felt confident that this fact would sway his obstinate mother. But she remained intractable and was already turning her attention away from her son's useless arguments. Searching and finding a distraction through the window of their palatial apartment in the heart of Saigon, she glared at the large, smooth, elephantine fronds of tropical galangal, ginger and jasmine painting the lush courtyard garden a deep emerald, laced with lime and saffron, and sniffed in their elegant tropical scents first without pleasure, then again with some resignation. In the heady atmosphere of the mid-summer evening, the delicate fragrance of the white flowers mixed perfectly with the subtle smells of the kaffir lime and the intoxicatingly sweet scent of ripe papaya. Joël mistook her resigned expression for capitulation and opened his mouth to speak, but she pre-empted him, rallying her substantial forces once again and laying siege.

"Non!" declared Madame de Vogel-Larochette. "We are French royals. *We* ... cannot dilute eight hundred years of European royal blood with those from these ungrateful colonies!" She turned toward her son with an expression of absolute tyranny, and brought her carefully manicured fist down upon lacquered teak. "It is just not possible! You will be disinherited if you dare to defy me again!" With this final ultimatum, she left him shocked, withered, and defeated in the lounge room, as she disappeared into her boudoir.

For three years, while attending university in France, Joël sustained a wall of silence against his mother and made few friends. Eventually he finished his law studies at the University of Paris-Sorbonne, and left for far-away Québec for a year of graduate studies. There he met Lorraine at a Law faculty party and they became friends and eventually lovers. When he returned to Paris, although he never lost his love and yearning for Mae, the political separation between their two countries was immutable and he began to lose heart and consider alternatives. Communication by telephone and even post between Hanoi and Paris became unpredictable, difficult, and then impossible. All seemed lost. In his lonely, vanquished, and defeated state, he considered Lorraine for a partner. Marriage was an unwritten requirement of diplomatic service, and he decided that she might make a decent and not unpleasant wife after all.

In the serenity of his hotel-apartment, he considered her pedigree. As a commoner from the colonies with half-Scots, half-French, albeit Breton, heritage, she would be a perfect candidate to test his mother's motives behind her ban on his love for Mae. Not surprisingly, his mother gave her immediate approval as soon as she saw a photograph of the lovely girl, learned of her background, and heard that she had a solid Catholic education. The breach between the maternal and filial relationship seemed mended finally — superficially, if not whole-heartedly. On the mother's part there was never a real breach; for the son, however, it was another matter. He let go the fact that the "colony question" was never broached, and kept that small observation to himself, reserving it for another time, perhaps another place. He was determined that someday she would regret her unjust and entirely dictatorial judgment against his true love in the oppressive heat of that desperate and precarious summer evening in Saigon following what he considered his unforgivable capture, as if he were a wild and untamed animal.

When Lorraine wrote back to accept his proposal, Joël was somewhat regretful. But, it seemed the only way he could resolve the long-standing issues of his career requirements, his mother's financial support, and his own personal needs. The unspoken rules of his desired diplomatic career dictated a certain marital status that could be resolved with this simple solution. He could never really love her, not like he loved Mae, but he was willing to look after her financially, if she looked after him "politically." But how could he tell her this in a simple letter?

Such a practical-minded young woman was Lorraine that he convinced himself she would accept his complex personal situation without question or drama. He was correct to a certain extent, but when she arrived in Paris somewhat emotionally on edge and not quite herself, he found difficulty in divulging his plan. He put her lethargy and evasiveness down to the hardship of being away from her family and the familiarity of Québec, but he could not bring himself to expose his duplicitous scheme while she was not entirely well. Then finally, when the truth was ultimately revealed after the wedding, her level-headed reaction to it confirmed for him the aptness of his choice.

The next hurdle was to convince Mae Anh that this was the best resolution to their problem. Several letters were begun expressing his excitement at the imminent possibility of his return to her country, but when he tried to explain the delicacy of his situation, to explain the complex turn of events and relations, no expression or collection of contrite words could properly convey what he knew he must do. He had to give her a choice to refuse him, of course. But that made him sick with sadness. With a passionate optimism he dreamed of them becoming united, and with the blessing from his surprisingly open-minded wife, she would join their relationship as an equal partner. His son would have two mothers; he especially liked this fantastical idea. But the letters became complex and inconclusive, like a half-constructed city in a futuristic fiction novel or an unfinished symphony.

Though his personal petitions were not successful, his professional appeal for an assignment in Vietnam was, and the confirmation of it finally came about in the middle of the French summer. With his background in the region, familiarity with the culture and language, and understanding of the delicate nature of the current political climate, his placement was hardly in question. A full year in Paris was required before he would be permitted to relocate to Hanoi. This would allow for his child to be born on solid French soil and for the official negotiations with the new Vietnamese government to continue apace.

Prior to the diplomatic assignment, their life was quiet, almost retiring. For Joël it seemed interminable. But the quiet life suited Lorraine, whose burgeoning belly became harder to obscure behind loosely flowing couture dresses, not unlike her antique eighteenth-century wedding gown. After the assignment, everything changed. Suddenly, the constant string of mandatory cocktail dinners and soirées of varying cultural significance became the routine. As an aspiring diplomatic couple, Joël and Lorraine were required to host their own dinner parties, and they did so on a regular basis. Occasionally, an impromptu guitar concert would be demanded of Lorraine to entertain the guests, and once following a particularly impassioned performance, she was invited to travel to Madagascar to perform with a guitar ensemble which was in Paris at the moment for an official government-hosted tour. Ever graciously she declined, pointing out her expectant state, but she accompanied her husband to official function after function, smiling demurely, courteously kissing the air above elegantly coiffed temples and sipping champagne, even as her feet began to swell in the final trimester and her stomach swelled to a monstrous size.

Philippe Stewart de Vogel-Larochette was born in early October, an extremely large, weighty, but placid child. Cherub cheeked and bright-eyed, he won the affection of the entire clan, his busy parents, the society press photographers, and particularly Madame Marie de Vogel-Larochette. Gifts flooded in through their front gate like a flotilla into a port under siege from every corner of Europe and around the world. It seemed she had written thank you notes to every single friend, former friend, colleague and acquaintance from current and previous diplomatic assignments, as well as distant relatives. Exquisitely made garments from the exclusive French fashion houses arrived. Little blue and white sailor suits with matching caps and an oversized red pom-pom; gilded specialty toys and 24-carat charms, Louis XIV baby furniture and fine Belgian lace linen, exquisite gold-leafed albums, porcelain-ware — there was nothing more the small lad could possibly require.

But Lorraine was nearly ruined by the exhaustion of pushing out such an over-sized infant, followed by an incessant string of official visitors and royal relatives. The only consolation was that she was temporarily excused from her diplomatic spousal duties until sometime in December when celebrations of the Noël would begin in earnest. During this time she was free from the soirée circuit, and began to consider how she might be able to convince her husband to let her travel to St.-Gérard with the child in order to introduce him to her parents. The traumatic birth left her anemic and constantly fatigued, and nearly psychotic from the excruciatingly painful nursing; in truth, she never completely recovered from it.

The delicacy of her health worked in her favor, for Joël was feeling very contrite towards his good wife, and yet quite excited about the imminence of his overseas assignment. A decision was finally made — when the posting was to commence in April, Lorraine would return to her family in St.-Gérard with the infant for a spell, and he would travel to Hanoi in advance to set up their residence and ensure the safety and viability of his position in Vietnam. When he sent word for her, she and their son would join him. These plans immediately set Lorraine's heart at ease. By December, she was beginning to recover her energies and the baby thrived with her rejuvenated spirits and improved lactation. Fortunately, she knew it was her own desperate attachment and retention of the baby that caused her son to be born so late and with a full layer of mature fat, so her depleted state and inability to lactate properly during the first few months since his birth was no cause for real concern. More life-threatening had been her own physical deterioration. She was emaciated, her hair limp, lifeless, and falling out in large handfuls.

But the news that she would be going home soon buoyed her spirits, and her thoughts began to wander to the cabin on the lake. Many times in the past year she had begun to compose a letter in her mind, but there was nothing really she could explain to him that would not be painful in one way or another. The apartment, she knew, was no longer occupied, as she had her father arrange for her lease to be terminated and her furniture and possessions placed into storage at their family home in St.-Gérard. There was no news of Bernard from her parents and she did not know if he had stayed on in her apartment in the city for a while without her, or whether he returned straightaway to his lakeside cabin. Her guess was the latter; he had the quiet grace of an animal of the wild and his rightful place was really in the embrace of the evergreen trees and shoal of the lake. The dream-like quality of her memories of him made her believe that he was just a fantasy — a dream lover, a phantom of the passionate embrace, a silent winged angel bestowing beautiful music upon the world.

In the spring, preparations for two separate departures were kept entirely as independent affairs. A large leather traveling trunk inherited from his great-great-grandfather who moved only once, from Russia to France in 1812, provided Joël with a case large enough to pack his most treasured possessions: his entire bookcase of legal reference manuals; a stupendously large collection of Vietnamese and Chinese poetry in the original language, also translated into French; a collection of six eighteenth-century oil paintings of French country landscapes, and one of his great-great-grandmother as a very nude Turkish courtesan — the soft curves of her perfectly rounded breasts and the rich pink of her areoles repeated on her rotund cheeks and rosebud mouth.

Into the trunks also went a full briefcase of stationery implements — parchment, linen papers, drawing pads, pencils, brushes, quills, ink pens, calligraphy brushes, wax seals, charcoal pencils, water-colors, and gouaches; a family photo-album and a gilt-framed photograph of the fat and smiling baby Philippe entwined in the folds of Lorraine's silk brocade. A wardrobe which included four seasons of formal and casual wear and an arsenal of personal items to ensure he did not lose his up-to-the-minute debonair style while he was overseas in the fetid jungles of Hanoi was sent separately in four large table-high matching Louis Vuitton suitcases.

Lorraine's travel baggage was directly opposite of her husband's. Packing only for one season, a chilly Québécois spring, she kept it to the bare essentials — the very things she had brought with her only a year ago. She abandoned all the fashion-house couture outfits of the past year, but made room for her wedding trousseau, a wedding photo-album, an album dedicated to baby Philippe — his birth, homecoming, christening, with various members of the extended family, first of everything — toys, cot, outfit, shoes, tooth — and two personal notebooks which contained a diary of her time in Paris. The last item to be prepared for travel was the guitar, newly dusted and polished, and packed carefully in a new custom-made black leather case lined in chartreuse silk moiré.

It had become not only a good luck charm, her rabbit's foot, but a nanny of sorts to baby Philippe. The guitar resided permanently now in his nursery, for his mother became accustomed to playing him a quiet lullaby to put him to sleep after she laid him in his cot for the night. There were times when she was certain the guitar was possessed by a spirit — just before Philippe spoke his first word, Lorraine heard an excited chorus of notes rise from the guitar in the nursery at the end of the hour during which the baby would have his afternoon nap. The mother, no longer surprised by the independent and never predictable music of the guitar, calmly strode into the room just in time to hear the baby softly utter the words, "Mamma … mam … mamam!" When he heard his mother rush in and saw her lovely face hover with a smile just above his wee cot, the animated words repeated themselves excitedly, spilling out of his baby lips like cupid's arrows — the sweetest sound.

Mother and child sang the words to each other for another hour, dancing joyfully around the nursery and composing a little song in time with the melody of his utterances. Instinctively she looked to the guitar and heard it chime in with an *allegro* — a sound like a whale rising through a foaming sea, spouting its glee into the receptive arms of mother air across planetary distances. This animal channeled its song to a companion guitar — the echo of those bellows from baleen and blowhole was then transformed into a falling *allegretto* in an empty schoolhouse on top of the world.

Once Col was able to bring a spark of flame to the half-burnt log embers of its last fire, the drafty fireplace in the main classroom of the schoolhouse warmed the traveler sufficiently, if not well. Downstairs there were four classrooms, varying in size from one large room for nearly fifty students down to one for only a handful. A small administrative office with built-in shelves was at the far end, adjacent to a large eat-in kitchen with bare cupboards, and two spare dressing rooms complete with showers. The outdoor toilet was yet to be discovered by the exploring couple. It stood thirty feet away from the house, on the edge of a precipice which fell away to nothing.

Feeling like a pair of squatters in an abandoned farmhouse, the couple nonetheless made the best of the situation and proceeded to settle in before it became too dark to make their sleeping arrangements. The electricity was no longer connected and they would have to work by candle or flashlight as soon as the sun dropped below the horizon. Col calculated that they had about three hours of sunlight left. By dark they had succeeded in hauling in the bulk of their transported possessions and the scant items of furniture they had posted ahead of themselves in case of emergency. With foresight, two folding camp chairs and rollout bedding had been packed along with cooking and dining utensils and select items of personal hygiene and comfort — on the occasion that third-world housing and plumbing would require them to camp in the great outdoors — as true Canadians they were experienced wilderness survivalists and masters of the self-catered holiday. Their temporary new abode was more than they could hope for, particularly under the circumstance in which they found themselves.

But after a cold and uncomfortable night on the floor of the classroom, Col was keen to find better sleeping quarters. At the top of the stairs to the upper floors they had found the doors securely locked. From the look of the deep scars sustained around the locks, several enthusiastic but unsuccessful attempts had been made to break and enter. In the morning light, Col carefully unhinged the door of the doctor's studio using his Victorinox Swiss Army knife and efficiently made his way into the residence, at ease now in his new role as the proprietor.

Timber shutters provided a complete black-out of the room, except for the rectangular-shaped perimeter of sunlight straining to shine through. He dislodged the shutters with a bold pound of his substantial fist around the bottom and top edges where they were stuck and flooded the room with a near blinding light. A single bed with a dark green quilted cover came to view in the far right corner. Beside it, a large pine writing desk supported a small, neatly stacked pile of newspapers. On closer inspection he found a copy of the

Sydney Morning Herald, dated 15 March 1948, on top of two copies of the *New Zealand Herald*, similarly dated, a well-worn copy of *The Merck Manual of Diagnosis and Therapy (7ᵗʰ Edition)*, and an appointment book. Cracking open the cover of the diary, Col glanced at the last entry penciled into the book. 2 PM, Monday, 1 September 1947. *Strange,* he thought to himself, *half a year before the newspapers.*

On the blank back facing page of the diary the doctor had drawn a picture. It was a sketch by an amateur illustrator, but he could see the care in which the ink drawing was rendered. It appeared to be a message carved in a huge flat stone in Tibetan Sanskrit, appearing like a row of tangled shoelaces hanging across a taut clothesline. The drawer had even sketched in the shadows of the stone cast by the crisp, clear high-altitude Himalayan sun. Below it was written in English: *Don't let the love die.*

This mysterious message had presented itself to him somewhere before and he pondered it for a few minutes. Could these sad parting words mean simply "Goodbye"? He considered it further and suddenly the realization dawned on him, a revelation that seemed to come over him, rather than to him. They should be taken to mean that every visitor must come back again and again. *Don't let the love die.*

Col closed the notebook and glanced at the newspapers. Over ten years had passed since the doctor was last here. The driver had made it seem the doctor and the school had been here until recent years. Evidently, his last patient must have put an end to the service. Or perhaps the doctor left for his annual trek up the mountain and never returned? Or something more sinister, like abduction by insurgents? With these dark thoughts in his mind Col moved away from the desk and toward a narrow free-standing pine wardrobe which stood alone in the opposite corner. He hesitated before opening the door. This timber box looked ominously like an upright coffin, as they are stored before being laid on a trestle table to receive their newly dead. Over the forty-some-odd years he supervised its operations, the timber mill made its share of them — raw pine coffins — the only product the mill took orders for and they came in steadily on a daily basis, from as far as St.-Jerome, Sherbrooke, and even once from St.-Johns.

They were made on individual order and never stockpiled, for no one wanted to see them in a storeroom. They came in two sizes, he recalled: adult and child. It was never a joyful occasion to craft a coffin. Over the years Col observed, however, that the child boxes were the most common — their doll-sized dimensions brought grief even in the hearts of the most hardened men. Here in this country at the roof-top of the world, the dead would be burned, sometimes without a coffin, their short prematurely aged bodies sent as ashes into the oxygen-vague air. Where was it, he wondered, that bodies of the dead were "buried" in the tops of trees — he had heard about it somewhere: a tribe of American Indian or in Africa perhaps? Left presumably for vultures to pick clean until the bones could be more readily cleaned and stored as relics in the family's curio cabinet? The wardrobe handle was in his hand when Ellen halted his exploration with a loud rap on the open door and a loud clearing of her throat.

"Uh...hum. Are you sure you want to do that?" she cautioned, her eye suspiciously on the pine wardrobe as if she had read her husband's mind.

"Well, why not?" he retorted feigning nonchalance. "Are you expecting a skeleton?"

"Certainly hope not. But if there is one in there, you'd better leave it alone — at least until *after* breakfast."

"Yes, excellent idea. Could be quite a business to try and get it to go back in."

"I agree. Okay then, breakfast is served. Would you prefer it in the kitchen, or on the veranda?"

"Veranda, for sure," he answered brightly.

"Then, veranda it is." She turned and descended the stairs slowly, uncertain whether her husband would open the closet door or not, but hoping he wouldn't. The probability of there being something untoward in that abandoned cupboard was middling to high. Not prone to superstition or squeamishness under normal circumstances, she had been under a bit of strain lately by the unpredictability of their lives since leaving St.-Gérard, and the constant miscommunications and out-and-out lies that had been told to her were a shock to her normal equilibrium. She could tell from the layer of dust about the place that it had been abandoned for quite some time, certainly for longer than the military truck-driver had let on. But they were under shelter, a fairly fine one at that, and skeletons could stay in their closets for just a bit longer without them being the worse for it.

Breakfast consisted of a shared tin of pears from their transported boxes and two thick slices of bread from a loaf Ellen had brought on board the Thai plane. The morning air was decidedly cold from a night of winter-like temperatures but at this altitude the sun would warm the air and soil within hours of rising. The house was built off of the main road where the truck had rounded the hillside and deposited them the day before. A few dry oak trees spotted the area around the house, and a dry gray-brown cover of brush and tough sandy-colored grass spread from the edge of the rear veranda where they sat at breakfast to the clean line of the back boundary edge which dropped several hundred feet presumably down the mountain and back into Kathmandu.

The calamitous monsoons that sweep across South Asia each summer ensure that fertile soils are washed down the mountain, leaving the low-growing shrubby vegetation of this area marginal at best. Further up the mountain, lush stands of rhododendron greet travelers on the vast alpine plains and tea bush border the cultivated hills where rice is grown on curving terraces like wide staircases to the heavens. The forested Himalayan mountain ranges open out to infinite forests of cedar, fir, oak, birch, and other pines.

The village was literally on the cusp of the national park which contains the network of yak trails that lead virtually up into the stratospheric peaks. The thousand-year-old trading route between Kathmandu and Lhasa over the Tibetan plains has become over the millennia the same route of trekkers and mountaineers like Sir Edmund Hillary and Tenzing Norgay, who made the first successful ascent on the summit of Everest. Dotted along the route are a string of one-inn Sherpa villages like a bracelet of charms from Jiri to Junbesi, Kharikhola, Namche Bazaar and Pangboche before the trekker arrived at their prized destination beyond the moraine: the Base Camp, Gokyo Pass, Kala Pattar, or the great peak of Everest — or Sagarmatha herself. Around and beyond this fixed constellation, the southern ice fields of the great Himalayan Range are home to only a small population of mountain goats, snow leopards, and the inimitable Yeti.

Yesterday's fiasco at the airport terminal and the unbelievably precarious cliff-side drive seemed like a lifetime away to the Tenderfields. Here they were now, deserted it seemed in an unwanted and abandoned schoolhouse, their personal goods delivered unexpectedly, and an unknown future ahead of them. There seemed no way they could escape this fate that was thrust upon them. For lack of an alternative, they settled into their first meager breakfast in the Himalayas, and contemplated the view that rose before them like a crisp but surreal backdrop to an imaginary film set.

"*Himalaya! The Musical,*" Ellen thought out loud with full irony.

"*Namaste, namaste!*" her husband called back, like an attentive whipbird answering the call of its distant mate. Smiling wryly, her heart swelled with the rise and fall of the orchestral number in her head, as emotional as a captain on the verge of capsize and riding the last waves of his mistress the sea, and then she realized that the musical undulations were emanating once again from the guitar, still inside its case on the dining room table where she had left it, never for long letting them forget that it too was a fellow traveler on their improbable journey through this rough, uncertain, and unfamiliar terrain.

It occurred to Ellen at this particular moment that the increased frequency of its musical emanations suggested that the spirit that inhabited the guitar was in its element here in the easy uncomplicated surrounds of the earth's primordial summit. The tanned-leather faces of the Sherpa were so familiar, their beautiful black-haired children smiling half-naked up to them, with never a harsh look or word amongst them. These people must be linked to our native people in North America she realized. Iroquois, Cree, Sherpa, Tibetan, a shared prehistoric ice age continental heritage. It was like a revelation.

No longer a surprise, the musical interludes were like a barometer of her mood and seemed to facilitate communications between the couple. The music was particularly a comfort to Ellen, as she felt captive to an unplanned present. Col, on the other hand, relished the adventure and the challenge of starting something new, reminiscent of the early days of the mill when he was a capable young recruit full of ideas of how to make the mill grow and make their lives the stuff of dreams. He would do it again in the sunset of his life, here in the land of refined air and unbelievably breathtaking and crystal clear views. Like a picture frame, a keyhole in the cover of clouds would suddenly throw up intimate glimpses: Ama Dablang at dusk in her pink crystalline beauty like a pristine goddess.

The plane journey home to St.-Gérard was a far cry from Lorraine's erstwhile sojourn to her Paris adventure. Her six-month-old infant Philippe was the ideal travel partner: passive and cherubic, and with a wide-eyed look that motivated others at every turn to stand aside and let his mother pass to the front of long queues, or to proffer the last seats.

Even with these courtesies and polite gestures, she was exhausted by the transit, but luckily, as soon as they landed on the tarmac of Montréal-Dorval Airport, adoring grandparents swept up mother, child, guitar, and luggage. A nursery had been set up in the A-framed attic guest room of their St.-Gérard home. Nightly Lorraine kept a vigil over the infant as he slept, the guitar always beside the nursing chair adjacent to the cot. The slanting walls of the nursery were painted a pale blue and three light-filled dormer windows curtained in filmy white lace welcomed the spring air into the room. The breeze exited again through two windows on the other side, giving one the sensation that they were ensconced in the clouds like an eagle on a lofty thermal.

One bright morning the boy opened his eyes to find the familiar presence of his mother's face. He reached up with a chubby hand and touched her lips. This was the precise moment she noticed that the baby blue of her infant's eyes had crystallized into an emerald green. His gaze upon her was as contemplative as that of an old familiar spirit, and glistening like sun-soaked pastures. Three months had passed and Lorraine had not dared to contact Bernard and her parents never mentioned him, but the color of her son's eyes unleashed a sudden torrent of tears, an eruption of remorse bottled up in eighteen months of anxiety and confused loyalties. The enormity of her subterfuge still weighed heavily, but it was balanced against the triangular truce she formed with Joël on behalf of Mae. His secret was safe with her. She had sailed along on her precarious sea of denial for so long that she nearly forgot about the deception.

One early autumn afternoon she found herself at the cabin on the lake. The studio window was open but she dared not approach. There were moments when she felt she was being watched, particularly when she brought the little boy, but her visits continued to be uncomplicated by unvoiced sorrows and bittersweet greetings.

That evening on her return, Lorraine's mother read to her a telegram from Joël — his appointment had fallen through. It read:

HANOI NEGOTIATION AT STANDSTILL STOP IN SAIGON STOP TAKING POST IN COPENHAGEN IMMEDIATELY

The cable was terse, but Lorraine read in it urgency not only from a political standpoint, but also from an emotional one, one which she knew would be edged with heartache. She would send a cable back the next day, informing her husband she and baby would join him in Copenhagen in two weeks' time.

Parking her mother's Renault a short distance from the cabin she picked her way down carefully along the wooded path to the front door. She sat in silence on the veranda for hours watching brook trout nip out of the water at unsuspecting flies. The riotous autumn colors of the birches and maples scattered like confetti low across the water-fringing landscape. Sheaves of bright yellow, garnet, and sunset-struck orange mellowed the deep evergreen overhang of the tall and shadowy conifers.

Finally, she descended down the path to the edge of the lake, as the whirring noise of a wood lathe met her ears like a little gasp from a sleeping baby confirming its precious life. Accompanying the whir was a faint music which resonated from somewhere deep within the cabin. It had an unfamiliar ring and the tune was cheerless, sending a thin unexpected shiver down her spine. Was it self-reproach? The sound was deep, but not fearful. Like a tear it descended, heavy with restraint like a mother's sacrifice.

7

JOËL (CHIANG RAI), 1960–1976

Like a bull in the pit of European politics, Joël became impassioned to keep his petition alive after his first effort to gain the Hanoi position proved unfruitful, dispatching brilliant internal mini-campaigns dramatically in the halls of the French parliament and in the Paris social press. He refused to believe that the failure of negotiations to secure his rightful office was purely geo-political, not personal. But to prove to himself and the others that a failure at the start of his career was an aberration, he channeled his energies into perfecting the art of power politics. His powers of subversive and not-so-subtle manipulation won him a reputation throughout the extensive French diplomatic network as *Le Taureau*. The Bull.

By the mid-point of the 1970s, however, Joël's reputation had grown and he became better known as a consummate strategist. His effective behind-the-scenes negotiations during the high-profile Paris Peace Accords of 1973 reflected his own personal intent to establish peace in Vietnam. As early as 1968, he was instrumental on behalf of the French government in negotiations that led to the Accord. As a result of the treaty, the United States National Security Advisor Dr. Henry Kissinger and Vietnamese politburo member Lê Duc Thọ were awarded the 1973 Nobel Peace Prize for their efforts, although Lê refused to accept it, and Joël felt he and his French colleagues were slighted.

He assigned himself to a special mission during the summer of 1976, to accompany a French and Belgian medical team traveling to a besieged refugee camp on the Laotian border set up by the Thai government to intercept the tide of Lao and Hmong refugees flooding into Thailand not unlike the muddy waters of the Mekong after a relentless season of monsoons. He would then move on to Hanoi, where it was arranged through tentative diplomatic channels for him to gain an audience with representatives of the Communist leadership.

It was a politically subversive operation and later branded a secret war, but French intelligence reports told of hundreds and thousands of refugees fighting their way haplessly through the bullet-infested jungles to possible freedom, in hot pursuit by Pathet Lao soldiers intent on stopping their progress. All but a handful were picked off by the gunmen before they could reach safe haven. It was Joël's job to ensure that the Thai army could guarantee protection for the humanitarian medics searching these perilous jungle tracks for survivors injured en route to the camps.

For six days he sat in negotiation first with low- to medium-ranking Thai officers, backing them against linguistic and diplomatic walls until they caved and called in their superior. More than once he endured tedious waits in a visitor's chair ending at long last with the arrival of a young houseboy gingerly bowing to him in apologetic gestures, and presenting him at the end of a long hallway to an officious middle-aged bureaucrat in the long white uniform of the Thai military official, who would invariably be seated behind a heavy darkly ominous mahogany desk, strangely devoid in Joël's mind, of the piles of official documentation, correspondence, and bits of paperwork and writing utensils that cluttered his own industrious desk back at home. This official's shiny jet black hair would be oiled to perfection and not a strand would waft as the whirring rattan ceiling fans swirled laboriously above them.

Joël launched immediately into his main demands, not waiting for the coffee or tea to be offered, making deals and brokering promises in French and English, and resorting to Vietnamese, and then rudimentary Thai when no other words seemed to make the connection. He paced the humid yet sterile room with its wall-length rows of portraits. Thai royalty looked down sternly upon the Frenchman as he resolutely walked the line of the carpet, refusing to be seated and waving off the houseboy, leaving his opponent silently fretting over the sanctioned iced tea. They put up ever weakening blockades to his demands, and then only after signs of imminent capitulation began to show did the diplomat allow the tea to be poured. After three afternoons and one evening of masterful entreaties, it was the Thai General himself who approved the use of an armored convoy of six military jalopies headed by one tank to protect and carry the doctors and their supplies.

It was a successful negotiation and a potent win for Joël and he felt he was at last at the height of his diplomatic powers. But most of all he was relieved that his mission was accomplished and he could now focus on his long-awaited return to the one place he felt most at home. As he prepared the official dossier on the mission, he also made enquiries into the state of travel and safety in the former French colony. His colleagues, now well aware of his power and influence within the diplomatic channels, responded to his questions with alacrity, and obliquely voiced their hopes for a recommendation by him for the Home Office. In due course, he secured a special diplomatic flight to Hanoi from Chiang Rai.

Joël was prepared for anything to happen, but he was not prepared for the news he received by telephone the night before his departure. He had retained his neutrality in the great political debate of the time, enabling him to negotiate with less difficulty, and underneath his crisp white shirt, his heart did not beat for any Fascist, Communist, or Socialist. A conservative by nature and a true believer in the Keynesian School of Economics, Joël was as distanced from the proletariat as he was cosseted by the wealth and refinement of his family and diplomatic position. He was a sophisticated and well-educated connoisseur of fine French wine, cognac, Scandinavian beer, and all things intellectual. That his only son was interested in Asia for its disruptive political and social upheavals was a complete anathema to the diplomat.

When Philippe was six, the family left Europe for diplomatic assignments in Tunisia and Senegal, and after nine years in Africa they had returned to Paris. Philippe was now nearly seventeen and through the tinny, cacophonous transcontinental noise of the embassy telephone call from Paris, he beseeched his father to allow him to join him on the next step of his diplomatic assignment in Southeast Asia. He was on the verge of completing his terminal year and graduating early from the lycée, and had already secured his Communist membership through some sort of underground student network. He had received an official letter of endorsement from the regional Party Chief in Paris. Knowing his father was a senior official in the French Ministry of Foreign Affairs, the Party Chief had allowed special dispensation for his age, making him the youngest official member of the Socialist Party in France. The young man was convinced that if his father would grant him his wish to travel to Hanoi to meet the Communist leadership, he would be assured of a great career like his father. While the father haunted the halls of power like a man possessed, the son sought to level the playing fields of the underclass.

It was the beginning of the monsoon season in northern Thailand, yet Joël clutched the phone with uncharacteristically cold and clammy hands. His son was his most formidable opponent and against the younger man's precocious negotiation skills he was sometimes left quite astonished and without a retort. It seemed Philippe had learned through proximity the art of persuasion, enough to sway the seasoned diplomat to agree to a three-week trial period. He was not to wear his red armband in public or identify himself as a Party member to anyone. The diplomatic attaché would postpone his departure from Thailand for one day only. If the boy was not at the Chiang Rai airport the next day at the designated time, he was on his own. The Embassy would see to it that he had a return air ticket back to Paris, but that was his only concession.

So, while the son made his excited departure for Thailand to follow in his father's footsteps, the mother prepared to leave Paris for Québec for the last time. Through nearly two decades of global unrest, Lorraine had supported her

increasingly irritable husband through his internal political contests and pursuits of career advancement. She kept
an immaculate house and single-handedly homeschooled
their son both in French and English before he became not
only matchless in scholarship but fearless in his pursuit of
social justice. She felt her work had been done and she was
prepared to retire gracefully from public life in France to her
home in Québec.

On the tarmac of the Chiang Rai airfield the small plane
alighted. The first to exit was a young man with tousled
hair in crinkled shirt, dungarees, and a fisherman's cap,
followed by a long snaking queue of slightly less disheveled
older men, and the occasional woman — volunteer medics
who would soon be transported into the jungle to implement their rescue mission. Only when Philippe waved to
him did Joël realize that the tall, wiry young man dressed
in the faded worker's blues was indeed his son. A blood
red kerchief encircled a thin neck above his wide square
shoulders. He did not on this occasion look like a diplomat's son but more like a dock hand or a street musician.
He carried a black leather case over one shoulder and a
small khaki rucksack over the other. His rusty black-brown
locks tumbled in waves across his forehead and over one
eye below the black felt of the mariner's cap. On approaching his father, however, he tossed his head back and the
unruly locks parted to reveal the intensely green eyes of a
young Party member on a mission. It seemed the generation
gap had widened like the maw of an angry lion while his son

was away at lycée, and now the father felt uncomfortably hot and overdressed in the intense humidity.

The letter sent by the Paris Regional Party Chief was full of praise of the young man's early achievements, having recruited a full eight times as many new members from the inner and outer *arrondissements* — from the furthest suburbs and from the university student ranks — as any other member. Everyone lured into his sphere of influence was charmed and impressed by this young man, whose rhetoric and arguments made so much emotional and logical sense that it was impossible to reject his invitation to attend a local meeting just to see what his enthusiasm was all about. Even young women who under normal circumstances would not have engaged in such political discussion were enlightened to the rights of workers, what the labor unions were advocating for, and why they should support the ground floor movement that would eventually change the direction of the national leadership.

He tirelessly recruited the local clergymen and invited schoolteachers and headmasters to attend lectures and meetings, and when the opportunity was offered to make a speech and talk on behalf of lycée and university students across France, he did not hesitate. Once he brought along his guitar to a large gathering and led the rally with stirring patriotic ballads he composed impromptu as the ever-enlarging crowds gathered. During the less impassioned speeches of the other Party leaders, the guitar seemed to play itself in low dulcet tones as he strummed quiet chords in accompaniment to the instrument's stirring melody.

And now, as the snaking queue of medics and nurses began to converge at the entrance of the hangar, Joël dutifully offered cordial embraces, kissing both cheeks of the ladies as if they were his own family members. He voiced his welcome with as much enthusiasm as he could manage, while beyond him the Royal Thai Army officers rounded them up indecorously, ushering the doctors into the building while cursing silently under their breaths. Philippe saw the waiting limousine and for a moment hesitated before turning toward the building and disappearing through the doors in the wake of the *médecins*. Once inside he quickly caught up with an older woman whose pale silver-blonde hair was swept up into a weary chignon, her blue eyes tinged with red after a long sleepless night. But she smiled warmly as Philippe reached her from across the long warehouse, clearly surprised but pleased to see he had not disappeared into the conspicuous black vehicle that pulled onto the tarmac near the entrance of the building as they landed.

Sophie Morens had sat in the narrow seat beside Philippe during the arduous journey and their camaraderie was at once conspiratorial and familial. They embraced like old friends, kissing each cheek with a tender reverence. Sophie was forty-six, recently widowed and without children. As a trained pediatrician, she was one of the rare female doctors that worked at the Paris National Hospital, and she had taken a six-month sabbatical to volunteer on this urgent medical mission. She had heard about the horrors in Southeast Asia and beyond, and had a clear opinion about Ho Chi Minh, Pol Pot, and their collective ruthlessness in the false name of Socialism. During the relentlessly long flight, conversations with this disarmingly charming and convincing young man at first put her on edge, and then slowly they made her think critically once more about the many sides of any given story, and she was struck by the contradictions of the atrocities.

"In my opinion, any violence and torture inflicted on innocent people, particularly children, is evil," she retorted vehemently to her seat companion on the small plane en route from Bangkok. The parameters of her life's work, and the Socratic oath which bound her profession, were immutable. To prevent death and alleviate suffering was the sole impetus for her volunteerism.

"I do not condone violence, per se," Philippe replied. "But when the masses have been lied to for centuries, what can one do to resist the constant brainwashing?"

"Your political philosophy," she continued, "is perhaps a wide-eyed idealism."

"You may see me as an idealist, but the reality is that change to the status quo must always be preceded by violence. Extreme methods must be employed when complacency achieves nothing, which is exactly what the elite want ... "

Listening to his oration on the utopian ideals of students everywhere from Paris to Copenhagen to Beijing, she nodded silently in agreement to those ideals. And their philosophical and political debate and discourse ensued across the transcontinental flight, and only when the plane experienced turbulence did they call a truce and offer each other a comforting hand until the shaking of their seats and rattling of their teeth abated. Sophie never enjoyed traveling by plane, forever plagued as she was by memories of old prewar two-seater prop planes that flew her and her husband across the sands of Africa to tend to critically ill patients in remote sites in Algiers and Tunisia. She looked on in awe as the young man sat nonchalantly in his seat as the plane pitched and rolled through storm clouds. He was a veteran of the small military plane, having traveled with his parents to nearly twelve countries in less than seventeen years. She wondered to herself about his experiences and perceived that he was mature beyond his years.

His youthful enthusiasm reminded her of her late husband during the early years of their courtship. Jean Luc had been a brilliant philosophy and biology student at the Université d'Auvergne Clermont-Ferrand 1, where they both matriculated. Two years of military service in Tunisia and another two years of travel and research in Papua New Guinea and East Timor prior to commencing medical studies had given him a maturity that she respected, and when they served together at the maternity hospital in Auvergne, she felt his worldliness was a badge of honor. For nearly a decade in Africa they undertook hospital work together and then married just before returning to France and settling in Paris at the National Hospital, where he was offered a new position in internal medicine and surgery, and she in the infant ward.

During their first years in Paris they tried for children, but never conceived. The bitter disappointment faded as the years passed by, both busy with their important work and the satisfaction of saving lives and helping others. Then Jean Luc was abruptly struck down by a brain aneurysm at the age of forty-six. He was gone within three days. Eighteen months later Sophie herself turned forty-six and she knew that she could not continue her routine any longer, and felt that a guardian angel must have heeded her call when she received news that a group of French doctors had put out a call for more volunteers to travel with them in aid of the unfortunate victims in war-torn Indochina.

Sophie did not hesitate. The very next day she called the colleague who knew the organizer and readily signed on.

They were glad of her credentials in infant medicine and particularly relieved to finally induct the first woman onto their team. She had only three weeks to receive permission to leave the hospital and settle her private affairs for her long absence. And as she sat now next to this boy, barely out of lycée but already a citizen of the world, she felt a pang of reminiscence for her youth and the heady days of young love with Jean Luc, her lost soul mate, her guiding light.

Philippe opened the case on his lap, his young face breaking into a broad smile as the guitar gleamed presciently under the dim glow of the cabin lights. Sophie watched him in silence, her tidy pale head leaning against the window, its shade pulled closed in front of it. She glanced across the aisle to see the other passengers' eyes closed against the light.

"You might disturb the others..." she began, but Philippe put his finger to his lips and silenced her. "No," he whispered. "I hear the music others don't. Those times are the best; the vibrations go deep."

"Like now?" she asked, curious that perhaps he was joking with her, but no jest seemed suggested in his serious demeanor, the charm of his liquid eyes still intact.

"Yes. It has just started. It is a very beautiful sound. It will put everyone to rest even if they don't hear it. I think the air of anxiety around us with every roll of the plane has made it — I don't know how to explain it — but, perhaps *sympathique* might be the word? I cannot suppose that you hear it, do you? It seems that only my mother and I can actually hear and feel the *simpatico*."

"Are you hearing it now?" she asked, straining to catch the sound of the music he spoke of. Under the incessant hum of the plane engines she imagined she heard a melody among the roar, but she could not be certain.

"Yes. Listen with your heart. The music is low and droll, a kind of *barcarolle*, a lullaby sung by a gondolier in the clouds." He closed his eyes and began to hum the melody that filled his ears. Suddenly her eyes felt heavy and then, surprising herself, she relaxed willingly into the humming of the plane which now receded seamlessly into the background, blending and pitching perfectly into his tune. It entered her head from a place all around her, engulfing and welled up through the vessel of her body and then settled into her very core. The music was rich and deep, as he had said. Like a love song full of plaintive yearning, it rose and fell in waves like a sterling sea lapping and overlapping upon itself. She could feel hands softly upon her hair smoothing the tresses as they did nightly before he was gone. Through the silver of translucent lashes, a delicate hand gently caressed the strings as if they were strands of her hair, quietly stroking out a melody that would transport her to the place that she once shared with him.

The rudimentary airstrip in the interior of the Laotian jungle was primed for the arrival of Joël and Philippe's small military plane, which would take them to Hanoi. It had been a five-hour jeep ride across the border from the refugee camp, and it was the closest airfield from which the North Vietnamese military would agree to pick up the diplomat. His French intermediaries in Bangkok had bargained hard with the North Vietnamese government to allow him to negotiate, but they refused to fly into Thai airspace to retrieve him in Chiang Rai. The landing area was merely a long, temporary clearing on the edge of the jungle and two young Lao soldiers accompanied them with their guns at the ready as they all watched impassively for a small plane to clear the top of the rainforest. But after a fruitless five-hour wait and much vociferous swearing, the plane failed to show. Joël's consternation nearly unhinged his son, but the two soldiers stood impassively deflecting the angry epithets with disinterest.

Joël's immediate task in Hanoi was to ask the powers-that-be to rehabilitate a well-respected doctor whose plight had reached the French diplomat press in the weeks before his departure from Paris. He knew he did not have much time to spare. This particular doctor was married to an academic who had trained at the Sorbonne as a scholar of early Asiatic linguistic history, and had published a definitive work on ancient languages before returning to Vietnam after Independence. He had been instrumental in re-establishing the department of Languages and Linguistics at Indochina University on his return from Europe and had held the highest honors, including President and Dean of Linguistics.

Twenty-one years later, the Communists developed a disdain for intellectuals interested in preserving the past. Professor Huey was banished to hard labor and re-education in the countryside alongside his "useless" academic brethren, but he was sent further still into the rural backcountry for his audacity at receiving a foreign doctorate. It was whispered among those who had witnessed the round-ups that all reading materials were confiscated and eye-glasses destroyed before these former scholars were sent out to perform hard labor.

The diplomatic press article had landed on Joël's mahogany desk one Paris morning two months before the plane was to meet him on the jungle tarmac. The article raised alarms that now academics were being singled out for exile and harsh labor. It was reported that many scientists and professors were being particularly mistreated if they were known to have a French diploma and connections with Europeans. What caught the diplomat's attention however was the black and white photo of Professor Huey and his wife standing at the front of the University entrance during less tumultuous times. Joël's eyes opened wide with surprise and disbelief. Her face was fringed with strands of smooth black hair streaked with gray — the face was more familiar to him than his own hands, which now rustled the newspaper with its slight trembling.

With all the alacrity his official position could afford him, Joël collected intelligence on the current situation. He discovered that the professor had been sent to an undisclosed location, but his wife was still in Hanoi under house arrest. She was a physician and head of staff at the Hanoi General Hospital, which had been taken over by the People's Army in recent months. All the while working through her external contacts secretly to find the whereabouts of her husband and to reach out to French and European governments for assistance, Mae Anh stoically administered to the wounded. After so many years of civil war she knew instinctively that the press in France was her only hope to reach out for international assistance in a situation that had no hope of internal resolution.

As guerrilla fighting escalated on the fringes of her country, she heard of scores of villages being scorched to the ground and hundreds, perhaps thousands, of refugees from Cambodia, Vietnam, and, more recently, Laos, trying to flee into Thailand across hostile borders. Mae Anh wrote letters to hospitals and aid organizations in Paris, Brussels, and Geneva asking for doctors and medics to consider coming to the aid of these innocent refugees who were being wounded mercilessly by guerrilla gunfire and caught in the crossfire of chemical warfare as they attempted to cross borders. The Thai government, in an effort to remain neutral in the conflict and not be seen as a haven, refused to treat these unwanted patients. They begrudgingly set up refugee camp-sites but forbade their own hospitals and doctors to send either supplies or personnel. While Mae Anh's letters slowly made their way into sympathetic hands in various agencies, it was at the National Hospital in Paris that they finally found their champion.

But Mae Anh found herself under house arrest one morning when it came to light that the French embassy, which still had one office in the region, was looking for Dr. Anh to discuss the cooperation of the Hanoi General Hospital in assisting a European medical corps arriving to aid refugees in Thailand. The soldiers who held Dr. Anh captive had strict orders to bring the prisoner to the makeshift jail they erected at the town hall, but to let her first contact relatives and then she was to remain there until further notice.

Philippe watched his father from across the tarmac, as he ducked his perfectly combed head under the hatch of a small plane that eventually arrived eight hours later. It was, however, to Joël's great annoyance, not taking him to Hanoi, but to Bangkok. The Royal Thai Army pilot had received radio communication instructing him to bring the

French diplomat to the capital city to deal with a crisis that had arisen due to the Thai government's sudden refusal to cooperate with the European medical team. It had come to light that the head of the Hanoi General Hospital had been arrested by the People's Army and they were threatening to execute her if the medics continued their mission to help "the traitors" leave Laos to escape into Thailand. No plane from the People's Army ever materialized. Rather than go to Bangkok or return to the medic camp near Chiang Rai, Philippe asked his father to leave him with the two soldiers at this camp in the Laotian jungle that also served as the temporary airstrip and outpost for the Pathet Lao.

"I must spend time learning and observing their job. I cannot come this far, and not see for myself what it means to be a real soldier. I must feel their passion and experience their plight. This is the time to live our lives as if it matters!"

Joël marveled silently at the young man's oblivious-ness to danger and stubborn idealism. "You are mad. These so-called 'soldiers' are just children — no older than the youngsters being treated at the refugee hospital. You should spend another week there, and then you will have learned the lesson of war. It is not glamorous, nor is it glorious as your Communist propaganda machines will tell you. Has no one told you yet the collateral damage of idealism? The machine gun wounds, the amputations, the severe burns — are those *not* the real lessons in your Socialism?"

The son remained silent and looked at his feet as he remembered Sophie's tears as she swathed a three-year-old girl in bandages around her nose and eyes, which had been irreparably burned in a village fire. He had only spent one evening at the refugee camp as his father had already sched-uled the special flight to Hanoi for the following morning.

The father continued. "Those boy soldiers — they are taken from their villages and promised many outrageous things, like 'Glory' and 'The Greater Good of the Proletariat.' 'Comrades' they would all be, but they are all lies and propaganda. Those boys are taken by force or simply killed if their parents do not hand them over obediently. We have intelligence on this fact. It is not the great glory of Socialism that you idealize." The father paused, and then continued, "Come to Bangkok with me. I will find a way to get us to Hanoi after that. I must go negotiate for the lives of a doctor and her husband, a professor of languages there. She is an old friend of mine from when I was your age, attending *lycée* in Indochina."

Philippe shut his ears to the warnings, although he knew in the back of his mind that his father might be speaking truths. His father had always been a conservative career politician and as risk-averse as any bureaucrat in a comfortable office in Paris. The fact that he was now in the jungle on his way to negotiate for the lives of a local doctor and professor did not fit into the square box he drew around his father's image. His own radical, youthful passion forced him to seek the truth on both sides of any story, but he could not know yet that it was also a blindfold obscuring the truth amongst so many lies being told.

The father watched his son's expression carefully as it changed from resistance to surprise and back to resistance. He knew there would be little he could do to dissuade his radical and intractable progeny from changing his mind once he was resolved to do something. So he expressed a change of heart and surprised his son by agreeing to allow him to continue his stay in the interior of the Laotian countryside, promising to send a diplomatic plane when his negotiations were completed in Bangkok. Joël knew it was the only way his brilliant but stubborn son would learn the bitter truth, but he hoped the boy would be safely back home before his mother ever found out.

The young soldiers were roughly Philippe's age, and although they were uneducated country boys, they were sufficiently francophone to understand Philippe's offer to teach them to play the guitar, if they taught him to load and shoot their Russian-made AK-47 assault rifles. By the second evening at the small encampment, Philippe learned the basic gun handling techniques taught at the boot camps, and began the first guitar lessons. By evening of the third night, he found his reluctant companions had suddenly become his best friends.

These two young men felt particularly fortunate because they had been randomly chosen to hold the fort at the obscure landing strip, and after six months they only ever had one plane visit and it was from Joël and Philippe. Analu and Thao did not know each other prior to the assignment but they became fast friends as they were from neighboring villages and could reminisce about local swimming holes and what-not to pass the time. When the occasional official came to give orders or instructions and supplies, they pretended to be enemies and spoke harshly to one another. It seemed to be the way comrades spoke so they continued the tradition while in the presence of others. Philippe's company under these austere circumstances was welcome although it took more than a few days for the initial chill to thaw. Joël had brought food supplies along in case of an emergency and these were unloaded alongside Philippe's duffle bag and guitar. They were plentiful compared to the rations the soldiers had in their spare makeshift larder. The young men allowed themselves to savor the exotic fare on the fourth night around a campfire.

When the guitar rang out in the jungle night, it was unlike anything either of them had ever heard, including Philippe. In all the years he had played the instrument, never had the sounds rung out the way they did in the rain-forest, like a murmur of voices. The sounds defied being tuned and as soon as Philippe tightened a string it loosened itself and emanated its own sound so hypnotic that the deafening drone of cicadas was drowned out temporarily by this human-like chant. The jungle felt to Philippe like an acoustic sound shell. The canopy of phayom, pinang and white meranti trees created an arena of faultless perfection while the scent of rosewood filled his senses with a heady fragrance redolent of tropical cardamom.

"This is wild and beautiful country," he mused out loud, stroking new sounds from the strings. "It's like a forgotten land."

"Yes, and it is rough and dangerous if you do not know your way," Analu began. "We search sometimes for a way out. You move slowly, bashing and slashing your way. Once we found a clearing and what seemed like an old rice paddy. But it was abandoned. The trees and vines grew over whatever might have been there. There is a river also about half a day's journey that way," he continued gesturing over his left shoulder.

"We followed the river once," Thao interjected, taking up the story. "We camped for two nights far away from its banks." Philippe stopped playing and his questioning face was met with menacing laughter. "Crocodiles, don't you know? They will grab you by the head or foot while you sleep and drag you into the water to drown you, and then they eat you!"

"But, the river only took us further into the jungle," Analu continued. "Nothing but jungle every direction. When we came back we realized that without the plane we could never leave the jungle. We would die in there."

"We were actually more worried about running into drug smugglers," Thao finished. "You know, opium growers. They grow them here and nobody knows where they are, but they are in the middle of the jungle. Only secret planes know where to land. This here...I am sure it used to be a drug trafficking strip!"

"Ahh! And how often do they bring food and supplies here for you?"

"Not often enough!" the two soldiers replied in unison. He then heard the boys give their first confidential account of the truth. They told Philippe about how enlisted soldiers of the Pathet Lao like them were predominantly very young boys — they were as young as seven and never older than fifteen or sixteen and were basically dragged forcibly from their homes by the recruiting soldiers if they or their parents dared resist. The boys were invariably promised expert training, mentoring, and good treatment by the older soldiers and a future as leaders in the Righteous Government. What they found, instead, was months of grueling marches, very little food, long stirring speeches and lectures by their elders, and a severe, sometimes fatal beating if they ever questioned authority. Philippe felt a dread in the pit of his stomach. His father's words echoed in his ear.

The guitar then unexpectedly resonated with a reply — an approving crescendo of a melody like a rushing river with crashing and frolicking waves of sound. The young men all looked at each other in turn, the soldiers standing at attention and looking around to see if the sound had come from an external source beyond the camp. A cry from a monkey pierced the night and this sent the boys abruptly into their tents, ending the camaraderie.

Before the first rays of sunlight could break through the thick fog of the jungle the next morning, Philippe was awakened by noisy chattering just outside his tight fabric-walled enclosure. When he poked his head out, he found his hosts arguing loudly in their sing-song dialect just beyond the tree to whose canopy he had fixed his canvas tent.

"What's the matter?" he called out. The two boy soldiers stopped momentarily and then continued their bickering without an answer to his query. Philippe pulled himself out of his enclosure and stood up to his full height to stretch before he ventured toward his comrades. But he found suddenly both boys pointing their guns at him at waist level. Their stances identical, both were simultaneously menacing and comical. "Hey! Hey — what's this?" the young Frenchman asked, putting up his hands to show he was still friendly and unarmed. "What's going on, my friends? What's the purpose of the guns?"

It was Thao who answered, first in his dialect, then slowly in French. "That guitar, where is it?" Philippe opened his eyes in wonder.

"The guitar? It's in my tent, of course. What's wrong with the guitar?" Then he remembered the sound that had emanated from it which had sent them undercover several hours before. "Do you want me to get it?"

"Yes. Wait. No, Analu will get it. I want you to come here closer to me, and keep your hands up." Analu grabbed Philippe by the arm and spun him around and placed the barrel of his sub-machine gun into his back. He walked him abruptly over to Thao and then left them to open the flap of the canvas tent. Philippe kept his hands in the air, but cried out.

"Wait, please, don't damage the guitar. It's just a guitar... nothing more! It was my mother's, it was made by a friend in Canada. I swear — it is nothing more than a guitar!"

"We are not so sure. We believe it is a spying machine. And you must be a spy of France, or the U.S.A. government. You are under arrest!" Thao forcefully pushed Philippe to the ground so his knees and forehead hit the dirt before his hands could brace his fall. The light was just beginning to break through the canopy of trees and the two captors were surprised by the amount of blood that flowed from the fallen prisoner's head. He remained recumbent as the two soldiers fell back into their dialect and continued to argue over what to do next. After some time, Philippe slowly sat up and removed his khaki shirt and held it to his head as he applied pressure to the wound. The other two ceased their arguing and stared at their dusty boots. Neither would lift their head to see their handiwork.

"Eh, look here, I will bring the guitar out and show you. There's nothing to be afraid of. There is no radio or spying device. I do not work for the French or the U.S. government. It just plays its own music when it feels like it. I didn't think you could hear it. Most people cannot."

The two stood fast and eyed their prisoner sheep-ishly without a word. Philippe felt lightheaded and nearly vomited, but he steadied himself and sat for another few minutes. He noticed in the corner of his eye that neither of his captors raised their guns as he slowly gathered himself up and lumbered toward his tent. He lifted the canvas flap and peered in. The guitar was in the farthest corner where he had laid it last night in the dark. He fumbled with the clasp. It fell open and he was able to draw out the instrument with his one free hand while the other continued applying pressure to his head. When he exited the tent, the morning was well and truly upon them and in the light of day everything seemed calm and less frightening.

His captors were mere boys, probably a year or so younger than he, and they stood now rather cowed and shaken. Neither one of them had ever beaten anyone. They had each fired a gun twice during training — anything more and it would have been considered a waste of bullets. Several times they had seen bruises and blackened eyes when a boy was misbehaving and one of the camp leaders had to punish him, but they had not seen so much blood pouring from a wound, much less from a foreigner's head. They were frightened that they might have killed him with the single blow which would have caused an international crisis. Even they knew it would have been a major incident.

Philippe approached them now with the shining guitar in one hand and the blood-soaked shirt in the other, and they both began to see the levity of the situation. They had been alarmed by a simple musical instrument and had barely slept because of it. Philippe found a tree stump and crouched down on it with the guitar, plucking out a slow melody as he did it. It was a Jacques Brel tune from a movie that might have recently shown in a cinema in Vientiane. But both boys were from the countryside and movies would have been a luxury they never enjoyed. Philippe now gestured for them to approach him — without the guns. Before long, he was playing by ear and picking out tunes from their childhood that they sang or hummed for him, songs their mothers and grandmothers sang to them when they were very young, before all this war, before a gun was ever strapped over their shoulders. Always they shuddered when they heard the sound of gunfire in the far distance and the occasional explosion.

"Have you heard of that terrible bomb? Called 'na-palm'?" Analu asked calmly.

"No," Philippe answered. "What is it?"

"It is worst kind of bomb. It makes you burn, choke and die. Sometime even make terrible windstorms up to 100 kilometers an hour. They drop them from airplanes. If you hear an airplane flying too low, you run into that hole and you stay there for four days." He pointed to a large metal plate on the ground. "Do not come out or you will die." Philippe looked ominously at the plate and imagined himself in a coffin for four days. It was the first time that he felt un-heroic. Analu and Thao laughed nervously at the sudden somber air their new comrade invoked. They themselves had experimented with staying in the underground cellar with the gas-masks on, but were only able to withstand less than two days.

With fists clenched tight Joël sat impassively on the seat of the military cargo plane ascending slowly above the jungle on the northern edge of what had been known for nearly a century as the Golden Triangle. The opium trade continued to churn mightily like the roiling waters of the Mekong River delta here, and at this ancient crossroads the fringe elements of the black market trade gave rise to independent gun-runners — another black market that fomented revolutionary zeal, fueled the endless fighting, and financed the mercenaries paid to do their worst. Night was falling fast and quickly blackening the orange and navy hues of the setting sun through the small window of the aircraft. Not far below was his only son, whom he'd left with two unknown and questionable guerrilla soldiers who could easily have executed him without hesitation in this wild jungle. Joël had marveled at the young man's complete lack of fear or sense. He was so adamant that he stay and learn the lessons of the jungle.

"I am required to learn the life of the revolutionary," Philippe had argued. "What good am I to come this far and not take the opportunity to live the life and learn what needs to be learned?"

"What is it you hope to learn?"

"How to show my true worth in all this change that needs to happen! I must, if only for a few days or weeks, learn to fight and be a man."

"Don't be a fool."

"I am not a cool-headed diplomat like you, *mon père*. I cannot simply stand back and hold my toe in place always behind the Party line like you. It matters not to you whether that line is Conservative, Fascist, or Communist!"

"That is enough. You will come as I say, Philippe. This war is not ours to fight. Neither France nor the United Nations sanctions this rebellion, and I will not let you sacrifice your life to this wretched fighting — no matter how stubborn or naive you are. Your mother, first of all, would never forgive me."

"Please leave Maman out of this. No, actually she would be on my side. She was resistant at first when she knew I was attending the rallies and organizing meetings back in Paris, but soon she realized that for me to take a stance and work for something I believed in would be more valuable than any diploma I could earn at University. I am a doer, Father. I need to use my hands and my heart to do what is right. I cannot stand by passively while others fight for change and struggle for the rights of the workers."

Joël's patience was truly tested at these last words and he felt the blood vessels at his temples throb and threaten to burst. But he eventually capitulated because of his own desire to imminently flee the scene. He was also honor-bound to allow his son to become a man — it was true that this young man had all the traits of a leader, and not a follower — the traits, he had to silently admit, of an officer or warrior, unlike him. After the endless wait for the delayed airplane, Joël had let his humiliation creep beneath his skin and scorch his very pride. It was the impossibility of the son's demand that made the diplomat feel both surreally detached and incensed at the same time. He had never felt so ambivalent and out of his depth during his entire career.

As he boarded the plane for Bangkok, he knew his rash decision would have consequences at some point. But he was a man in a hurry to make headway. As he sat down on his small cushioned seat, he pulled from his pocket the picture of Mae Anh at the entrance of the University standing proud next to her hero-like husband. In that picture he imagined his own features on the face behind the wire-rimmed spectacles. The professor's shoulders were as square as his own, but he was not nearly as well dressed, and his heart dropped ever so slightly.

Just prior to departure there had been a quickly worded follow-up cable from Paris about Dr. Anh. Apparently, it was now Mae who was in jeopardy. She was under arrest by Communist soldiers near the Hanoi General Hospital because of her connection with the very project for which he was here in the former colony. It did not come as a surprise to him that she was somehow involved. Their lives had been intertwined from the very start. He would find a way to get word to her that he was here in her country now to both secure her freedom and to ensure her efforts were not in vain.

Then all at once the plane shuddered with a violent rumble as if it were a truck hitting a rut in a pocked back-country road. As it began to pitch and roll, Joël gripped the arm of his seat and called out to the pilot, who was now frantically reaching across his instrument panel with both hands hitting switches in a vain effort to regain control of the craft.

"What was that?" he called, straining toward the cockpit as smoke began to waft up from its under-carriage. "What's happening?" he demanded.

"I'm not sure," the pilot called back. "Everything was normal just now." Abruptly, another round of enemy fire hit its target and the plane dipped precipitously on its right wing in mid-air. "Sir, that could only be gunfire from below in the jungle. I think I saw flashes just then. We are losing altitude quickly!"

"But we are a diplomatic plane," Joël replied impertinently, too exasperated to be afraid. "We should be immune from enemy fire! Get me on the radio to base — now!"

The tops of the trees were already within striking range before the radio dispatch could be sent and there would have been little that the base command could do even if they were reached. As the plane continued to plummet both men signed the holy cross before them and braced for the inevitable.

Mae Anh heard the news from a prison guard one morning three months into her captivity and she refused to believe what she heard. She had been held as a prisoner with no outside contact, served a small ration of rice and old vegetables three times a day, and allowed no exercise or access to any news or information. Thin and weak from starvation, she offered little resistance to the guards who kept her there only because they heard no further instruction. She was considered a counter-revolutionary of the worst kind, locked in a windowless room, and only given permission twice a day to use the toilet or to freshen herself in a small basin. She pleaded with them to allow her to at least use her skills as a doctor to administer to the wounded back at her operating hospital during the day, but even that rationale made little difference. They kept her hostage and tortured her with inactivity. But one morning a new guard who had replaced her usual one came to release her to the bathroom and quietly commented, "The French government is demanding that you be released in exchange for the persons who shot down the airplane."

"What airplane?" she demanded, surprised by this sudden piece of news. "What airplane? Did someone shoot down a French airplane?"

"Oh, haven't you heard? The Vietnam government they say they found the fighters responsible for shooting down the foreigner's plane in Laos, across the border from Chiang Rai. One French official and a Thai pilot were killed — everybody very tense for the past two and half weeks. No one told you?"

"No, they have kept me here like an animal in a cage for three months. I demand my right as a citizen! Let me go!"

"Whoa, whoa, sister, stay calm! I am only doing what I am told. They demanded your release, but my leaders they say they don't want the shooter. They say probably one of those drug smugglers — protecting their territory. Not one of ours. Those French have no right coming here anyway to interfere with our movement. Those doctors should stay in their own country and mind their own business!"

"The French doctors are here to do what our own doctors will not... or cannot do!" she fired back. "Our people and the people of Thailand have lost their way. This revolution is a big mistake and will be the end of Vietnam!" At this last cry, the soldier's dark hand flew up and struck the doctor across the left side of her face as he shoved her forcefully back into her prison.

"Shut up! The Revolution is all about getting rid of stains like you, who don't care about the People. You and your fancy doctor title! Don't you think the People know that doctors are just as dangerous as those fancy professors who only try to tell one side of history and make Vietnam look weak and poor? I hear your husband was one of those they sent out to the countryside and committed suicide... so weak. The People will make Vietnam strong again. Not doctors or professors like you."

Mae Anh remained on her right hip on the floor where she had fallen and stayed there bruised and stunned while her captor slammed the door and turned the key. She felt sick to her stomach and vomited until she could no more. Her temperature soared for the rest of the week and she could eat nothing. On the fifth day, the French government again demanded her release and at last her captors agreed to release her to be delivered to a nearby hospital. As she was being transported Mae Anh learned the name of the diplomat who had coordinated the refugee camps. The attending doctors assumed it was dehydration that made her lose consciousness. After nearly three days she regained consciousness only to be overcome with tears and delirious with grief for nearly four days.

Philippe became worried only after the military plane failed to return after one week past due. His father had said he would send for him in a week's time and after the extra week passed, he began to wonder what had befallen him. Food and supplies had been delivered earlier that week and he had hidden himself well inside the interior of the jungle while the drop was being coordinated. Thao and Analu acted as nonchalantly as they could under the circumstances. Thao, however, did ask casually as the pilot was checking the plane's landing gear after its rough touchdown whether there was any news about the diplomat who visited with his son a fortnight ago.

"Haven't you heard the plane was shot down on the way back from here? Don't know if it was one of ours or an opium runner. No one has claimed the deed. Right now the French government is blockading any food, guns, or supplies being brought into this country and the Thai government is about to join them. We may not be able to continue to drop the food here any longer."

"Is that so? Then we would like to return home." Thao and Analu looked into the older man's eyes and saluted. "Can we ask, Comrade, that you take us back on this plane?"

"Well, with this food and both of you, the plane will not take off."

"Then, let's leave the food behind. The animals will eat it."

"No, they wouldn't!" The older man laughed. "Even monkeys have better taste than for these hard loaves and dried meat! Okay, help me unload these sacks and then get your things; we will leave while there is still light."

Philippe heard the airplane take off shortly after it arrived and he stayed hidden until the sound of its propellers faded with the dying light. When he returned to the camp it was in near complete darkness and he knew immediately that his comrades had deserted him. He scanned every corner of the camp with his torch and found only a large sack of food provisions left in a heap beside the tin shack. In the bag he found a quickly scrawled and rather cryptic note from Thao or Analu, with no explanation for their sudden disappearance, but the terrible news that his father was dead. Philippe's heart sank deep into his soul. He reared from the note, as if some invisible fist pummeled him in the chest. In a daze he pitched his tent by the dimly lit glimmer of dusk above the canopy of the jungle, and fumbled with the flint until he lit a small fire. The haunting cries of the monkeys in the distance were no comfort.

He never in his young life felt so utterly alone. His head throbbed with the shock of his father's death as he paced back and forth from his tent to the fire, to the shack where his former campmates had slept, and back to his tent again, repeating this route for nearly three hours, remembering his father fearless and strong, mostly at odds with him but always fair. He found he could not eat. With the last bit of his flagging energy, he finally sank down beside the flickering embers of the dying fire and wept until he fell into a deep undisturbed sleep devoid even of the strains of the music from within that usually burnished his slumber with their gentle melody.

Lorraine felt the panic in her heart as soon as she received the telegram from the French embassy in Québec. She had sensed that her husband and son were somehow in danger several days before the message arrived. The heaviness in her heart was palpable. It had been less than a fortnight since she had returned and she was only just beginning to enjoy the old familiar rhythms of the city. At the residential hotel in the heart of Old Town where she was staying, she had begun to get her bearings again. She was starting to make plans to find a large property in the countryside on the edge of the city where she could move her elderly parents to be closer to her. Glen and Sylvie-Marie were now in their mid-eighties and not so sure on their feet. The old rambling house where they still lived was drafty and the shop had been sold to a young entrepreneur several years ago before it was taken over by Les Marchands. The daughter's entreaties to uproot them were met with great opposition. Not a week after Lorraine's return, however, Sylvie-Marie slipped in the backyard while hanging out the laundry and broke her hip. That, they all knew, was the beginning of the downward slide.

Her mother was still in the hospital when Lorraine received the telegram from Paris saying she must pack her bags immediately, and a limousine would be at her hotel the following morning to take her to the airport where she was expected on the official state flight to Thailand. When she landed in Chiang Rai and alighted from the empty plane, she knew it was going to be the most difficult day of her life. She realized something terrible had happened but no one was willing to apprise her of the situation; neither the limousine driver nor the air staff seemed to have any news, and the telegram itself was uninformative.

Now she was sitting at a long table with a small cohort of French officials who had flown in themselves only a few days prior. When Lorraine entered the room directly from the tarmac, all the men stood up, but none would look up to meet her eyes. She recognized an older gentleman amongst their ranks, Mr. Henri Dansereau, one of Joël's superiors from the Paris desk. She had met him several times at official functions and now he was moving toward her as she arose from her chair.

"*Condoléances,*" he began. "*Je suis trop désolé, Madame…*"

"Please, Henri, what has happened to Joël? What has happened to my husband? Where is my son?"

"Your husband, I am afraid, is dead."

Lorraine reeled on her feet in shocked silence for a few seconds.

"Madame, we are very sad…"

"No. It cannot be!"

"His airplane was shot down."

Lorraine saw the room blur in her vision and she collapsed against the older gentleman. He guided her carefully back into her chair as a doctor came to her aid. She quickly came back to her senses and began to shake her head in defiance, until at last choked-back sobs broke through her wall of denial.

"I am so sorry. We did not know for some time, but finally last week, the Thai government was informed by some insurgents and they contacted us. I flew here as quickly as possible, but it was several days before they would allow us to collect the bodies ... *excusez moi* ... your husband's remains."

"And, Philippe," she asked through her tears. "Is he dead too?"

"Your son," the older man replied tentatively. "He is missing..."

"What?" she cried, looking up at the older gentleman. "He is not dead? Where is he? Tell me!" This news seemed to bring some hope to the distraught mother.

"We are still negotiating with the Thai government to get any information they have on his whereabouts. He has not been seen since he left with Monsieur de Vogel-Larochette on the plane several weeks ago."

"Then he has been missing for nearly a month! If he is still alive, he must be in grave danger, or injured!" With this realization, she began to sob once again.

"Madame, your husband and the pilot were recovered after a long drawn-out negotiation that ended in a bloody battle where the responsible party was eventually captured and the bodies recovered. But we have no information on your son. It is a mystery."

Lorraine looked up through her tears at the man who gave the news, then looked at the others around her. They shook their heads in sympathy but none spoke.

"Where do you think he is? Why is he missing?"

"We are not certain at this moment, Madame. But we have heard from one of the doctors that he may have gone to spend some time in the interior to do research before being picked up again and returned. But, unfortunately, the mission was aborted when your husband's plane was shot down. We know nothing more. We are doing all we can to request the Thai government's cooperation. But it is very tricky. We are in deep negotiations with the Communist forces for the release of a prisoner in Hanoi. Joël was working on this when the plane was shot down. It is a delicate situation."

Later that evening, Lorraine was visited by Dr. Morens, the only one among the group who knew Philippe. Sophie told Lorraine of her attempts to gather a search party for the lad, but the Thai soldiers were not sympathetic, and the French diplomat who had arrived to replace Joël was useless. But now Joël's boss was here and his widow as well, so as a team the two women pleaded with the French officials to begin the search for her son in earnest. After Lorraine attended to the terrible business of identifying her husband's charred remains for them to be flown to Paris for interment as a war hero, Henri Dansereau gave his condolences once again and reassured them that he was trying his best, but the situation remained incredibly tenuous. Apparently, the Communist authorities were now demanding the release of Joël's murderers in exchange for the doctor in Hanoi. Paris did not feel this was an even trade since the doctor was a Vietnamese civilian, while Joël was a French government official, not to mention distant royalty.

Their only recourse now was to rally the coterie of physicians into an ad hoc search and rescue team. Sophie beseeched her colleagues as Lorraine sat beside her with quivering hands covering her tear-stained face — to lose a husband and not know the whereabouts of an only son deep inside a sniper-infested jungle? What, she asked the reluctant men, did they leave their comfortable homes in France and Belgium to become? Was it not their duty as husbands and fathers themselves to come to the aid of an unfortunate family? But the doctors knew that without the cover of the soldiers they would simply be moving targets for the mercenary snipers. They felt their medical skills would be wasted in this risky endeavor. Couldn't they wait for assistance from the Thai government, once the negotiations for the exchange of hostages were resolved?

When news of the downed plane first reached the camp, panic struck in the hearts of every single person in the entourage, in particular, Sophie, who had had a premonition in the form of a dream two days before the news arrived of the fate of the diplomat and the pilot. When two bodies and not three were finally allowed by the mysterious and ruthless perpetrators to be retrieved by the French government from the plane wreckage, she felt an ominous portent of things to come. Philippe had told her he would be away for a mere week or so, and no more. Sophie was obligated to tell the officials but the information was not taken seriously at first.

The arrival of Madame de Vogel-Larochette, however, changed the tune of the French officials, and they were prepared to negotiate with the Thai military but found themselves in a political stand-off. Apparently, the Vietcong officials had already warned the Thai government that the French doctors were in violation of their sovereignty by coming to the aid of the "traitors" fleeing across into their borders illegally. They demanded the deportation of the doctors immediately, and closure of the refugee camp. They also threatened the execution of a certain Dr. Mae Anh, who was obviously one of the French government's spies in Hanoi. When Lorraine heard the name Mae Anh and heard the danger the woman was in, she felt a certain sensation in the back of her neck, as if Joël himself were speaking to her and urging her to take action. Certainly she would make it her mission to not only find her son, but also come to the rescue of this long-suffering woman whom her husband had been forced to abandon so many years ago. As negotiations continued with the Thai military authorities, weeks went by and the two women grew closer and maintained their resolve to initiate action. They would find the young man if it was the last thing they ever did on this Earth.

Lorraine and Sophie sat together in their shared tent that night huddled over a large map spread out on one of the low beds. An oil lamp was the only source of light and the two women strained their eyes to make out the hairline trails marked on the faded chart. A small red "X" marked the spot where Joël's plane was discovered. They were surprised to find the location was actually across the border inside Laos, and not closer to Chiang Rai. It had taken them nearly two weeks to secure this map, and as they surveyed the area surrounding the "X" their certainty that the young man would be somewhere in this vicinity increased.

"Perhaps he was injured in the crash, but not fatally, and wandered off into the jungle?" Lorraine suggested.

"In hot pursuit by insurgents and drug runners," the other woman continued. Neither woman expressed her fear in words, but the flickering of the oil lamp reflected the ominous mood. "I heard just this morning from one of the medics that an explosion was heard shortly after your husband's body was retrieved. They do not know who was responsible. Possibly the C.I.A. It was discussed on Radio France."

"A bomb?! It's so close to villages? Would they do that?"

"All governments are hypocrites, no less. No negotiation with terrorists they claim. Yet now they act like one themselves. It's a travesty!"

"Dear God, I hope my Philippe was not still in that area!" Lorraine began to cry again, the fourth time this day. The friend drew her close and let the widowed mother express her deep pain.

"I've got it!" Sophie suddenly exclaimed. "All we need is a helicopter and a pilot. We can put together a collection of funds between the physicians here to hire a pilot! Why didn't I think of this earlier? Why not, eh? A helicopter perhaps could be procured from the Red Cross or United Nations? Do you have a friend at the United Nations? Joël must have known some of these people?"

Lorraine slowly dried her tears and blinked until her eyes cleared. "I know a family back in Canada who had five brothers and four pilots amongst them. The oldest four trained as bomber pilots in Europe during the war, and after they came home, including one in a coffin, the third brother became a helicopter pilot for the regional news and weather station, as well as for the Primary Reserve, if I'm not mistaken. The youngest brother was a l-..." she stopped herself, "... a dear friend, although I have not seen him in many years," she continued. "I could perhaps ask his brother to come?"

"That sounds like the best course of action, Lorraine. Perhaps our government could also contact the RCAF. We will still have to hire a helicopter locally. That may prove to be more difficult in the end than hiring your friend to come to Philippe's rescue. You must contact him immediately. Let us go now to see if we can send a telegram to Canada — tonight!"

Bernard was surprised to find his brother and sister-in-law at his cabin door one summer morning. Clutched in his brother's hand was a telegram. Both wore a worried smile on their faces. He ushered them in and they sat down at his kitchen table as he turned his back to prepare a pot of coffee. He was not used to company and it took him several minutes to locate two additional cups.

"Bernie," Callum began, walking across the room to face his younger brother. "Don't worry about us; we aren't here for coffee. We're here to ask you something important." He paused for a moment for his brother to register the words and nod in understanding. "Well, it's urgent actually, and very unexpected. I got a call from the Reserve boss this morning." He continued, pausing again. "According to the coordinator, there is an urgent need of a helicopter pilot out in Thailand right now. A call from one of our own apparently — a wife of a diplomat." He waited for the younger brother to nod. "The diplomat and his son were on a special mission several weeks ago and their plane was shot down by insurgents over Laos. The father is dead but the son is now missing. Neither the Thai nor French governments want to send out one of their own for a search party for him."

Bernard sat without expression listening and reading his brother's lips.

"The mother is Canadian, from around here, and she is sure he is alive, but no one is willing to go into the jungle to find him."

Bernard nodded.

"This is where I, or you, come in. The mother has asked for help from the Canadian government, but they don't want to do it either, at least not for another two weeks. She thinks her son would be killed by then, and is begging someone to come. She is willing to pay privately and will supply the helicopter through the I.R.C. or U.N. I will go if you cannot, Bernie, but under the circumstances, we believe..." and here he paused and looked at his wife, "...that you might be the better person to go. You're a better helicopter pilot than I. And besides, Missy's wedding is in two months and it's too risky for me..."

Bernard put up his hand at that moment and spoke out loud. "Stop right there. Tell me where and how, and I will go tonight."

His brother Callum had been an excellent instructor from the very beginning. When Bernard returned from Québec City that New Year's Day in 1959, he seemed to all his brothers a changed man. His heart was no longer fixed to his woodworking. Not a word was spoken of the cause of the heartache, and like all the rugged silent men of the Canadian woods, they carried on as if nothing was amiss. Bernard closed his shop for three months and sat silently on his veranda, staring at the frozen lake until it thawed and cracked, and again jumped with trout.

Aidan and Callum had come with their wives and children for their usual Easter weekend fishing jaunt on Lake Aylmer, but Bernard was not in his usual spirits and the boat obviously had not been used since the previous spring. With some coaxing from the nieces and nephews, Bernard found his fishing lines from the shed and swept the damp leaves from the boat hull. When the uncle returned at dusk with the tired but happy children, both brothers and wives knew it was time for Bernard to find a woman who would make his cabin a home. Callum's wife, Jane, sent two of her favorite nursing assistants over to help him with his food shopping the following week, but they came back with smiles but no invitations to return.

The day a recruiter asked Callum if he knew of any men that might be interested in becoming a Reserve pilot, he knew straight away his younger adopted brother Bernie was the perfect candidate. It was 1962 and North American involvement in Vietnam had begun. Canada had no conscription but the Reserve was on constant alert for possible mobilization. Helicopter pilots were needed urgently and although his brother was deaf, he possessed intelligence, a calm demeanor, attention to detail, bravery, and a sense of altruism that nothing could waiver.

A geriatrics nurse at the local hospital, Jane had heard of a new experimental cochlear device that would make it possible for him to hear sufficiently to pilot a plane. Bernard agreed to have a special frequency radio device and headset manufactured for him. This, with the especially made earphones all pilots wear as a matter of course, suited the use of the new technology. For Bernard it was a turning point. Callum knew that this would be a way for his younger brother to serve his country despite his disability, particularly as he could not serve during the previous wars. As Callum guessed, Bernard took to the skies naturally like an eagle to flight. There was no turning back. He seldom returned to furniture making, for he enjoyed the flight work and enthusiastically took odd jobs in mail delivery, woodland fire emergencies, and the occasional search and rescue mission. He remained with the Primary Reserve along with Callum and anticipated his first mission in Vietnam for the RCAF, but it never came. His hearing impairment was still an obstacle which grounded him, even though technically he was allowed to remain in the Reserve. Callum's request now, was like the answer to a long-sought question.

Lorraine did not sleep for a moment the night before, but was ready and wide-eyed to meet the plane as it arrived onto the pre-dawn tarmac. She had received word from the Canadian Embassy that a pilot was being sent by the RCAF Primary Reserves and was arriving via a special air cargo plane the next day. A helicopter, however, would not be available for another several days. The bureaucracy was swift with personnel, but equipment was harder to come by. A helicopter, she was told, was being secured via the International Red Cross, which had the proper markings to allow it into enemy air space without fear of being ambushed. This convention, however, was not guaranteed and few pilots would have been willing to undertake the dangerous task.

When the helicopter pilot stepped off the plane and onto the tarmac, Lorraine was disbelieving. She watched from the window of the terminal and forced her forehead hard against the glass trying to get a closer look to see if her eyes were not deceiving her. It was unexpected to say the least and she was not sure if it was indeed he, but her heart leapt into her throat and she choked back tears as she rushed for the door and descended the stairs toward him.

Bernard saw Lorraine approach him from across the tarmac as he disembarked. She seemed in a restrained rush and it was a long moment before he could clearly recognize the familiar heart-shaped face. The sad but radiant smile was hard to miss. Without a word he caught her up in his arms, and for a moment they were lost in time. All the years, all the pain washed away in that brief moment of reconciliation. He sought out her tear-soaked face and kissed her on the eyes while she wept. There was nothing between them that could not be brought back to health and goodness with this kiss. There was nothing, Lorraine felt that could not be done now that he was here. But she struggled with the truth held so long inside her closed heart. Her love and the long-held secret devotion she had to him was the treasure inside a long buried chest, hard to fathom once in the light of day. She finally resolved to tell him the truth only when — or if — their son Philippe was ever found. It was only fair.

8

WALK-TALL (SOLPETRIÈRE), 1881–1886

While others merely engaged at one level of reality and consciousness, Father Jacob straddled two worlds continually. The priest spoke directly with God. His was a direct line to The Divine. Father Jacob avoided excessive contact with his niece on most days because the delicately balanced scales of his mind were easily disturbed. A finely tuned spiritual receptor that balanced the constantly disequalizing forces in nature and the universe allowed Father Jacob to receive simultaneous messages from natural and supernatural sources — from differing transmutations of time and reality.

This man of the cloth, although bound by his allegiance to God and his will to do His daily work, struggled tumultuously in a super-existential limbo. His inability to separate the real from the supernatural — or rather, his ability to engage the two simultaneously while appearing to be on the plane of normal, material existence — could easily be seen as some kind of insanity. Luckily he kept it mostly to himself and his extremely small coterie of confidantes, namely Madame Lowell.

From the time he was a young boy working the fields of his father's farm in Haute-Provence, Jacob Sébastiani had a certain knowing.

"*Nous sommes partout ... pas plus, rien de moins.* We are everywhere ... no more, no less." It was a silent Gregorian chant in his mind as he scraped the fertile soil with a steady plow and threw out seeds with an arcing wheel of an arm, as if he were extending a perpetual blessing over the land in an anointed sermon of toil which flowed as a perpetual monologue he shared with no one in particular.

"*Nous sommes tout le monde ... partout dans le monde. Rien de plus, pas moins.* We are everyone ... everywhere. No more, no less. Life is not a straightforward plain ... no linear pattern, simply from A to B, and on to C and inevitably ending us up at Z, where we are then inevitably tossed by angels into heaven or hell. Progression is immaterial, time relative." For Jacob, life ebbed and flowed into complex woven conundrums of interrelatedness, of stops and starts and intervening presents transforming over and into elaborate and repeating futures.

He believed that at all times man existed with one foot in heaven, another in hell, and everywhere in between and within lay his soul.

"There lies the truth of God, where never an end will be or a beginning hailed — no beginning because everything has already begun. At the all-knowing turning point of existence, eternity bellows in a great exultation; turbulent circularity increasing metamorphosis — the antithesis of time. Would Earth exist if it He did not create it to support us? Why would He then create time to confine us? Earth contains within it neither designation nor destination. Connectivity to the larger continuum is embodied in it — Earth is beholden to it."

For his lifetime of convoluted and confounded wonderings, Jacob received answers from God himself, transmitted to this inner ear from the trees that grew around the farmhouse in the Lubéron, in the clumps of upturned soil, through whispered triumphs heralded from the brilliant summer skies. He received them in the half-lit barn, the scaffold half-creatures of living and past, souls not quite completed and not yet evolved. Meanwhile his father simply tried to beat the autism out of him. His punishments did eventually succeed in silencing the boy as Jacob eventually taught himself to distinguish conversations from the material world from communication during transmigrations of souls from other times, places, and levels of consciousness.

By the time he reached adolescence Jacob eschewed contact with other people of his age. The exception was Adrienne, his twin sister who protected him and respected his articulated fantasies of other worlds. Until the summer when they were twelve, nearly thirteen, and Jacob's feverish and boiling-over mind conversed with an unseen ghost who instructed him to force himself upon her. He did not recognize this act as an abhorrent trespass, nor his sister's sudden and intense aversion to him. For Jacob, yesterdays and tomorrows were inconsequential, spirits immaterial.

The siblings had found a mutual purpose, however, when their father brought home a new wife, like a stray cat who eventually took over the household. To escape the avaricious chiding of their unwanted stepmother, brother and sister both eventually escaped to the hills and mountains and the embrace of the monastic life. The father was not sad to lose both his children to houses of God. With a new wife, he felt he was finally blessed after so many years of loneliness and hardship. But when his new baby died in infancy and, following another pregnancy, his second wife died in childbirth, the new baby also succumbing after two weeks without sufficient nourishment, Arnaud Sébastiani fell into a stupor and eventually lost his failing farm in a drunken gambling bet that same year. When his father was found by the farm help hanging in his barn by a bullock rope, the son already knew because his father had paid him a visit offering unwanted advice from the other side. After some time the young man left the Trappists and journeyed to Canada as a missionary priest in the new country. Eventually he became the resident pastor of a new parish in Solpetrière.

When he inherited his niece's welfare, the letter he received via the Catholic archdiocese offices in Canada, written by Father Pascal, roused his sense of duty to his beloved, now deceased twin sister Adrienne. But the sense of obligation did not arise immediately, as the responsibility seemed somewhat below what he believed to be his exalted, higher calling. He did, however, consult with his trusted housekeeper, the well-meaning Amalie Lowell, in one of his rare earth-bound moments, who helped him see the way to accepting this responsibility, and she agreed that together as a team — mostly led by her — they would act as legal parents to young Isabelle. Madame Lowell, however, saw herself as the mother to an entire parish, some one hundred children and their needy souls. Her sense of duty and her maternal instinct was unquestioned. The Swiss-French woman had been born in Lausanne, but her family moved to Québec when she was a child, and with her family's blessing, she had married an Anglican minister from Toronto and had two sons. She lost them all in a tragic accident one winter day when their steam train collided with a mule-train on a bit of muddy track. Miraculously she survived but her husband and seventeen- and fifteen-year-old sons were killed.

Several years later she received a letter from the complicated French priest whom her husband had known through their unusual nondenominational religious affiliation. He wrote to her in Toronto, extending his condolences, and said that he had received a message from her family which he wished to pass on to her. They arranged a meeting in Montréal several weeks later and when they met, she knew that he had a special ability to communicate trans-spiritually for he immediately channeled her youngest son whom she called "Pauley" even though his real name was Alexander. Pauley's message to his grieving mother was that it was time to move on; their father's spirit had returned to his native Scotland where he missed the mist on the moors, but he and his brother remained in Québec and were sorry to see her alone. She accepted Father Jacob's invitation to assist him in Solpetrière as soon as he offered it. Over the eight-some-odd years she had worked for him, prior to Isabelle's arrival, she had never felt anything but respect and compassion for the odd priest, and through him she kept up a regular communication with her sons.

The opportunity to be a mother again appealed to the middle-aged woman. The memory of her sons never left her; even as she cooked, cleaned, and organized baptisms, weddings, and other special sacraments, their strong young faces graced her every waking thought. She was a naturally maternal person, and although Father Jacob could never be a husband, she thought they would make a fine pair as parents.

When Isabelle finally arrived at the small, well-served parish, Madame Lowell could hardly contain her excitement. Father Jacob, however, had no illusions about being a father — other than as a priest — and had become painfully shy in the presence of his new charge. Particularly during the passage across the Atlantic, his equilibrium worked exceedingly well in attracting lost souls to the steamer ship, but the awkwardness he felt in the proximity of his niece was rather disconcerting, and on occasion he wished he had not accepted the challenge. So many souls! And most of them sad and still drifting on the open seas. They popped up on the ship's deck at all hours of the day and night, and even frequented the dining cabin when it was unpopulated by the living. Like a floating Tower of Babel, their multitude of languages confused the priest, but eventually the noises calmed down and funneled into a single ongoing monologue in his own language, a built-in simultaneous interpreter in his head that he had never experienced before, certainly not as effortlessly as he did now.

Madame Lowell took to her new role like a fish to water. Isabelle was the daughter she never had, and naturally she saw herself in the young girl. But during most of the early years of the girl's new frontier life, Isabelle remained in a forest of fog. Madame Lowell could never replace her Maman, and because she never had a father, only the elderly Father Pascal who seemed ancient even when she was a toddler, Father Jacob's role in her life was more as employer. Isabelle remained aloof, but helpful, and over time she grew to appreciate the efforts of Madame Lowell and her awkward uncle. As adolescence settled in, however, a new independence took over. It was subtly refined and finely tuned by fearlessness by the time she approached seventeen, a trait her uncle soon recognized as a vestigial inheritance from her mother.

Despite Madame Lowell's best efforts, Isabelle would mourn her mother's death for many years and lament the loss of the rich soul-preserving tenure of music her mother had granted her. Isabelle's life had been simple: do her mother and God's work, and the rest will be provided. But now, without a purpose in life to guide her, she found the beacons of her life on the headlands of her private sea journey by searching within herself. Opening her heart to God's messages had always been her path in childhood, but if His love was the greatest gift of all, it could just as easily be lost in the blink of an eye, just like the simultaneous loss of her mother and her bearings.

She felt the smallness of her existence, and a keen sense of isolation, and could not explore the forest around the camp without trepidation. Then she met the young brave who would change everything. Walk-Tall was a bridge to another world that existed beyond the forest. His entry into her life suddenly created an unfamiliar expansiveness; it opened the world out to her. It was a world of newness that made redundant the dull safety of her every day.

Their bond transcended time, place, age, culture, experience, and language and flourished in the infinitesimally small space between their kindred spirits. Isabelle and Walk-Tall had no conflicting loyalties between their desire to explore and be possessed of one's own freedom. Love found its way in the equalizing deaf-mute blindness of their silent physical gestures. Walk-Tall actually knew quite a few words in French and English, but during their first meeting he chose not to reveal this, and she, new to the New World, had been led to believe that the Red Man still spoke the savage's language, rather than the languages of Europe. On discovering this language bridge, their childish laughter gave way over time to feelings of intensity that were facilitated by a desire to communicate and to begin to truly experience life's reality. They drew joyfully together. Isabelle's talent for perspective and the fine details of the forest and the everyday found fodder in Walk-Tall's notions of the natural world and spirit life. An easy uncompetitive desire to improve drove their exploration.

After the first day of their meeting when Isabelle's horse brought her to the bend in the creek where he lay resting and then disappeared again, she thought only of her new friend. His softly chiseled face another beacon in her life, the image burned into her mind's eye like a lighthouse on a dark cliff — it was inviting, intriguing, beckoning, and strangely safe. The latter came as a surprise once again, so indelibly etched was the prejudice of her times. If his face was a map of the territories they explored, they were the waterways and the tall trees, the span of natural bridges, the expansive sky full of hawks, osprey, peregrines, eagles' nests on cliffs, and the clouds that fanned and cooled them at that great height. His laugh was the tripping of water over the rocks in the river running up to their knees, his hands the beautiful rough bark of the birch trees.

For every day they saw each other there were a hundred reasons to do it again. They agreed to meet every third day at the bend of the river throughout the summer, at the place where old gnarled cedar and spruces pummeled the ground and beat through it with roots like tentacles.

"I feel so alive exploring the forest with you," she said, treading lightly on the familiar path.

"Here," he replied pointing to another native plant she did not recognize. "It is one of the medicine herbs my mother uses for setting a broken bone. My brothers come home often needing that medicine."

"But not you?" she asked innocently.

"No, I am my mother's son — I am more careful!"

Together they searched her uncle's great botanical guide for the illustration to match the rounded leaves and she read them for him out of the book, which she carried secretly to their meetings.

They learned two, sometimes three or four, sets of words for every object they came across, and their expanding vocabulary was like growing fresh new skin every day, for how they changed in appearance to each other was an ever-evolving experience; with each interaction they could attach a new word, like infants new to the world testing new skills and exploring new phenomena as they experience them for the first time. Once words were ascribed to something they used them over and over again, with different intensity, in different contexts to see if the meaning was firmly imbedded, to ensure they were on the same path, soaring on the same thermal. They were birds destined to be mated for life, staying unabashedly close to one another, taking turns to lead and then follow. It was an emotional watershed for both.

They rode the old mare together on occasion and explored farther downstream and upriver, spotting signs of the oncoming season of the salmon run like it was a spring dance. It was not difficult, as two animals of the same species, to eventually fall in love. Though their playful partnership became unwittingly flirtatious, their innocence was preserved. But over the course of five years, a chaste but very emotional love blossomed between them in the quiet garden of their cedar creek-bed. Isabelle was sixteen and in her heart she knew that the stirrings she felt in the presence of his solid and grounded being were going to grow stronger by the day and at some point she would want to allow their powerful physical attraction to make them wholly one. He was more than a bridge to another world now; his *was* the world she wanted to live in.

It was on a late summer's day, as Isabelle admired the last elderberries of summer, that Walk-Tall dropped to his knees beside her and looked up at her as if he were her loyal hound, his brown eyes moist. Earlier this afternoon he had met her on the edge of the trees and they had walked together to another bend in the river, this one a much broader curve where the water spread out unusually wide and unnervingly quiet. The trees were different here as well; unlike the giant cedar, spruce, and fir of their familiar creek bed, this area was populated with willow, birch, aspen and poplar, along with the ubiquitous pine. In the midst of the lake-like expanse of wetland, a dome of twigs and leaves stood like a rotund castle encircled by a very large moat; it was a beaver lodge, its underwater entrances making entry impossible for any other animal.

Taking one hand in his, Walk-Tall led her down a separate trail to see the tightly interwoven beaver dam wall of logs, branches, twigs, and leaves which was nearly seven feet tall. In several undisturbed parts the dam was a solid bank, resisting a great force of water; some of the broken-down willow, poplar and birch had taken root, shooting up here and there forming a regular planted hedge, in some places so tall that herons built nests among the branches.

All at once Walk-Tall grasped Isabelle's arm and placed a finger over his lips and then pointed to a ledge on the dam where two of the dam builders abruptly popped up out of the water. They appeared to have surfaced to tend to some repair and suddenly seemed to be in a race against time, chattering and worrying over where to put which branch. They ignored the human pair who were admiring with awe their human-like antics as well as the impressively large amount of water they had successfully dammed with their concerted effort. They were a team, a mated pair, a couple. This was the shared future the two observers could have one day, if they cared to achieve it. The concept dawned first upon the young man. They had walked along together now hand in hand until coming to a large stand of white elderberries, their fruit fermenting on the forest floor and sending up an acrid sweet smell. Isabelle reached up to grab a few and unexpectedly saw her friend drop to his knees on the ground beside her, his liquid brown eyes seeking out hers, tears threatening to break their dams and fall to his cheeks.

"Walk-Tall! What is the matter? Are you sick?" she cried, trying now to raise him from his knees upon the forest floor.

"I am fine, Isabelle," he replied, surprised it seemed at his own tears. "You look so beautiful — your dress white, like your face, and so lovely in the sunlight." A wan smile now came over this face, replacing the sadness of the tears. She wasn't entirely clear what he had said because he used his own native language to express his feelings. But from the undeniable look of love in his eyes, she knew his confession would have been important, requiring the use of his native Iroquois instead of French or English, which was understandable. Then he continued in her language. "I am fine.

I feel a weakness in my knees. I am thinking how much I love you."

She laughed out loud and bent over to him, their lips meeting halfway as she leaned toward him, and he half raised himself. The kiss was perfect, calming the emotional tremor he felt in his heart, and melting away the nervous twinge she felt in her stomach when he had dropped to the ground. He rose fully to his great height, and held out his arms to her. They held onto one another in a full-bodied embrace that was filled with hope and a slight anticipation.

"Shall we go back now?" she finally said.

"Back to the creek?" he replied, hoping for another kiss.

"No, I mean, back to my camp. And you back to your family."

His eyes fell to the floor. "All right, of course," he replied in his language, an agreeable phrase she learned very early in their meetings years ago.

"Tell me," she said, turning away from his downcast eyes. "Would your family be happy that you are spending time with me?" The question was not said as a challenge, but it might have been seen to be. She hoped for a kind answer.

"I cannot say they would be happy about it. The mixing of our peoples has occurred for many generations," he replied diplomatically. "The life of the *Métis* is not very secure. They have no rights on either the Indian side or the European side. They have had a difficult time."

"I see ... "

"I cannot be sure of what my family would say if they knew I came to the forest to be with you!"

"Yes. I cannot tell my uncle either. I know he would not approve. He is a very religious man, you know."

Walk-Tall did not respond. He did not understand what the word "religious" meant, but he did not ask.

"Madame Lowell is really my guardian in many ways, but I think she might also be cautious about our friendship."

"She is like your mother."

"Yes. And what do you tell your mother — about where you are?"

"Oh, splitting maple trees with my tomahawk for sap!"

"Really? But you do not return with firewood, do you?"

"Sometimes I do after I leave you. There is a wonderful stand of maples just beyond your camp."

"That is very clever of you, perhaps I should help you, and take some back with me?"

"Yes, but that might cause some... what do you call that?

"Suspicion?" They both laughed nervously.

"But a *true* Mohawk, he would slit your throat and leave you here to be torn to pieces by bears." This grisly comment he said tenderly while stroking her neck as if it were a flower.

"Then I am most happy that you are your mother's son!"

"Yes, you are beginning to understand. You know I would never hurt you. I am a not a warrior like my brothers. I am the youngest in my family, and it is our tradition that the youngest does not have to become a brave if he does not need to. As you know, my family has not given up our land yet to move to the reservation; we are one of the few family clans that are trying to preserve our tradition in the face of you *intruders*."

She was taken aback at first, but knew he spoke the truth.

"I hope you don't really mean that," she cried.

"Although we have long ago moved out of our long houses and now live in timber houses like the White Man, I think the unhappy relations between the Iroquois Nation and the French are still very strained. We had many, many years of bloody wars between our peoples, particularly against my peoples — Seneca on my mother's side and Mohawk on my father's."

"Yes, I have heard these things said. It is a shame on our side, I believe."

"I think my mother would approve of it. The Seneca are great... how do you say it... philosophers? We Seneca observe the gentle world around us and constructed the medicine wheels of self-knowing and self-understanding to explain it, and to teach us how to live our lives. The Mohawk, however, only believed in war. I am my mother's son!"

"Yes, that is a good thing. The French have a philosopher named Jean Jacques Rousseau. I read his book from the library when I was younger. He believed that all people are born good — even you *savages*." The insult was returned and they now both laughed heartily.

When their mirthful laughter ended, a feeling of mutual calm came over them and they stopped briefly to kiss again. It was a gentle kiss, not as perfect as the earlier one, but rather brief and not quite satisfying. This inadequacy necessitated another union to achieve a more satisfying kiss. He sat her down on a soft patch of grass and kissed her deeply, his arms supporting her as they rolled together to the ground, his lips not leaving hers for a moment.

She was surprised at how soft and supple his lips were. They were full and dark but gentle it seemed, and soft as a baby's, not at all what she expected, but much better.

He kissed her and stroked her hair. Neither of them had ever felt so at peace, and yet so excited. In the distance the haunting cry of a pair of loons broke the silence.

"Ahhh, listen," he said excitedly, breaking away from the kiss to better hear their cry. "Listen to these wonderful birds. You know, they only nest in pristine lakes. They hide along the shores, or on small islands. They mate for life and lay one pair of eggs a year, at most. After hatching, they carry their downy little chicks on piggyback for the first three weeks of their life."

"It is so sweet. But that song... it is beautiful, but so sad, is it not?"

"No, not sad, just solemn... like the way I feel about you."

As they returned to their kiss, the silence was interrupted again overhead by a very different sound — the raucous squawking of geese in formation, reminding them that autumn had arrived and the great migration would soon commence. Winter was around the corner. Their previous winters had been difficult for private meetings in the forest. With the snow thick and difficult to travel through, and temperatures freezing, they could not meet as frequently as they would have liked. When the blizzards had stopped and they had not seen each other for several weeks, they grew restless and irritated at their separation. Reuniting again in the great blankets of snow, they no longer played like children. With their first kiss, it seemed suddenly they had grown into adults. Winter would be a real test of their patience.

Reaching the outskirts of the camp again, the lovers separated, reluctant to release each other. It was a bittersweet parting, but one so full of promise and unknowns. It would soon be a matter of loyalties and negotiations, but love always holds sway over demands of propriety, creating grand schemes for continuation in the face of obstacles, great denials, and the trials of miscommunication and mistrust. No soldier patrols the heart, nor can love be overprotected. They made a vow to bring their families together and if possible find a path to open and share their happiness with their loved ones.

In three days' time they met again. Isabelle rode Béatrice to the creek-side meeting place that day, and on the ride she lost her bonnet and her hair fell in auburn waves down her back as she rode into the clearing. Walk-Tall had never seen it that way, and the surge of desire he felt in seeing the deep burnished red color of her hair, like the rippling back feathers of a majestic eagle, was intoxicating. She trotted the old mare into her usual space, and straight away Walk-Tall leapt on the back of the horse and took the reins. He led them through a series of switchbacks, which the old nag did not like one bit. But he had brought the horse apples from his family garden and she appreciated the reward and made the effort. After the uphill climb they reached a summit. On the other side, a steep ravine fell away. Below, the cedars stood so high their tops nearly reached up to them, even as their roots disappeared into the dark of the forest floor.

Quickly the old mare trotted down to the bottom and there they came to a bend in another creek which bordered a large stand of giant, ancient cedars, their old gnarled roots reaching out of the earth like sea creatures. Walk-Tall swung himself over the side and led the horse to the water's edge for a drink, holding onto her harness as Isabelle slipped off her back. When the horse had drunk her fill, he led the mare to a sapling and tied her reins to it. He swung a woven brown striped knapsack off his shoulder and dropped it in the niche created by the great-grandmother of all the great cedars in this ring of trees. The ancient cedar was seven hundred years old at least, its girth nearly ten feet around and its height over fifty.

Walk-Tall opened his rucksack and removed a blanket. It was thick white cotton and emblazoned with a dark native design. He laid it out on the soft, ferny, and pine needle–bedded ground space between the arms and motioned for her to sit upon it. She sat down gingerly against the base of the giant feeling rather small and dwarfed by all its greatness, and leaned her elbow on one of its roots as if it was the arm of a chair. This soft landing was welcome after the calamitous ride up and over the ridge that left her a little sore. Never having experienced a ride like that before, she was relieved that it was over and they were now safely in the embrace of the old tree.

"'Old Grandma Tree,' I call this one." It became obvious to her that this place was one of his favorites.

"Do you come here often?" she asked with some amazement. It seemed so out of reach, so genuinely remote. Contemplating the distances, it was like the farthest reaches of her small world here in Canada.

"I used to come quite often with my brothers when we would go moose hunting. But we don't do that anymore. We don't have to. Now the caribou and moose come to us on our orchards and farms and we feed them instead of hunt them!" Not knowing if he was joking or whether this was true, she grew uncomfortable with the idea of coming up against a caribou, and a look of fright must have passed over her face. He sat quickly beside her and placed his arm around her.

"I'm sorry; I've frightened you," he continued. "Never fear, I have brought my hunting knife, so if we are stalked by deer or moose or caribou, I will protect you!" He laughed a light-hearted guffaw that put her at ease. His laughs were always genuine and showed his beautifully large straight teeth, gleaming white against his tanned skin, and her fears fell away, along with her reticence.

"You may kiss me then," she declared, parting her lips in a half-smile which brought a misty look to his dark eyes, like the day he knelt beside her under the elderberry bush and declared his love. Her wait for the kiss seemed too long, so she brought his head toward her lips with her hands, his thick hair tied in his usual long braids warm in her hand, the sparse collection of eagle feathers and wooden beads swaying rhythmically at the ends of a leather thong. Their kiss lasted so long that they both felt faint at the end of it. Its magic still worked its way in for some time after they detached. For hours they kissed and stared into each other's eyes. They listened to each other's heart beat against their ears.

They marveled at the calls of different birds chiming, replying, tooting, or scaring away predators from their nests. The cauldron of trees seemed to funnel all sounds, from the smallest beetle to the grandest birds of prey, down into the human-like embrace of the tree around them. He did not enter her domain, but they made love passionately, desperately, like bees busy with the discovery of their young love, swarming each other with kisses, caresses, and questions about the feeling of each sensation. Their new experiences were stacked on top of the next: the feeling of skin on skin, the softness of anatomy never familiar until now, the smell of hair, the scent of musky sweat on virgin territory. His eyes were like a barometer of his emotions, the windows into his soul; they became clouded when he was overcome with desire, and cloudier still when the woozy state of sexual delirium flooded his body. The release forced his eyes closed, but brought clarity to them later, like those of a hawk that has nailed his prey. But his love was nothing like a predator's strike; it was gentle but strong, fervent and grateful.

At home, it was Father Jacob, not Madame Lowell, who noticed the change in Isabelle as that autumn came to a close. She seemed brighter and happier and he could see a new spirit that followed her about. She went about her business in her usual way, efficient with the cleaning chores, generous with her time and attention to the needs of her uncle, Madame Lowell, and members of the parish who occasionally dropped by to request a private audience with the priest. The church had finally been completed after several more petitions to the Archbishop, and although it was never adorned or furnished to the level they would have wished for, nevertheless the job was done and Father Jacob was generally lauded for his Herculean efforts to bring about the conclusion of that great debacle to the satisfaction of most, if not all, of the community members.

Meanwhile, the niece continued to come and go as she pleased. The old mare had grown lean with the exercise she gave it; both girls became like new fillies, full of life once again, and galloping off into the woods to explore new territory. She often packed a small meal depending on the time of day it was when she was able to escape after completion of chores. Isabelle still occupied that small closet, for in the morass of church-building, the house itself was never extended as was announced on her arrival.

For the amount of time she spent in the room, its size never imposed upon her. She liked the close cocoon intimacy of it; it had made her feel safe in her first year in what felt like the vast interior of a frontier with no bounds. After the tight confinement of the sailing ships, it seemed palatial. And now, as winter was setting in at the end of her fifth year, the intimate closeness of the four walls was akin to the embrace of her lover; however, it could never replace it. She dreamt of his weight upon her, his smooth hairless stomach, hips, and thighs pressing down on hers, and the way his elbows kept his chest from crushing her as he laid kiss upon kiss on her face, neck, lips, and bared shoulders. All the while his arms encircled her, one diagonally beneath her back, and the other cradling her head against the solid surface of the forest floor; their horizontal waltz rotating in breath-taking sweeps, to the swing of their own heart-swelling music. With the first light snow they agreed that they would wait until the spring thaw — if they could wait that long — to make their love complete. She would be almost seventeen then and old enough to know a man; he would be nineteen and truly one. They would together approach their families for a truce of some kind and bring their love to the open air and let it fly freely with the eagles and peregrines, whose grace and beauty were the same hallmarks as their feelings for each other. The anticipation was sweet.

But they could not stay away for the duration of that interminable winter. Each week a desperate agreement was reached to meet the following week at the cedar. She came wrapped in Madame Lowell's wool coats and shawls, and he in layers of buckskin and cotton blankets. Their horses complied with a tolerance beyond the norm of the noble beasts, but it seemed their master and mistress's love and desire to be as one drew them into a cooperative truce that was rewarded regularly with dried apples, pumpkin skins, and much affection. Temperatures dropped below tolerable levels, but the lovers remained oblivious. The old cedar offered them the sanctuary of its cavernous and labyrinthine roots. Adding to this Walk-Tall brought blankets and hides to line the damp pine needle floor and together they wove pine and aspen branches together to form an intimate hut, like a large cradleboard hung with dream-catchers and Isabelle's knitted shawls. Isabelle and Walk-Tall inched toward the consummation of their love in a slow but steady dance whose finale was as thunderous as their beating hearts.

April brought the first early buds of spring and the lovers happily plotted an introduction of Walk-Tall to Father Jacob and Madame Lowell. As clergy and devout Christians, it could be expected that their Catholic charity would prevail over their prejudices, even if absolute approval could not be expected. Did she expect a battle? Would they put up a fortress of excuses and denials to break her heart? The day after Easter Sunday, which always brought a measure of goodwill to the faithful after an end to a long fast, was a window of opportunity, Isabelle surmised. She would prepare dinner as usual before she went out of doors, but she would prepare an extra place at the table. They spent the early afternoon together exercising the horses over the steep ridge, gathering pine-cones and logs for the fire. This was the day they would receive a sanction for their love and she would bring her special guest home to meet her guardians.

When they arrived at the camp, however, they found that Madame Lowell had fallen ill with a stomach upset and retired to her bed. That left Isabelle alone with Father Jacob at dinner to attempt the introduction, a possibility that struck a frisson of fear and nervousness into her heart. Madame Lowell was the intermediary between the uncle and niece; she was also the light of reason, while Father Jacob in his increasingly befuddled mind confused the real with the surreal without distinction. He would hold forth at the table rehearsing ad hoc sermons while they listened attentively, and then he would sit supping in absolute silence, punctuated occasionally with a murmur of something or other to someone they could not see or hear.

Although his spirits spoke to him regularly now at the dinner table, almost nightly in fact, Isabelle never quite got used to his mutterings. She dreaded the prospect of introducing her uncle to her unsuspecting suitor, without her ally present. She had a slim chance of winning Father Jacob to her side. Ultimately it was the uncle's decision whether he would bless their union or not, but the inevitable disaster of this first meeting could spell catastrophe for their overall plans. It would have been much preferable to garner Madame Lowell's support and approval first, and then rally together as a team to find a way to win the priest over with her direct recommendations. Father Jacob, after all, valued her judgments above all others when it came to most things relating to members of his congregation and the household, while it was his duty to look after their souls, *and* the other spare souls that never waited for a private consultation with the priest, arriving and interrupting at their invisible leisure.

Isabelle contemplated sending the young Indian home and rearranging a time to re-launch their campaign of acceptance, but decided against it, naively optimistic and impatient to bring her love for Walk-Tall into the open. Walk-Tall entered the dining room of the residence with Isabelle, and Father Jacob froze in his tracks. He muttered something incomprehensible and reeled around, turning his back to them. Together the young couple managed to get him to the dinner table before he collapsed and he sat staring at Walk-Tall from across the large oak dining table while they all ate their meals in absolute silence. It was then that Father Jacob left the table and entered his bedroom.

Father Jacob returned to the dining room where his niece sat anxiously at the rustic timber dining table, her back turned to him as he approached. Opposite her, the young scout watched, first benignly, then, rising up cautiously from his chair as the tall priest approached them, muttering menacing words in a low unrecognizable growl — words — or a name — unfamiliar to the guest. With his next step, the priest raised a revolver from the folds of his black cassock and fired a shot as the younger man stood up fully from his chair.

Taken by surprise but already on guard, Walk-Tall twisted his body as the shot rang out. The lead bullet pierced his body through the muscle at his waist, threw him back diagonally against a corner of his chair, and toppled him to the floor. The priest was now above him leaning over to fire another shot to ensure his demise, but the wounded young man, with a swift motion like a reflex, pulled out a hunting knife from beneath his buckskin vest and swiftly dispatched the priest through the heart as the second bullet tore through his thigh.

When Madame Lowell heard the gunshots ring out and the subsequent screams emanating from the other room, she came running as quickly as her stout legs could carry her. There she discovered the incredible mêlée at the dining table and ran immediately to Father Jacob, who lay supine on the floor with the large knife in his chest and the heavy pistol still in his hand. It took very little time for her to scan the room to find Isabelle crumpled on the floor cradling someone in her arms, to surmise that in his increasingly deranged state of mind her employer had caused a blood-bath. Nonetheless, she gathered up the priest in her arms as he laid bleeding, muttering and tossing his head in a delirium. Meanwhile, Isabelle supported her lover in her arms, her hands pressed upon his body as blood oozed from his wound between her whitened fingers, his stillness like an island in the stream of pandemonium and panic that stormed the room.

"No! No! Please ... oh please," Isabelle cried. "Don't die! Please don't leave me. No!" The young woman cried inconsolably, her tears flowing down her stricken face upon her limp and dying lover. Peering through red swollen eyes she looked up momentarily to see Madame Lowell crouched like a small animal at the side of her uncle, still moaning softly and muttering incomprehensibly in the housekeeper's arms.

"Why, Father Jacob? Why?" Isabelle called. "What did he do to you? Why did you do it? No!" For her uncle she felt the welling of the largest hatred a young heart could summon. She felt an overpowering sense of anger, shame, and regret for having brought the innocent young man into this house of insanity. "What have I done?" she wailed, pressing her hand deep into his bleeding wounds desperate to stop the flow of life that seemed to be seeping from him.

Amalie Lowell looked across at her young charge, no longer a girl, as she rocked her dying lover in her quaking arms and wailed like a wraith. She shook the now silent priest until his closed eyelids began to quiver, and then slowly parted. "Why? Why?" she demanded. "Why did you do such a thing, Jacob?"

The priest struggled but could not answer for the thick coagulating blood that was welling up in his throat and choking back his words. But then, the unspoken surfaced and broke through the quagmire of bile that clouded him, and with the few words he had left in his wretched soul, the dying priest uttered a name, and then a second name.

"Adrienne ... Tomàs ... no friend ... traitor ... must not ... "

Madame Lowell cradled his head, beseeching him to answer. "Who is he? Who is Tomàs, Father Jacob? Who is he?"

"Tomàs. Adrienne ... she is mine ... cannot be his. He ... he ... must die." His last gasp was a death rattle as the priest fell limp in Amalie's arms.

For many months, like a macabre circus performance enacted over and again on a revolving carousel of a stage, scenes from the ill-fated meeting of Isabelle's uncle and her beloved played repeatedly in the young woman's mind. How the two men in her life could clash so brutally in a single irreversible moment was a question with no answer. It was an unexpected blow of the bitterest kind, which spun her into a tumult of confusion and longing. During that time, Isabelle lay in a fetal clutch in the womb of her small dark bedroom. As she lay limp and wordless on her small bed, her regret scraped away at the insides of her soul like the blunt edge of a rusted hunting knife. Hate, love, and anger mixed so thoroughly throughout her wracked body that she could not willfully move, her rhythmic rocking driven by another source.

Meanwhile, in her infinite capacity as housekeeper and caretaker, Madame Lowell took charge in the mounting chaos that swept across Father Jacob's church like a tidal wave, until even her capacity was breached and she could no longer stem the tide of mishap that decimated both church and township. Stoically she marshaled Isabelle through the crisis without letting on that there was unrest in the parish, hand-feeding her young charge twice a day and each week bathing her. It came as no shock to Madame Lowell finally when the entire parish began to abandon the sinking ship; it was as if Moses himself stood at the top of Mont-Mégantic and declared the church spiritually bankrupt.

The decline in numbers of the faithful had been precipitous in the months before those defining events of winter. The priest remained oblivious; his once impassioned sermons escalated into incomprehensible liturgical ravings which bewildered, then offended his already beleaguered patrons. At first they came to his mass believing they would receive succor from the worry and dread of further decline in the mill-town, but when they received instead the hell-fire and brimstone ranting of a street-corner madman, disbelief and unrest began to reign. Those who returned to the church every week came out of politeness if not loyalty or sheer habit. But they grumbled less than politely as sermons segued into belligerence and misplaced hostility. Names said in the confidence of confession were unabashedly disclosed and individuals whose crimes were imagined in the priest's fevered mind were personally vilified, their libelous actions decried as direct affronts to him, the Right Hand of God.

The whispered half-veiled criticisms and apologetic notices of complaint threw the fiercely loyal Madame Lowell into a momentary black mood, but she rose above the fray and expertly turned them back upon the accusers, pointing out their lack of faith and spiritual fortitude. Father Jacob's ultimate act of insanity, however, left the poor woman with no defense. With his death she was forced to write a letter to the Catholic Church headquarters in Québec informing them of events, underplaying the drama and admitting only to a minor loss of parishioners. By the time her letter touched down upon the Archdeacon's desk, however, the scandal had already reached as far as Rome. Madame Lowell could do nothing but wait until a new priest was sent.

But no reply to her letter arrived. It was nearly summer by the time she was finally approached by the eldest daughter of one of the last remaining families in Solpetrière, a devout but meddling young woman named Cécile, the local shopkeeper's daughter. She had been a willing volunteer for Madame Lowell at the many after-service church gatherings, but when she stepped boldly into the church one late afternoon that spring, she was full of well-meaning but misguided help. She found Madame Lowell busily cleaning and preparing the church for the next service, as if nothing out of the ordinary had happened.

"Madame Lowell … " she began, clearing her throat hesitantly and waiting for the church caretaker to turn about. "Madame Lowell, you know that I will always be God's servant and your friend, but I must tell you about what everyone in this town — and those who have already gone — are talking about behind your back." Madame Lowell had turned around, but now she stopped her dusting and looked the young woman in the eye. Cécile continued carefully, avoiding Madame Lowell's expectant stare. "What Father Jacob did — God rest his soul," she began, lowering her eyes and crossing herself. She then dropped her voice to a low whisper, "What he has done has brought onto this town the wrath of … the umm … the uhh … the Indians … those

Mohawk. I think that's what they call themselves. We must keep looking behind our backs for a tomahawk in the scalp!"

Madame Lowell's eyes widened with disbelief. "What are you saying?"

The girl continued, now emboldened. "Madame Lowell, I am most serious. My father says that the construction of a new Church is already under way in St.-Gérard. Before the Indians... have your scalp and ours. You should come with me now."

"And, what of Isabelle?" Madame Lowell replied, placing her feather duster upon the vestibule where she had been cleaning, her two small round fists coming to rest on the curves of her matronly hips.

"Isabelle? What of her?" The young woman spoke with complete fervor and conviction now. "She must most definitely stay!" She continued. "They will come to claim one of 'Us' for the killing of one of 'Them.' That's what they do — you must know. I think SHE should have thought about it all before she started her... her... dalliance with that Indian. She should give herself up to them — for all of our sakes!"

The young woman's words rang through the rafters of the church like a bat through a belfry, forming a gust of wind that subtly shook the dusty windows loose in their casements like a death rattle. The younger woman looked to the other with a shudder. Cécile spoke earnestly and was taken aback when Madame Lowell picked up her feather duster and briskly escorted her out of the church. She closed the door and locked it securely, and returned to her fervent dusting and cleaning. The more she dusted the angrier she became. How the townsfolk could be so fearful and backward in their regard for the native people was more evidence of their deficiencies in Christian charity and spiritual fortitude. Little did the specious young woman know that the Indians she feared had already come to claim their dead from her doorstep, and from her assessment of them, they were more civil than many of the local parishioners themselves in the face of destruction.

Walk-Tall's father had come to claim his youngest son's body from the priest's house only hours after the incident — news of events having traveled faster than the eagle flies — but he came calmly with his four remaining sons bearing no malice. And, although a mixed incendiary flame of anger and despair burned in his liquid brown eyes and his broad shoulders shook visibly under his thick buckskin coat, he entered the house solemnly and placed a hand over his son's eyes tenderly without an angry word. Something in his face showed leniency, showed he understood what had transpired in this desecrated house, and showed that he had already forgiven whoever was responsible for his loss. He looked sadly at Isabelle, who sat slumped in a wicker chair at the far end of the room where Madame Lowell had left her, head in one thin hand, loose dark curls damp with tears and blood, wet swollen eyes closed shut and pale lips quivering.

This must be the girl, he thought silently to himself. For some time his son had been like a young buck in the mating season. As a father he watched secretly proud as his son seemed to grow by bounds over the course of several months from a reedy and quietly assured boy into a strong-minded and almost imposing young man. There was a new strength in his brow and a chiseled appearance in his jaw. Into his eyes came a softer light, where before frequent flashes of a too-clever, all-knowing, and sometimes benignly mischievous glare would reign, revealing the confidence of a youngest child upon whom parents doted.

The father had seen his older sons paired with young maidens from their tribe and three had already made vows of marriage. One was about to make him a grandfather. But with Walk-Tall, this awakening was different. He was completely transformed. Between the summer months and the intervening autumn, a new articulation of words had suddenly formed and a refinement in his mannerisms became subtly apparent. Always a cooperative child and a considerate helper around the home, he now became like a courteous servant to his mother. She smiled as she tended her extensive medicine garden and also silently reveled in her son's new maturity. When spring arrived they waited patiently for him to come forth with some news or reveal the source of this transformation.

But when news finally arrived it was not at all as they had hoped for or expected. Word had been sent through the Indian grapevine from one of the sheriff's sources to find out which young Indian was not where he should be, and before long, one of Walk-Tall's cousins came urgently to their home to give them the terrible news. Not a soul uttered a word as the stoic father gestured for his four sons to walk with him to retrieve their brother, while their bereaved mother retreated into their home to pray to the gods for her youngest.

The constable and his men arrived shortly after the mêlée and, after questioning Madame Lowell and examining the victims, they left her to attend to the bodies which they had lain out for her — one on the priest's bed and the other on a wide bench beneath the dining room window. Madame Lowell removed the hunting knife and dressed both the priest and the young brave the best she could, pressing bandages and towels into the mortal wounds to stem the tide of blood. The knife wound no longer bled, but the flow from the gunshot wounds seemed to defy her efforts. She righted the overturned furniture and mopped up all but a tiny smear of the blood from the timber floor by the time the young Indian's family arrived. Solemnly greeting them at the door, she said nothing as the father removed the leather holster from his son's belt and replaced the hunting knife into it. This he held for a long moment in his left hand, his eyes lowered, before he walked over to the weeping girl and laid it carefully beside her on the wicker divan. Madame Lowell held the door open silently as the small soundless band lifted their fallen brother and son into their arms and carried him out of the house, onto the back of a tall palomino, and into the dark of night.

By the time the new stone and brick façade cathedral in St.-Gérard was completed some three months later, the town of Solpetrière and its already struggling timber mill was completely deserted. It was now late spring–early summer, and the turbulence in Isabelle's heart had subsided to a low uneasy burn. Her grieving took the shape of work, and each passing day she applied herself to the cleaning of house, stable, and church and the grooming of the vegetable garden and orchard with a dedication looked upon by Madame Lowell as a sign of her emotional healing.

Madame Lowell had long ago removed all of Father Jacob's clothing and personal items which could not be given to charity, and locked them into two large leather cases. With the assistance of the sheriff and his men she buried the priest in the small graveyard beside his church, waiting just long enough for a young priest newly arrived from Lyon via Québec to travel to Solpetrière to give her old friend his last rites posthumously and sprinkle dust upon his lowered casket. The modest stone cross was inscribed with Jacob Sébastiani's name and dates. No mention was made of his ordained status or the nature of his demise. Madame Lowell did not cry, but that night she prayed for his salvation on her knees at her bedside for much longer than her old body could bear. She prayed this way nightly until the day Isabelle finally arose from her traumatic stupor.

She was still a painfully frail frame of skin and bones after her long convalescence, but when Isabelle finally arose, she sprang into action as if wound up like a spinning top. Although the housework brought color to her cheeks somewhat, it did nothing to put flesh upon her frame. From that day onward, the two women never addressed the fact directly that they were the only two remaining inhabitants of the town, preferring instead to go about their chores, stopping only briefly to make a meal twice a day from the remaining stores in the larder, and what was sprouting in the garden. Each night after supper they knelt together in the empty church and prayed in silence for an hour. Early one morning Isabelle arose from her bed and strode into the kitchen in her bedclothes to find Madame Lowell dressed for an outing.

"We are nearly out of staples. Flour and salt," she announced when Isabelle appeared in the doorway, wrapping a light shawl around her rounded shoulders and brushing off an old straw hat which Isabelle had never seen off the small nail in the pantry where it hung gathering dust. "I will make us some bread this day. We need to bring you back to health, my girl. You mustn't stay this thin, it is not right for a girl — a young woman — your age to be thinner than a willow switch."

"I am fine, Madame Lowell," Isabelle replied, leaning subtly against the breakfast table to steady herself. "I have not had an appetite for a while. But today seems a bit different. I will be fine. Please do not go to any trouble on my behalf." She sat down now as her head began to spin slightly and her stomach grumbled with something like a hunger pang at the thought of fresh bread.

"No such thing as trouble," the older woman gently cooed. "I will go around to the stable and rig up Béatrice with the old horse cart. It has been many years since this old housekeeper has ridden that trap, but God willing, I shall be fine for a careful jaunt into St.-Gérard."

"I'll go, Madame Lowell. The mare and I need to get re-acquainted ... "

"Oh no, you will not. I'll not have you falling over halfway to St.-Gérard from here. I'll manage. I may be old and too round for my own good, but I do have excellent balance. My mother was a fine equestrienne, you know." She planted the straw bonnet upon her upswept gray chignon and tied the faded blue ribbon resolutely under her double chin. "Now, make yourself a good breakfast, all right? Old Renate and Brigitte have left you two beautiful brown eggs. I'm off ... shall be back before noon." Madame Lowell swung the door closed and briskly trotted off to the stable, leaving Isabelle alone again in the quiet sun-lit kitchen.

For the first time in over three months Isabelle was gripped with a hunger pang so intense she nearly fainted. Staring at the two perfectly oval hen's eggs nestled on a kitchen towel on the stove — one a deep rust color and the other a pale creamier tan with a sprinkling of light brown freckles — she thought to herself, *they are a beautifully mixed pair.* A tear escaped one eye just as she heard hesitant hoof steps treading over the hard ground behind the house and the roll of heavy cartwheels. Wiping away her tear, she waved the horse and rider goodbye through the window as they strode by, and for an instant forgot about her momentary lapse into longing.

As the horse-cart careened along the unfamiliar road, Madame Lowell's thoughts lingered on what she would propose to Isabelle in the evening. Going to St.-Gérard that morning had initially been something of a frightening prospect for her. Not only was it the unfamiliar road that bothered her, for it had always been Father Jacob or one of his loyal young volunteers who rode into town for items that could not be bought in Solpetrière itself — but it was also the prospect of meeting up with former parishioners of Father Jacob's church that had put her off the trip for as long as it did. But provisions were getting too low to ignore and the deed had to be done.

In her traveling bonnet and lurching her way into town on the old-styled horse-cart, Madame Lowell felt self-conscious and not a little ashamed — but of what, she could not rightly place her finger upon. Was it the fact that she had written an official letter to Québec and been ignored? What did people think of her now? Was she seen as a silly old woman without a sense of the obvious? Or was it the fact that she was fiercely loyal to Father Jacob, right up to the moment he revealed his true colors? But Father Jacob was truly a good man; she remembered how he had reached out to lend a hand across Canada at the time her husband and her sons had died and left her all alone. He had been a ray of hope and a conduit across the grave to her loved ones.

It was true, his ranting had become beyond outlandish, but she never thought he would ever do anyone harm, particularly to a guest in his own house. But what he brought upon himself, his niece, and the entire town was unforgivable. Without a doubt, she needed to let go of her saintly image of him and move forward to do whatever was needed to help Isabelle, who was now without any family. Like herself.

Quickly she found the general store just inside the town's limits and made her necessary purchases: a twenty-five pound sack of threshed flour and a double smoked ham shank wrapped in muslin. The shopkeeper, Cécile's father, recognized Madame Lowell immediately but their conversation remained formal and at a polite minimum.

"Good morning, Madame Lowell...I trust you are well," the shopkeeper offered, avoiding her eyes in a way completely foreign to the normally convivial man.

"Good morning, Mr. Lonsdale," Madame Lowell answered, watching him as he hung his head, busily examining the ham hock. "I am as well as I can be. Thank you for your kind words."

"Well..." he answered awkwardly smoothing the muslin around the ham. "It has been some time since we've seen you." He wrapped the cured meat in brown paper and tied the package in twine. "Tis a warm day, must keep this out of the heat..."

"Yes. Thank you. I will."

He handed the bundle to her, adding, "The young Miss Isabelle is well too?"

"Yes. Not too badly. I will tell her you asked after her."

"Good. Thank you. Shall I help you with the sack and ham?"

"Yes please."

The shopkeeper carried the packages on his shoulders, hefting them carefully into the horse-cart and tying them expertly, one on each side of the carriage. He helped Madame Lowell climb with some difficulty onto the driver's seat, and gave the horse a pat.

Just as Madame Lowell brought up the reins to start up the gray mare, he added, "Today is a special feast day, and me mum and dad have just left for church a moment ago. I'm sure they would be happy to see you if you were planning to stop in for Father Maurice's service. They think very highly of him."

Madame Lowell had not planned to attend the service but she arrived at the church just as the service was about to begin. She crept in quietly taking an inconspicuous seat in the last row of pews. Nearly three times the size of Father Jacob's, the church was but half full. Occupying the forward seats were recognizable personages, some clutching new babies unknown to her. This observation made her realize just how long she and Isabelle had hidden away inside the small cabin like bears hibernating through an inhospitable winter. Sitting stolidly there in the new church, she felt liberated having conquered her self-consciousness and riding now above any possible ridicule she might receive for her futile attempts to salvage Father Jacob's tainted church. Her only purpose now was to find some sort of employment to keep herself and Isabelle fed and clothed. If she could secure a caretaker or housekeeper role with this new priest here, or even one as a cook, she would be grateful.

The grandeur of the church was wondrous to behold, with its dark-stained timber rafters spanning a breathtaking expanse of masonry and brick, imposing a heavy celestial weight upon the heads of the congregation. Dropping her head in prayer as the priest's words wrapped themselves like a penitence upon her shoulders, she realized then that she had not attended church or confession for many months, so ensconced was she in the duties of nursing her young charge back to health and tranquility after the traumatic events of the spring.

The yoke of prayer was so overwhelming and complete that Madame Lowell lost all sense of time and place. In her prayer she saw marvelous sights.

Jacob was dressed in his finest priest's cassock and above the collar was the face of the younger man she knew from her first meetings of him. But he was floating just a few inches above the ground and the rim of his gown where the black cloth would have skimmed the earth as he walked glowed with an ominous half-ring of flames flicking steadily as he glided. Trailing not far behind in a similar airborne fashion was her husband, just as she last saw him, replete in his finest ministerial gown. The two men guided her along as they hovered just ahead of her in this silent pantomime, moving assuredly toward an opening at the edge of an unfamiliar forest.

She was young again, but it was winter in this other-worldly trance in which she found herself. The arch of the cedars and firs about her loomed precipitously high like the overwhelmingly vaulted ceiling of the cathedrals of her childhood. They were ancient and imposing, venerable and oppressive, but at the same time they brought an abiding sense of comfort and awe in which only the truly devout can revel. Like a pair of dolphins skimming the waves of a frigid green ocean, the two angels of men rose high up into the canopy of the forest. Parting the sea of trees among them, a golden ribbon of river strangely lit from an unworldly sun above was revealed to the earth-bound traveler below.

In its pristine grandeur the ravine widened out at this wintry bend in the river, but the bold bristling pines pressed in with inconceivable closeness and evoked a sacrosanct intimacy; it was a clandestine cathedral lit from within with its own other-worldly luminescence. Rows of giant cedars parted their veils and peered out through the stillness like young maidens receiving first communion in the silence of the snow. Freshly sprouted pine needles curved like eyelashes over demurely downcast eyes; soft mounded snow drifts rounded shoulders sheathed in white lace undulating over young bosoms quivering with anticipation.

As she stood frozen at the bend of the river, Jacob's sweeping robes enveloped her for a moment and doused their flames upon her, transferring the heat of an early summer's day to her in a blanket of warmth that suddenly filled her with a protective yet stifling sense of assurance. It was with a contradiction of fear and certainty that she surged forth into the forest as the apparitions began to recede into the thick pine foliage above. She called out to them but no sound came from her lips, except for the muttered words of prayer that her enslaved mouth pressed her tongue into forming. She found herself creeping deeper into the forest as the echoes of her own prayer filled the cauldron of trees in which she was submerged.

Even before the sound of the cart wheels was fully dissipated, Isabelle was weeping again, head bobbing and eyes streaming a flood of tears into desperate hands. The gnawing sensation in her belly demanded her to put food in it but she could not bear to look at the eggshells, much less break them. Through her tears she peered about the kitchen but found nothing at hand to feed herself, and could do nothing more than continue to sob hopelessly until finally, the tears came to a halt. It was only then that she heard a few slow hoof steps approach the house, this time from the opposite side of where the housekeeper had departed on the horse-drawn cart. Perhaps it was the mixture of surprise and fear which gripped her that dissolved the pain in her stomach. Isabelle rose out of her chair, rushed into her bedroom and pulled the bed covers off the bed to wrap around herself. She stood stock still cowering in her bedroom for an eternity it seemed, listening intently for footsteps at the door or any sounds of entry into the house. But there was none, only her loudly beating heart underscoring the hum of a horsefly and the incessant warbling of a distant bird.

Then, the hoof steps passed slowly by her window and Isabelle drew up her courage to walk soundlessly over to the window and step onto the footstool that she kept at the base. What she saw then through the small window nearly toppled her from her perch. The horse and rider had already passed her window so the male intruder had his back to her. But what was this? The figure was familiar, and furthermore it bore more than just a small likeness to her deceased lover — she would know it anywhere and from any angle.

It was he, she was sure of it, perched slightly bent upon the bare back of a white and brown pinto, his black hair tied loosely down his back.

She almost called out to him, and then realized that she must be seeing his ghost, in broad daylight. Could she halt the figure from receding away into the garden and into the ether if she simply willed for the rider to stop and turn around, she asked herself? What if it is not him? Maybe it is one of his brothers? Maybe they are here to seek some sort of revenge? Or payment for their loss? What could she offer them? Herself, as a hostage? She would gladly do it. And with this thought she rushed out of her room and out of the kitchen door in her bare feet, rounding the corner just as the rider stopped and turned his head to see her coming around it, and then brought herself up short at the sight of him.

Walk-Tall was startled to find her looking so pale and thin, and even more so when she toppled over onto rocks and grass in a faint. Quickly he brought the horse around, urging it into a canter to the place where Isabelle had fallen. With some difficulty he dismounted, tied the horse to a tree and was at her side before she returned to consciousness. As if under water, her hands reached up to touch his face, not believing the reality of the beautiful but blurred image she was seeing. He was a vision she thought she would never see again, but here he was in flesh and blood. It was all too much for her and she fainted away again. Painfully aware that he could not pick her up and carry her into the house as he wanted to do, Walk-Tall simply pulled the bed covers tightly around her, and lay down beside her, his arm cradling her head and the other resting across her body. Small ruts jabbed his back and arms but he relaxed his body and patiently waited for her to awaken. When she finally did, it was with a jolt, her emerald eyes opening wide and her mouth forming a silent circle.

"Ahhh, it *is* you!" she cried, rolling them into a full embrace oblivious of the sharp rocks and tufted grass that formed their impromptu bedding. "You are real! You are real! I cannot believe it!" she repeated, stroking and squeezing his shoulders and arms to prove to herself he was not an apparition.

"I am real," was all he said. Tears flowed and each felt as if they had regained a most treasured possession thought to have been lost forever.

"But, you were dead. They carried you away and you were dead! I thought I was dead too. I wanted to die... I did not want to live without you! But how did you come back? And why did you not come back to me straight away?" He could only close his eyes and smile wanly as she blanketed him with questions. "Oh, my poor darling... I am so sorry for what happened... I am so sorry! Oh... let me see what he did to you. Are you in much pain?"

He stayed her hand and prevented her from peering at his wounds. But he felt the excruciating pain sharply in his body where the bullets had torn large irreparable holes in his muscle, and he clenched his teeth to stifle a cry. It was ecstasy and agony entwined as he was in her arms, but he would have forfeited his right leg to be able to feel her body against his just one more time. He relaxed his body into the pain and drew her to him and kissed her deeply, first on the eyes then on the lips to quiet her sobs, and waited to begin his explanation.

"My mother is a medicine woman. She always had the touch. Her father — my grandfather — was the tribal medicine man and she learned everything from him, just by watching, understanding, and knowing." She now cradled his head in the grass and listened intently as he told his story. "I was already dead, they told me, when I was brought back to my home. There was almost no breath coming out of me or into me. But my mother refused to believe I was gone. She shooed everyone out of the tent where they had laid me and she immediately undid the bandages and applied her magic poultices and rubbed my body from head to foot with her special medicines. No one knows what she applied to me or which god she made a deal with, but in the morning I awoke.

"I heard the rooster crow like I have never heard a cock cry before! It was as if my ears had swelled to the size of maize, and I felt all my senses like they were bolts of lightning and the crash of thunder upon my body. Yes, the pain was unbearable. I wanted to die again so I would not have to feel it. I got my wish, for my brothers tell me that I fell into a deep sleep and did not wake up again for nearly three weeks. I only remember the awakening part, of course, and by then the medicine was doing its work and the pain became more like a painful memory, coming and going rather than always there.

"She sat at my side every minute, I was told. Those three weeks were a test for everyone: a test of faith and test of our family's love. The weave of my family's basket was torn and my life was leaking out. My life hung by a small thread and they told me my fingers turned black and my mother rubbed them every day ten times a day until their color returned. I think she chanted every chant she knew, sang every spirit song she remembered. The tribal medicine man came, but she turned him away, telling him that in my fragile state his magic would be too much for my spirit and would drive it away instead of inviting it back. She told him that she saw my spirit and it was an owl that sat in a large cedar tree in the forest beyond our home. She was right; for exactly an hour before I awoke, a large owl kept watch in a tree beside my tent and flew away the minute I made my first move."

Isabelle was transfixed by the story. She had been visited by the snow owl too, many times, as she had lain like a child in her bed. The soothing sound of the hoot in the night was like a lullaby, but in her dreams the bird was more like her mother, silent and watchful. Still in the dream she would find herself in the forest alone leaning against the large old cedar tree. She would be waiting for Walk-Tall to join her, but each time she heard a sound in the silent cathedral of trees, it would be the owl, arriving just after her and lighting upon a low branch just above. It would look down upon her with its stern yellow eyes, soft snow-white wings folding silently into their perfect position. If she closed her eyes and let go of her pain, those wings would grow and expand into a feathery embrace and she could lose all memory, lose herself in it.

Then one day a momentary panic descended. She listened for the plaintive cry of the owl at the expected hour but none came. Those visits and dreams were the only things that kept her from rising from her bed and finding a way into the frozen lake. *Abandoned again*, she thought. But what small grace the owl had brought in the days and weeks prior had buoyed her spirits enough to give her the strength to continue. With the passing days she came to realize that it only meant her lover had finally gone to heaven, to a beautiful place where someday they would be reunited. In her dreams that night, the owl came to visit but she no longer waited for her lover to arrive. The bird kept its watch silently from its perch in a nearby tree. It was then that she began to sense a small stirring of life deep inside her. It was nearly summer and Isabelle knew that come winter she would be a mother. It was with this realization that she arose that morning resolved to begin a dedicated regimen of manual work.

And now, as she held the father of her child once again in her arms, it was with relief, gratitude, and joy, unbelievable joy. She sat upright with the joy, and then retracted as Walk-Tall gave a grimace of pain. His wounds were on the mend, but far from healed. Carefully helping him into an upright position, she held back the tears, silently crying with remorse at his wounds, but her joy was like a heady brew and instead she gave a mirthful but genuine cry of happiness. "You must have been touched by an angel, Walk-Tall. Perhaps your mother is an angel? I must meet her some day and thank her. She must be a wonderful woman."

"She is, my love," he replied. "But I have bad news to tell you next."

"Oh no. I hope you are not going to say what I fear you are going to say?"

"I am afraid, yes." Walk-Tall reflected for a minute then reached for Isabelle and held her to him, even as the pain in his abdomen nearly made him cry out.

"Oh no, Walk-Tall! I am so sorry. That is why you did not come to me straight away!"

"Yes, that is why. She was an old woman already; please do not cry. She lived a most wonderful life. I was the much younger child that she did not expect. She sat by my side chanting for the three weeks of my long sleep. This is what they told me. Without sleep or food. When I awoke the second time, the final time, I saw her small body sitting on the floor beside me. Her eyes closed. In her hands was her most powerful talisman."

"She was a good woman. The kind of mother I hope to be one day." Isabelle sighed.

"Yes. And for a moment her eyes opened and she smiled at me. Then she gave out a long breath. I think it was with that breath that she left for the spirit world. When I called her name, she did not answer. I tried to get up, but the pain stayed me to the bed and I could only call out with a weak voice. Soon, my father came in and when he saw her, he knew right away that she had already left us."

They held each other and said no more words. Isabelle thought about the dream she had of their unborn child. But it was Walk-Tall who turned her face to him and looked deep into her eyes and seemed to read her thoughts. She grasped his hand and placed it under her bed-cover wrap on her stomach through the cloth of her night dress. Beneath the sharply carved cliff-line of her lower ribs, the swelling mound was a sun-warmed hillock. Their eyes met in a moment of corresponding vision and mutual understanding.

Walk-Tall could feel the life in Isabelle's belly like the deep waters of a hot spring rising in an otherwise cool lake. The warmth emanating from her womb and into his hands had healing qualities that made the pain in his own abdomen and leg subside. Almost with gratitude the young man allowed his eyelids to close and his wrinkled brows to smooth out with relief. Isabelle mistook the action momentarily for returning pain. But when a beatific smile crept across and transformed his face, her fears were immediately allayed. That beautiful face was so familiar to her; the rapturous expression brought to her the memory of her early childhood so many years ago, and the gilded angels swoon-

ing in ecstasy between the covers of the books in Father
Pascal's library.

Like a sleeping child himself, Walk-Tall remained in a
blissful otherworldly state for a long while, wrapped as he
was in the warmth of his lover and unborn child's embrace.
Isabelle was loath to disturb him, but she was aware that
Madame Lowell might shortly return with the horse and
cart. They pondered the effect Walk-Tall's return would
have on the older woman and agreed that the right time
would come when they would bring her into their secret.
For the time being, it seemed unfair to burden her with such
unexpected news on so many fronts. He unwound his body
slowly, unwilling but wise enough to know he must return
to his home to recuperate fully before attempting to see
Isabelle again. Both knew without discussion that his family
would disapprove of his return to Isabelle, even though in
his tribe it was custom for a man to join his wife's family,
and regardless of the fact that her murderous uncle was no
longer of this world. Their union had already brought infinite misfortune on both sides.

*In the midst of this expanse of virgin snow a solitary
figure, wrapped from head to foot in a thick white cotton
blanket emblazoned with a dark native design, soundlessly wends its way slowly through the forest, listening intently with eager ears swathed in cloth, searching for the sound of water, running water. The figure
is a woman, a mother — cradled in her arms beneath
the blanket, a small sleeping bundle provides ballast*

to her slow mincing steps. Even as the bundle stirs she inches forward, certain that the water source must be here where the colossal line of trees stands guard against an unseen and unknown enemy, their territory the domain of the regal peregrine falcon and the black bear in spring. In this stillness a thawing creek bed gives way with a trickle then a gush of running water, resolutely terminating the once vast silence with the tentative first notes of its intimate musical offering.

The distinct sound of water stops the young mother in her tracks; her head tilts up to search the tops of the trees and to pick out the old woman amongst the ring of giants. An old stately cedar stands before her, its towering height and formidable girth giving clues to the colossal measure of its life. Standing like a monument to this wild wonderland, the tree itself is her destination. She finds a familiar crevice in its impressive gnarled trunk where the 700-year-old roots heaved themselves above the earth to provide a human-like embrace and there she settles as she did many times before.

Softly she begins to sing, rocking the bundle in her arms, inured to the tears that fall upon her sleeping child. The blanket slips away from her head as she rocks, her body involuntarily moving in a rhythmic trance. Like a trail of blood after a successful deer hunt, a loose wave of auburn hair escapes from her small black bonnet, forming a meandering creek across the thick white weave of the blanket around her shoulders. Her eyes are closed and the lashes quiver; pale skin on her cheeks glows as translucent and wet as the thawing creek bed beyond.

Her singing becomes sleepy and sonorous; it summons a young scout who appears before her amongst the snow drifts. Unsure momentarily if the vision is real or a cruel trick of light, she draws in her breath sharply, and then slowly releases it again to the familiarity of his image. It makes her heart jump into her throat even as she continues her trance-like singing and rocking. The young brave is draped in deer skins below the waist; above he is bare, his wide brown chest emblazoned with the bold black markings of his people. Long jet black braids are tied at even junctures along both sides of his chiseled face and down to the narrow of his waist; loose eagle feathers trickle down from his ears to below the broad shoulders. His arms are held out before him as if he is making an offering of some treasured but invisible burden.

The scout slowly makes his way across the short distance of snowy ground to the woman and child, his moccasined feet making no sound at all. As he draws closer his image dissipates, dissolving into the frosty air like a soft word spoken from her lips. Around her the blanket draws itself tighter and the weight of his familiar body leans up undeniably against her. The old cedar welcomes them anew, shutting out the world around them and providing a shelter for their enduring but interrupted love. The mother closes her eyes and releases herself to a deep sleep, joining her blissful child in a place safe from the sorrows of the snow and ice. Content with their sleep the brave begins to climb the great tree, clearing the highest branches and disappearing into the tree top.

It was at this point, in mid-dream, in mid-prayer, that Amalie Lowell's heart abruptly stopped.

For as long as there was light on the horizon Isabelle remained in the garden tending the trailing vines of potato and humming a soft song to herself. She listened diligently for the sound of the horse-cart in the distance but Madame Lowell did not return that afternoon. That evening, however, someone else arrived at the cabin in Solpetrière, and she watched as Cécile slowed down the horse and called out to Isabelle as she swung the horse and cart around the garden toward her.

Behind her, another horse carriage followed in which rode a young man, Cécile's new husband-to-be. Isabelle approached the visitors with alarm, fearing the worst for Madame Lowell's absence. Both visitors alighted from their vehicles and slowly came up to Isabelle, who was wrapped from head to toe in a thick cotton blanket. Cécile suspected it was an Indian blanket but pursed her lips in uncharacteristic silence.

"What is it, Cécile? What brings you here this time of the night?" Isabelle demanded. "Have you seen Madame Lowell?"

"Isabelle," Cécile began. "It is about Madame Lowell. I'm afraid ... I'm sorry but ... " she could not complete the sentence. "I wanted to come earlier, but ... "

Isabelle covered her mouth with her hands and began to tremble.

"No. Stop. Don't say it, Cécile," she cried, "don't tell me. She buried her face into the sweat-soaked neck of the old gray mare. "No, no. It can't be. No!"

"I'm afraid so...Belle." The young woman had not called her by that childhood name and now it sounded hollow even in her own ears.

"No. No." Sinking to her knees on the gravel path of the kitchen garden, Isabelle's world spun in an unbelieving whirlwind. Nearly in a faint she pulled the blanket over her head and sat in the darkness of the hood as visions of Madame Lowell swam painfully in the black backdrop of that narrow cave. It was only when she felt arms folding themselves around her that she finally came to terms with her loss, and through the stiff cotton weave she slowly pronounced her words. "All right...please tell me. I am ready to know what happened to Madame."

Cécile relayed the shocking news of the morning to her former friend as her fiancé looked on in silence. "Madame Lowell made a surprise appearance at our church in St.-Gérard this morning," she began.

"Did she? I'm not surprised," Isabelle replied now more calmly.

"She took a seat in the back row and several people said they saw her immediately bend down on her knees in prayer," Cécile continued. "She did not seem to expect to meet anyone, and greeted no one. She just knelt down in prayer, and never rose up again."

Isabelle gasped. "She never rose up again?"

"No," the other young woman continued. "After the sermon ended, we all walked around her quietly, thinking she may have fallen asleep. No one wanted to wake her."

"No one wanted to wake her?"

"No...but then Father Maurice came to speak to her, and he realized that she had joined the angels while deep in prayer."

"Deep in prayer," Isabelle sighed, imagining her rosary held between her palms and her forehead resting upon the back of the forward pew.

"Deep in prayer," Cécile repeated. Isabelle's tears now flowed like the melting of spring snow onto the banks of a thawing river. "I'm so sorry," Cécile offered, placing a comforting hand upon the distraught woman. With her other hand she gestured to her fiancé to bring the horse-cart around. "Father Maurice will take care of her burial in the new church yard."

"But I think she would have wanted to be with Father Ja..."

"No, I think it is best this way," Cécile interjected. Isabelle fell silent. "We brought the provisions Madame Lowell had bought this morning from my father's shop," she continued. "Twenty-five pounds of threshed flour and a ham. There are also a few things my mother sent along. Abel will take it all into the house, if that's all right with you?" Isabelle continued to sob into the horse's gray neck as Cécile looked on quietly. With a nod of her head, a sack of flour and a ham wrapped in muslin were procured from the cart. Hefting them upon his broad shoulders with his chin firmly pressed into his chest, the stout young man delivered the packages into Isabelle's house.

Isabelle stopped her sobbing and thanked the other woman for bringing the horse and the provisions back. Leading the gray mare to the stable, she wiped her eyes, stowed the cart away, and filled the feed bucket before returning to her visitor. Cécile and Abel bid their farewells and left

Isabelle soon thereafter in her kitchen all alone with a cup of tea and Madame Lonsdale's apple cake. Straightening herself up, Isabelle moved automatically to gather the things she needed to carry on. A few handfuls of flour were strewn on the kitchen table and slowly the preparation for the baking of bread commenced. It was an activity that soothed and relaxed her, and the sad young woman was glad for the opportunity to sink cold hands into yeast-warmed dough and to light the oven against the coming evening chill. More than a few tears fell into the soft pliable dough which, when ready to sit in a dark place to rise, fed upon the salty addition and rose to a towering dome.

Isabelle never felt so utterly alone as now in the dark of her empty home and deserted village. Although she lit as many lanterns as she could justifiably light, it still felt dark and alone. Wrapping her shawl around her and grabbing a hurricane lamp, she braved the dark to walk around to the *potager* to pick up the wicker basket of vegetables she had left on the stoop. Béatrice would be pleased to get a freshly pulled carrot or two after her long journey, the first after a long winter in the stable, and happier yet to get a languid stroke on her long nose. As Isabelle approached, the horse whinnied and excitedly nudged her as if to say, *I know who you saw today.* Isabelle put her arms around the mare's sturdy head and whispered the secret into her large white ears as they switched energetically in opposite directions.

"Yes, my girl, you are right. I did see him today, and I will see him again soon. How did you know?" she asked as she brushed the horse and lovingly draped a light blanket over her. "You missed him too, didn't you? But, we must be patient." Isabelle turned toward the house and slowly walked the brief distance with bittersweet excitement. Just as she got her best friend back, she lost her other dear old friend. She cherished the prospect of living a life of truth and beauty with her small family-to-be, but was sad that she had no one with whom to share this excitement, nor anyone from whom she needed to keep her secret.

"I will be strong," she said out loud now as she entered the warm and well-lit kitchen. "I will be strong and there will be no more tears. Madame is in heaven now," she said as she punched down the rounded dome of bread dough, "And Walk-Tall and I will live in ours soon. Be patient, Isabelle."

Isabelle wrote a long letter to Father Pascal. She remembered a certain book she once perused within the dark wood and leather of his old library, which described the *medicinal* plants of the Americas, a companion to Father Jacob's directory of common New World plants. The book was not extensive, but within its sheaves of parchment were copious watercolor renderings of strange and exotic plants — leaves, flowers, and fruits that called out to her now many years later in a faded but distinct recollection. At the time of her first reading these surreal herbal depictions had no relevance, but in their soft exoticism she remembered them to be fascinating. Some of these plants were described as poisonous and to be administered with utmost caution, while others were nutritious, and to others were attributed a cure for every known ailment. In her mind's eye, Isabelle ran her hands over the pages and the healing essence of those medicines entered her with a warming sensation she could feel in her very being.

Two months to the day she imagined her hands on the book of extraordinary miracles three large cases arrived in a horse carriage from Halifax and were delivered to the old cabin porch by two straining, large, and dusty young men. The cases occupied a large portion of the veranda and Isabelle was just able to squeeze in between them to accept the letter one young man held out gingerly to her from the front steps. It was addressed to Isabelle Sébastiani and written in an oblique and official hand.

Messrs Lafayette Frères, Avocates
Forcalquier, FRANCE
12th July 1886

Dear Mademoiselle Sébastiani,

We are in receipt of your letter addressed to Father Pascal Gagnon. This was most fortunate as the Father had passed away nearly six months ago and left a will which includes your name, without address, as the recipient of a portion of his library collection, as well as two separate items which he believed to be of genuine interest to you.

If you are reading this letter, you will have received three parcels containing the book collection, in addition to the two individual items aforementioned. Please acknowledge the receipt of these items by placing your signature upon the bottom of the packing inventory on the following page and resealing it in the envelope wherein this letter resided. Return the envelope to the delivery courier and it will be remitted to our offices.

We thank you for your timely correspondence and wish you success in your endeavors.

Faithfully yours,
J Lafayette

Isabelle lowered the letter slowly from her scanning eyes and approached the cases as if they were three winged chariots alighted from Heaven containing the font of all knowledge. She never imagined that those volumes, precious beyond their monetary value, would ever leave Father Pascal's library much less the country. But here they stood now as her hand nimbly unbuckled the strap of the first case. Pushing aside the suede cloth that swathed the volumes, Isabelle peered at the first title that revealed itself: *The Divine Comedy*. Dante Alighieri. Her heart pounded in her ears as she lifted the volume to her chest. Beneath it was *The British Museum Botanical and Horticultural Guide*. A miracle, the books are here, she shouted silently. Tears began their trek down her cheeks as she recalled the kindly old priest who in the first years of her life was the only father she ever knew. The volumes were large and luminous like the priest himself, and as they stood before her now like a tripartite mountain range; it was as if the old man presented himself to her here as The Holy Trinity itself.

Quickly finding a pen amongst her things, she placed an awkward initial on the second page as instructed. The two men hoisted the trunks into the cabin and took their leave as Isabelle sat herself down in the aftermath of the excitement, Dante's allegories still clutched tightly to her chest.

By nightfall the majority of the volumes were removed from the first two of the traveling cases and placed neatly in rows in and alongside Father Jacob's twin bookcases. Culpepper's *Book of Natural Herbs* held a place of honor beside the *Book of New World Medicinal Plants* — the single pied piper of handbooks that brought the others to Isabelle's world in an unexpected windfall of nostalgia and opportunity. Isabelle's lantern burned late into the night and into the early morning as she reviewed each book lovingly and ran her eager hands over the gilt-lettered covers and renewed her familiarity with the hand-inked drawings and press-printed texts.

On opening the third case, Isabelle was overcome with emotion. Cradled in the midst of the volumes was a small black leather case whose beautiful familiarity alighted upon her like a flash of brilliance from an angel's trumpet. A note was attached to the inside of the case.

Dear Isabelle,

At last this instrument has found you. It was returned to me from the ship which delivered you to the New World. I have kept it with much care in the Library amongst the books that you will now have in your possession. There is also a special book which I am assured you will treasure. It was found beneath the mattress of one of the beds we were preparing to donate to the orphanage. I trust you will take care of all of these treasures of the Old World as you find your way in the New World.

May God's Blessing be with You for Eternity.

Père Pascal Gagnon

She drew the guitar from its case and clutched it to her as she discovered beneath it another parcel wrapped in a black cloth. Placing the guitar on her bed, she unwrapped the cloth to find inside a red leather-bound notebook. With shaking hands she opened to the first page — it was her mother's writing, still so familiar. The fine feathery words were like black birds embroidered in flight across the sky of a medieval tapestry. She remembered but once seeing its red cover escape from the black cloth in her mother's hands just before she died. Thinking Isabelle was asleep, she had quietly taken it out and opened it to a page and written in it a few words before returning it to its secret hiding place. And now Isabelle was reading it for the first time.

As she leafed through the notebook, small passages captured her attention, snippets of observations about the birds in the garden one spring morning or one day when she harvested finger potatoes in the *potager* while Isabelle was still in her cradle beside her while she worked, and another when she was sick. This last entry was full of sadness and the knowledge that she was not long for this world. In it she addressed to no one in particular:

It is my fate to pass from this world without full under-standing of my true purpose in this life. I have brought into this world my daughter Isabelle. Every day I cherish her wondrous life and bear witness to God's love in her beautiful eyes. But I know not the fate of my brother, the poor lost soul who understood better than the rest of us what mysteries lay at the bottom of one's heart. Nor what has become of Him, the one whose light carries on with my Isabelle. He is forgiven, as the Lord I pray has forgiven me for my trespass.

After Madame Lowell's passing, Isabelle and Walk-Tall met every day at the old cedar. As she listened to his gentle words like the soft contours of the summer forest, she could feel his life essence growing more ephemeral and his once-strong body increasingly limpid, almost fluid. And as they lay together in an embrace imagining their future together, she felt the growing child within her pulse and vibrate, as if it were drawing its very life-source away from its father. With sadness and trepidation she listened to his entreaties for her to come to live amongst his family. They would show her the way of his people and teach her the multitudinous uses of the medicinal plants she eagerly pointed out to him from her book.

But Isabelle remained at the cabin, where she kept a sad and watchful eye on the abandoned church, its slow ruin like an unread book fading and yellowing upon a shelf. The old cedar became their sanctuary for the remainder of her term, but the wounds Walk-Tall sustained nearly eight months earlier never healed completely and the pain once again slashed through the muscles of his stomach like a harvesting reaper through brown grass. The lingering infection now held him captive and the shooting pains returned, punctuating the lovers' tranquility with its cruel reminders.

Struggling to dismount his regal paint horse for the last time, Walk-Tall arrived early at the meeting place dressed in his finest buckskin vest and a pair of dungarees Isabelle had sewn for him. He still made a fine strong silhouette, even though his thick black hair was matted against his sweat-soaked forehead and even with the frosty bite of late autumn, his face and body were flushed with heat. The sound of his horse's even footsteps together with his heavy slow tread through the shrubbery told her they were near, and she lumbered across the wooded terrain to meet him on the path.

A single glance at his flushed face and she was gripped with fear. Directly to the cedar she led him. There she removed his drenched vest and laid him down on the bed of blankets and pine needles and retreated to fetch water from the creek. On her return, she found him sitting slightly hunched over, his lower back against the old roots and his steed anxiously pawing the ground nearby. He gestured to the horse's saddle bags — there she found where he stowed the large pieces of white willow bark collected on his journey to the cedar. She administered these natural analgesics to her patient, gripping the pieces with her bare fingers and stripping them finer for easier mastication.

Desperate now to dull the pain, Walk-Tall chewed the bark like a good patient and eventually fell into a deep sleep as Isabelle tenderly drew her damp handkerchief over his brow. With her other hand she fanned him with a small Chinese fan of red silk that Madame Lowell had bought her years before from a passing frontier trinket salesman. While he slept she managed to hoist her own body and its rotund burden beside him. In this way she could keep her eye on him as she herself reclined. Fanning them both with the faded red silk fan, she extended a tired arm over his body and swept it over her own face at alternating waves. Slowly the tune came to her. A soft melody sung with the sweetest voice. Her mother's favorite piece, a nameless tune she played with such passion and sadness that Isabelle often wondered where the wellspring, the source of that intense emotion, could be. "Sleep now," Isabelle whispered as the soaring music reached its summit and loosed its final crescendo of falling notes. "Sleep now, my love, and when you awake, you and I will go to your home and I will join your people."

In her repose, with her mother's beloved guitar clutched to her body like a child's blanket, Isabella slipped into a slumber so deep her breath came sporadically... angels and ordinary men wept from the sheer beauty of its sound. Engulfed with the sense of Walk-Tall's presence in the embrace of the old tree, she saw her own body of flesh and blood recede into nothingness. She knew that when her own time arrived to leave the world for eternity and to pass into the spirit realm she too would return to this old cedar. But that would be a time determined not by her will but the will of the marching seasons upon her soul. For now, however, she must find the resolve to carry on, to raise her child — the very fruit of their union, and protect him from the fierceness of this sparsely charted frontier.

9

NEENA (CHITWAN), 1974

From the moment they arrived in the Himalayas, Col Tenderfield knew that it was going to be an exhilarating journey. A glance about him toward the undulating peaks and monumental valleys and he felt like Moses at Mount Sinai staring into the rugged landscape, waiting daily for a message from God. It would come, he had no doubt, maybe not in flames, but perhaps on the wing of a Himalayan monal, or on the back of a rambling yak, or more likely from the lips of a young Sherpa lad.

Fifteen years in this part of the world, although a mere page out of the weighty well-worn tome of his life, gave him a new perspective on the relativity of time and the value of human life. His students arrived as children and within a short five years were adults. Meanwhile, Ellen and he were like ghosts to the children. They never aged and every winter they vanished off the mountain to a world beyond which they had never wandered.

On one such vacation, the couple retreated to an elephant safari for a glimpse of the one-horned rhinoceros and Bengal tiger. The newly established animal sanctuary at Chitwan, or *Heart of the Jungle,* was used by the government at the end of the nineteenth century as the favorite winter hunting ground for Nepal's ruling class. In an area known as Four Mile Forest, visitors' camps were set up for the feudal big game hunters and their entourage, where they stayed for months shooting hundreds of tigers, rhinoceroses, leopards, and sloth bears, now nearly extinct from the sport. The Tenderfields held no desire to shoot game, but the possibility of seeing for themselves the majesty of the Bengal in such close proximity that only could be achieved in a loosely regulated animal zoo like Chitwan brought them that late autumn to the park ready to behold the beast in awe.

Chitwan did not fail to deliver. Ellen held her breath as she was allowed to move closer to the caged tiger than she'd imagined. Nearly within her reach, if she dared to do it, was a beautiful male specimen, his massive regal head held high as if he knew his captivity was a mere formality. One large pliable paw extended beyond the palings of the wire cage and Ellen observed that its width across was wider than her own head, and one unfriendly swipe from that clawed hand could certainly have caused serious damage, if not death. Yet she edged closer, and immediately Col reached out to restrain her. He did not like the look of that powerful arm from which the paw extended, its girth about equal to his wife's slender waist but surely twice as muscular.

A soft voice immediately came upon them from behind. "Don't worry. Shahim here was raised from birth in the Park. He was found quite helpless as a newborn kitten after his mother was shot by game hunters. He is rather tame for a young adult Bengal of his age."

Ellen and Col both turned to find an attractive and petite young woman of Asian descent peering at them expectantly. Her long dark brown hair was parted down the middle of her tidy head, and below her arched eyebrows a pair of gold wire-rimmed glasses perched studiously upon a small freckled nose. Below it a full mouth was shaped in a friendly smile.

"You don't say?" Col replied, immediately charmed by her proper English diction. "Hello. I'm Col Tenderfield," he continued, extending a hand. "And this is my wife, Ellen." The young woman took his hand and introduced herself.

"Dr. Neena Tan. I'm Chitwan's bird expert." She shook Col's hand firmly and observed the older man's look of mild surprise. "Oh," she continued. "I suppose you are surprised that they have a bird expert here? The burgeoning number of tourists frequenting this oasis of species diversity has warranted the employment of a specialist like me. An Australian government grant. I was hired to interpret the calls and clicks of the various flycatchers, vultures, and cuckoos that reside here."

"Not surprised at all," Col replied, "Very pleased to meet you, Miss Tan."

"That's *Dr.* Tan, Col." Ellen extended a hand, which the younger woman took and shook softly. "Pleased to meet you too."

"We are running a missionary school up at Jiri," Col added, smiling broadly.

"Oh, really?" she replied, reciprocating the broad smile. "I had heard that someone had come to restart that school. So pleased to meet you!"

"So tell me, *Dr.* Tan. How did you come to have such a lovely Oxford accent? You don't come by that accent around here much."

"Please call me Neena! Well, it is a rather uninteresting story, really," she began. "I received my education first in Australia, then in England. I originally completed a medical degree at King's College before enrolling in Oxford's doctoral program and becoming an ornithologist."

"You're a medical doctor?" Ellen asked, amazed at this young woman, who couldn't possibly have fit in all that education in so few years.

"Yes. That is so. I practiced as a GP briefly in a hospital in Surrey, England. I did enjoy the work, but I found it disconcerting that my patients often asked for a 'real' English doctor, even when I was in the room. Very disappointing. I suppose it didn't help that I look much younger than my years. Of course, I did start at King's College at fifteen. Anyhow, I enrolled in the doctoral program in ornithology."

"That's quite a jump," the older woman replied.

"Yes, but not really," she returned. "While I was studying medicine, I also studied several Asian and European languages. I found languages fascinating. I was quite good at intuiting and hearing patterns and quick at mimicking sounds — basically the building blocks of all phrases in human language. Just like music."

"How many languages do you speak?"

"Nine. I speak French, Spanish, Portuguese, German, Swedish, Norwegian, Danish, Sherpa, and Nepali. Well actually, that's *fourteen* with English, Mandarin, Malay, Hokkien, and Vietnamese," she added. "I forgot my familial languages!" She laughed with a light chirp like a bird.

"Fourteen languages!" Col exclaimed. "That must be a record?"

"Hardly. Then again, the Scandinavian languages are all quite similar, particularly in writing, so they might even be considered as one language with three dialects, with German a close relative; same for French, Spanish and Portuguese; and of course Hokkien, Malay and Vietnamese." She did not mention that her command of languages could have been considered thirty, if the call of birds could also be considered dialects.

Neena was on her third field research trip in Nepal. After Col and Ellen's two-week stay at Chitwan, they invited her to visit their school, and it was on one of these visits that Col inquired about going with her on one of her visits to witness the arrival of the hawk-eagles in spring near the highest peak in the world.

"There is a wonderful village called Namche Bazaar, which was an amazing crossroads of Tibetan, Nepali, and Chinese trade in the Middle Ages, as it still is today. It is more vibrant and enterprising than one would expect at such altitude — today's mountain explorers have made enterprise here viable. Sir Edmund Hillary recruited his Sherpa aides for his historic climb of Everest from this village."

"Will it be OK for us to go, at our age? Is it a long walk?" Ellen asked.

"She means *me* to go," Col corrected.

"*Both* of us, Col. You are as fit as a fiddle. *I* am the one with the arthritis in my knee."

"Don't worry, Mrs. Tenderfield. It is a serious, but not impossible trek for an elder person. And altitude sickness is not an age affliction. I have heard that a ninety-year-old woman from the United States recently completed the trek from Jiri to Namche without incident. She had been doing the trek every seven years since she was fifty!"

"Is that right? Then I am in! I shall be fine, Ellen. Don't worry!"

"I shall also arrange to hire two mountain guides or sherpas. They will carry your packs and also help with the trail navigation should we require it."

"Ellen, are you in?" Col felt a new excitement that he had not felt for some time. Ellen remained quiet, but she nodded as Neena reassured her.

"We shall go at a comfortable pace. The mountains have their own rhythms for anyone who goes there. And," Neena added for reassurance, "in the unlikely event that you — or anyone of us — cannot walk any further, we can always take the plane that transports climbers between Kathmandu and an airstrip in Lukla just before you reach the Bazaar — it cuts the trail time by half to three-quarters."

"It does sound like a trip-of-a-lifetime," Ellen agreed.

"*This* lifetime!" Col exclaimed with finality. Both women nodded and Ellen smiled at the look of delight on her husband's face.

"When do we leave?"

"Spring is the best time. Late April?"

Neena returned fortnightly to help her friends prepare for the one-and-a-half-month-long trek, arriving early to the schoolhouse to lecture on the flora and fauna of the area to the small clutch of schoolchildren in the single classroom. For her fellow travelers she expounded upon the breathtaking vistas that they could expect to see in the highlands of the Everest Trail and at Sagarmatha herself. Frequently she stopped to ask the children if she was correct. The little ones looked on in wonder, but the older ones readily participated in her dialogues, citing the location of colorful stands of rhododendron, the names of various local birds, or where a large yak herd could be found grazing on Uncle Kili Sherpa's pasture.

Her research skills were well-honed by her academic achievements, but on a personal level, she also liked to be diligent, in particular with the safety of her companions, and so she mapped out the entire route in advance, researched the possible flora, fauna, and landmarks they would encounter, and made extensive lists of all the provisions they would need. Adding twelve more bird "dialects" to her repertoire was also on her personal and professional list. Each new distinct sound of a bird species was another feather in her cap. She needed no recording devices to help her remember those whistles and clicks, for her facility at distinguishing fine nuances of sounds was so well developed that she could hear a new call and instinctively identify its purpose simply by distinguishing the final two seconds of the call. If it went down it was a mating call by a male, if up it was the answer of the female. If it was sustained, it was a distress call. If simply communication for communication's sake, she knew that as well. Each species had its distinct tune which helped maintain the integrity of the species, and each theory had its exceptions.

Neena usually trekked alone. In the dark of her camp she would light an old camp-stove and prepare to cook her spare meal of potatoes or rice and tinned salmon simmered in coconut milk. She most often traveled alone as she wished only for the chatter of the birds to break the silence of the mountains or the rainforest. But some nights, as she waited for her pot to boil on the campfire, she would bring out her *dan nhi*, a simple two-stringed violin that she played with a horsehair bow. It made a stirring melody which she imagined was like the dulcet sounds of a lullaby to the baby owls that listened quietly inside the darkened trees.

Neena arrived at the Tenderfields' door just before daybreak on the morning of their long-arranged trek. Wearing a wide brown leather drover's hat atop her dark brown hair, which was braided in a glossy plait over one shoulder, and the Hasselblad around her neck, Neena was the picture of an Aussie sheepherder-turned-photojournalist. Tucked in every pocket of her khaki field-jacket was a film canister or map. Her canvas backpack, with a sleeping mat rolled up tightly and tucked into the top section crosswise beneath a curious-looking black leather instrument case, was nearly as wide as she was tall. Two water bottles strapped on either side hung like soldiers flanking a castle door.

"Are you ready?" she called cheerfully from the veranda just as the dawn broke above the mountain range. Col opened a pink-sky reflected window and waved his trekking guide inside.

"Good morning, my dear. I'm ready!" he called. "Ellen's just packing the last of her things. Won't you come in and have a cup of tea before we head out?"

"Cup of tea sounds lovely. I'll leave my pack here and help Ellen with hers. Let me inspect yours too, sir," she joked.

"Be my guest, dear. I trust you completely. You are our leader, of course. I am at your command."

"You are too kind, Mr. Tenderfield. I am but your humble servant."

The young woman bowed before the towering older man, who gave her a fatherly bear hug in return. Arm-in-arm, they entered the house before Col released her to busy himself with the tea preparation while Neena made her way into the rear of the large house to find Ellen in the bedroom struggling to close the flap of her pack. On the bed was the guitar, open and gleaming in its case.

"I didn't know you played the guitar, Mrs. Tenderfield," the girl stated.

"Oh, haven't I told you? I'm hoping to introduce it to the class next semester, as an extracurricular activity, for those interested. Do you think there will be interest?"

"Most surely. Who would not want to learn to play music? I play the violin. And a little bit of the guitar. I hope you're planning to bring it along,"

"Well, I hadn't thought about it. My sister played the violin as well. We had wonderful family concerts when I was young, back in Boston where I grew up. I haven't played the guitar much since then."

"You haven't? Well here, let me strap it in." Neena moved closer into the bedroom, and then suddenly stopped in her tracks when she heard a low but clear melody emanate from the guitar. She looked to Ellen, who looked back at her curiously.

"Are you hearing the music, my dear?"

"Yes," the girl whispered back. "Do you hear it too?"

"Yes. If you hear it, then you have a special place in this family." Ellen replied with a smile, as the girl stared at the guitar in wonder. "It was hand-made by my son, Bernard. He is a woodworker. I hope you meet him someday."

"Yes — that would be most amazing and absolutely fabulous!" the girl replied, moving closer to the guitar and picking it up gingerly. The melody stopped when she placed her fingers upon it. She held it upright like a cello on the bed and worked out the melody by moving her fingers on the fret-board until she worked out the first note. From there she readily picked out the melody and repeated it three times, finding chord patterns to express the sad melody in a variety of keys. "You must bring this instrument with us. We can play together in the moonlight tonight. It will be a full moon. Perhaps the spirit in this instrument will speak to us again! Come on, let's get going ... never a minute to waste when the trail beckons, Mrs. Tenderfield."

"Please, Neena-darling, do call me Ellen."

"Okay. How about I call you Auntie Ellen?"

"I would love that. Yes. That would be nice."

"Shall we, Auntie?" Neena packed the guitar in the case and closed it firmly. Holding it lightly in her arms, they left the room together to find Col in the kitchen ready with two thermoses of milky tea for the lady travelers.

"Neena heard the ghost guitar," Ellen remarked.

"Did she?" he asked with one eyebrow raised and a smile on his craggy face. "And what did she think of that?"

"Most extraordinary, sir!" was the reply. "Uncle Col, you never told me you two were ghost-whisperers! In Singapore, you would be most revered!"

"Aahh! Now that would be something!" All three heard the guitar reply and it was with strains of this melodic refrain that they started out on their long trek to the highest peak in the world.

At Bhandar they spent their first night in a rustic teahouse. "You should know that this trail is centuries-old," Neena explained. "It is an old Tibetan trail, and also the route originally taken by Sir Edmund Hillary, Tenzing Norgay, and their crew when they made their first ascents onto Everest."

"Ahh, Sir Edmund Hillary! He is quite the celebrity in these parts, isn't he?" Col replied.

"Did you know that, with his brother Rex, Edmund Hillary was a beekeeper — a summer occupation that allowed him to pursue climbing in the winter?"

"A most clever fellow!"

"And remember, in Hillary's day, there were Sherpa homes in these villages, but no trekking lodges nor an airfield. We are lucky today. Tourism has found root here in the 'Mountaintop of the World.'"

And with this bit of happy information, the trekkers took the first steps of the many thousands they took before they were near the peaks. They followed the trail over several passes, descending over 1,000 feet through fir and rhododendron forests just on the first morning, visiting a Tibetan Buddhist monastery, Thupten Chhuling, where Neena was anointed by one of the monks when she took his photo with her special camera. Crossing the Junbesi Khola and Dudh Koshi rivers and several picturesque streams by wooden bridge, they followed the waterways through endless forests before climbing through sweeping terraces to reach a village in a tributary valley. Neena stopped their progress in the midst of a particularly lush forest to photograph a pair of mountain hawk-eagles perched in a prickly black oak. As soon as they stopped, the birds took to the air. Their voices filled the valley with a soft soprano call as they soared above the canopy, their flight undulating and forceful.

"They are trying to distract us from their nest, I would wager," Neena whispered. "Nest-building for these mountain hawk-eagles is a joint enterprise — the male fetches the material, and the female performs the actual construction. It's quite economical. They work as a team actually.

The single egg is incubated entirely by the female, who is brought food by the male throughout the incubation period. During this time the female will be very aggressive to any potential intruder. She will remain in the nest with the young, not leaving until it has fledged. The family will remain together until the fledgling is able to fly strongly and hunt independently. Eventually they become a competitor to their own parents and then the parents will chase them off and encourage them to relocate."

"They are predators after all," Ellen observed.

"Langur monkeys and red pandas can also be found here from time to time," Neena added excitedly as she scrambled up the steep side of the trail and positioned her camera nearly above her head to capture the swooping forms. "And, if you are extremely lucky, a snow leopard!"

"Neena," Ellen asked their knowledgeable guide when she slipped back onto level ground, "that is an impressive camera."

"Oh, this Hasselblad? For an ornithologist like me it's a little unorthodox, but I like the quality of the photos. They come out almost exactly as I see them — in black and white and crystal clear. Without it I would have to visually memorize each new bird species — which I do, but it's a lot more scientific to have actual visual and forensic records. My sketchpad is useful too. I often render them in pen or pencil and record the size, shape and markings — the camera, however, is the more artistic medium."

"And where does one get such a magnificent machine?"

"The camera was a gift from my father, who was an employee at the Swedish consulate in Sydney, Australia. He received this Hasselblad from a visiting dignitary one summer when he was newly in his job. He had the good fortune one day of saving one of the dignitary's children from drowning at sea. He had been delivering a very important and urgent package to the Swedish diplomat while his family was enjoying the Manly Coast. The youngest of the children had drifted on a raft too far out to sea and could not swim back. Her father was a decorated captain in the Swedish Navy but curiously could not swim. My father had been a Nipper — a junior surf lifesaver — during his early years of grammar school in Sydney, before returning to his native Singapore and becoming a soldier, then an officer in the Malayan army."

After he left Malaysia, Neena continued, he took a job at the Australian embassy in Singapore where he met and eventually married his wife, a pretty, young Aussie girl whose family had been in Asia for a century as missionaries. She was in the typing pool and fluent in Chinese. Bruce and Joan Tan were still without children after ten years of marriage when they asked one of their well-connected diplomat friends to assist them to adopt a baby from a Catholic aid organization. Neena was only four months old when she was brought by the nuns to Singapore from Vietnam. Mr. Tan's adopted daughter inherited his passion for photography and at a very early age learned to play the violin, and later an instrument her mother gave her when she was eight.

"It is called a *dan nhi*," Joan had told the girl, "a two-stringed traditional Vietnamese violin. It is best known for its expressively emotional and somewhat melancholy sound." She did not tell the curious child that the exquisitely inlaid lacquered instrument had been included with her official paperwork when she was delivered to them by the nuns so many years before. The daughter assumed her mother had purchased it for her from the nightly markets in the Old Chinese quarter.

Several days into the trek, at a large scattered village called Chauri Kharka, which boasted a monastery and high school built by Sir Edmund Hillary, the party stopped at a large white-washed tea house for the night. After they peeled off their steaming boots and Col organized the Sherpas to place their packs onto their corresponding bunk beds, Neena pulled out her musical instrument and invited Ellen to bring hers into the dining area where the hosts were preparing their meal of potato curry and *dhal baht* — lentils and rice — on the white earthen stove.

"Chauri Kharka is the 'breadbasket' of the Khumbu region," she began, tuning the strings by turning the two large pegs at the top of the long round wooden neck. "The land is fertile and they harvest crops like barley, wheat, and enough green vegetables to supply the many buyers who walk for days and weeks from throughout this mountainous region to come here. They send out boys as young as six years old to bring back rice and vegetables to the higher altitude villages." Without skipping a beat she drew her attached bow across the silk strings. The whole mountain range seemed to reverberate with the sound. "They would strap a large hunting knife to the back of these six-year-olds — to defend themselves against mountain lions or wild yaks! Imagine doing that with your average six-year-old in Québec?" she said nonchalantly, drawing the bow back again as the sun began to set in a pale pink glow and the temperature dropped precipitously. Neena's melody drew an immense smile across the faces of their hosts. Before long the tea house was filled with the neighbors and several guest trekkers who gathered to listen to the soaring emotional sounds of her sonorous two-stringed violin.

Ellen silently observed the young woman and wondered to herself how one thinks one knows a person, and then they completely surprise you with their personal talents and secrets. She tentatively joined with her guitar, but it was at first a tenuous accompaniment, because she had never before heard such hauntingly soulful melodies as those which Neena coaxed from her violin.

"The sound of the *dan nhi* is said to imitate that of a singer," she explained. "Think of it as the soloist, and accompany it as such." As her delicate fingers held down the strings at varying distances from the bow, the sound became mesmerizing, and Ellen's strumming accompaniment stirred the audience in a way that none had experienced before.

One of the Sherpa lads exclaimed something in the language and Neena immediately translated it for the Tenderfields to the thundering applause of all the local listeners.

"He just said: 'This is how one feels when they make a steep descent before crossing at the confluence of two rivers!'"

"What do you call it? Ellen inquired, amazed that her young guide was also fluent in Sherpa.

"It is called a *dan nhi*."

"*Dan nhi?*" Ellen repeated.

"Yes, in Vietnamese. In Chinese it is called an *erhu*. It is a two-stringed fiddle. The strings are made of silk. Its soundboard is made of wood and snakeskin. Have you never heard of it?"

"A two-stringed fiddle made of snake-skin? Never!"

"Well, it's a violin, really — only much richer and more emotional," she said trailing off, her fingers finding their positions as she again drew her bow across the strings in a sinuous undulating line that was reminiscent of the graceful flight of the mountain hawks, complete with their soprano song.

Ellen listened in awe, and then heard the guitar take up an accompanying arpeggio. The swelling melodies held her in thrall for as long as the soaring continued. Mid-flight she joined in. "My sister played the violin when we were young. But I have never heard anything like this."

On the morning of their departure, the hosts made Neena promise to return with her husband when she was married. The young woman only smiled and said, "Yes, Uncle Kili. Namaste!"

A half hour later the trekkers crossed a large suspension bridge high above the river where they caught their first glimpse of the peaks of Sagarmatha, Lhotse, Nuptse, Ama Dablam, and Taweche in a miraculous keyhole in the clouds, appearing at a height impossibly high and unfamiliar. Neena felt a particular pulling at her heart as her eyes panned across the breathtakingly beautiful panorama before her. The scenery had a surreal quality that set her soul alight — it stunned and amazed her the way only a spiritual experience can manifest a desire to know what lay beyond, beyond the known boundaries of this earth-bound existence. She heard the crystal clear strains of her *dan nhi* in her inner ear; they made her heart soar, and she had a sudden urge to cry at the enormity of the mountain peaks.

They had been walking for over three weeks by the time they reached their first destination, Namche Bazaar, and decided to remain there for two or three nights to acclimatize to the extreme altitude they now entered. Col felt tired and retired early to bed while Ellen tried her hand at the

dan nhi as Neena walked her through it, the bow feeling
unfamiliar to the older woman yet apparently so effortless
for the younger. She closed her eyes and let the melody
emerge from the silk like a waft of perfume or a cloud of
breath in the thin mountain air. These nights Neena felt
particularly sad, an emotion she did not often experience.
The feelings seemed mixed up with the cold brisk air and
with the melancholy call of the nightingale in the dark. By
morning Neena was able to turn to her lectures for some
solace. To focus on the scientific facts she knew was a form
of comfort.

"Situated in a large protected hollow, this village gained
importance during the period when Tibetan salt was traded
for the lowland grains of Nepal. Today trade still exists here
and Tibetans can be seen trading rugs and Chinese-made
goods, clothing, salt, and dried meat."

On the fourth day, Col was feeling much more energetic
and insisted on pushing on to catch a sight of Everest at
Kala Pattar. Ellen looked worriedly at Neena, who looked
into Col's eyes and saw that they were clear, inspected his
tongue and took his pulse and was satisfied with his energy
levels, so she cleared him to continue.

From Namche, they ascended steeply to Khumjung,
the largest village in the region. "Towering above Khumjung village is the sacred rocky peak of Khumbila, home of
Thangka, the guardian goddess of the region, often depicted
in religious painting as a striking white-faced woman on a
white horse."

The trail contoured around Khumbila's lower slopes,
passing through beautiful birch forest and on to treeless
grassy slopes to a stupa, a mounded structure containing Buddhist relics on top of a rocky ridge. After trekking

through a picturesque village set in a patchwork of stone-walled fields, they descended onto a series of switchback trails to the river again, 900 feet below. Leaving the bridge, they ascended steeply and enjoyed excellent views of the mammoth Cho-Oyu at the head of the valley. They were now trekking beyond the tree line and passed some imposing waterfalls. Although they felt the effects of high altitude, the barren alpine scenery with small clusters of scrub juniper did not escape them and they appreciated the beautifully stark contrast they made to the snowy white peaks and deep blue skies above.

"Keep an eye open for Tibetan snow cocks," Neena called behind her. "These steep grassy slopes could reveal colorful fauna. The valley here widens onto the moraines of the Ngozumpa Glacier, the largest in Nepal and the source of the Dudh Kosi River."

Countless towering snow-peaks and rock spires filled the horizons at Cho La Pass. The breath-taking altitude was now asserting itself on the travelers as they climbed the ridge beside the trail for excellent views of Everest's North Face. To acclimatize, they lingered for three days in Gokyo, a village surrounded by yak-settlements. The herders were particularly good and jovial singers and when Ellen and Neena plied their instruments, they were delighted to find some of the brown-faced men with creased and weather-worn smiles joining in with their own chorus of chants and yak-like bellows to accompany their rhythmic strumming and bowing, with Col providing a low bass counterpoint to the occasional bellows.

Over the three nights the women traded instruments again; one learned to strum with passion and the other to draw a bow with emotion. The convivial atmosphere and spirited music warmed the hearts of the travelers and inspirited all the villagers in a way that no travelers had done before them. They were invited to stay at a different Sherpa family's home each night, but the whole village showed up promptly after dinner for the sing-along. After three days it was difficult to say goodbye, but it was not sad since everyone knew they had to come back again on their way down. There was only one path up and back down from the peak of Chomolungma.

From Lobuche a gradual ascent enabled them to build the slow, steady rhythm required for high altitude walking. A series of small ascents and descents over a rocky trail lined with cairns eventually led to the surprising glacial sands of Gorak Shep. It took them several hours to cross the glacier, technically the hardest and most dangerous section of the mountain, which wove its way between translucent ice pinnacles and past bottomless crevasses.

"The trek to the base camp from here is about three hours. We will encounter yaks and porters supplying food and equipment to climbing expeditions. From Base Camp we do not get views of Everest but we will be able to see the notorious Khumbu Ice Fall. That will be our destination." And just as the words slipped from Neena's lips, Col suddenly collapsed in a heap on the icy path.

"Uncle Col! What's the matter? Are you all right?!" Neena called out.

"Col, what's happening?!" Ellen was beside her husband, shaking him, but he seemed unable to hear and respond, his eyes rolling slightly in their sockets and his body rigid. Neena methodically implemented the CPR methods she knew very well, but after twenty minutes of pumping his chest and breathing into his mouth, there was nothing more she could do. Ellen kneeled to one side, holding his hand tightly while the other woman worked diligently. Eventually, a small band of mountain climbers arrived and carried the unconscious man fireman-style back down to Lobuche, but acute mountain sickness claimed Ellen's husband before the rescue helicopter arrived to take him to lower elevation. It developed so rapidly and quietly at that altitude that descending would not necessarily have stopped the swelling of his brain. *High altitude cerebral edema*, Neena sighed.

By the time they reached the airfield in Lukla with Col's body a day later, Neena and Ellen had walked in the mountains for over seven weeks and were fully acclimatized to the rhythm of the villages. They were sad that they could not visit the Sherpa families they had earlier stayed with, but instead rose early for the arrival of their twin-prop aircraft for the flight back to Kathmandu. On the precipitous journey which felt dangerously close to falling off the mountain, both women were emotional and on the verge of tears.

Neena was silenced, her mind reeling from the enormity of her feelings, her remorse for having allowed Col to continue up the final ascent on the mountain. Ellen, on the other hand, felt distressed at her loss, but somewhat buoyed by the fact that Col, her husband of over five decades, had died a happy man walking nearly to the highest peak in the world. If he had had time to say it, she was sure he would have said, "This is as close to heaven as I'll ever get!"

Neena traveled to Canada from Kathmandu with the Tenderfields, one sitting beside her and the other in a casket below. Neena had undertaken the painful tasks of retrieving her elder friend's body and signing the death certificate as the attending physician when they reached St.-Gérard. It was Bernard and Neena who held Ellen's hands tightly in each of their own as the casket was slowly lowered into the ground. Two weeks later, Neena prepared herself to return to the little schoolhouse at the rooftop of the world. The children she knew would be surprised to find someone other than the Tenderfields in the classroom, but Neena was ready. She knew of no child in the world that was not fascinated by stories of wild animals or backyard bird calls. She had a whole arsenal of defense against the protestations of small children, not least of which was the rich sounds of a guitar which Ellen had urged her to take as a gift for her friendship and loyalty.

The classroom became her new wilderness and the children her own, until one day nearly two years later, she chanced upon a tattered copy of a newspaper amongst the litter at the Base Camp on her annual summer trek to Everest. The edition of *Le Monde* was nearly four months old but this was still news for her in far-away Himalaya. She scanned the page casually and then stopped at a special advertisement calling for doctors to sign up for a new endeavor organized to help save the lives of children at a refugee camp on the Thai-Laotian border. She knew instinctively that *this* call to action would be her new *frontier*. Even before she could sling both Ellen's guitar and her *dan nhi* back across her shoulder alongside her rucksack, she heard the arpeggio ascend like the angled rise of a falcon's wingspread as it skims above a mountain thermal high upon the open skies.

10

PHILIPPE (CHIANG RAI), 1976

In the early morning dawn, Philippe arose from the dirt where he had collapsed the night before. He wandered aimlessly through the camp; the unfamiliar rainforest beyond beckoned to him as he gathered his meager belongings, collapsed his tent, and stashed the sack of provisions and guitar. It was at that moment he heard the sound — the haunting music, refined and familiar, coming to him through the silence. It was a cool breeze on a humid night. He absorbed it, drank it deep into his soul and with it felt a renewed sense of purpose. Something in this music drew him out of his body and he was visited by the vision of an old growth forest in a land he hadn't seen since he was a small boy.

It flashed vividly before him. His feet paced out the rhythm of the music and although it took him eleven hours of walking before the music allowed him to rest, he felt no tiredness, his sense of purpose still strong. Philippe's journey through the deep of the rainforest was slow-moving, but the extreme patience and equanimity required of the young man was equal to his resolve. His exhaustion and loss of directional certainty distressed him to a point of paralysis, but the thought of returning to the medics' encampment and finishing the business of saving the children was the essential vision he formed and held firmly in his mind with clarity only surpassed by his purpose.

At this point he had been in the midst of the rainforest for nearly two weeks. In that period he had partaken of only the provisions he could carry with him, supplemented sparely but sufficiently by edible vegetation found along the forest, mostly jackfruit, wild guava, and elephant ear stalks. He was now grateful for the knowledge bestowed upon him by his camp companions on one of their short treks into the interior. This resourcefulness sustained him through the extreme measures of his exodus through the rainforest. Since the first day of his journey, a strange music filled his head. It led him, the spirit of some sort of guide. It featured nightly in his dreams as he slept on the soft forest floor, and each evening it was the same dream.

Floating over the treetops by moonlight, bringing him to a tall cedar whose nightly calamity befalls with a thunderous roar. Two spirits rise up to join him in this mystical flight, their presence stirring like the shifting fog of music filling the night air with its crescendos. Then suddenly they disappear, as swiftly as they appeared, back into the forest as the music explodes into a cacophony of sound.

Abruptly Philippe sat up in his sleeping bag. A mixture of shock, sadness, and relief overcame him as the music ceased and the solid reality of the ground below him conspired with the early morning mist to fully awaken him. When he gathered his few belongings and the guitar, he had to close his eyes and trust his instincts to deliver him to his destination, like a young beast tracking its own scent to return to its den. But every turn seemed identical to the last. Conjuring up the music in his head served useless; nothing came to him except the weak confidence he felt in his gut that he was on the right path. After two weeks, disorientation and exhaustion became his companions — he did not know for sure whether he had been walking in great circles through the unfamiliar forest, or whether his progress was linear. But with the assistance of the weather and the elements, the alignment of the stars and sun, an ancient and well-worn footpath through the thick rainforest, and purity of heart and spirit, he pressed on. *What does not kill me,* he repeated to himself, *will sustain me.*

Then all at once, crouching down in the thick of the foliage, Philippe heard it. A very distant roar of a plane overhead, then an explosion. It seemed far away and yet the voices shouting and the horrific cries were perceptible, drifting as they were in on the wind, and immediately his heart quickened and stomach clenched with fear. A few minutes later he received the slightest inkling of an acrid smell in those winds and he retraced his steps, running purposefully for hours, grateful that he had marked his path with his machete on the way inward. After three full hours of retreat and feeling now that he was out of danger, he collapsed in a heap at the side of the trail, wedging himself under the cover of a huge stand of elephant ear. After a while his heart stopped pounding and he fell into a fierce deep sleep.

He was floating down a river in a canoe. By the position of the sun it was afternoon and he was somewhere between the headwaters of a creek and the junction of a river. He scanned the horizon for landmarks. There were no mountain tops to give geographic proximity, just a sea of green — luxuriant waves of emerald, jade, viridian, khaki, olive, lime — washed across the landscape in infinitely watering-down layers one behind the other on both banks of the river and beyond them.

The unstoppable lateral movement of water downstream shunted him into an illusory sense of progression in the opposing direction although his canoe was at a virtual standstill in the slow churning of the eddy. Then he saw it in the corner of his eye — a silvery flash, a flicker in the water that could only mean one thing.

He lay low for six days before preparing to retrace his steps back into the jungle toward the awful explosion. It had rained for several days after the event and this he saw as extremely good luck. The rains would have diluted some of the chemical impact of the bomb, and although it wasn't entirely safe, he knew he had to return in that direction to get back to the refugee camp across the border.

His pack was now empty of food and he found that he could stuff the guitar into it if he strapped his sleeping bag to the outside. This allowed him to travel at a faster pace. After almost running back along the beaten path for several hours, he began to smell the burnt acrid odor once again. He carefully pulled the sleeping bag around his head as he got closer to the site, covering his mouth and breathing through the fabric layers. Even his eyes were beginning to burn somewhat, to a point where he knew he would run into trouble if he kept advancing. At this juncture, he deviated from the main path and took a 35-degree angled turn. Walking as swiftly as he could, he bush-whacked with his machete as he traversed through the undergrowth of the jungle. After several hours he angled again in the opposite direction and continued his progress, hoping to skirt the bombed area and regain the path out of the jungle.

He listened carefully for signs of wildlife, knowing that if a bird could be heard here he would be in a safe environment. Alternatively, he listened for a melody in his inner ear, any sound that would help him sense the right direction. But it was eerily silent. Not a sound was present when he ceased his bush-whacking, except for the occasional roll of distant thunder. And then he saw it. A body strewn across his path face down, the clothes burnt to shreds, and skin charred black and brown exposed through the gaps. He nearly stumbled and retched once he recognized it, but avoided the obstacle just in time. He tramped carefully through the undergrowth for another thirty feet or so before he found the second corpse, this one also a soldier it seemed, with clothes shredded in the back exposing the blackened skin underneath. It looked like he had been crawling on the ground for some time and his prone, face-down position showed that he had died as he dragged his painfully destroyed body on all fours as far away from the explosion as he could manage, succumbing eventually.

By the fifth body, Philippe was gagging with repulsion, grasping at his sleeping bag and pulling it as tight around his mouth and nose as possible, averting his eyes from the carnage. He came across fifteen bodies before he found the last one quite a distance from the others in the midst of a meranti grove, lying chest down, curled in the rooted embrace of an old bodhi tree, the face turned sideways. He could just make out that this one was alive — still breathing, the back rising ever so slightly with every breath — not quite dead yet barely alive. The profile was blackened by the blast but the filthy shirt was in one piece. He could not tell if it was a boy or a man, a few years younger than himself probably... fifteen or sixteen perhaps. In his right hand he clutched a sawed-off machine gun, its magazine of bullets still engaged. Philippe approached the body gingerly, removing the machine gun carefully as a first safety measure. The hand did not give up easily at first but then the gun was freed and he placed it a safe distance away. He then sat back for a moment and removed a water bottle from his pack, holding the cloth against his mouth and nose with one hand. He had recently refilled his four bottles with rainwater collected from the crook of tropical leaves in the rainforest, and this he poured now into the mouth of the dying boy and spoke to him quietly.

"It's okay now. You are going to be okay. Are you in pain?" The boy did not answer, but his eyelids fluttered for a few seconds before they relaxed again. Philippe poured another small amount of water into his open mouth and watched as the lips closed slightly as if to savor the water. He stayed for several hours with the boy repeating the water dose every few minutes until at one point the eyelid fluttered again and the eye seemed to actually move in the socket. Several minutes later the eye opened a tiny slit and he asked once again if his patient was in pain. A slight nod was just perceptible. At this point he felt confident enough to turn the boy over gingerly onto his back and could now see the whole of the damage on the young face.

One side of the face was blackened, blistered, and caked with blood from the hairline to jaw and partially on the neck, and the other side was burned only from the hairline to the cheekbone. There was a pristine section from the cheekbone to the neck which remained untouched although it was lined with mud. Luckily, the rest of his body was intact, although his exposed forearms were also blackened and blistered. Philippe slowly dissolved four aspirin pills in the cup of the water bottle and fed it slowly to the patient, also dripping a little of the liquid onto the blackened skin where he could reach it.

That night he built a small fire and read a book by firelight to the boy, wondering whether it might be his former camp-mate Analu. He could not be sure because there was very little left of the face that would have given him that knowledge. The boy's voice was also gone; whether from pain and fatigue or taken away by the chemical burns, he would never know. All he knew was that as long as his patient was breathing, he would not leave his side. Every few hours he poured the pain-relieving liquid onto the cracked and blistered mouth-hole and stoked the fire until all the dried wood he could find was exhausted. In the near dark he swept away the leaves and debris from a small area beside the fire and climbed inside it, stretching his long thin body out beside his companion and continuing the story in a whisper. He had finished reading the novel weeks ago at the camp, and in the dark he repeated the chapters as best as he could remember them, not sparing any details or leaving out a character description.

Sometime in the early hours the boy's breathing stopped mid-contraction with a death rattle that startled Philippe awake. He peered into the darkened face to find a thickened whitish substance oozing from the mouth-hole of his patient. The dawn brought stirring strains of the ghost music in the air and he mourned the passing of his friend and wept with the whole of his being.

Mae Anh lay on the low bunk in the hospital prison with her bruised back turned to her cell door, while the warden, a barely pubescent Vietcong soldier holding his gun high across his chest, his young brown face impassive, guarded the door on the other side. Beaten and starved by her captors when she refused to confess her crimes as a traitor to the Righteous Government, the woman weakly drifted in and out of consciousness, intermittently visited by dreams of an earlier time, decades before the tragedy of this horrendous civil war.

She is young and happy and in love with a man whose life is laid out before him like a lotus flower of good fortune and he invites her to share it with him for the rest of their days. They walk hand-in-hand along a paved path which runs alongside a large placid lake brimming with fish, turtles, and water lilies. Hoan Kiem Lake. She is dressed in a flowing white silk áo dài that he had given her as a gift for her eighteenth birthday.

She turned her head slightly, thinking she heard the door open, feeling his presence for the first time in so many years. Her fiancé is holding his hands out to her, palms open.

The warm breeze flutters the long skirt of her tunic and the rustling of silk triggers a memory of her home where the washing of the silk is the woman-folks' ritual. It is here, peering across the shimmering water to Turtle Tower Island that he brings her delicate hand up to his lips, kisses it tenderly, and he asks her to run away with him to Saigon so they can be married. They have no bags or much money but together they hire a bicycle taxi to Lao Cai Station and board the south-bound train. They feel fully alive and at last fulfill-ing their destinies. In his arms and beneath his kisses, her body unfolds as she receives him in the dim light of the cabin. As the lush green countryside peels past them through the window against a darkening black and orange sky, her love like the budding vessel of her young body blossoms into full womanhood.

But the happy tale does not end well. Once she is home in Saigon, her parents are not as receptive as they had hoped. Within hours the word on the diplo-matic grapevine is received and several persuasive guards in the employ of the French intelligence are sent to her parents' humble home and the young man is forcibly taken into a waiting car, where he is whisked away back to Hanoi before he could even say farewell to his beloved. He is not there to see the baby girl in her arms, her beautiful round infant eyes blinking away the tears shed by the young mother as she hands the small bundle to the waiting nuns. Tied to the bundle is the young mother's treasured dan nhi, the family heirloom given to her by her own mother when she was six. "Please don't let her go without it," she sobs. "She must always know where she came from."

Hours later, the soldier rapped on the hospital prison door and opened it to announce: "Get up. They are releasing you." But the woman did not awaken.

He was crouched under cover of an old banyan tree in the courtyard of an ancient deserted temple when he heard the chopping wave-like sound of a helicopter before he saw its boxy metallic form in the early morning sky. His skin was now blistering in all the exposed areas, particularly the palms and fingertips, and he soaked his damaged hands in the old stone fountain in the courtyard for as long as he could, occasionally splashing its cool water on his blistering face as well. The machine had passed by once earlier in the day but Philippe was too fearful of leaving the safety of the stone structure to peer into the open sky for it. He had fled from the carnage of the bomb's aftermath and wandered in a state of shock for a day and a half before stumbling upon the abandoned temple and finding adequate refuge in it. His breathing was rasping and labored now, his body weakened and his head splitting down its middle as he relived in his mind the desperate day and a half attempting to rehabilitate the helpless bomb victim. Philippe was sickened by the horrors of this bloody war, and for the first time ready to abandon all his convictions.

The old stone wat was completely overgrown with persistent figs and banyans that grew into the crumbling structure, twisting their languid arms possessively like miasma or ghosts petrified mid-stream while passing through the walls. After the helicopter's first pass he had convinced himself that it would have been too miraculous to be a rescue plane, and he fell into a deep sleep. But on the second approach, he felt a sense of enormous relief and forced himself to investigate from under cover of one of the banyan trees to see for himself whether the aircraft was friend or foe. As it drew nearer, his relief turned to exhilaration when he saw the large Red Cross on the helicopter's sides and viewed it again on its undercarriage as it flew directly above him.

He stumbled out from under his cover and stood in the center of the courtyard waving his arms. When this did not register with the pilot, Philippe willed the helicopter to circle around again, but instead the machine continued unabated in its original direction. With the last vestiges of his strength, he re-entered the wat as quickly as he could to retrieve his battered flashlight, wedging it between his ruined hands, now more like the claws of an animal or bird, and returned just as the helicopter was quickly disappearing into the sky. He switched the torch on with his mouth and waved it frantically with both hands, arching its light as his arms passed over his head several times. But it was to no avail; the pilot missed his second signal and was out of sight as quickly as it came. Philippe's panic was complete but he struggled mightily to not let it annihilate him. He remembered the bodies, fifteen or more, and imagined the others who would have lain closer to the detonation site, ground zero. He wept for them, and then himself.

After two days of waiting for a helicopter to be secured from the International Red Cross, Bernard was eager to begin his work. Once a machine was secured, he spent the first two days making wide sweeps across the forest canopy with a medic in the navigator's seat, but they found nothing. It was now the third day and he had taken to the skies alone but it was becoming apparent the mission could quite possibly be unfruitful. He had a picture of the young man on his instrument panel and he marveled at the likeness to the boy's beautiful mother. He had never seen the father, but he was sure the man was handsome.

As he surveyed the forest canopy for the final time, he was beginning to feel the frustrations of possible failure, yet something in his gut told him not to give up. With this vague assurance he decided to do something he had never done before while in flight. In one motion, he swept off his headphones and shut off the electronic radio that regulated his hearing device. *Tell me now if this is the place*, he whispered to himself.

Almost immediately a long-unheard music began in his inner ear, its familiar strains as soothing as a love song. He had covered nearly forty square miles of this area already on an earlier day, but had seen nothing although its proximity to the red "X" marked on the map which the French intelligence officials had given him indicating where the diplomat's plane crash had taken place made this area prime for finding the lost fellow. On this second rendezvous he decided on a ground-level reconnaissance. Nodding to himself, he turned the helicopter sharply around 180 degrees and there below him, as clear as day, was a structure that he had not seen before — an old temple perhaps that was being reclaimed by the forest. As he swept around the west side of the landing area at a low cruising speed, he caught a movement in the near distance through one corner of his eye. He replaced his headphone and radioed back to base that he had seen a signal and was going in to have a look. He gave his coordinates and then prepared to land his craft onto the temple grounds.

Although over a ten-year veteran of helicopter piloting, Bernard felt his heart pound excitedly. He felt an urgency and exhilaration that was almost inexplicable. Less than a mile away and descending in a straight line at a ground speed of twenty knots, he brought the helicopter into a hover above the clearing, being careful not to rush the landing. He settled the machine to the ground, and then turned his eyes toward the ancient ruins to see a young man stagger his way out of it with the last vestiges of strength. His arms were over his eyes to protect them as the helicopter blades in the narrow clearing swept the grounds clear of leaves and debris, sending them into the air like a tornado.

Bernard carefully climbed out of the helicopter with his head down low and then saw the boy teeter in his boots, steadying himself against the stone wall, an exposed tree root snaking above his head like a stream of smoke above a candle. The older man immediately leapt into action and just missed catching the lad before he fell in a crumpled heap at his feet, face blistered and gaunt, hair matted, shirt and trousers dirty and damp with mud. When the man lifted the unconscious boy, he seemed only slightly heavier than an armchair, perhaps no more than a large musical instrument, like a cello.

Lifting the unconscious patient into the rear area of the helicopter with ease, he checked the boy's breathing, which was slow but steady and rasping, and placed an oxygen mask over his nose and mouth. Carefully wrapping him in several blankets, he strapped him onto a stretcher fixed to the floor. Just as he was climbing into the pilot seat, he heard the familiar music rising from the ruins where the boy had collapsed. There on the temple steps lay a large canvas rucksack where Philippe had dropped it when he fell unconscious. The pilot retrieved it and noted its bulky weight with surprise but did not open the pack. He simply placed it carefully into the navigator's seat and hopped in beside it, radioing back to the station to inform them that the mission was accomplished. He would be returning immediately and would a medic please be available at the tarmac on his return, which he estimated to be in one, or one and a quarter hours?

Neena stood quietly on the makeshift helicopter landing waiting for the transport to arrive in the half-light, the air heavy with jasmine and the vapors of fuel. She had only arrived at the medic base near Chiang Rai two days beforehand, but she willingly took the assignment to meet the search helicopter and bring in the latest casualty. Neena had worked in the burn center of a hospital in Surrey during her early years of training as a doctor, and even though she insisted that her experience was limited and she had been out of practice for several years, the organizing staff was overwhelmingly amazed at their good fortune to receive an experienced burn physician. Her command of French and the local languages, furthermore, set Dr. Tan apart from the others.

Philippe remained unconscious for nearly three days while Neena, Sophie, and a whole team of medics treated him for first- and second-degree burns, toxic inhalation, and carbon monoxide poisoning.

When Lorraine returned from France where she had flown with Joël's remains to bury him in his family's catacombs, she stayed constantly by her son's bedside, strumming the guitar softly as she did when he was a baby until the moment he opened his eyes. Immediately he sat up and tried to explain in a state of delirium that he was all right, not realizing that he had been in a coma for several days. He had no recollection of the helicopter rescue, or his ordeal in the forest. An intravenous drip tethered him to his bed in the recovery ward but he agitated for immediate release, shouting that he had to return to the camp to meet his father. Lorraine eased him back onto his bed and brought him the news of his father.

"*Mon fils,* please do not try to get up. You are not well." She held his chest while he coughed violently, bits of spittle with blood making its way up with every vociferous cough. When his spasms ceased, she continued gently, "You cannot go to your father — you don't remember this, but your father is dead. His plane was shot down on his return from the interior. You were with him, weren't you? He's dead."

"He's dead?" Philippe replied incredulously. "But he..." He stopped short, the memories abruptly flooding back. Like a film reel he saw in his mind's eye the camp where Analu and Thao first smashed his head and then became his friends over the campfire where they shared a fortnight of music and companionship. They trained him on the use of the Russian machine gun, and showed him the underground trenches and the spiked bamboo booby-traps. He remembered the scribbled note and the stirring music once again.

"He is buried in the family estate now, Philippe, next to your grandfather in Aubigny-Sur-Nère. I will take you there when you are better." She saw her son's eyes darken and his head drop to his chest as he began to cough again. His breathing became labored and she called out to a nurse to administer the oxygen. The young man sank back into his hospital bed and turned his head away from his mother so she could not see his tears and shame.

"It's my fault," he cried. "I asked him to take me out there. So I could learn to be a guerrilla. I was such a fool!"

"Philippe, please do not say that ever again. You were brave to go experience what others are afraid to see. If our politicians could..."

"No, Maman. I am a fool! The guerrillas...? *Communistes*...? Americans...? Us French? We are all fighting a dirty war. No one is virtuous. No one!" Lorraine nodded sadly in agreement and her own tears found their way to the rims of her eyes. But he continued, "And, no, I was not with him. He left me at the camp and promised to return in a week. He was supposed to fly to Hanoi."

"Hanoi?" she asked, surprised, hearing this information for the first time.

"Yes, Hanoi, he was meeting someone there. He did not say who. I was to stay at the camp until he came back. I asked him to do that for me. But then they all left. They abandoned me there." Philippe pictured the empty deserted camp and relived the sickening fear, and the dread in his stomach as he realized there was only one way out. The walk would be treacherous with poisonous snakes, without maps, and worst of all, amongst the opium smugglers and ruthless mercenaries wielding the Russian machine guns he knew too well. "Father was shot down and could not come back to me."

Lorraine now understood. He was flying to Hanoi, at long last — but he never made it. The sadness stuck in her throat and the guitar moaned, articulating the heartbreak of both a life and love cut short, and a father lost. Lorraine looked sadly at Philippe as the young Australian doctor entered the tent. Beneath the layers of bandages that covered his face Lorraine could only guess at what her son looked like. Neena knew, though, that his face was blistered and reddened and his eyes frighteningly bloodshot — not permanently disfigured but certainly a shock for anyone who knew his handsome face before the ordeal. But it was his fingers and hands that worried her most. Lorraine had explained to her that the young man was an exceptionally talented guitar player, a musical prodigy who had picked up his mother's instrument at two and half years old and already knew how to play the tunes she had introduced pre-birth. Neena, being a virtuoso violinist herself, knew that although he might regain the use of those fingers, to play a musical instrument at master level required a highly sensitive sensory touch and manual dexterity that he would never regain fully. Even with physical therapy for several years, the likelihood for rehabilitation of his guitar mastery would be slim.

When Philippe awoke again, he opened his eyes. It was early morning but he could not see any light. Bandages completely covered his eyes and face and he lay helplessly for hours before he heard anyone enter, his mind returning again and again to the bodies he had discovered in the jungle, and the last survivor before him. His friend Analu? Of this he would never be sure, but it did not matter. He was his

brother-in-arms; they shared a deep grief for youth and idealism lost. He mentally searched his body for pain, and then
for his hands but could not find them, nor could he move. It
seemed he was strapped to the bed and immobilized but he
could not be sure since his sight was completely obscured.

Then he heard someone enter and he sensed them watching him as he lay completely still, almost feigning death.
Neena had entered the tent silently and stood beside his
cot observing him quietly. She had an idea. The *dan nhi*.
This was the instrument that would rehabilitate him. Its
two simple strings were much more forgiving, and it was
the wielding of the bow that required true genius. Damaged
hands like his could still fulfill the promise of a song from
the harvest moon on an autumn night with sounds from
such an emotional instrument. She knew instinctively that it
would be his element. She drew the bow now slowly across
the first string, its sonorous sound like a falcon's cry.

He wanted to call out, but feared that he might still be
in the jungle, or in an enemy camp. He could not be sure.
Then he remembered the rescue. It all came back to him in
a flash, and he let his mind wander to that miraculous event
while the strange but stirring melody wooed him into a state
of complacency.

The helicopter flew over the temple and it was as if the
silence of the forest had suddenly intensified and only the
sound of the helicopter blades in a slow pulse reverberated
across the sandstone ruins. It was an eerily familiar sound.
He wanted to try to replicate the haunting sound with his
guitar, but was debilitated at this point from lack of food
and the intense burning sensation in his hands and face,
and in his lungs. His entire body ached from several days
of coughing. He lay himself low and waited, hoping in deep

prayer that the helicopter would come back eventually. He willed it to but fell into a deep sleep while doing so.

Jagged rows of conifers wound down, down, and down yet more; layer upon green-black layer, from where he kneeled on the ridgeline to the very bottom of the ravine. There it was, that sharp bend in the creek and a beautiful giant lying waiting on her splintered back. It was several hundred feet down below, but the tree appeared as clear as day. Almost as if clouds had parted and the vision was thrust upward in a perfect moment of transference. The vision was crystalline and inspired in him a sense of infallibility.

He was awakened again several hours later by the sound of the whirling blades overhead. He remained still for a moment, sensing relief wash over him and noticing that his lungs burned a little less as it did so. And then there it was again, that familiar strum.

Epilogue

THE CONCERT (SYDNEY), 2000

Under the resplendent proscenium arch of a world famous opera house *not* reminiscent of any of the great cathedral halls of Europe, a tall man in dark sunglasses holding a baroque guitar emblazoned with a red sunburst in one hand moves purposefully to center stage towards a pair of carved wooden chairs. He eases himself slowly and deliberately onto the one to the left, while from the opposite side of the stage a woman enters, joining him at center stage. She is dressed in a flowing white silk tunic, with swooping sequined scarlet swallows, her dark hair falling in soft waves down one shoulder. In her delicate arms she carries like a child a black lacquered lute-like instrument covered with burnished gold, snakeskin, and mother of pearl, with a long white silk-string bow entwined. She now holds her instrument out to the man, and receives his guitar with her other hand.

Behind them enter four musicians — two hold guitars, the other two violins, their eyes fixed in front of them toward the endless sea of faces in the audience. The man brings the *dan nhi* upright against his torso, draws the attached bow, and turns the keys one at a time until both are tuned, and then returns to a stirring single-string melody. The woman begins a rising arpeggio on the guitar in tune with the one-string note, opening the concert with an uplifting master-work, a work of intimate subtlety. He bends it and shapes it with his fingers, as her singular accompaniment begins to fan it with the winds of a fertile river valley. Seven strings now meld with a single drawn bow, before twenty more add their voices to it. The mesmerizing melodies take their audience aloft with the great churning stick of the sky, ringing a symphony of disparate voices six in total.

Over two thousand pairs of ears are trained on the trilling melody which skips above them like a nightingale's warble from a wood surrounding an alpine convent. Another strain blows in on a high thermal, straddling the rocky peaks of a different shore. Fired one upon the other, and then back again in a continuous overlapping point-counterpoint, steaming like lava flowing into a cold sea. It is an aural phenomenon to behold: the musicians and their ancestral forebears all contained in those furies. A string of chimes set against a melodic measure, from the moraine of a bare-breathed mountain down to ancient temples and watery passageways.

When the last strains of the symphony finish, the audience is silent for a full seven seconds while each individual allows the dulcet notes of the musical brilliance to sink fully into their bones. The sound waves of those four thousand hands clapping caress the small nautilus-shaped cochlear device inside the ear of an old man in his seat beside me. On the other side of my grandfather is the woman he has loved for a lifetime, my grandmother's thin hand in his, fingers lightly squeezing his as their son and daughter-in-law — my parents — allow their prodigious music to sweep across the many frontiers they both know deep in their hearts, deeper yet in their soul and sinew.

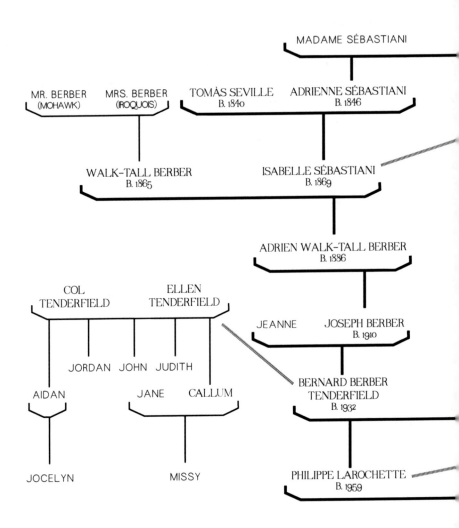

MADAME SÉBASTIANI

MR. BERBER
(MOHAWK)

MRS. BERBER
(IROQUOIS)

TOMÀS SEVILLE
B. 1840

ADRIENNE SÉBASTIANI
B. 1846

WALK-TALL BERBER
B. 1865

ISABELLE SÉBASTIANI
B. 1869

ADRIEN WALK-TALL BERBER
B. 1886

COL
TENDERFIELD

ELLEN
TENDERFIELD

JEANNE

JOSEPH BERBER
B. 1910

JORDAN JOHN JUDITH

AIDAN

JANE CALLUM

BERNARD BERBER
TENDERFIELD
B. 1932

JOCELYN

MISSY

PHILIPPE LAROCHETTE
B. 1959

FAMILY TREE

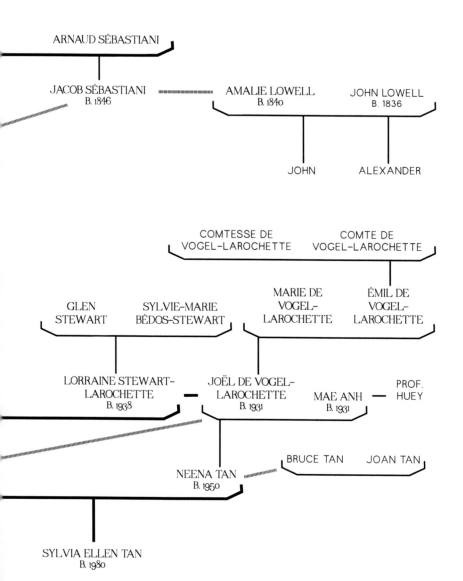

Acknowledgements

A writer needs her champions. I thank my family and friends, some who read early chapters and encouraged me to keep writing, including: David Smith, who gave me my first glimpse into the world of book publishing. The Divine Six: Ellen Sherwood, Martha Jeffers, Daphne Vandergrift, Merry Parrish, and Ruth Klein. My family: Susan LeClair; Jean Young-Jones; Mary Young; John, Linda Young and the Girls; Peter Young. In California: Chi Bui; Mike Burchfield; Jane Lin; Victoria Link; Pablo Miralles; Alex Perel; John Spielman; Cindy Steffen; colleagues at Long Beach Public Library Foundation. The folks at Inkwater Press: Linda Franklin, Emily Dueker, Sean Jones, John Williams and Jeremy Solomon. In Australia: The Meyers Family; Laura Brennan; Mark Bromilow; Ben Davison and his guitar; Rod Howard; Sian Lauw; Janine Lewis; Jacqui Tyack; colleagues at Arts Queensland and Australia Council. And last but not least, my daughter Marina, to whom I dedicate this book— you let me disappear for hours and days over many years to write it.

CPSIA information can be obtained at www.ICGtesting.com
Printed in the USA
LVOW10s2038040913

350649LV00006B/14/P